bad

girls

burn

slow

Also by Pam Ward

WANT SOME, GET SOME

Published by Dafina Books

bad
girls
burn
slow

Pam Ward

KENSINGTON PUBLISHING CORP.
www.kensingtonbooks.com

DAFINA BOOKS are published by

Kensington Publishing Corp.
850 Third Avenue
New York, NY 10022

All Kensington titles, imprints and distributed lines are available at special quantity discounts for bulk purchases for sales promotion, premiums, fundraising, educational or institutional use.

Special book excerpts or customized printings can also be created to fit specific needs. For details, write or phone the office of the Kensington Special Sales Manager: Attn: Special Sales Department, Kensington Publishing Corp., 850 Third Avenue, New York, NY 10022. Phone: 1-800-221-2647.

Dafina Books and the Dafina logo Reg. U.S. Pat. & TM Off.

ISBN-13: 978-0-7582-1801-8
ISBN-10: 0-7582-1801-X

First Printing: August 2008
10 9 8 7 6 5 4 3 2 1

To Mari;
Hana, my mama;
and Guy

Acknowledgments

There is something sinister and delicious about laying souls to rest. The sadness. The wet cheeks of uncontrolled grief. The woeful talk of "going back home." But there are some folks who aren't above helping death along. They relish in seasoning the earth with fresh meat and hover over decay just like crows. As a business, death has grown and hellishly changed. Cremations have brought doom to unheard-of profits and the rituals themselves have put Hollywood to shame with the lavishness of their productions. But some of us do need a final resting place and a good soul to navigate the way. That said, I'd like to thank the cemeteries I visited: Rosedale, Forest Lawn, Hollywood Forever, Holy Cross, Rose Hills, and the ancient Evergreen. I thank all the parlors that entertained my calls. I especially thank my mother, the beautiful Bonnie Moore, who told me gory and good stories of redemption and loss and has gone to more funerals than anyone I know. To Guy, my sweet husband, who shows the true meaning of love and gives everything under the sun. To my children, Mari and Hana, for the best gifts in life; and for Ryan and lil' Ryane, who keep me smiling. To my sweet sisters, Linda and Lisa, my great brother Jimmy; to Rachel my cousin, who gives friendship soul; to Grandpa, Aunt Joyce, Aunt Steph and Uncle Jarrett. To Aunt Donnie; Uncle Lantz; Aunt Linda; Uncle Ed; Uncle Morris; and, of course, the Abrahams clan including Mich the Peach and Ron Sweeney. To Cousin Robin and especially Eddie who gave me grizzly graveyards facts from the parlors along Pasadena. To Claudia and Jeannie; and my agent, Stephanie Lee, who sang praises for me all the way. To Rakia

Clark at Kensington, who shoveled through these sheets and got this whole book in the ground. Lastly, I thank those who are no longer breathing: my father who warms my heart like a 1,000-degree oven; my sweet GrandMarie who got this family thing started; and my neighbor, Demora, whose artful hand made death look stunning. May all of your souls rest in peace.

Oh Death

What is this that I can't see
With icy hands taking hold on me
I am death, and none can excel
I'll open the doors to heaven or hell

Oh death, oh death
Can't you spare me over till another year?

Oh death, someone would pray
Couldn't you call some other day
The children's prayed, the preacher's preached
The time of mercy is out of reach

Oh death, oh death
Can't you spare me over till another year?

'Tis Death, I come to take the soul
Leave the body and leave it cold
To drop the flesh off of the frame
The earth and worms both have a claim

Mother come to my bed
Place a cold towel upon my head
My head is warm, my feet is cold
Death is a-moving upon my soul

Oh death, oh death
Can't you spare me over till another year?

(excerpt from ancient American folk song)

1

Margie

Fowler, Alice H.
Age 78, slipped away peacefully into eternity, on Tuesday, October 9, 1985. Born Alice Hughes, daughter of Gladys and Rupert Hughes of Texas and heir of the late Howard Hughes' estate. She is survived by her husband, Edward Fowler and their only son, Bernard and will be interred at 4:00 p.m., on October 12, at Rosedale Cemetery, in Los Angeles.

It began as a con. Something you did and got away with once. But the next thing you know, the whole con was your life and you couldn't stop even if you tried.

A small girl watched the sky turn from light gray to grime. She was melting the feet of her doll with a lighter while sitting in the back of the car.

It was three. The funeral parlor was now in full swing. The place ran year round and eighteen hours straight. It turned crystal clean air into rancid cologne. A horrible mixture of putrid and sweet, like fruit going bad in a bowl. You wouldn't know. No, not unless someone told you. That this scent, this burnt licorice rotting aroma was a skin searing, two thousand degree human oven. With a flame so intense, that flesh dissolved from your bones, cooked you clean until nothing was left but scorched limbs and a puddle of smoldering grease.

The girl's mother sat in front, hunting the obituary section. She read the obituaries each day like they were racing track forms. Who was born where. Who died when and how. Who was the last surviving kin. She was from Memphis but knew all the funeral homes in town. She kept track of death like a bookie does his nags, with both eyes trailing the cash.

"The service is about to start in ten minutes!" Margie wiggled in her seat like a puppy at the screen, panting to be let back in. Her infatuation with death was shrewd and direct. She was like a vulture, soaring over fresh deceased meat with her keen beak-like nose and squat little fingers, she hunted through each fallen bone. She read the obituaries gleefully, drawing rings around names with the red pen she kept in her purse.

They were sitting in a banged up Buick, parked a few cars from the funeral home's doors. They were grand, hand-carved doors like the front of a hotel lobby, but the paint was such a shiny grotesque, freak show gold that they mocked the cracked side-walk outside. Two trees in gilded planters added regality to the place, but their leaves were black from soot and their branches so bent they looked like two hunchbacked women clawing at the door.

Margie shifted her gaze to the headstones and grinned. She grabbed her purse and car keys and fluffed her hair in the rear-view mirror. She sprayed her cologne along her fat, mole-filled neck, and the cheap drugstore scent filled the car. Along her throat was a gold necklace, sparkling in diamonds. She'd gotten the necklace from her con in Nevada, and it gleamed like the sea in July. Sorting her curls behind her ears, Margie smiled at the picture of Alice again and then carefully drew on some freckles. But her smile evaporated quickly when she saw her kid in the backseat, and Margie let out a big, I'm-so-sick-of-you sigh.

The child was still frying her doll's feet with the flame. The smoke began filling the car.

"Put that damn fire out!" Margie yelled at the child.

Obediently, the girl blew the flame off the doll's feet. The rest of the legs were pitted with marks.

Margie shot the child a mean look in the slim rearview mirror and then hastily turned to the street. Staring at the child made her sick. But she was stuck with this disaster. She was trapped damn fool in Texas. He took our last bit of money and gave you this cheap awful perm."

But the disgusted look switched to a hint of a smile, which raised the thick mounds on her cheeks. "But I must say," she said, pulling a long reddish strand, "that straightening junk really worked. Your hair looks completely different. You'd never even know it was you."

The girl was ghoulishly cute with mascara and lip gloss lips like one of those six-year-old beauty pageant kids. She sat perfectly still. She didn't smile or frown. Exhibiting the mannequin face of a skilled poker player, the girl showed no emotion at all. But then, ever so slightly her left knee started to twitch. She tried to sit stiff but began shifting back and forth and then mildly shaking across the seat.

"Mommy?" the girl asked, using a mild-measured tone. She said the word as if testing a stove to see if it was still hot.

"What?" Margie asked, putting another rubber band between her lips.

The girl looked hesitantly at her mother. She tugged the hem of her pink chiffon dress.

"What is it? Speak up!" Margie demanded.

"I have to go," the child offered meekly, bringing her hands to her face as if waiting for the next blow to appear.

"What? Are you saying you have to go now? Why didn't you use it at the gas station like I told you?"

"I did. But now I have to go again." The girl bit the meaty part of her palm.

"Well, you can't go right now. It's too late," Margie told her. She noticed an older man sobbing alone by a tree. Both his arms circled a headstone.

The girl panicked. Her legs twisted across the cold vinyl seat. "I could go in those rosebushes over there." The girl pointed to some shrubs near the cemetery's entrance.

"No you can't! Are you crazy? You're a lady for God's sakes! You can't just go pee in a bush." Margie pulled the girl's hair so fiercely her head slammed against her chest.

"But we did it before," the little girl offered.

"The hell we did! Don't you ever mention that again, okay? Listen, you're a lady. Everything's changed. You have to be respectable. You have to act decent and look clean. Little girls don't pee in a graveyard of scrubs. They sit quietly and learn how to hold it."

Margie watched the old man standing by the lone tree again. "Besides," she said, keeping her eyes on the man. "People could see you out there."

The little girl stared at the rosebush and squeezed both her knees She tried to will the strong need down, but it would not go away. She turned toward the mortuary's door.

"I bet they have one in there," the girl offered hopefully. "It looks like the same kind of place we put that dead man in Memphis."

Margie whirled around and slapped the child hard across her mouth. "I don't ever want you to mention Memphis again, hear?" Margie watched an orange tractor lower a casket in the ground. "I sunk lower than I ever did in life in that town, and I'm never going down that dark path again.

The girl cupped her jaw and rubbed her sizzling cheek, which felt like she'd held a hot comb too close to her ears.

Margie didn't like hitting the child and avoided these confrontations. She was glad she was sitting behind her and didn't have to look at the child head-on. She avoided her at all costs, tossing the child magazines to read instead and stacking big piles of books near her legs. Reading kept the child occupied and quiet. It kept Margie from doing what she dreaded more than anything in life, having to actually sit down and deal with the child face-to-face, to have to look inside the miserable child's vacant eyes, having to see what she'd done to her own flesh and bone. Just the thought sent a horrible chill up her spine, rattling her teeth like a bitterly cold night, and torched the soft hairs of her soul.

Margie frowned to herself, keeping her lids toward the ground, burying the sorrow that burned inside her stomach.

The worst part was that she couldn't talk to anyone about her troubles. A naturally talkative person, Margie was forced to bite her tongue. She couldn't utter one word. She kept their secret locked inside her tightly clenched jaw. It stayed shut like the arsenic she kept in her trunk and the fine jewels she took from her marks. Margie was a natural con artist. As good as it gets in this game. But things had gotten out of hand lately, and they barely escaped their last scam. She had to rearrange their lives to get out of the state. All she had to do now was sit quietly and cool her heels. Wait for things to simmer down and turn back around. If she gave it a little more time, the fire would eventually burn out. If she could just get through winter and wait for summer to heat up, then maybe she could put the past behind her. Maybe by June or July she could undo this lie and finally begin to breathe deep again. She was living with a ticking time bomb, but there was a definite end in sight. And at ten, the girl was more than halfway done being a child. In a few short years—not many more now—the child would be grown and hopefully gone and then things could be normal again.

Margie sighed deeply. She studied the birthmark on the girl's neck. Normal seemed a long way from now.

Margie wrinkled her nose and sniffed toward the sky. Life was different now. Things had gone tragically wrong, but if she sucked it up and played one last little con, she could relax and be done with this drama.

"Come on," Margie said, getting out of the car.

And then slowly, the girl daintily slid out one of her feet. She was wearing a white patent leather boot, trimmed in soft rabbit fur, which licked the taut meat of her calves.

"My name is Paula Green," the girl said to herself. She curtseyed, pinching her dress between her index finger and thumb. But before she got all the way out of the car, the girl stopped to look back at her mother and let "slut," casually slip from her lips.

Margie grabbed the girl's hand and walked toward the mortuary door, oblivious to the girl's hostile curse.

A protester held a cardboard sign etched in red letters, blocking the Chapel of the Pines entrance.

"Bake bread, not bodies," the scrawling type read. The protester's hair was the color of used coals. She looked a hundred years old.

Lately, people had been protesting Rosedale Cemetery. They didn't like the noise and the dust, and there was no mistaking the sickening odor. It was like rancid cologne mixed with pungent rotting leather. The neighborhood smelled like the bottom of a worn thrift shop purse.

Margie ignored the protester and tightened the grip on Paula's hand.

"The dental work from burning puts mercury in the air. The EPA should shut this place down."

Margie ignored the woman and kept chomping her gum. She glanced at the obituary announcement once more and then tossed the newsprint down on the ground. Alice Fowler. Alice Fowler's husband was in there. A nasty smile crept from Margie's painted mouth. Marching up the cathedral steps and pulling Paula behind her, Margie took a deep breath and grabbed the brass-handled door.

The protester rushed her, rapidly following her up the steps. For an older woman, she moved as fast as a graveyard rodent. "The homeowners have complained. We have signatures now," the woman explained. "Our property values dropped when that smokestack went up. Don't give them any more business!" she warned.

Margie swung open the door against the protester's shoulder. Paula had to duck to get out of the way. "So what?" Margie said, holding the door with one hip, popping her gum in the old woman's face.

The first thing Margie noticed in the room was the cool fragrance. A heavy natural scent of hundreds of freshly cut carnations perfumed the dense air. "What a waste," Margie said, scowling at the floral arrangements. She took her gum out and smashed it under the holy water dish. "People spend so much money on this junk, and it's all going to die in a week."

Paula ignored the flowers. She fiddled around. Almost bursting, she did a torturous I-have-to-pee dance. Scanning the room, searching for some kind of bathroom, she broke loose from her mother when she spotted a blue sign.

"Wait!" Margie whispered. "Where do you think you're going?"

Paula was halfway in the men's room when Margie snatched her arm.

"Mommy," the girl anxiously held her own crotch. "I really have to go bad."

She looked agonized and pranced back and forth on her feet. Her pleading eyes looked desperate and wet.

"Okay, but can't you read? You're in such a hurry to pee, you're going inside the wrong one!" Margie pushed the girl into the women's door across the hall. "And make sure you lift your dress and do it the way I showed you. And come right back out when you're done."

The girl nodded, broke loose from her mother's firm grip, and went inside one of the stalls.

Margie turned her head and walked toward the front pews. She saw a bald man trying to loosen his tie. *That must be the son,* she thought.

Struggling with the knot at his throat, he finally opened it up and took a breath like it was the very last one of his life. He sneezed, rubbing both of his eyes with his fists as if the flowers had triggered an allergic reaction.

The chapel was sprinkled with a variety of withered, time worn souls, people that had already lived the summer and fall of their lives and were now in the middle of a hard winter storm. Margie saw an ancient-looking broad holding a casserole pan in both hands. Another dried up crow carried a pink dessert box, and a third clutched some wine in her age-spotted hands.

"Bitches!" Margie murmured, a little too loud, while slipping on a laced pair of gloves. She knew lots of women who worked the funeral circuit like her. Parading from one death to another, carrying casseroles on their hips. Dressed to the nines wearing broaches and pearls, hunting through widows trying to nab a new husband.

Margie took a close look at old Mr. Fowler to see if any woman trapped him yet. Two old women were huddled in the pew behind his chair. One rubbed his shoulder. The other held his hand.

"Go 'head ol' bitties. Shoot your best shot," she said to herself. Margie shifted her dress and popped out her bosom. She had studied the picture of Alice, Mr. Fowler's dead wife. To look more like Alice, Margie had cut and colored her hair. She'd already snipped it once to avoid the cops in Nevada, but now it was dyed midnight black to make her look exactly like Alice.

"None of you heifers have a chance," Margie laughed. She strutted down the aisle, jiggling her frame and then suddenly she stopped, dropping down on one knee, and making the sign of the cross, dabbing her head, chest and shoulders. Then she got up and boldly sat in the front pew reserved for family.

Margie was a natural beauty, with high cheekbones and pouted lips and a body to make Marilyn Monroe cry. At fifty-six, she looked sensational from way across the street, but up close and underneath her good friends Maybelline and Revlon, she was twenty miles of long, beat up road. Looking good was a hell of a lot harder to pull off. Being in California didn't help matters either. This was definitely no Memphis. It wasn't Shreveport or Dallas either. Shoot, in those states, plenty of men would have noticed her already. Three or four would have approached her and she'd be sportin' a man's arm by now, without giving up anything but a semi-cooked grin.

But this was L.A. This place was a lot different. L.A. was a bitch for scheming women like her. In fact, Los Angeles was another league altogether. There were beautiful chicks every single place you went. Margie would suck in her belly, but then just let it fall because it didn't matter what she sucked in out here. There were fine women all over, in the banks or at the mall. Even the scags bagging her groceries were beauties. So Margie had to be more practical. She concentrated on much older cons.

The sixty-year-olds wouldn't even look in her face. The seventy-year-olds glanced but ran to women in their forties. Sadly, Margie was aiming at octogenarians now. She couldn't believe she had to deal with these wrinkled old stiffs who had one foot in a rest home and the other hovering near the box. But these men felt lucky to have a foxy chick like her and loved squeezing her with their age-spotted arms. Margie wore extra makeup when working a con. Her face was so completely done, she was like a hazy Cézanne painting. She wore an eighteen-hour bra and a reinforced girdle, and though she struggled to breathe from all the armor under her dress, the old men sitting in the pews for the funeral thought she was a breath of fresh air. They stared at her and felt like they'd died and gone to heaven, and she smiled at them all, pretending to nod and wave even though she didn't know a single soul there.

Blowing his nose and trying not to sneeze, Bernard hurried down the aisle toward the bathroom in back. Floral walls met up with solid wood molding, and large planters exploded with exotic fake plants.

Bernard saw the mortuary's owner, Mr. Reynolds, talking to another family down the hall. Mr. Reynolds held the shoulder of a slack-jawed old man. The man was wearing a jacket with elbow patches, and his lids were so red he looked like he had a nasty bout of pinkeye.

Reynolds was a broad, commanding man, who was used to comforting others. He stood 6' 7" and wore dark expensive suits and glossy black wingtip shoes. His shock of gray hair only made him appear more grand. People liked him. He had a great gift for gab. His name was the main reason they came to this parlor. Reynolds. People remembered the place. Generations had been coming to see Reynolds. He was like a friend of the family, a long distant cousin, a favorite uncle you saw from time to time. He was there when your favorite uncle fell down the stairs or when your sister swam alone at the beach and drowned or when your grandfather stopped breathing in his sleep. Reynolds had viewings or wakes and celebrations of life, where you sang to ornate caskets of silver or gold that gleamed like a brand-new waxed Rolls.

People said things like, "Reynolds sure made her look good," and "Call Reynolds, honey, he'll handle the whole thing for you." They admired the beautiful living room elegance of his rooms, the chandeliers, the rich carpets, the burgundy drapes, and the espresso machine he kept in the corner or the warm cookies on the buffet. He worked hard to make the living feel relaxed with departure. He made death so damn pretty; people lingered in their seats, marveling at his grandiose altars. Reynolds was making a killing. People came to him in all kinds of imaginable contraptions. In cars or in limos, pickup trucks or wagons, in buses or bicycles and even on foot, but it was his white vans that delivered the bodies. The white vans were blank with no hint of signage at all, except for a singular "R" on the driver's side door, done in a beautiful, hand-painted, calligrapher's scroll. If it weren't for that one single letter on the door, you'd never know Reynolds was there. But he was everywhere you looked, once you realized the score. He was at parks, schools, or hospital wards—wherever death came knocking at your door. He came unannounced and least expected. His van would just roll up and park at the curb, and wheel out a vinyl green gurney. Everybody eventually saw Reynolds. His parlor was over a century old. He never advertised or printed brochures or put signs on bus benches. He didn't make sales calls or knock on anyone's door. His funeral home was like an undergound, word of mouth kind of business. He didn't need to find clients. His clients found him. There was always a steady supply of corpses.

But when the crematory became the profit-making arm of Reynolds' business, the parlor started to get a bad name. People started complaining about the odor and soot. The chimney stacks emitted a thick ash that covered everyone's cars. The ash eased through their windows or underneath doors, making dusting each day a necessary chore and the locals began to abhor it.

"People are larger," Reynolds explained to some protesters once. "Those big ones, hell those suckers take forever to burn.

Stinkers, they can burn for eight hours. Shoot, we used to do stiffs for under ninety-six minutes, but those good old days are long gone."

And with the popularity of crematories on the rise, Reynolds couldn't stop burning bodies.

"Hell, people can't afford to lay folks out anymore," he once told Bernard. "Caskets and plots and the rental of limos can run you way up in the thousands," he would go on. "Now don't get me wrong. I appreciate this business. My daddy would have keeled over if he knew what I charged today. Shoot, the average funeral costs you upwards of ten grand at least. But cremation is as easy as making popcorn on a stove. Next thing you know, it's all done."

Bernard liked working for Reynolds. He didn't require him to talk. His boss seemed content with hearing his own voice. All Bernard did was sit back and listen.

Reynolds winked as Bernard passed him to go to the bathroom "I'm sorry, son," he said, smacking Bernard on the back. "At least your poor mother doesn't have to suffer no more."

Ever since Bernard's mother had gotten sick and he'd started working at the parlor, that was something he heard Reynolds tell people each day. But today Reynolds was talking to him. Today they were burying Bernard's mother.

Bernard could hear Reynolds talking to the other grieving family again.

"Now, your basic cremation runya close to eight hundred. You can take Grandma out in a nice plastic box. Or you can put her in one of our decorative urns." Reynolds waved a mottled hand toward a shelf of small vases. "We got blue ones and pink ones and some inlaid with pearl." His smile revealed a row of new shimmering teeth.

Reynolds winked at the red-eyed man. "If you're slick, you can sprinkle her from a skyscraper downtown, or the Neptune Society will take her for three eighty-five and scatter her ashes at sea. I had a feller take his wife's ashes out in a bag. He sprinkled her all over the parking lot at Ross, which had always been his wife's favorite store."

The red-eyed old man trembled and burst into tears. His whole back quaked as he sobbed. Mr. Reynolds guided the man to the waiting room in the back and handed him a brochure about caskets.

"You folks ready to start?" Reynolds looked at Bernard.

Bernard glanced at his father, waiting for some kind of nod.

Mr. Fowler was squeezing the wheelchair's arms. His lips were clenched so tightly they were practically gone. His white hair was long and flowed down to his shoulders, but today it was woven and pulled back in a braid that cascaded over his black woolen collar. He was elegantly dressed, wearing a full tux and tails, saved from his wedding day over forty years ago. He looked like royalty in the long coat, satin vest, and gray tie. Only his Ray-Ban sunglasses knew the whole truth, but his dark glasses weren't talking. They only reflected other people's faces back or the blue and white sky-colored ceiling. No one could see the misery in his eyes or notice the wet on his cheeks.

Slowly, gesturing to his son, he lifted one of his age-spotted wrists.

"Yes," Bernard told Reynolds. "We're ready to start."

Mr. Reynolds excused himself and ducked in a door. He emerged one minute later donning a white preacher's collar. Greeting people along the way he walked down the aisle smiling, shaking hands, and offering condolences. His capped teeth looked slimy, and his eyes were always focused on a person across the way, like a prostitute peering inside a john's car while scanning the street for police.

He shook Margie's hand roughly. "I'm so sorry," Reynolds said, but before she could comment, he was on to someone else, shoving an obituary in her palm. He did this all the way up the aisle, turning from left pew to right until he reached the front of the flower-drenched altar.

When he got to the front, he stopped at the wheelchair of Bernard's father.

"Mr. Fowler, sir, I'd like to express my regret." He shook the old man's hand and then patted his back. "Your wife was a very fine woman," he said.

He coughed loudly, and suddenly an organist started to play and a blind man sang "The Lord's Prayer" in a throaty falsetto as Mr. Reynolds squeezed his eyes shut and quietly hummed along, looking the picture of sanctified glory.

When the song was finished, Mr. Reynolds opened his eyes. He breathed deeply and picked up a worn, tattered Bible.

"Dearly beloved," Reynolds said, flipping the onionskin pages. He was stalling, trying to recall the deceased person's name. "We are gathered here today on this solemn occasion . . ." he stopped in midsentence and started to hum wildly as if taken over by glory again.

"I say, we are gathered here today . . . can I get an Amen?" Reynolds barked this request like he was trying to wake the dead from their graves outside.

As if on cue, the small congregation said "Amen" together.

Seeing a copy of the obituary on a chair, Reynolds could finally go on and stop stalling. "We are here to honor our dear sweet sister, Alice Fowler."

Margie scanned through the pews, looking around for the child. Paula should have been back from the bathroom by now. Margie rose from her seat and walked down the aisle. When she got to the bathroom, she lightly knocked on the door. Since no one answered, Margie jiggled the knob, but the small door was locked tight.

"Paul-la," Margie called, knocking louder this time. "What are you doing in there?"

Bernard turned when he heard Margie knocking on the slim door.

"Paula, open this up at once!" Margie jiggled the handle in her hand. Pressing her ear to the door, she heard an older woman's voice.

"Oh, I'm sorry," Margie, said. "I thought my daughter was in there." The voice was too deep to belong to her child. Maybe Paula used the restroom and slipped out the front.

"Damn it," Margie snapped, walking toward the front marbled entrance. The funeral had started. They were reading the obituary now. She needed to get back to the chapel. She and the child were a team.

Maybe the girl was playing outside near the graves. She'd kill her if she ruined that dress.

Margie walked to the entrance and opened the door. "Paula," she called.

"Where are you, dear?" Margie blotted her lips and then smeared orange gloss across her mouth. She walked farther down the steps and saw a large family outside, gathered around a huge mound of dirt. The tractor was gone, and in its place was a pink casket. The casket was perched on an AstroTurf platform and completely drenched in hundreds of primroses. Surrounding the mound were tall, weeping reefs of more flowers and white chairs with foam-covered seats.

"Paulaaaaaa!" Margie screamed across the vast lawn, forcing her voice through the trees. It was freezing, and Margie pulled her sweater around her shoulders and glanced in the wild angry sky.

The large family turned toward Margie and stared. They were in the middle of a graveside service, and Margie was yelling from the steps with both hands hoisted on her hips.

Some of the family members shot Margie long dagger glares, but Margie couldn't care less.

Margie desperately searched through the cemetery plots. She carelessly stepped over graves and kicked the flowers left next to headstones.

"If I snag my new hose, I swear I'll make her pay!" Margie was livid. She snatched a twig from her face and kicked her pumps through the leaves. But she didn't see Paula anywhere at all. The only kid she saw was a three-year-old brat, sucking his thumb in his fat father's lap.

Margie went back inside the chapel again and looked around the opulent room again. She decided to try the bathroom handle once more, only this time the door twisted free.

There was Paula, standing with another woman at the mirror. The woman was a small, platinum blonde with beautiful, long, swirling hair. She had an athletic body with perky tennis ball breasts and an autumn's worth of hazelnut skin. She was the prettiest woman at the chapel, and Margie scanned her hard. The woman was half Margie's age, and if she were working a funeral con like her, then the woman would be steep competition.

Margie opened her purse and took out some gum. Chewing aggressively, while examining the scene, Margie popped her gum in the younger woman's face.

"What are you doing?" Margie asked Paula, shooting the woman a look.

"Didn't you hear me calling your name?"

"Look, Mommy, she gave me a Snickers bar, see!" The girl smiled, revealing a baby row of teeth, filled with chocolaty chewed nuts.

The strange woman smiled at the child and at Margie.

"Hi, I'm Val. I hope you don't mind, but I saw your daughter all alone. I was helping her reach the soap." Attempting to placate Margie, Val offered her hand.

Refusing to take her hand, Margie mimicked Val's speech. "I hope you don't mind, but I saw your daughter all alone," Margie snatched Paula away and hid her behind her back.

Ignoring Val's hand, Margie glared at her hard. What was this blonde tramp doing in here alone with her daughter? And why was the door locked before?

Margie pretended to panic. She pretended to be alarmed. She twirled Paula around. "Did this lady touch you, honey? Did she lift or touch your skirt?" Margie gave Val a cruel head-to-toe stare. Everybody knew there was a horrible pedophile scandal in the news, and Margie used it to accuse anyone who dared to intrude.

"Oh, I'm sorry. I swear, I didn't mean anything by it. I just helped her with the soap and gave her some Halloween candy."

Margie stared at Val without blinking an eye.

"Listen, you sick freak," Margie said, pointing to Val's chest, "stay the fuck away from my kid or I'll have you arrested. Touch her again and you'll need to buy some teeth, at the same place you bought all of this fake bullshit!" Margie pointed to Val's brimming chest.

Val immediately turned to leave. She grabbed the handle of the door, but before walking out she looked in the mirror at the child and blew a kiss.

Paula waved good-bye as Val strolled out the door.

Margie shook Paula fiercely and whispered in her face. "Didn't I tell you not to speak to strangers? Now tell me everything! What did that blonde lady say? Did you show her anything? Did she touch your privates?" Margie shook Paula again trying to get an answer from the child.

"Noooo," Paula sputtered. "She didn't do anything wrong."

"Come on, what did she say? You were in here a while. Did she follow you in the stall? Did you say where we are from?" Margie shook her again, her anger looked worse in the mirror.

Paula began to weep, and mascara ran down her cheeks.

"Oh, for God's sake! Are you going to start crying again? I don't have time for this now."

Margie grabbed a paper towel and scoured Paula's face. Then she grabbed Paula's chin holding it tight. "Telling a stranger the wrong thing could ruin our plans. My God, you're as dense as a rock!" Margie dropped the girl's jaw and checked her own make-up again while rapidly popping her gum.

Taking a paper towel, Paula slowly wiped her own eyes, smearing her makeup into a watercolor painting.

"Holy shit, you're just useless," Margie scolded. "Here," she said, shoving the young girl her keys. "There's no time to redo it. Go sit in the car and stay there 'til I call you, okay?"

Margie made sure Paula got all the way inside the car before going into the chapel again. She looked for the blonde, but the woman was gone.

When she entered the chapel again, everyone turned around and stared. Mr. Reynolds had just finished the eulogy and asked if anyone wanted to speak and share a few kinds words about Alice.

One woman sucked her breath, stifling a scream. She clutched her fist between her teeth and watched Margie closely. Margie looked like a bad imitation of Alice. Though she copied Alice right down to the freckles on her face, Margie's version was sinister, menacing, and sick, like Alice having a a torturing dream.

Ever the actress, Margie walked straight to the stage. She looked at the funeral party and smiled like a queen. "Hello, everybody, my name is Margie Green, and Alice was my cousin and very best friend." And with that, Margie fell down and burst into tears. She sobbed mightily, and Mr. Reynolds had to gather her up with both hands. He helped Margie's limp body toward a pew, but she stopped him, genuflected, and made an elaborate sign of the cross and then knelt on both knees and stayed there bent over her pew, pretending to pray while scanning the scene with one eye.

"Dearly beloved," Reynolds said. "Does anyone have anything else to say?" One by one a few old souls said some kind things about Alice.

Margie didn't know Alice Fowler from Adam. She'd only been in L.A. for a week and a half. She was an almond-colored woman, from Memphis, Tennessee, who wrote bad checks and preyed on the elderly and weak. She sat in the chapel looking sad and serene. Dabbing her eyes with a white embossed hankie, she looked like the epitome of anguish and grief.

When the services were over, she ducked her head in the pew. She slathered on more lipstick and rubbed vanilla-scented lotion over both breasts until they glowed like two buttered rolls. She waited for the guests to file out of the chapel one by one, so she could be alone with Mr. Fowler.

Fixing the seam around her hips, Margie rose from her seat and did a hot, jiggling stroll to the pew where Mr. Fowler sat.

"I'm so sorry about your loss, sir," Margie said sweetly. She used her charm school voice that she saved solely for her cons, and it chimed like a small music box.

Scooting up to his chair, she touched his shoulder with her glove. "I don't know if you remember me. I'm Margie Green from Texas. Alice and I are related on my father's second cousin's first wife's side. She and I were very dear friends all through school. I'm going to miss her so much!"

At this last line, Margie broke down and wept in both palms. Her cheeks were as red as a virgin's first time. She looked agonizingly sorry and stricken with grief and could have won an Academy Award for the miserable soul she played if it wasn't for the quick sidewise look she gave.

Mr. Fowler was touched by how choked up Margie was. He couldn't believe what a dead ringer she was for his wife. He didn't remember Alice having any friends named Margie and especially no kin that looked brown. But Alice was from Texas, and those fools were crazy. They did a whole lot more mixing than he did in Kentucky. Seemed like everybody in the whole state was related.

He squeezed Margie's palm when she offered her hand. "There, there," he said, putting his arm around her waist. Margie easily slid her ass onto the arm of his chair.

Now even though Mr. Fowler was at the funeral of his dead wife, even though he was grieving and mournful beyond compare—for a second, he totally forgot where he was. For an instant, he was just Mr. Fowler the man. So when Margie's beefy butt spilled over into his chair, as a reflex, he slid his hand up and over the curve of her knee and stroked her leg as if no one else was there.

Margie sniffed in her hankie, dabbing her eyes, while letting his hand explore the thick, juicy silk of her thigh.

"I apologize. I get so emotional sometimes." Margie's lace gloves stroked the older man's cheeks. She shifted her Playtex bosom until it was right in his face. Squeezing her shoulder blades together, she lifted her breasts slightly and gyrated them in front of Mr. Fowler's lips.

In that moment, Mr. Fowler didn't feel eighty anymore. As the sexual heat rose, he stroked his thumb under her dress, and he was so glad he had put his sunglasses on that morning so no one could see the raw lust in his eyes.

With his hand at the rim of her skirt, he said smiling, "That's okay, darlin'. You ain't got nothing to apologize for. Grief can turn beef jerky into mush." Mr. Fowler opened his legs as wide as he could in the constraints of his metal chair. Under the weight of her girth, his muscles twitched, but he didn't mind. He loved a big-boned woman, and an inner urge he hadn't felt in months started to stir.

Suddenly, someone came up and tapped Mr. Fowler's shoulder. Startled back into reality, he turned and stared at the black man's face. It was his gardener, Mr. Wade, paying his respects. Mr. Fowler could have knifed him for killing his joy.

Margie looked at Mr. Wade and turned quickly away. She hated to run into other black folks while working her con. She was passing, but black folks could always sniff the truth. They were like Nazis pointing out Jews.

Bernard had his back turned. He was holding the ashes of his mother. He was talking to Reynolds, but Reynolds wasn't listening to him at all. Reynolds was more interested in the sexy scene happening right in Mr. Fowler's chair. Suddenly Reynolds laughed and smacked Bernard's shoulder. "Death hits all of us different. You never know what emotion will pop up. Some folks will bawl until their eye sockets bleed, others just want to have sex."

Bernard turned to where Mr. Reynolds was staring and saw Margie sitting on the arm of his father's wheelchair! It was the same woman who was making a ruckus near the bathroom door earlier.

Bernard excused himself from Reynolds and rushed down the aisle. The first thing Bernard noticed was Margie's tight shoes and how the meat spilled over the edge. Who was she? What was she saying to his dad?

"Hello," Margie said, not bothering to stand up.

"Oh, there you are, boy! This woman's a cousin of your mother's."

"Pleasure," Margie said, sticking her hand toward Bernard. Every nail was painted a Cadillac red.

Bernard shifted the box of ashes on his hip. He limply shook her hand, but let go of it fast. Her sweaty glove felt like a sink sponge. He tried to shove his mother's ashes to the lap of his father, hoping Margie would get the message and get up.

"I don't want to see that!" his father snapped. "Take it away!"

Bernard took the box and held it with both hands, as if it were a very special present. He scowled at Margie, but she continued to smile at him sweetly until he eventually turned his scalding head away.

Bernard was so embarrassed for his father that he walked out of the chapel.

Mr. Wade came closer and touched Margie's shoulder, but Mr. Wade wouldn't let go. He searched Margie's face, like a science student dissecting a worm.

"Stop pawing her!" Mr. Fowler said to his gardener. "Don't you have some weeds to trim or something?" Then grabbing Margie's hand again he added, "Thanks for blessing me on such a woeful day."

Mr. Fowler brought her thick meaty wrist to his cheek; he looked like a baby fingering its mother's succulent breast. Clinging to its thickness and buttery warmth, with his eyes closed, he imagined it was Alice right there. His lovely dead Alice was reborn again! He squeezed his eyes shut and smiled with all his fake teeth. He hadn't felt this good in ages. It had been a long time since he enjoyed a woman's soft touch. And even though she wore gloves, he could still feel her warmth as he held her hand against his face.

The truth was, Margie's body was very similar to his dead wife's. That's why Margie picked him for the con. They had the same pearl-shaped hips and extra ripe bustline. They both had slim noses, high cheekbones, small jaws, and wore the exact same style of black curly hair. The only difference in their appearance was that Margie was darker, but from where Mr. Fowler sat now, with her ass rimming over his knees, her tan reminded him of his wife in July.

"Please . . ." he said to Margie. "We're having a repast. I'd love you to come by the house." He laid his wife's obituary over his knee and drew a small map, right over the pallbearers' names.

"We're up in Hollywood Hills. It's a little bit tricky, but if you just shoot straight up Western and hook a left on Sunset and take that all the way till you hit Crescent Heights, there's an Arco gas station on La Cienega, that means you went too far. We're just before that, north of the Virgin record store. Just keep winding around until you reach Woodbridge Lane."

Margie took the map and kissed Mr. Fowler's cheek. And then slowly, as if she were a royal queen herself, she rose from the metal wheelchair's arm. "It's so good to meet Alice's people. I'd love to stop by. Do you like Southern fried chicken?"

Mr. Fowler licked his lips as if he could already taste it. He hadn't had a good chicken dinner since the summer before last. That's when sweet Alice took sick.

His son fixed things from cans or dragged bags from the freezer. And though other women showed up with food in their hands, they brought grayish casseroles or old slanted cakes with holes in the center that were as dry and unappealing as the prune faces that served them. He couldn't wait to see what juicy thing Margie would bring.

Margie waved and smiled broadly. "I'll see you all later!" Swishing her big ass down the aisle, she paused at the front door. She blew him a kiss and put on large black sunglasses and knowing full well they were watching, she added one last roll of the hips before going out of the funeral parlor's door.

Margie walked all the way out of the cemetery's gates to where her daughter sat in the car.

The girl was leaning toward the front seat. She was listening to a game. The Dodgers were in the last inning.

As soon as Margie got in, she switched the station until she found a James Brown song and began wildly popping her gum and bobbing her head.

The girl looked down at her hands. She looked like she'd been stabbed. "The game was almost over," the little girl offered sadly.

"So what! Who cares about baseball, huh?"

Paula knew better than to challenge her mother. Instead, she picked up a lighter and flipped back its flint, burning a hole in the seat.

Margie drove to the Kentucky Fried Chicken on Crenshaw and Venice. Heading north, they stopped at the 99-cent store on Vine where she bought plastic containers and aluminum foil. Margie dumped the chicken in foil and wrapped it up tight so it looked like she fried it herself. She scraped the mash potatoes in the plastic containers and poured the beans in another tub, sprinkling the top with cumin and the red chili pepper she bought just to doctor it and make it look homemade. She opened the car door and dropped the empty bucket in the lot and left the rest of the Kentucky Fried Chicken containers in a cart.

It was almost dark now. The streetlights were on. Margie waited for the last few stragglers to leave. But when she stepped on the gas to park, her left heel got stuck under the pedal and it lifted halfway off from the sole.

"Damn it!" Margie screamed, beating the steering wheel hard. Her left shoe was ruined. The heel was broken. It hung like an unhinged tooth.

Margie only had two dresses and one pair of high-heeled shoes. She'd left everything else in the hotel when she heard the police siren. All she had were bags of clothes for the girl. She walked slow, so as not to lose the wobbly shoe. She fluffed some of her black, tightly coifed curls. With forty extra pounds on her frame, no one would ever mistake her for the slim, light-haired beauty that pulled off that sick Memphis crime. All she had to do was lay low, get a quick sugar daddy and wait for her hot tracks to fade.

Tilting her neck toward the clouds, Margie took a deep breath. A hint of a smile broke her harsh face. Someone had a fire going.

She could smell the wonderful scent of hickory in the air. Margie scanned her eyes over the neat, well-kept houses.

"This is going to be easy," she said.

They were in Hollywood Hills. She parked on an immaculate, tree-lined street with wonderful forestlike yards. Queen palms and azaleas grew in beautiful ad hoc berms. The houses were modern, English Tudor, or Spanish stucco with multiple terra-cotta roofs.

It was fall, and Mr. Wade, the gardener, was raking up leaves. His black, rusty hands moved in the rhythm of men who'd long since given up moving fast. Without turning his head, he observed the scene in the street. A Buick pulled up with a busted-out light. It shook like a washing machine on spin. A stout suntanned lady sat in the front. Her head was filled with black curls, and her face was littered with freckles. It was the dimple-faced woman from the funeral today. Mr. Wade watched her through veiled eyes. The woman was probably a beauty, way back in the day; he peeked at her juicy hips and nice ample breasts and watched her look up toward the sky.

In the back, like a princess, sat a tiny white child. The girl was biting a doll's foot, squeezing it between her molars. Her lips were heart-shaped and dense and almost strawberry in hue, and they sat in a canvas of white Ajax skin. Her sharp eyes were translucent and lawn mower mean, like they could slice the tips off of wet grass.

Her color was pale compared to her mother's. Her wavy hair was long, and her limbs had a porcelain, see-through cast and were as pale as the mountains in Alaska.

The suntanned woman was whistling a tune Mr. Wade knew. She was wiggling in her seat, dancing to the rhythm and snapping her fingers to the beat. Mr. Wade came closer to get a look at her better. She'd left the funeral so fast. He didn't have a chance to really see her face.

"Well I'll be," Mr. Wade said to himself. The woman wasn't white at all. He came closer, hiding his body behind a tree. He stared at the child in the back again. She looked like one of his cousins from Natchez. Mr. Wade smiled to himself at the careful recognition.

The light-skinned child was black, too.

From the backseat, the little girl looked like a rich kid being chauffeured. A pink suitcase sat in her lap.

"Come on," Margie said, without looking at the child.

The girl clamped her teeth on her doll's skinny calves. Her mother had viscously slapped her face at the light for complaining about needing to pee again.

Mr. Wade waved to the child once, but Margie turned away. But the child stared at him fiercely and held his gaze for so long that Mr. Wade shifted his lids toward his wooden rake again and quickly began pulling the leaves.

No sirree. There was definitely no doubt in his mind. He could see all the asphalt that lived in the girl's veins. The red bee-stung lips, the mild ride along her nose, the subtle kink in her long flowing braids. Even though she had the skin of a bleached king-sized sheet with long auburn hair and swimming pool–colored eyes, underneath she was as black as a newly paved street, and he couldn't wait to share this news with Corleen.

Except for him and Corleen, the crossing guard up the block, there were not many blacks living in Hollywood Hills. Most of these people were white folks and rich.

The girl scowled at the gardener. She hated people who stared. She was very self-conscious and turned hostile when anyone gawked at her. She knew she looked different and hated this fact. But there was no turning back. Part of it was her fault, and she had to pay. So when she caught someone staring, she locked in on their eyes and held their gaze until they looked away.

When the gardener went back to pulling his rake, the girl smiled and sucked her doll's feet, happy about another quiet victory.

*   *   *

Margie studied the ancient mansion behind the gardener's back. Its green walls and garish burgundy trim made it look like a large Spanish olive. Wild exotic plants covered the windows and frame, shading the place from the dull L.A. sun. But the plants couldn't hide what sagged underneath, a tilting structure built in 1905. Its pitched peeling roof and rotting, leaning columns made it look like two broken legs. It was a wreck of a place that was hurriedly painted with colors so loud they yelled at all who passed by. The front porch was warped. The walkways were cracked. The inside was a raging sea of uneven floors. She saw rotted wood, gutters that were completely detached, and siding that was gone on one side. The other houses were fixed and beautifully maintained with smooth paint jobs and sanded-down wood.

"Well it's ugly, but got damn it, we got us a house!" Margie smiled at the horrible wreck of a place. Many of the rich people she'd tricked lived in establishments like this. People who were too scared to touch their assets and sacked away cash, refusing to spend one cent. They let their high yields grow and thicken in banks just like mold. The more they socked away meant a better payday for Margie. So when she saw this old wreck, she sucked in her breath. A place this bad meant they had to have millions.

Margie grabbed the bags filled with chicken and fixings. She glanced at Paula but didn't say a word. She sat the two bags at the curb.

"Can I help?" Paula asked from the backseat. She wanted to hold the food. She could smell the salty fumes. She hadn't eaten all day.

"Yes. You can help by keeping your lips shut. Don't talk unless someone asks you a question and practice those faces I showed you."

Margie struggled to get all their things from the car.

Mr. Wade walked closer. The girl was scrawny and extremely petite. She hadn't hit any serious growth spurt yet. She was as short as a bat and as flat as a board. A pink lacy collar strangled her thin pencil neck, and a four-inch hem covered her thin scabby knees. Her red hair was pulled so tight along her crown, it made her eyes look vaguely Chinese.

Margie struggled to lift a bag, but one of them ripped and a pair of ruffled panties floated to the curb.

Mr. Wade decided to be friendly and come lend a hand. He walked across the street and almost picked up the ruffled panties, but Margie snatched them out of his hand. He watched her fingering the satin material with her palms.

"Need some help?" he said.

But Margie waved him back. "Oh, no, I'm fine, really. I only have a few bags."

"Well I'll get those for you." Mr. Wade came closer.

"Oh please don't. I can get this myself. Besides, I'm trying to get as much exercise as I can. I have too much weight on my poor bones already." She waited for the gardener to go away, but he didn't. Instead he peered at the girl sitting in the car. He watched her gaze at herself in the mirror. Fiddling around with her hair, she seemed upset with her own reflection. Making an assortment of faces, mocking excitement or doom, she went from prom queen and blowing small kisses to herself, to a miserable hatchet-faced shrew.

When the girl caught Mr. Wade staring, she narrowed her eyes. Her face was an avalanche of hate.

Mr. Wade gripped the rake, holding it in one fist. "She ain't the friendliest thing in the world," he said to Margie.

"She's all right, just high strung is all." Margie sneered at the gardener. "Is there anything else you wanted?"

"No, ma'am," Mr. Wade said, giving her an all-knowing once-over. "It's just that there ain't many of us up in these hills." He said that last line to make sure Margie knew that he could see all the dark underneath her tawny skin.

"I'm sorry, boy," Margie said in her most Southern speech, "but I swear I don't know what the heck you mean." Margie fluttered her ultra-dark mascara eyes until they looked like two bumblebees whizzing around like a fan.

Mr. Wade tipped his hat and walked back across the street. "I got your boy, right here," he said, and grabbed the crotch of his pants.

Margie turned from the gardener and spoke to the child again.

"Remember, don't talk to anybody, especially colored men like him, and I want you to use that high voice we practiced." Margie forced herself to smile at the child. She needed her to go along with the plan.

Grinning sarcastically at her mother, the girl practiced a few lines. "How do you do? I'm very pleased to meet you. Would you like to hear a poem I wrote?" It was so high and squeaky and sugary in sound, it could rot your teeth right out of your mouth.

"That's right, that's good," Margie told the child. "Now where's the poem? I hope you memorized each line." Margie leaned against the Buick's fender and scratched the back of her leg. Everything in California was so luscious and green, but the mosquitos were hungry and mean.

Margie smacked one off of her elephant calf. Popping open a Coke, she took a deep, syrupy sip and stared at the neighborhood again. It might be a bit chilly, but nothing like the deep freeze of where they'd been. Hopefully, things would be a lot better over here. Margie hadn't slept well in months. She wasn't wearing the giant sunglasses she wore at the funeral parlor, and she had to add a lot of concealor to her eyes to hide a life filled with crying. She licked her lips and stared at the home's front door. She couldn't wait to sleep in a real bed again. On the road, she and Paula often slept in their car, and Margie always left one eye open.

Margie watched the girl suck her doll's mutilated toes. The feet were melted and marred from cigarette lighters and bitten all the way up to the thighs. It was the tenth Barbie she bought since they started this journey. Margie liked her holding a doll. It was the ultimate prop. No one would suspect a young girl with a doll as someone who was in on a con.

Downing the rest of her Coke, Margie studied the sky. She could smell the cool breeze from the ocean.

The girl looked at her mother and leaned up from the seat.

Grabbing her suitcase, the girl placed it up on her lap. She was about to open the car's latch but Margie told her to stop.

Rushing up to the car door, Margie tore the lipstick from her purse and smeared some of the color across the child's small lips. A deep satisfaction stewed in Margie's cruel eyes. She held the girl's chin in the palm of her hand. She turned her head left and then turned it right. "Yes," she said, examining her better. "You look pretty as a picture," Margie said.

But a horrible sadness swirled through the girl's braids. It covered her cranberry mouth and slid down to her spine. Her lips started to quiver. Her blue eyes brimmed with tears.

Seeing this, Margie immediately turned into a fireplace of rage. "Snap out of it, already! We can't go if you look sad. No one wants an unhappy kid."

Margie began to fuss. She dabbed Paula's face with a crumpled up napkin.

"Goddamn it!" she said. "You're gonna ruin your mascara if you cry!"

The girl stifled her tears and pulled herself together fast. She gave her mother a giant smile that was so counterfeit and contrived, it shined like a Las Vegas beach.

"Now remember!" Margie said, grabbing the girl by the arm. "You're Alice Fowler's goddaughter from Texas. Don't say anything more but your name."

Margie watched the child slowly get out of the car. Sinking into the red earth of her heart was sadness so dark, so brutal and deep, Margie shuttered each time that she saw it. Down the road, Margie had made a terrible turn. She had ruined the child in an attempt to save their life. This deception shattered Margie. It burned down to her soul. And because of this, and a few ugly incidents that occurred later, her own flesh and blood, the child she used to adore, had begun to savagely hate Margie's guts.

Paula developed mood swings and brooded all the time or simmered in a thick cloud of vengeance. She didn't dare do any awful things in front of Margie. Margie didn't tolerate such antics and would slap the girl in a red-hot minute. But Margie knew what Paula was capable of. She could see the evil simmering inside her veins, the same evil that simmered inside hers. There were little signs at first, way before the change. Like how the child always lied or would start ugly fights. Margie had ignored them before. But each fit had become more massive and meaner in size.

Margie's own life was spinning out of control. She was brutal, that was a horrible truth. But she never expected her kid to turn calculating or cruel. But one night, the child flipped out and burned down a garage. Though the child lied profusely, refusing to admit the truth, Margie had seen her sneak off with her very own eyes. She saw her creeping along with a tall box of matches, dragging a wagon's worth of newspaper to the priest's tiny house. Margie squeezed her lids shut, trying to block out that image. The blood, the dead dog he called Boots in the mud. It's head halfway chopped with an ax! This was all too much for Margie to bear. But she was suffering herself from a fling that had turned sour; never in her life did she think things could get worse. But then suddenly, things were worse, with an incident so brutally cold that Margie took pills to avoid feeling the pain.

It was so fiendish, they had to sneak out in the pouring rain. In the cruel freezing night, they left with no coats or shoes. Taking hard rattling buses and long putrid trains until they eventually lucked up on this old beat-down car. They rushed on highways, crossing tall slushy hills, going through back roads and farms, until they finally saw green. The California sign was the only reason they stopped because there was no more road left. There was nothing in front of them but the shimmering blue glass of the ocean.

Margie thought maybe living near water would cool the fire in the girl's heart and fan off her own flaming soul.

Margie watched the girl fool around with her hair. She was the one who started the child on this path. Even her birth was a series of lousy cheats and lies. She'd never run a con before the child was born. She was normal. She was a schoolmarm who sang in the church choir. But after having her heart maliciously ripped from her chest, something changed inside Margie. It was like Darwin said. Her species evolved into a much higher form. She'd reached the point where she was the epitome of rejuvenation, focused solely on her own survival. She'd taken many identities since her poor husband's departure. And the man she'd slain for wouldn't even take Margie's calls. There was nothing left but to live out these reincarnations. Cutting her hair, adding weight, changing the way that she spoke or walked, all of it took a huge toll. And the last con almost took both their lives. She didn't want to try anything like that again. She just wanted to rest, live in some peaceful spot for a minute, and stop running away from the law.

Margie watched Paula in the backseat. She seemed to relish Margie's inevitable decline. Although Margie kept her on a short leash, Paula was always up to something and was getting a whole lot harder to control. Although she disciplined her severely enough to curtail the child's wrath, it only seemed to make matters worse.

"Come on," Margie said. "And act exactly like I told you. We didn't come all this way for you to screw up."

The girl stuck out her tongue at Margie as soon as she turned her back. She reached for her suitcase and pushed it out on the grass. And even though the suitcase was too heavy for her frame, Margie let her drag the thing toward the front steps herself.

When they got to the porch, Margie reached in her purse and sprayed a perfume mist along her squat throat. She tried to spray Paula too, but Paula jerked away and the mist got into her eyes. The child was enraged! She tried to escape the smell, but the floral scent was everywhere she turned.

Margie rang the bell and started whistling at the door while Paula stood there seething in hate.

The man downstairs coughed and glared from his front picture window. An elderly white woman jutted her jaw while watering her lawn. They both saw a thick woman holding two trash bags in both fists and hobbling in broken shoes to the door.

Both of these neighbors had the same thought at the very

same time. They loathed the idea of this person on their street. It meant property values dropping, good neighbors moving out, and graffiti being tagged on their gates. They both hated this tan-looking woman on sight. Their malice was complete without ever speaking to her once. She was a signpost. A warning. A violent alarm, that said their neighborhood was about to go down.

The white woman turned off her water and yanked her hose hard. Black people didn't have any business here no matter how pale they looked. This was a nice neighborhood. It was quiet. They all had beautiful, landscaped lawns. Even the woman's car was a total disgrace. It had been sideswiped and was all dented up in the back, and had a smashed front light.

A loud buzzer sounded as the woman and child waited by the door.

Bernard made her wait for a very long time. He didn't like this strange woman. And why was she coming here so late at night? The repast had been over for hours.

But when the buzzer rang again, a voice roared from the back. "Open the door, damn it! What are you waiting for, fool?" Bernard's father beat the back bedroom wall with his cane.

Bernard ignored him. He looked out the peephole again. Margie was on the steps but next to her, halfway hidden behind her leg, stood a very small and frightened-looking little girl.

Slowly, he put his hand on the dented brass knob. He slid back the links of the metal short chain. "They'll be sorry they came here," Bernard said to himself and carefully clicked back the latch.

2

Val

Before Margie and Paula showed up at Bernard's house. Before Reynolds locked the cemetery's gates for the day. In fact, before Alice's funeral even started that morning, Val watched the mortuary door from Roy's car.

Roy smiled at Val as she sat in the seat. Val was absolutely stunning. Her eyebrows were arched, her blonde hair perfectly coifed, and her smooth skin looked like newly blown glass. Like a film star, in a silk dress and three rows of pearls, she peered from her tortoiseshell frames.

"That's him," Val said, looking back at her friend. Her sunglasses reflected the funeral home's doors in each lens. Both lenses sparkled in gold.

They watched Bernard struggle to open the large ornate doors.

Roy looked at Val again and mocked surprise. "Now tell me which one, honey, cuz they're both so damn fine! Is it the eighty-year corpse rolling down in the chair, or the pasty ass zombie behind him?"

"Come on, Roy. Stop playing. Look at his little plaid pants. Don't tell me you don't think he's cute."

Val looked at Bernard like he was the most adorable thing on earth.

"That's him! *That's* your dream man?" Roy was so shocked he was speechless. He kept shaking his head. Then he leaned over and pretended to feel Val's forehead. "Girlfriend, you really must be sick."

"Come on, Roy," Val pouted. "Don't talk about him." Val sat further up in the seat, straining to get a last look.

"I thought you told me you wanted a good-looking man, not some bald-headed, two snaps from death, cadaver!"

The wheelchair got stuck, and Bernard struggled with it madly.

"Idiot!" They heard the old man say, frowning up at his son. His sunglasses contrasted with his ultra-white hair. And his whimsical locks laughed at his grimacing face.

The pair in the car watched Bernard rip the chair up and over the crack as the old man grumbled in the seat.

"Come on! Let's go with them down to the grave. If we hurry we can watch them put poor Alice down."

Val started pulling the latch on the car door.

Roy rolled his eyes. "You've got to be kidding. These are the people you wanted me to meet. Didn't you see the Plymouth they both pulled up in? That jalopy is probably worth twenty dollars."

Val held the obituary section in her hand. "Roy, that old man is sitting on billions." Val thumped the paper with her long, lacquered nails. "He's Alice Hughes' husband! Can you believe our luck?"

"So what?" Roy shot back. "Who the fuck is Alice?"

"Alice Hughes! You've never heard of her?" Val smiled at Roy with slot machine eyes.

"Sorry, but nothing is coming to mind." Roy looked bored. He glanced at his watch. He hated this part of L.A. It was seedy and cheap. There wasn't a single Starbucks in sight. The sidewalks were busted and cracked wide open and dotted with flat, blackened gum. Though you could see downtown's slick buildings, screaming loud in the east and the beach was just fifteen miles due west, there was nothing right here in the middle of town but broken glass, tall charcoal palm trees, and chain link that went on for days. Roy's BMW gleamed like a jewel in this jungle. There were no cars like his parked on Normandy and Western. This area was as dead as the cemetery behind the brick fence. He didn't want to be here at all.

"Alice Hughes was Howard Hughes' niece! She's the only descendant from the Howard Hughes clan. Howard never had kids. Both his parents died young. It was just Howard, Uncle Rupert, and Alice."

"How do you know? Where do you get your facts?"

Val pulled a *National Inquirer* from her purse. "The whole story was here last week."

Roy snatched the magazine out of Val's hands.

"A tabloid! Honey, they're notorious for their lies. They'll say anything to get you to buy these damn things!" Roy looked at the ancient cemetery again. "Why would Howard Hughes' niece be buried in this dump? I bet none of that's true!"

"It is true! I read it!" Val snapped back. She believed everything she read in her magazine stories and couldn't understand people who didn't.

"What about this, huh?" Val shook the *L.A. Times.* "Obituaries don't lie. It tells you right inside here!"

Val cast her eyes toward the mortuary door again. "Bernard and his father are Howard's closest kin."

"Let me see that!" Roy snatched the paper from Val. His eyes scanned the front page. "Girl, the McMartin trial has started! You know I substitute teach." Roy traced his finger across the page as he read. "One of the mothers claimed her son was molested in a stall. Many students admitted to being fondled and raped or forced to watch dogs being slaughtered. Oh my God! I bet I get fired! You know they go for us first. They don't like men like me in schools. I bet they drag me by the hair and toss me right in fire and torch me like my girl, Joan of Arc." Roy bit his fist while he read.

"Listen to this," Roy said. "Listen to what the woman told police. She said a helper named Ray, wearing a Santa Claus suit, sodomized her son while holding his head in a commode."

"Oh, that's gross! I don't want to hear about that crap!" Val put on more mascara.

Roy brought the newspaper over his face. "I'm telling you, I'm cooked. I bet they don't call me at all. My new car is going to get repoed."

Roy stared at the paper again. "Look at his face," he told Val. "He's got the evil eye." Roy shoved Buckey's picture right in Val's eyes.

"What?" Val said, staring at the sad homely man.

"Look at that photo. Who does he remind you of, huh?"

Val gazed at Buckey's picture. He was a thin, balding man. He was sitting next to his wheelchair-bound mother.

"Who?" Val said. "I don't have a clue."

"Bernard!" Roy shouted. "He and his dad look the same. They're the same kind of weird, creepy wheelchair pair. I'm telling you, I wouldn't be bothered if I were you. Bernard could be a nut job. He could be a wild raging fool, and you want to go play with him near some grave."

Roy saw a homeless man creep behind a fender to pee. It splattered against the cemetery wall. "Oh, hell no! Can we go? I've seen enough." He turned on his engine and sprayed cologne in the air. "Can't you smell that? My Lord, it stinks over here." Roy narrowed his brows like something smelled real bad.

"Roy, don't be silly. This is our chance. We're talking Howard Hughes money. Those people are related to a dead billionaire. This is our entry into the big leagues at last!"

"This is *your* entry, doll. I'm not involved. I don't do anything but weaves, rolls, or twists." Roy reached over and fussed with Val's large buoyant hair and then slid his convertible in reverse.

Roy wrinkled his nose and waved a hand over his face. "Come on! The air quality sucks. We might as well be sitting in Downey." Roy dropped a small Snickers bar on his tongue.

"That's the crematorium, Roy. They're going to bury her ashes outside." Val glanced at the giant golden doors again. "Poor Alice," she said under her breath.

"Poor Alice! You act like you know that damn bitch!" Roy pinched the tip of his nose and grimaced. "So you're telling me, I'm breathing in an eighty-year-old's ashy stuff? My God, do you test our friendship." Roy put his finger inside of his jaw, gesturing like he was about to gag.

"If we stay we can catch Alice before they lay her down proper! We can meet the whole Howard Hughes family!"

Roy looked at Val as if she were insane. She was a dreamer. She always came up with weird hair-brained schemes. She lived somewhere between tabloid ink and her delusional smeared mind.

"How can you go to a funeral of someone you don't even know? You know, I don't do death. I hate funeral parlors! How can you even ask after all I've gone through? And, honey, news flash! Howard Hughes has been dead. I bet these poor folks have nothing to do with his money. I don't see one single nice car in this lot."

"Okay, okay, wait. I'll tell you what, Roy. You just sit tight. I'm just going to run inside a second."

Val looked so excited he thought she'd pee on his sheepskin seat. Val opened the door and was halfway out of the car. Her black patent leather heels glowed in the sun.

"No!" Roy said. "I have to get back. My four o'clock is probably waiting at the shop. Besides, you look dangerous. Shoot, you could get plenty. Why waste your time with some cemetery folks?"

Val lowered her sunglasses and flashed him a smile. "What are you talking about? Roy, this is fun. I can't believe you don't want to at least go and see."

Roy watched his friend and rolled his eyes. "Haven't you been bitten by enough vampires in this town? Every time I see you, someone's sucking you dry."

"That's why I'm here!" Val told her friend. "I came because I saw his sweet face in the *Inquirer*." Val pulled a picture cut out from a magazine. "Come on, I know he's nerdy, but isn't he sweet? And I'm sorry, but a little cold hard cash would be nice." Val kissed his picture and put it back in her purse. A heartbreaking smile cracked her perfectly made up face.

"I know it seems calculating, but I've got to increase my odds.

I just want to put myself out there, increase my chances, is all. It's just as easy to marry a rich man as it is a poor man. I just want to roll the dice and see where they lay."

Val checked her face one last time in the mirror. "Now I'm just going in for a minute to pay my respects. I'll be back in a second."

Roy rarely saw this Val. She seemed so vulnerable and naive. Even with her killer blonde hair and her stunning black pumps, she still looked like a vanilla cream pie. He saw past her hairspray to her pure beating heart. She looked like a squirrel, with a nut in its jaw, about to race across a treacherous highway.

"Listen, girlfriend. Don't go in there, okay? Looks are deceiving, you don't know who any of these people are. I bet that McMartin kid thought Ray Buckey was nice too, until he flipped and dunked his head in the toilet."

Val wickedly smiled and shook one of Roy's knees. "Come on, Roy, stop being a killjoy, okay? Why are you tripping? The news is filled with stories like these. They feed us this stuff, 'cause everyone eats it up." Val snatched the newspaper out of Roy's hands. Randomly flipping the pages, she stopped at one. "Look, here's a story about a poor kid. 'A nine-year-old boy murders his Sunday school teacher.' See all the pages are loaded with this crap. Don't be so spooked! I know it's Halloween, but crazy shit happens everyday. I'm just shooting the dice, okay? I'm not doing anything but trying to have a good time. Who knows what's going to happen. None of us have crystal balls." Val glanced at her friend's lap and gave Roy a sly wink. "But from the quantity of fine things you have inside your shop, maybe you're the last man who does."

"Shut up," Roy said, laughing. Val really was cute. He lifted a wisp of hair from her eyes.

"I don't want to play life safe. I could take my last breath tomorrow. What about Doug, huh? Who'da thought Douglas would die. Doug played by rules. Did everything right. No one would have guessed in a million and one years that Douglas would drop dead." Val snapped her manicured fingers in Roy's face.

Roy bit his lip and gripped the steering wheel tighter.

"I'm sorry, Roy. I know he was your friend. But come on, man! How much life do any of us really have? Don't rain on the last parade I have left."

"Last parade! Girlfriend, you're barely past twenty!" Roy popped a small Milky Way bar in his mouth. "I'm thirty-six, and you don't see me tripping hard." But Roy stopped chewing when he saw the tortured look on Val's face. She'd lost some friends, too, and was one step from the street herself. Although she had a job slathering makeup on fifty-year-old mugs at Macy's, she hadn't been there long, the hours were erratic, and it was difficult for her to make ends meet. She was starting to look a bit more tired around the eyes. Oh, she laughed loud and seemed to be having a grand time, but he could see she was desperately searching for a raft, a place to lie back and float along a little. How could he blame her for that? Shoot, if it wasn't for his friend's RV when he first came to town, Roy might have ended up on the hard streets himself.

"All right, all right. I guess you can handle yourself. You made it this far without any gross bruises or scars." Roy glanced at the Rolex on his arm. The band dug into his fat skin. "But listen, hon, I've got to get back to the shop so don't take all day." Roy smiled at Val and pinched her behind. "You bad, girl. The Howard Hughes clan is the one in trouble," Roy laughed as Val got out of the car.

"He's sweet-looking. I bet he's easy as grass. Did you get a look at his brown and gold pants! Plaid! Come on, Roy, weren't they just darling!"

"Oh my God! You're making me sick. You have no fashion sense when it comes to men. You'll hang any old rag on your arm."

"I bet I could have him eating out of my hand by tomorrow."

"See, it's that cocky shit that always gets you in trouble," Roy gave her tight ass an open hand swat. "Now if you would have given me some, I'da worn that ass out."

Val smiled at Roy. She grabbed her purse and thin sweater. "You're too slick for me, Roy. I like the shy, quiet type."

Roy watched Val go through the mortuary's doors. He rolled up his windows, turned the air conditioner on high, and watched the flies buzz around the dash.

After a while, a little girl came out of the door alone. It was cold, and she scrambled into a car with such speed and spread apart feet that he could see all the way up her dress. The girl didn't see Roy sitting alone in the car, and she lit a small flame in her hand. The next thing he knew smoke filled the whole car.

Probably stole one of her mother's 'smokes, Roy thought to himself. What he couldn't see was the girl burning the hair off her doll's skull. The entire scalp dripped over the vinyl seat like wax.

Roy looked at the girl. He could hear the radio coming from out of the girl's car. She was listening to some kind of ball game.

Suddenly, Val came outside again, too.

"Thank God!" Roy said. "I thought I was going to have to go in and get you."

When they passed the small girl, she meekly waved back at Val, and Val vigorously waved her hand back.

"Who would leave a girl like that in the car? Don't her parents know this city is filled with sick, sadistic freaks? Especially around Normandy."

"You know her?" Roy asked.

"I met her in the bathroom," Val solemnly told him. It was cold. The wind had picked up. Val brought her sweater closer around her chest.

"Well somebody needs to slap her mom's ass for that hairdo. I'd put five hundred degrees of my Remington on those locks and flat iron that mess into submission."

Val watched the girl as they slowly passed. The girl was shivering in the front seat.

"Stop the car, wait!" Val jumped from her seat. She rushed to the Buick, pulling her sweater off both arms and handed it to the small girl. The girl grabbed the thick sweater and put it across both goose-bumped legs, covering herself like it was a blanket.

"Thank you," the girl said in a well-mannered tone.

"No problem, honey," Val smiled at the child.

They stared at each other for a very long time, until Roy tooted his horn for Val to come on.

"Hello! Oprah! You can't save the world, honey. Get your Mother Theresa ass in the car."

Val slithered on the leather seat and stared over the dash. "That's the saddest child I ever met in my life. Her eyes were a cesspool of doom."

"Earth to Val. Can we forget these cemetery hicks for a minute? I've got a four thirty coming, and I can't be late. Tyrone turns into a hurricane if he has to wait, and I'm not clipping him while he's fuming in my chair."

Roy tooled his car all the way up San Vicente, and he gunned the engine to let folks know he was there.

Later, inside the protection of his beauty shop again, Roy took a deep breath and blew it out slowly. He plopped another miniature Snickers bar in his jaw and rolled it around while he talked.

"Listen, hon, you're young. Listen to someone with wisdom and age." Roy washed his hands ferociously in the sink. "Don't mess with nobody's children, okay?"

"Oh come on! What do you think I was going to do, grab her and push her into the trunk of your car?"

Roy ignored this remark and put lotion on his hands. "You young things think you're cool, walking around like pool sticks." Roy swallowed the candy in his mouth. "But if you don't watch it, someone will come by and snap you in half."

"Please. You're always so dramatic."

"Life's a bitch! It's not like skipping to Oz, Dorothy. This is no time to be playing with somebody's baby, not with the McMartin case in the news every day."

Val rolled her eyes. She outlined her mouth in lilac filling the center with a cherry dayglow gloss. "You worry too much, Roy. I found my cutie pie jackpot. I'm going to meet Bernard Fowler."

"I can't believe you want to date some cemetery dude! Just 'cause you've walked through a few backyard fires, don't mean your skinny ass can't burn." Roy was plump, and to him skinny people had big egos. "You may fool around and get singed, playing with cremations and shit." Roy sniffed as if he could still smell the bad air and went back and washed his hands again.

Even the Botox couldn't hide all the worry lines on his face, which zigzagged across Roy's tanned forehead. He was teasing, but deep down he was very concerned about Val. She took so many chances. And was gullible to the bone. And besides, he had a bad feeling after seeing those people. The father looked dry, and the son looked downright creepy. Roy didn't like the whole vibe.

"Well, look who cleaned up and turned preacher," Val smiled. "Why don't you quote some scripture and save me a trip to church on Sunday?" Val kissed his rough cheek and left.

"Just watch your back," Roy yelled. "That's all I'm saying."

Val teetered down the street on murderous stilettos. One of her heels caught a dead leaf on the ground. When Val bent to yank it off, she almost tumbled in the street.

"Mercy," Roy said under his breath. He rubbed his cheek where Val kissed him, slightly shook his head, and shut the shop's frosty door.

Even though it was sunny, it was a coat-wearing October. A veil of worry draped across Roy's face. Val was an amateur. She didn't have the stomach to do scams. Hell, she'd only been in L.A. for two years. But it was long enough for her to think she knew the whole town already. Those were always the first ones to fall. He'd seen lots of girls like Val in his shop, some desert town hick trying to make it in pictures. Thinking Hollywood was a slick place to live. Most of them ended up in the streets, working way after midnight. Selling it for two hits or a few nights at the flophouse. Traipsing up and down Santa Monica Boulevard, dragging their high-heels on cement, shoving sad, messy wigs inside steamy car windows and trying to grin without showing their scabs. Lots of them became junkies or bottom-rung whores. Some became so diseased they looked like death wearing pumps, stumbling through life in their cliff-hanging shoes. He went to a lot of their funerals in this part of town. Three or four of them could be seen sharing one cigarette or huddled around a single cup of coffee at Denny's. But most of them you never laid eyes on again.

Hollywood had definitely changed since the Howard Hughes days of glory. It was a hellhole of spit with smooth sidewalks of piss, syringes, and big gangs of poor roaming kids, who stayed alive by eating the dead food from restaurants at night. And even though they just threw a new mall in the place, planting trees and hammering up these gaudy fluorescent lights, Hollywood couldn't hide what crept out at night. Late at night, it was a cesspool of slime.

3

Bernard and Mr. Fowler

"**I**'m sorry we're so late. I got lost in these hills. The roads are so winding, and some of these streets don't have signs."

It was after nine at night, and the streetlights were on. The repast had been over for hours.

Bernard stared at the woman without one hint of welcome. "May I help you?" he asked.

"Oh," Margie said. "Maybe I have the wrong address." She dropped both bags and fumbled through her badly abused purse. Pulling a rumpled obituary, she smoothed it out against her thigh and asked, "Is this four-thirty-five Woodbridge Lane?"

Bernard ignored her confused face and glanced at her kid.

She had a wide grin on her face. She smiled at him with such big freakish eyes that she looked like one of those carnival kids trying to lure him on a cheap rickety ride.

Suddenly, his father wheeled himself in the room. He examined the scene at his door. He'd been wondering the whole time when Margie would come and had looked up every time someone else rang the bell. But the person was never her, it was always another cadaver in a dress, holding an old pan of noodles and cheese, smiling with a few missing teeth. He was so depressed that Margie didn't come, that he left the room right in the middle of somebody talking. And when the sun dipped behind the garage and the entire street turned navy, he wheeled himself into his room, closed the door fiercely, and was too sad to even watch *Gunsmoke.*

"Oh boy," he said to himself, licking his tongue across his dentures. He could smell the cooked chicken seeping out from the bags. Bernard's father rubbed his old mangled hand over his gut and gazed at Margie with new life in his eyes.

"Let her in, fool! Why are you standing there staring?" Bernard's father rolled his wheelchair around Bernard's legs. "I told you she was coming." He waved Margie and the girl in and wrinkled his large nose at his son.

"Close that door, boy! Stop wasting my good heat. I don't want any of that cold air on my legs!" His wheelchair groaned across the uneven floor.

Mr. Fowler rolled his chair sideways, reached and locked the door himself.

Bernard bit his hangnail, stepped out of his way, and examined the strangers inside his front room. Though the girl kept up a fastidious appearance, the mother was another story completely. The rest of the day must have taken a heavy toll on Margie. Her black funeral dress was gone, and now she wore a clingy low cut floral, which was stained and showed a road map of horror. Her huge breasts were swollen and covered with moles, her ass spread as wide as the 405 freeway, and her feet were shoved into some scuffed peek-a-boo shoes.

She looked used. She had passed the last breath of forty, and the highway to fifty had definitely not been kind. Although she and Bernard were probably exactly the same age, she had a soggy warped body, with large rippled folds, like a loaf of bread that had been left in the rain.

Bernard was livid that this woman was here in his house. He ground his back teeth. He'd seen many women like Margie before. In the funeral business, lots of women came in looking like her. A savage face, that collapsed and laughed at itself, a harsh overripe life, where the water smashed through the dam way too many times, leaving nothing but a weather-beaten frame. Most of them arrived at the funeral parlor on gurneys. They had wounds at their temples or their stomachs bulged from pills or their skulls were cracked in half from slippery tubs. They looked cooked. They looked bleached or too greasy, wearing gobs of thick makeup to hide the sinking ship underneath. They wore cheap, crooked wigs over their white thinning hair. Their arms rattled with bracelets and giant grotesque rings, and multiple chains circled their multiple throats making the whole effect look like a grossly decorated Christmas tree. They reeked. They slathered on too much perfume, and it hung in the room long after they were gone like a bad song you couldn't get out of your head. They did everything they could to try to look young. They bought clothes that didn't fit or bought memberships at gyms, and when that wasn't enough they went straight to the surgeons and bought cheekbones and chins or a new set of boobs or injected a goo in their lips. They took reve pills to burn off the fat while they slept, and when that didn't work, they got liposuction to suck out the rest.

But death's savage arm snatched them up in the end. They found them lying on the floor in a growing pool of red, dead from botched beauty treatments or mixing too much codeine with vodka, trying to block out life's ugly claw.

Mr. Reynolds called them "butter." They were the bread of his business.

Their deaths were as violently staged as their lives. Heads stuck in ovens or blasted by guns or mangled to pieces from car wrecks. Reynolds had a devil of a time putting it all back together. Sometimes the families complained. Though they looked dignified and nice, people thought they didn't look quite right. Jaws were slightly off. Necks were engorged or their teeth protruded through too much lip. Details like skin tone would be analyzed and compared. Hair and makeup were scrutinized without end.

Once a woman rammed her arm next to her dead sister's face.

"That's not Sandy," she screamed, pulling the clothes from the dead girl's body. The funeral party had to wrestle the woman down to the floor but not before she tore off her dead sister's dress.

"That's not her, I tell you. That's not Sandy's nose. Sandy had a cute nose and she had the same skin tone as me and everyone knows it." She clawed at the body until her fingernails were filled with gunky cadaver makeup. She yelled at Reynolds, demanding the color be redone, screaming, "nobody in my family looks that color." But without any pictures or if a body was badly bruised or mangled, the makeup could easily come out wrong. And what could Bernard do with a face smashed to bits? He used wax, glue, false eyelashes, and rubber cement, trying to reinvent the right mixture of skin parts and color, correcting things while creating the perfect look of calm. A quiet, sleeplike vision of the face. The dreamy state before death's brutal clutch.

Mr. Reynolds didn't balk. These sad deaths were big business. And the men were just as reliable as women, only the men came in younger and younger each day. Men fooled around with snakes or tried to fix the electrical themselves or caught their hands in mowers and bled out over their lawns or drove drunk, crushing the family to death. Men who blasted their chins with rifles or stuck 45s along their tongues. Men who murdered their women and then shot themselves, or maybe they couldn't stomach the fact that they were fired from their jobs and gassed themselves up in cars. It didn't matter what vehicle wheeled them in. To Reynolds, each twisted face meant a steady flow of cash. Each body brought in was a hot buttered roll. They were delivered. They just kept showing at his door. He sent Tommy, the grave digger, to fish out the bodies. In an instant, they were picked up and put in his van and delivered like pizza or a bag of Chinese food, rolling in like a metal cart of groceries.

Bernard looked at Margie and loudly sucked his teeth. What was this miserable sack of potatoes doing in his house at this hour? Who was this overly made-up trollop who was one wink from going to seed, like an overly bruised peach on the sink. Bernard ran or worked out each day. He did pushups in his room with lightning speed. Except for the slightest little paunch around his taut belly, Bernard was as fit as a tree.

"I'm so happy you came," Mr. Fowler smiled. He reached for Margie's hand, guiding her closer to his chair, and she slid on the chair's arm just as she had done at the funeral, except now she circled her arm around Mr. Fowler's neck.

Even when Bernard glared at her, she didn't take her fingers away. But suddenly her lips pouted, and she appeared a tad more glum.

"I'm so upset about Alice." Margie's lips grazed his lobe. She took a tissue out of her purse and dabbed at her eyes.

"Yes, we all are," Bernard said, standing in front of Margie's knees. He looked at the greasy food in the plastic bags on the floor. "I'm afraid it's getting late. We've already eaten. My dad was getting ready for bed."

"What are you talking about, huh? I'm your father not your kid. Where do you get off telling me what to do?" He didn't make it sound as bad as he usually did. He didn't want to get too ugly in front of these special guests, so he raised one bushy eyebrow as a warning instead.

His father was a bit loopy. He'd been drinking Bombay gin. He'd been pouring himself shots since the funeral car brought them home, and with the liquor now wildly racing through his veins, he was definitely feeling no pain.

He smiled wickedly at Margie. He was drunk off her eyes, and he never turned his nose away from her sweet-smelling neck as his hand buried its way under her hem. He was working his hand further up Margie's thigh; he was so excited he felt like a dynamite stick, just before the hot spark ate the string. His wife's death took a toll, leaving him famished from the loss, and his hand almost savagely searched for the silk between her thighs. He'd never had a woman this much younger than him in his life. He felt like it was the Fourth of July.

Margie giggled and fingered the old man's long braid. Maybe she'd feed him antifreeze, hidden in fluorescent Jell-O wedges, or sprinkle arsenic on his pillow like that Florida man, or strangle him with her nylons.

"I really miss Sweet Alice. That's what we all called your wife. I don't know if you knew this or not but she was the godmother of my daughter Paula."

Margie pushed Paula forward with her leg.

As if on cue, and like a small wind-up doll, Paula said, "How do you do, sir! I'm pleased to make your acquaintance." She curtsied and smiled in a grossly overdone manner. "I'd like you to read the poem I wrote."

Bernard stared at her. She was almost too ghoulish to be cute. She straightened her dress and then completely dropped her smile and sang in a haunting falsetto.

"Oh merciful Lord.
Have pity on me
Lend us your bounty
Leave me your sheet.
Let charity exist
On each stranger's tongue
Let them be giving
Let each sun burn slow
And we will find mercy
When you call us home."

The girl spun around elaborately and then fell dramatically to both knees and after making the sign of the cross, pressing both hands together, she said a hearty, "Amen."

Margie clapped wildly and then clasped her hands tight. "Save us, oh Lord," she said, bending her neck, squeezing her eyes and mumbling her lips in a prayer.

"Amen to that," **Mr. Fowler** said low. He was watching Margie's breasts shake mildly as she clapped, and he nodded his own head in respect.

Bernard stood there amazed at their unabashed theatrics.

"Thank you," Paula solemnly said.

She completely transformed from the extrovert on stage and now stood mute staring at the floor.

"She's a cutie pie!" Mr. Fowler said, but he was looking at Margie. "Spitting image of you." He held his nose close to Margie's neck, like he was smelling a rose.

Bernard was the one who raised his brows now. One of his father's hands had completely disappeared. His hairy wrist was under Margie's hem. But Margie's eyes were closed, and she didn't seem bothered by the hand. Bernard was embarrassed for them both.

"So, how are you related to my mother? I mean, obviously it's not by blood."

"What the devil is wrong with you, boy? Have you lost all your senses? These people are your mother's relations." Mr. Fowler looked like he wanted to take off his belt and whip Bernard right there.

Margie opened her lids and smiled at Bernard. She could see the large question marks inside his eyes. There's always a road-block or two in this business. She started filing a knife inside her brain, imagining his throat in her lap.

"We're not related, you're absolutely right, but we always lived on Howard Hughes land. My people worked for Alice's folks back in Texas. We used to play as kids. And used to stay in touch, but I haven't heard from her in months," Margie said, dabbing her lids for effect.

Bernard looked at Margie. He studied her face. Even with the graph paper lines etching her mouth and her eyes, she was still way too young to be a childhood friend of his mother.

"Excuse me," Bernard said. "I don't mean to be rude. But aren't you a little young to be a friend of my mother?"

That's it, Margie thought. She would have to use a gun. She touched the outline of the gun on the bottom of her purse.

"Bernard!" his father said. "Shoot! Show some respect! Don't you know better that to question a lady's age?"

"Oh, that's okay. He's actually right." Margie smiled sheepishly and then turned toward Bernard.

"My mother died when I was a baby. Your mother took care of me back then. She was more than a friend and really like a mother herself." While dabbing her eyes with a hankie, Margie glanced at Bernard. Yes, the gun would be the best thing for him.

"What about your husband? What happened to him?" Bernard suspected this black woman didn't have any husband. She didn't even own a decent pair of shoes.

"Oh, I wasn't married long. My friends say I was spared." Margie fluttered her mascara lashes at Bernard and pushed her Playtex brassier toward Mr. Fowler's chin.

"I've seen my daddy," Paula offered. "I saw his picture before it burned."

Margie looked as if she stuck a fork in a socket. All her black curls were standing on end. She got up and stood behind Paula's pink dress and pinched her skin hard, twisting her flesh like a lock, until the girl's lake blue eyes gushed with tears.

Oblivious to her kid's pain, Margie strolled to the dining room casually and placed the food bags on the table. She scanned the elaborate room just like a cashier, the crystal, the silver, the huge chandelier, taking note of each item's worth.

"What happened to your dad?" Bernard was interested now.

"He got shot in the hotel," Paula happily admitted. She was pissed about being pinched and was testing the limits now. She hated this charade her mother made her play and although she would pay dearly and was often beaten with a stick, she enjoyed finding ways to get Margie back.

Margie dropped the bag of chicken and a breast rolled from the foil, splatting greasily on the hardwood floor.

"Paula!" Margie screamed wildly. "What did I tell you about lying?"

Margie turned to Mr. Fowler. She lowered her head. Her voice turned into a wilted bouquet of sadness. She had to cover this infraction. "That's not what happened, sweetie." Margie dabbed her nose and looked to the ceiling without speaking, like she was trying to make the tears rush back inside her eyes.

"I wish to God it was something as merciful as that." Margie covered her face with her hands and then burst into full-blown sobs. "My poor Henry died of lung cancer," she sputtered. "He was lost in a blink of an eye."

Mr. Fowler wheeled himself to the table and rubbed Margie's back. "Lung cancer took my Alice, too. Ate her larynx and tongue, and none of them doctors did squat, just made me sit there and watch."

Tears began to roll down Bernard's father's eyes, and Margie sat inside his chair, circling his neck with both arms. "There, there," she told the old man.

Mr. Fowler immediately felt better, though he hid this from them. He pretended to weep long and hard, but secretly he couldn't be more pleased with his face wedged between Margie's rose-scented breasts.

"Oh, sugar, it's all right." Margie stroked his large shoulders. "Cancer's a mean thief in the end."

Bernard was disgusted by this scene and turned to Paula again. This little girl was brave. He would have never had the guts to counter his father. And she took that hard pinch and didn't bat an eye.

"Isn't it late for her to be up?" Bernard glanced at Paula.

She didn't look anything like Margie. She didn't have the same features, skin tone or hair. She was as translucent as one of his mother's crystal jars, with skin so clear he could easily count all her veins. There was something odd about her, too. Something he couldn't put his finger on yet. "Is she adopted?" he asked Margie point blank.

A sadistic smile grew in Margie's orange painted mouth. You could almost smell the fire brewing inside her cold charcoal mind. Her eyes were as veiled as a white lacy bride, slyly claiming to still be a virgin. Margie was on a mission. She didn't mind comments like these. She could talk about anything they wanted and not get upset. She didn't mind explaining how some black blood mixed. Besides, the story always came out the same. Dousing gasoline on their beds or putting strychnine inside their coffee or stuffing plastic bags over their heads. She gazed at Bernard like a cat eyeing a canary. As a con artist, she used every comment that came her way, twisting it into her advantage.

"No, she's not adopted, my husband was white."

There was a long awkward moment before anyone spoke.

This was such a bold-faced lie Margie had to bite her own tongue just to ward off a burgeoning smirk. If her husband was white, there would have never been a problem and no reason to do that first killing.

But the truth was, her husband was a dark-skinned politician, and Margie ran off right before the election. She and his campaign manager had a torrid affair. Neither of them thought her husband would win.

Margie got up and slowly walked to the kitchen. All this talk dredged up memories Margie worked to forget, memories that lived like a short film running inside her brain. And though she tried to ignore these thoughts and took pills to dull the pain, she could never get the projector to stop. It kept playing the same movie over again, rewinding the horror in her mind. All of it was her fault. She created this drama. She was the star in the most horrible role of her life. And no matter how hard she tried; all the scenes were the same. Sometimes the scenery changed or day became night, but she was always dressed the same and always spoke the same lines. There was still a car chase, a gun, a long bloody knife, and the agonizing screams of her husband. It was that last image that tortured Margie the most. It gnawed on her soul, drilled deep lines in her face. What puzzled her was how she had changed so much in one day. In one moment, in one instant, she became savagely cruel.

Looking back, it was still hard to believe it was her. But those were her clothes, and that was her mouth speaking those lines. She wasn't the happy-go-lucky teacher anymore. If someone had told her she would commit murder, she would have spat in their face. She wasn't a killer! She was a Catholic schoolteacher for God's sake! She kept a red string of rosary beads in her purse! But suddenly, there she was, playing the worst scene of all. All these facts and much more bore big holes in her brain. They ate her stomach lining and dug crisscrossing lines over her face. Sometimes she imagined how it might have turned out different. Like if she'd never taken the campaign manager's call, or never went to his room in her husband's new car. But these were dead useless thoughts, fantasies at best, that never saw the light of true day. She was a fool who'd chased the wrong merry-go-round ride. At the time, the campaign manager lived a flamboyant life, more extravagant and much too rich for a plain woman like Margie. She was bitterly alone. Her husband was always on the road. But that life was over. And the next thing she knew, her husband was back and then the child came and holy hell broke out in her house. There was the car chase and her husband with a gun and the sharp steely blade in her hand. Everything after that happened in a flash. The damage was done. There was no going back. And her husband, like her normally long auburn hair had been cut down and buried in a cold unmarked grave, unrecoverable and irrefutably lost.

Margie was thinking of this while lathering her hands. She had the unfocused look of someone standing at a door, wondering what she had come to the room for.

Coming to her senses, Margie began searching the kitchen. It was a hideous, shipwrecked room with tall wooden cabinets, which were warped and hung slightly ajar. Margie started opening the doors and peering inside. She found the plates and started lifting them up one by one. Lots of folks hid their savings in between stacks of china. Holding a plate, she continued poking around. When she turned around, Bernard was standing right there. She dropped one of the plates on the floor.

Margie clasped a hand over her chest. "Oh, you scared me! I didn't know you were there."

Bernard took the other plates from out of her hand. "Why don't you sit down? I'll take care of this."

But Margie didn't sit. She noticed a basket of lemons. "Do you have any sugar. I can make some lemonade in a jiffy." Margie grabbed a knife and skillfully sliced the lemons in half. She found a pitcher and filled it up with water and poured the lemon juice on top. "Where's your sugar, honey?" she said, batting her eyes as if sugar was the last thing on her mind.

Bernard didn't know what to say. Margie was so capable and aggressive. The next thing he knew, everyone's glass was full and floating with sugar and ice cubes.

Margie smiled and took another plate from the shelf. "Wow, these are beautiful. Alice always had good taste."

Bernard quickly took the plates from her hands. "I'll do that," he said. He didn't like her nosing around his kitchen. He wanted these strangers to go.

Margie smiled at Bernard and opened a silverware drawer and grabbed a pile of knives and forks in her hand.

If he didn't stop breathing down her neck, Margie thought, she would slice Bernard right here and now.

Left alone, Paula walked over to a large crystal bowl. It was brimming with all kinds of beautifully wrapped candy. Halloween was almost here. She'd seen the decorations in stores. But her mother never bought her any treats. Her tiny tongue started to water.

Creeping, making sure the old man couldn't see, the girl tiptoed backward to the full candy bowl. With her arm behind her dress, she picked up a fistful of candy, secretly shoving it inside her pockets.

"Where are you from, honey?" Bernard's father asked the child. His wheelchair squeaked as he moved closer to the girl and one of the candies fell to the floor.

Just then, Margie came back in and put forks and knives on the table.

Angrily, Bernard followed her with a stack of plates and napkins.

Paula looked scared. She stared at the candy near her foot. She didn't want to get in trouble, so she kicked it under the couch and walked to the table just before her mother looked her way.

"What's the matter, gal? Cat got your tongue?" Mr. Fowler's crooked smile was a fun house of dentures, like the kind of teeth that moved by themselves when you wound them up. He ran a skeletal hand along her slim arm.

The girl stiffened and grabbed her knife, squeezing it in her fist.

This sudden aggressive movement made everyone stare.

Margie ignored her daughter and kept cutting her meat. Curling her lips like a kitten, Margie purred when she spoke. "Poor thing is just hungry." She patted Paula's hand. "We Texans can get vexed if we go too long without food." Margie took the knife out of Paula's clenched hand, but she had to pry loose each finger to do it.

"Want me cut your food, honey?" Margie asked her daughter. "Give Mama a big smile first."

Paula smiled ghoulishly, but then glared at Mr. Fowler.

"She's a pistol! Man, oh man, you have a real hellcat on your hands." Mr. Fowler broke out in loud laughter.

But Bernard didn't laugh. He studied the child, but she jerked her head from his stare.

Paying extra attention to Bernard's father, Margie tucked a napkin under his chin. She gave him another mound of potatoes, refilled his glass, and buttered his bread with her knife.

"You cook just like a Southerner," Mr. Fowler said. "Exactly like my wife."

"Well, we Tennessee women are in the kitchen at four years old."

"Tennessee?" Bernard questioned. "I thought you said you were from Texas."

"We're from Texas originally, but we've skipped around a lot. We've been trying to find a good place to rest for a spell."

"Got itchy feet, huh?" Mr. Fowler smiled at Margie's legs.

"Why'd you leave Texas?" Bernard wanted to know. He looked at the girl, hoping she'd answer this question, but the girl was gnawing her chicken and sucking the bones like she was starving, leaving a stack of stripped-down sticks on her plate.

Margie used his probing question as an opportunity to paint a new story. "Paula's daddy owned a whole bunch of oil fields in

Texas. When he died, I didn't have any reason to stay." Margie flipped what was left of her sawed off black hair. "There was nothing but sad memories there." She had a faraway look on her face.

Paula looked at her mother and then smiled at her own plate. "I took a train ride from Memphis. I bought the ticket myself," Paula announced this fact like she had just won a prize.

Margie dropped her fork. She looked horrified at the child. She knew better than to ever mention Memphis again.

"Honey, have some more." Margie plopped a breast on the girl's plate and then kicked her leg under the table.

Masking her pain and gazing angrily at this new piece of chicken, Paula stabbed the breast hard, leaving the fork in the dense center. "Who am I?" the girl asked, smiling at Bernard.

Bernard smiled back. The girl was playing a game of some kind.

"I don't know? Who are you?" he asked.

Paula stabbed the meat three more times. "I'm Mommy," she happily told Bernard.

Margie ignored this charade. She knew exactly what Paula was doing. The child could be as coy as a warden, herself. She'd deal with her little behind later.

"This is delicious!" Mr. Fowler said, licking his chops. He hadn't lifted his head since they put his food down. "I haven't had yard bird this good since I left Kentucky! You put your foot in this meal, gal!" Mr. Fowler made this statement with a mouth full of food, and some of it splattered from his lips. He smiled admiringly at Margie, wiping his mouth with the back of his hand.

"Alice taught me how to fry. The secret is seasoning your grease and heating your fire just right. I use bacon drippings and mix it with fresh buttered lard and keep my flame set on high. Being a good cook is a lot like being a good wife, you can't fake it and you can't skimp on flavor and taste. Who wants to marry powdered potatoes or a frozen bag of peas. Food, like a woman, should be completely authentic. It should be genuine. There's got to be some realness in each bowl. I put my heart and soul in each plate." Margie smiled at her fingers before swallowing her roll. She was thinking about the Kentucky Fried Chicken containers she left at the curb as she licked chicken juice from her thumb.

Bernard's father was hanging on each and every word. He looked as gullible as an eighteen-year-old soldier on leave.

"I haven't had a good meal like this in months. Once the lady who lived upstairs made me a nice meat loaf sandwich, but that was a long time ago."

Margie's ears perked. "You have tenants in here?"

"It's a two-unit house. Used to be one great big mansion, but me and Alice chopped the upstairs and rented it out. It was way too much house for just the three of us. Old Howard was really bent out of shape when he saw it. He used to live here first, when he came to California to make pictures. He thought we ruined the architecture. He went wild when he saw it. Hell, I didn't care what that maniac thought. I told him he was crazy and unless he was paying us money, I had a right to rent the place and make some cash from it myself."

Mr. Fowler loudly slurped from his lemonade glass. "Crazy as a loon, that Howard fool was. My wife didn't like me saying that, but she knew I was right. And the world found out in the end!"

"Howard Hughes, my goodness, how can you stand it. He lived here? Oh my Lord," Margie placed a hand across her chest. She wore a brilliant diamond ring on her pinkie. "What was he like? Was he really eccentric? A billionaire, my God! How could you stand being around all that money?" Margie's eyes looked like they had dollars swirling through the pupils. She was as lit as a Las Vegas sign.

Bernard didn't like talking about the Howard Hughes family. He thought it was boring and pretentious to even mention his name. He'd never met the man once. Had only seen him in pictures. He was a pitiful freak who lived his last days in a dark room watching the reels of his own movies over and over as his fingernails grew like claws on his hands. Bernard thought it was a bad joke that they were even related. And except for this broken-down, godforsaken falling down house, he never gave them one cent.

Since Margie was talking to his father, Bernard decided to talk to the child. He offered the girl more mashed potatoes.

"What grade are you in?" Bernard asked.

"Fourth," the girl said proudly, but then she glanced at her mother, checking to see if this was okay to say.

"Well all the schools out here are in a pickle right now. Public or private, it doesn't matter which. All of 'em are damn crime scenes now." Bernard's father wheeled to the living room and picked up a newspaper on the couch. "This McMartin case has got everyone in L.A. spooked. The whole system's running amuck."

"Have you heard of the case?" Bernard quietly asked Margie.

Margie shook her head no. She honestly hadn't.

"Well these hellions out here got a gang of folks fired." Mr. Fowler wheeled toward Margie and handed her the paper. His chair squeaked and almost buckled underneath his weight.

"I went to Catholic school," Paula said. "But we had to leave before I finished."

Margie shot the girl a strong, don't-you-tell-too-much look.

The girl looked down and played with her hands.

"People been pointing back and forth, lot of heads rolled this year and a whole lot more will go before it's all said and done." Bernard's father looked at the girl and licked his chapped lips while Margie read the article herself.

It was a very big story and with plenty of related articles, too. There was a graphic and morbid tale about a murderer on the loose, who killed three different men in cold blood.

Margie put the newspaper on the dining room table. She didn't like reading stories like these.

The old man wheeled closer to Margie. "I really like your dress." His vision wasn't that good even with Coke bottle lenses. He couldn't see that the dress was stained and starting to rip on one side. He touched it, fingering the delicate fabric. "This is real nice material," he said.

Paula got up and walked to a fireplace in the middle of the wall. She was tired of Bernard. He kept staring at her hard. She'd rather watch the flame leaping in the pit.

Margie looked at Bernard's father. "Is the apartment upstairs empty? Do you have any renters up there now?"

Bernard flashed his father a panicky glare.

"Oh no. It's been empty for years. I never had good luck with tenants."

"Well the reason I asked is we're looking for a place." Margie gazed at her lap. "Right now we're in a motel, until we get things together."

Margie walked over to Paula and started twirling her braid. Paula knew this was her cue.

"Mommy said we may have to sleep in the car, until her new job comes through."

Paula gave Bernard and Mr. Fowler a sad depressed look and then she spun around until her dress rose up her thighs.

"For heavens sake, honey! I didn't say that! Really, it's not that bad, Mr. Fowler. I had a few stepbacks, but I should be on my feet soon."

"Well why don't you folks take the empty room upstairs?"

"Dad!" Bernard bolted up from his chair.

"Really, we couldn't do that," Margie said. She was the picture of meekness. She had the humility of a saint. No one could see her cold pitchfork heart.

"You're right. My father made a ridiculous offer. The place is a wreck! It hasn't been rented in ages."

This time Mr. Fowler flashed the all-knowing smile.

"Come on, son, who are you kidding? We both know it's fixed. You worked on it yourself. Mr. Wade told me all about it. He took some great pictures for me last Sunday."

Mr. Fowler was agile and strong and rolled his wheelchair easily across the floor. The wheels creaked on the gold wooden slates. From a cabinet he pulled out a new stack of pictures.

"See. You can look for yourself." He handed Margie a stack of Polaroid shots. "My son did a helluva job," he said.

Bernard was enraged. He couldn't believe what was happening. He jumped up and looked over Margie's shoulder. There was his apartment. The one he'd secretly fixed. It was one thing for these people to barge in and eat, but to allow them to live here! Now, that took the cake.

"It's mine!" Bernard screamed. He sounded like a four-year-old boy.

Margie excused herself. She knew it was best to leave the room during these tense discussions. She hoped it was solved by the time she came back.

"Come on, Paula, let's clear up these dishes."

Obediently, the girl rose and gathered the plates from the table, following her mother to the kitchen. But when Margie went in the kitchen, she didn't wash a thing. She merely turned on the faucet at the sink and huddled behind the kitchen door, listening to Bernard and his father from the door's slender crack.

"The apartment was mine! I worked on it myself. How can you rent it when it is supposed to be for me?" Bernard screamed.

This was the first time Bernard ever confronted his father.

"You said you wanted me to stand on my own. I could live up there and handle my own affairs. You'd finally get me out of your hair."

Bernard's father stared at his son. He loved that he confronted him at last. But Bernard's hands were on his hips, which jutted out like a woman and seeing that pose only made him more upset.

"I never gave you nothing," his father said slowly. He opened another drawer and pulled out a pack of Pall Malls. He grabbed a tiny cardboard box and in a grand gesture, lit a match, sucking the cigarette slow.

"Let me explain something to you, son." Mr. Fowler blew out his smoke. "Something's yours when you go out and earn it alone, not wait for someone to hand it over like a damn welfare check."

"But you told me I could have it." Bernard clenched his fist. "You said it would be mine on my forty-ninth birthday. I'm the one who cleaned it all up!"

Bernard's father had promised him the apartment, about twenty years back. Who'da thought the fool boy would be living here that long.

His father sat quietly. He raised one eyebrow at his son.

"I'll pay you!" Bernard said, pounding his fist on the wood.

"With what? Your mortuary money?" his father burst into cackling laughter. He beat both his thighs with his large floppy hands. "Oh, please. You don't make squat at that job. Reynolds hired you because I asked for a favor."

Bernard didn't care if his father asked Reynolds or not. He liked his job. Reynolds liked him, too. He was making a name for himself in the undertaker world and could do wonders with skin glue and wax. "I work. I can pay my own way," Bernard shot back.

"Well, in my day, a man went out and worked with his hands. He didn't lie around all day rubbing dead people with soap, lathering Vaseline all over a stiff's face. You think it's work to put stockings on cold embalmed feet. Boy, sit down and stop crying, you're starting to make me sick." Mr. Fowler blatantly blew his smoke into Bernard's face.

The truth was, Mr. Fowler had become smitten by Margie. He wasn't about to let his son drive this fine woman out. This was his house! He made the rules. Besides, he couldn't believe he had gotten so lucky. The day had started off so morbid. The sun barely shined at all. He'd buried his good wife only a few hours ago. But low and behold, here was a peach of a woman right here! A live breathing beauty ready to move into his house. He wasn't about to let his son spoil that!

Bernard waved the smoke away. The nicotine made it hard to breathe. He plunged his hand in his pocket and snatched his inhaler out, clamping it down against his teeth.

"Look at you, you're weak. You need medicine just to breathe! It's too late to strike out on your own now. Good grief, you're way east of forty already, and the train ride to fifty is already in sight! You're a mess! You've never been on your own in your life, and you want to lecture me about paying your own way? Boy, I still put food on your plate." Mr. Fowler rolled to the fireplace and spat and a crackling sound filled the room.

Bernard's father took inventory of his son's puny frame. He was thin and didn't have a masculine bone to his name. He often wondered how he'd gone wrong with his son. He couldn't understand what had fouled up the process. He gave him lots of guns when he was young. He let him weld things at his job. He even left him alone in the forest one night just to see if he could survive in the wild. But as a man, his son proved to be a miserable failure. Bernard shot his own thumb and torched the wall at his job. And he cried all night long in the woods, screaming and clutching a rock for dear life, until his father yanked him down from the mountains himself and brought his sniffling bones home.

"I've rented it," his father said. "End of discussion."

Margie figured it was a good time to send Paula in the room. She told her to go over and talk to the old man.

Paula looked at Bernard. He scratched his forearms and his milky skin was covered in dark maroon marks.

The old man held his cigarette between his back teeth. A cloud of smoke hovered over his metal wheelchair. Reluctantly, she walked up to his knees.

"Do we have one of these?" The little girl asked.

The fireplace crackled and snapped at the silence.

"Well, you did once, but we had to seal it off," he said. "These fools didn't know how a fireplace worked and almost torched the whole house."

Bernard's father rolled closer to the girl and sucked his Pall Mall.

The girl watched the smoke swirl along his mouth.

"Show her, son," he said while exhaling slow, blowing the last bit of smoke through his teeth.

Embarrassed and turning a boilerplate red, Bernard slowly

rolled up one of his sleeves. Part of his forearm was melted from burns.

"I had to grab my boy here, right out the bed." he took a deep drag and held it down in his lungs. "His whole room was a dust bowl of smoke."

"Ever since then, I've had asthma." Bernard glared at his father. He waved the cigarette smoke from his face.

"You don't have asthma, damn it! Those damn doctors are liars. Those same doctors killed your mother, and I watched with my own eyes. That asthma shit is all in your mind!"

Mr. Fowler rolled across the floor and opened the cabinet again. He took a key out and put it in his palm. "So you want to see the place?" He liked the girl's eyes. "You're as pretty as your mother," he said.

He refused to look at the veins sticking out of his son's neck. "Why don't you show the people around?" He wheeled toward Bernard's legs and shoved the key in his hand.

"Please!" Bernard screamed as tears rushed from his eyes.

Paula was amazed. She'd only seen a man beg once. Right after her mom pulled out her gun.

Margie figured this was a good time to come back into the room. "Is everything settled?" she asked Mr. Fowler, ignoring Bernard. "We don't want to put anyone out."

"Naw, nobody's getting put out," he said. "Lessen they're wanting to go." When Mr. Fowler said this, he looked at Bernard. "Now, go on. I know my son fixed it up good." He wheeled his chair close to the little girl again. His face was right next to her collar. "As for a job," he said to Margie, "You and pretty can work for me. You can cook and clean, and she can help me read. That will help offset your rent."

Margie was excited. This was working better than she planned.

"Well then, everything's settled." He grinned at Margie's plump legs and rubbed his belly as she went up the steps. He could see her buttercream slip under her dress. But when the girl went upstairs she clung to her hem, holding it down around her legs.

"Let me know if you need anything!" the father's booming voice roared. "Bernard will get you anything you need, hear?"

Bernard's father wheeled himself into the living room and stopped, he rotated his chair by the fireplace's warm mouth. The heat made his shriveled face break into a sweat. He hadn't had this much excitement in ages.

4

Mr. Fowler

Within two weeks, the burn fumes had dramatically increased. A bus flipped on the 110 and leapt the divide. Thirty-nine people died. Reynolds was swamped, but he loved all this last-minute business. Though he tried to get all the cremations done at night, sometimes they were still burning by morning. The harsh cinder smell filled the calm, quiet block. If you looked up, you could see the dark swirling smoke, ballooning huge and then floating out of sight.

"Boy!" Mr. Fowler called in his baritone rumble. Though he wheeled himself to the porch and out toward the ramp, that was as far as he could make the wheelchair go without getting stuck in the mud.

It rained six days straight, and the sky was a dark, casket black with fat wheezy clouds floating by.

"It's going to be a hell of a winter," Corleen told them today.

Mr. Fowler grimaced and never looked at her face. He didn't speak to low-class blacks unless he wanted some work done, and today would be no exception.

Every day, Bernard pushed his father to the corner to get a Coke. Rain or shine, it was their daily trip outside. He could have drank one of the many Cokes they housed in the fridge, but that would deflate Mr. Fowler's list of daily chores for his son.

People didn't like Mr. Fowler. He was what kids would call

"mean." He was arrogant and rude and carried himself with an overseer's air, and even in a wheelchair he acted like he towered over folks, rolling by as if he were royalty. When they came back from the store, Mr. Fowler clicked on the news, and the television stayed on all day.

"Boy! Come in here and fix me my bath. I got a horrible itch on my skin."

Bernard ignored the call and grabbed the shovel by the fence. He was furious with his father. He dug a three-foot-deep hole, pitching the dirt over his back. He wished he could dig the hole three feet deeper and toss his cantankerous father inside. It was his fault the woman and the girl moved into his place. They took everything, every sanded floor and newly painted wall!

Bernard shoveled the dirt with venom and speed. His mother had told him where the strongbox was buried. She told him and him alone and said to not tell his father. Bernard dug until sweat dripped down his back and his face.

After shoveling for an hour, Bernard hit something hard. He jumped in the hole and pulled out a box from the dirt.

"I know you hear me, boy! Stop acting deaf. You better come in here when I call you, you fool!" The father leaned forward in his chair jutting his tight jaw, squinting through his Coke bottle lenses.

But Bernard did ignore him. He took the box to the garage. Snatching open a beer, he took two savage swigs and wiped the froth off his lips. He took a bolt cutter from his toolbox, snapped off the lock, and opened the dirty box's lid.

Staring back and sparkling like a Tiffany lamp was a treasure chest of heavy solid gold coins. Bernard scooped his hand in, picked some up, and let them spill back. Dispersed between the coins were gold cuff links and tie pins and what looked like a hundred thousand dollars in cash. Bernard's mother had always joked about hiding a treasure from his father. It was Howard Hughes' money. It came straight from the man himself. Howard had buried it there when he first bought this house but told Alice he could never remember where it was and after making all his billions he never thought of it again. Bernard's father was always after her about it, but she never let on where the money was buried, not even after Mr. Fowler cursed her and dug up the whole yard. The yard was her sanctuary. A place she spent most of her days, and it had taken three years to bloom into the abundance it was. But Mr. Fowler ripped it up in a drunken rage one night and pulled every plant up by the root. It was only on her deathbed that she told Bernard where it was. She said she wanted her son to have something to plant of his own. She felt his father would have lost it all in a Las Vegas minute, if she had given him the chance.

Bernard hid the box of coins in a panel inside the wall. He saw a mouse come out and sniff and then look around. Bernard cut up a sponge, dousing the bits in rat poison. He wished he could line these bits around his dad's bed. His dad was the reason his mother was dead, and he'd killed her just as easily as if he'd fired the gun himself. He never showed her any love or anything close to affection. Even in the hospital ward, when her watery eyes begged for mercy, he remained distant, unfeeling, and as silent as a tomb. He was a Southern man, raised to be hardworking and strong and to never show anything raw like emotion. He couldn't abide sickness or anything that could be seen as weak. He hated people who were unable to rely on themselves. That's why he rode in his wheelchair like a pillar of stone. He wanted to show the whole world he didn't need a soul, that he was better. Even though a cart carried his decaying body, he held his chin up like a king.

Bernard's father had yelled at him yesterday after seeing a mouse in the yard. He told Bernard to lay the small chunks of poison along the garage's floor. And for the first time in months, Mr. Fowler really smiled thinking about the horror of their maddening claws on the wall as the poison exploded inside their veins.

Bernard took off his suit coat and hung it on a nail. He loved the garage. It was his last bastion of peace, and he clung to it like a priest holding a cross in his sleep.

The place was a mess of old furniture and boxes of stuff people discarded when his mother and father rented out the top apartment. It had cobwebs and dusty old bottles of liquor, boxes of old tools, jars of lug nuts and screws, an assortment of long rusty saws, and a whole bunch of old worn out clothes.

But Bernard loved it. He didn't mind the spiders and bugs. He'd sit on a stool watching their intricate webs. He didn't mind the dust or big stacks of ripped boxes. This place was his. No one went in but him. The garage and all its grit was his private domain. He kept the place filthy to discourage any visits. His father would never step foot inside this disastrous trap. His father liked things clean and wiped down all the time. He'd made his mother a slave in the mansion like a twelve-dollar maid.

Bernard took an icy cold beer from the fridge. He opened one of the *Playboy*s an old tenant had left and stared at the beautiful bodies inside. Their cherry lips beckoned, their smooth skin begged to be touched. The ache in his bones made Bernard feel starved. He drew his finger along the length of a long milky thigh and held his face so close to the slick naked image that his hot breath rippled the page.

Scenes from his past started to play in his mind. Anything he ever wanted, his father squashed with hard fists. His brain flashed to the girl he wanted to take to the school dance.

"No son of mine is going around with some trollop."

"But, Dad!" Bernard whined. "Dolores is nice. You hated Eva. You said Hillary was cheap, but you told me Delores was nice."

The father had told him that. He thought Delores was safe. Five years younger, Delores was still playing with wood toys and paint. He figured Delores would never even look at Bernard twice. But his father was wrong. He'd misjudged the woman. It seemed Delores wanted his son very much. He caught them in the yard behind the dense fig tree once. His father said nothing. He'd crept toward the house. But he'd reached down and turned the sprinkler system on until both of them were completely soaked.

"Well, well, well! Would you look at you two? I swear you're a sloppy pair!" The father shook his head as he stared at Delores. His eyes drifted across Delores' budding body. The wet dress hugged her curves. Her calves dripped with water. Her nipples were like neat stacks of pennies.

Delores covered her chest and ran from the duplex. Bernard never saw her again.

A hammering scream knocked against Bernard's skull.

"Boy!" his father yelled from the screen.

Bernard's head bolted back up. He slapped the magazine shut and snatched the cap off his head, sliding the magazines in the box. Before leaving the garage, Bernard took his coveralls off, hanging them on the long nail. He slowly stepped back inside his nice work pants and buttoned the front of his oxford. He closed the garage and fastened the padlock.

When he got closer to his house, he saw Paula closing his back door. She was carrying a pillowcase in one fist. The case dragged on the floor from the weight.

Bernard watched her lift the thing over each step, which was met with a powerful thud.

"Hey, what do you have there?" he asked, walking toward the girl.

The girl was startled to see Bernard and scrambled up the tall stairs.

"Wait!" Bernard said, increasing his pace.

But the small girl moved quickly, taking two steps at once. At the landing, she looked back over her shoulder.

"Loser," the girl said low, shooting Bernard a glare and then slamming the door shut behind her.

He watched her go in as he got to the landing. He jiggled the handle, but the door was locked tight. With his eyes near the glass, he peered through the shade, but Bernard couldn't see anything at all.

Bernard thought for a moment, wondering whether to go inside. He fumbled with the passkey he kept in his pocket. He tried peering in again, looking between the slit under the shade, but the place was a murky sea of dark.

Just then, Margie appeared at the bottom of the steps. She watched Bernard jiggle the handle of her door.

"Can I help you?" She asked in a strong demanding tone. She examined Bernard's body, gliding her eyes from head to toe. She saw his white sweaty face, his red bloodshot eyes and one urgent hand clutching the knob.

"What do you want?" Margie said, taking another step forward.

Suddenly a horrified look crossed over her face. Like she remembered leaving a flame on the stove. Paula was inside the apartment alone. Bernard was trying to get inside. An awful dread crushed Margie's brain.

"Paula!" Margie called out to her child. Rushing her big body up the stairs she came to the landing with Bernard. Panting, she glared in his face.

Bernard stood there, trying his best to enlarge the narrow space between them. He felt guilty, even though he'd done nothing wrong. His body hung dangerously close to the thin rail. The old wood gave an agonizing creak from his weight.

"Paula, honey, are you all right?" Margie unlocked the door and called. "Did anyone try to bother you, in here?" Margie shot a final accusatory look at Bernard before slamming the door in his face.

Ashamed, Bernard descended the staircase with speed. He went inside his own apartment and closed the back door.

Fifteen minutes later, he heard her go outside.

Bernard usually ignored the girl, but she was definitely up to something. He wanted to see what it was. He followed her behind the garage. Bernard carefully walked across the grass, avoiding the dry leaves. He peeked through the vines that covered the dark narrow space.

At first he didn't see anything. It was horribly overgrown. He had to admit he hadn't been back there in ages. He saw the old cement grave of his dog. Letters on the gray concrete slab spelled the single word "Tess."

Next to the grave, he saw on the ground an almost-human

image. There was a small pair of jeans and a blue and green shirt. Some work shoes slept at the hem of each leg, and a baseball cap lay near the flat T-shirt's throat. The girl had constructed an entire body out of clothes. It looked like a scarecrow that fell back from his stick. Like a balloon, losing all of its steam.

"Boo!" the girl screamed, coming up from behind.

Bernard was so startled, he immediately started wheezing. He grabbed his inhaler from his sweater but it dropped over in the leaves. It fell in a green sea of ivy.

Bernard panicked. He fingered both hands through the dark waxy plant. Wheezing, he clutched one hand to his neck.

The girl watched amazed. She didn't offer any help. She cocked her head to the side and studied Bernard's face, like she was fascinated with watching a tiny bug die.

Bernard banged one fist against his suffocating chest. His eyes watered and blurred his vision, and he started to sneeze. With the other hand he continued to hunt through the leaves, searching for the tube that would get back his breath.

Gasping, he hit the cylinder, at last. He seized it inside his hand, and immediately brought it to his lips. He shoved the inhaler past his teeth and down the roof of his mouth and blasted it against the base of his tongue. After the blast hit the dusty cobwebs of his lungs, Bernard began breathing easy again.

"You're funny," the girl giggled inside her tiny, cupped hand.

Bernard glared at her, measuring the length of her neck. He wanted to squeeze her thin pencil throat in his hands. But even in brutality, the girl was astonishingly cute. She was a child beauty beyond all reason and compare with round cherub cheeks, a halo of swirling curls with skin as bright as a big tub of Cool Whip. He wanted to press his lips against her cheek and breathe in her luscious red hair.

"You almost died, huh?" the girl's smile flared her nostrils.

While wheezing, Bernard could see a curiosity in the child. She wasn't wicked. It was much more than that. It was natural to her to be mean, that's all she'd ever known. She didn't mind if he died, she wanted to watch the whole process. She was like a med student waiting to dissect a body.

"What's the matter with you? I was having an attack! Nothing about this is funny!"

The girl stuck out her tongue and ran across the yard. She looked back at him and did a cartwheel over the lawn, revealing a mile of white ruffled panties.

Bernard went inside the house and bristly washed his pink hands. A pool of gray swirled down the sparkling porcelain. His movements were hurried. He worked carefully yet quick. If he made his father wait too long, he'd have hell to pay later. His father was impatient and didn't like being left. If he lingered too long, he'd start tapping a wooden spoon against a tin metal pan until Bernard came into the room.

It was seven. It was time for their daily routine. There were certain things his father demanded of his son. His meals, his once a week baths in the shower chair, and brushing his long silver hair.

Bernard came with his head down and grabbed the brush off the dresser.

Something began to simmer in Bernard's desperate heart. When he stripped his dad's bed, he ripped the large sheet in half, tossing both pieces in the trash. He began to break glasses and plates and left his father's dirty dishes stacked in his sink. If they didn't have Margie to come in and clean, the apartment would have been a big mess.

Bernard was thinking of this when he brought his father's hot cocoa to his room. But just before he placed the cocoa on the stand, Bernard's father kicked out one of his thin legs and Bernard tripped and the cocoa splashed over the rug.

"Watch it! My God, are you a slob. Can't you even carry a mug?" Bernard's father had to bite his tongue this time, he really fought hard not to laugh.

Bernard stood up and grabbed one of his dad's flat worn pillows.

"Why on earth are you holding that pillow like a ninny?" Bernard's father patted the empty spot on the bed near his stomach. "Come sit with me and watch the eleven o'clock news."

Bernard clutched the pillow in both of his hands. He wanted to smother his face.

5

Paula

The gunmetal sky smelled exactly like fried grease. Dead leaves covered the street and the lawn. The row of clothes Margie hung on the skinny clothesline swung like ghosts in the October sky.

The girl waited for Bernard to leave the garage. She heard the old man calling Bernard's name over and over. Her eyes followed Bernard's head as he walked toward his house. She watched him open the screen door and go in the door. As soon as she heard Bernard's back door slam, she leaped down her steps and crept into the backyard. Passing the clothesline, she ripped one of her mother's dresses down and left the dress there like a corpse on the grass.

Taking a small key from her pocket, she unlocked the garage and opened its heavy wooden door.

Of all the stuff, she loved the metal toolbox best. There were pliers and screws and fishing lines and hooks and bottles filled with hundreds of squat metal tacks and black little bottles of poison. The girl grabbed the scissors and a small ball of twine and at the last minute she grabbed the poison, shoving it inside her panties and closing the garage shut again.

When she got to the house she grabbed her own hair. She stuck one of her braids inside the "V" of the scissors and started slicing her ends in uneven chunks until she cut two inches off on each side.

"Paula! Come on! It's time to go to school." Margie rushed around her room zipping in and out of dresses. She went shopping with Mr. Fowler while Bernard was at work and now had a few nice furnishings for the house. He bought her a queen-sized bed and a coffee machine and lots of lacy nothings just for her and a pink bedroom set just for Paula. Margie walked with him in the store as if she were his wife, and when the salesgirl said they had a beautiful child, Margie didn't bother to correct her.

"Come on!" Margie said. "Your cereal's getting cold." Margie was hell-bent on getting the girl out of the house. She couldn't bear the thought of being alone with the girl all day, and Mr. Fowler wanted to eat at the beach. Although it was hard getting him in and out of the van, Margie loved going out. The van parked right in front of the house, and she wheeled Mr. Fowler out, hooked him on an elevated stair, and loaded him into the van. The van hung around all day until they were ready to leave, and it felt just like valet parking.

Mr. Fowler really got a kick watching Margie struggle to lift his body. Sometimes there wasn't a van, and they had to use a cab. Margie would bust a gut trying to lift him out. He was downright fat in the middle, and it was work using a transfer board to get him in the passenger side. She had to push his massive girth across the board to the seat and then yank the transfer board from under his butt and strap the safety belt across his thick waist. After that, she had to lift the heavy wheelchair up and fold it inside the cab's trunk. The driver never helped. They weren't paid for that. Some kind of insurance crap they told her.

Today was one of those cab driving days. By the time Margie was done, her hair was a wreck and she was sweaty, but she was so happy to be able to get away and have some fun, it was worth all the arduous work.

That's why Margie enrolled the child in school right away. School granted her at least six blissful hours of peace. And if she and Mr. Fowler didn't go out, they had already settled into a mild routine of eating food she ordered from a delivery service and sipping mint juleps on the porch. Margie was having such relaxing fun, she decided to push back his murder. No use speeding up death when the living was so good! Who'd have thought dancing with a man in a wheelchair could be erotic? He wickedly spun around and expertly swirled back and forth and she shook her hips, swiveling all around his chair, both of them trapped in a hypnotic rhythm. Mr. Fowler had never danced to black music before. He closed his eyes tight and squeezed Margie's ample waist and here at the tail end of October, with winter closing in, he never felt more alive.

The other day, when Mr. Wade heard loud music at their house, he crept over and hid near a dense jasmine bush. When he saw them dancing in the living room window, Mr. Wade gasped, and his rake fell down in the grass.

"Paula! Come on!" Margie called.

Neatly, the girl placed the cut hair in a pie tin. With the skill of a person whose been burning for years, she lit a match in one hand, ignited the light auburn strands, and watched the gruesome flames leap toward the ceiling. The girl pulled a chair and stood on the seat. Holding the pan until the smoke rose to the smoke detector over the door, she waited for the alarm's blaring scream.

When the wild alarm shrieked through the entire house, Paula smiled.

Bernard heard the alarm and raced up the back steps. It was an awful, high-pitched, repetitive siren. If he didn't have to hold on to the rail, he would have held his palms over his ears.

When he got to the landing, he doubled over and stopped. With his hands on his knees, he breathed in the air. He could smell the burnt fumes. They rolled right under the door. Gasping, he sprayed his throat with his inhaler and banged his fist hard against the door.

"Paula! My God, what are you doing in there!" Margie rattled the door handle, but the girl had turned the latch and locked it.

The girl grinned in the mirror. She twirled her much shorter braids. This was the first time she actually seemed pleased with her own reflection. Usually, she avoided the mirror at all cost, hiding the pain in her face.

Her mother ran from her room and rushed toward the back door.

Bernard was banging it so hard the whole back wall shook.

"Hello!" Bernard said. "What's going on in there?" He had his mouth right over the glass as he talked. "The alarm's going off. Is there a fire inside?" Bernard rattled the knob and banged the door as the carbon fumes started making him sneeze. He wished he had his spray in his pocket so he could blast the awful itch out of his throat.

He was about to use the passkey and barge in, when he heard someone turning the lock.

Margie had done her makeup quickly and finished drawing the last of her fake freckles. She adjusted the knot on her robe and managed a slick smile. She glanced at Paula's locked door and fluffed her crushed curls while allowing the door to swing wide.

"Well, well, well," Margie said, twirling the sash on her robe. Her red lips were curved into a sweet wicked smirk. "Nice of you to stop by." She slowly pulled her left hand behind her wide back to hide the fact that she was wearing Alice's big diamond ring.

Just then, the smoke detector's wild alarm stopped.

Bernard stuck his head inside and sniffed the apartment. The burning hair smell singed his nostrils. "Are you burning something?" he asked Margie, but his eyes searched for the girl. He wondered what she was doing today.

"No," Margie said, hoping he wouldn't check Paula's room. "I was making some oatmeal and walked away from the stove." She fanned her hand in front of her nose for effect. "Unfortunately, the pot's totally scorched."

Bernard looked at Margie. She wore a sly guilty smile. The knot on her robe was about to fall open. He could see a lacy nightgown covering her breasts.

"Can you look under my sink while you're here?" Margie asked. "I can't stand hearing it drip."

Bernard didn't care if their sink dripped or not. He hated that his father had rented them the apartment. He didn't care if anything worked.

Bernard walked to the kitchen sniffing. He glanced at the girl's door. He looked at the faucet. A trickle of water seeped out. A tiny pool formed at the basin.

"It's not that bad," he said, ignoring the stream. He wiped his wet hands on a towel. He wanted to go into the girl's room where he smelled smoke coming out.

"Well, I can't stand this drip. It goes on all day and night." Margie jumped in his way and blocked his path down the hall.

But Bernard was skinny and easily pushed past her body and walked to the girl's bedroom door. He swung the door open and stared deep inside, sniffing and looking around.

Her bedroom was clean and impeccably arranged. The blanket was pulled tight. The sheet turned down just so. Not one book or doll lay out of its place. Her stuffed animals were sorted and propped up by size. Her dresses hung one by one and were lined up by color. Her shoes were so clean and shiny none of them looked worn. Every surface was spotless. The room sparkled and gleamed. There was not one thing lying on a table or over a chair. There was nothing on the bed but a white ruffled pillow. Nothing was left on the polished wood floor. In fact, the room looked like no one lived inside it at all. But there was something about it that seemed a bit fake and contrived, like a hotel or a movie set.

It was a garish room, brimming with bright pink and black. The Disney-themed colors gave it a cartoonlike gloom. Her blankets, curtains, and sheet set all matched and were covered with "mermaid," images. Margie had done the room completely in Disney. She had stack after stack of "Little Mermaid" coloring books. Ariel swimming under water. Ariel meeting the prince. Ariel trading her voice in for shoes. But instead of coloring the books, the little girl cut them up. She put fish heads on bodies and gave the prince sea witch fins. The girl smiled at her brand-new inventions. It pleased her to cut up and rearrange life. Sometimes she'd take her mom's magazines and slice the slick heads off models, putting them in pinstripes and pants.

If Bernard looked closer, he would have noticed the dark edge of her curtains, which were all singed from cigarette burns. And if he had looked under the bed, he would have seen the girl's retort, an assortment of ash-colored pie tins where she melted the bodies of her dolls.

Paula rushed to her window and hid behind the pink drapes. Staring out at Bernard from the wall, she looked at her mother with sheer panic in her eyes.

"Please," Margie said quickly, pulling the door shut. "My daughter's not even dressed."

Embarrassed, Bernard left and stood in the hall. He was excited by what he saw, but he tried not to show it. But his quick breathing gave him away.

"You like pork?" Margie said knowingly, watching his chest heave. "I make a real mean honey-baked ham." Margie saw a place that sold hams down the street, less than a mile away.

Bernard shifted on his feet. He kept his eyes on the ground. He didn't want Margie to think that he was looking at her child, especially with the McMartin case sizzling on every front page, branding anyone in its path as a sex fiend.

But there was something else. He had the distinct feeling Margie was hiding something too and it had something to do with that girl.

Margie was not shy and stared straight in his eyes. "Tell you what I'll do. I'll make it just us. We started off on the wrong foot, but I really want to make it up to you. I've been busy with your dad, and I know you help him a lot, too. Listen, how about this? I'll send a plate down to him and you and I can eat up here by ourselves. It'll give us a chance to get to know each other better."

Paula heard her mother behind the curtain and groaned. She didn't want to have dinner with Bernard. He always stared at her hard. Yesterday, while she was walking home after school, she saw him hiding under a tree on his hands and knees, watching her buy ice cream from the truck across the street.

A glass crashing sound filled the silence between Bernard and Margie.

The girl was dumping ashes from her window and accidentally knocked over a glass. It crashed to the concrete below.

Margie ignored the sound and kept smiling at Bernard. She turned her head and gently called to the child, "Paula. Are you okay? We have to get to school, honey. We've got to catch the seven-twenty bus. My car wouldn't start up again," Margie hinted. "I swear, when it rains it just pours. Her eyes rolled along the globe of Bernard's balding head. "Do you think you could give us a ride?"

Bernard didn't want to take them but had a hard time speaking his mind. He just stood there and looked at his shoes.

Margie rushed to her room and got dressed. She emerged squashed in orange, wearing a tight jogging suit and a rhinestone ball cap. She looked like she was going to a ball game in drag.

Bernard didn't want to give them a ride to any place in life! He hated them. They were strange and liked burning stuff up. He hated that they lived in the apartment that should have been his. But the thought of seeing the girl made him stop for a minute. And in a moment, he found himself nodding his head, and the next thing he knew, they were all in his car driving to Immaculate Heart.

The girl wore a plaid skirt and a white button down blouse. Her clean lacy socks fanned her black patent leather shoes, which gleamed like a showroom Rolls-Royce.

Margie kept eyeing the girl in his rearview mirror. She was enraged when she saw Paula's hair, but she couldn't do or say a thing with Bernard sitting here. Bernard tried to smile at the child, but she whipped her head away and stared at trees whizzing by.

At the stop sign, Corleen, the crossing guard, came over to the car. She'd been walking kids across the street since Bernard was a kid. "Hey, Bernard! I see you're a cab driver this morning."

Corleen smiled at Margie and then looked at the girl and grinned. "My, my, you're just as pretty as a peach. I rarely get to see little cute ladies like you. I bet the boys follow you all around school." Corleen gave the girl a warm, grandmotherly smile, waiting for her to respond.

But this comment enraged Paula. She hated when people called her cute. It inflamed her and made each hair stand up on her arm. She hated all references to being beautiful or pretty. Corleen was right about one thing; the boys did follow her at school. But they were mean and called her names, and the girls were fifty times worse. They mercilessly teased her and did ugly cruel things, too. Yesterday, a group of girls captured her behind the gym and one of them threw a can of black paint over her face and her clothes.

"That's your real color," a heavyset girl said, spitting in her face. "Now go home and wash your black face."

Paula cried pitifully that night, but Margie ignored her sobs and washed the paint off with nail polish remover and told her to be quiet and go to sleep.

A lot of folks assumed these things weren't going on anymore, but hate crimes were as regular as the *Sunday Times* on your porch. Just because they didn't make headlines or weren't featured in the news, didn't mean foul and grotesque crimes weren't going on all the time. They happened regularly in L.A. from Simi Valley to Orange County.

Margie looked at Corleen as if she were diseased. She pointed to two children, waiting to cross the street. "Shouldn't you be over there doing your job instead of standing here bothering me?"

Bernard snapped his head back. What a rotten thing to say! Bernard looked at Margie, but she seemed unconcerned. She was looking for something deep inside her purse.

Bernard grinned at Corleen, trying to cover Margie's infraction. "Nice weather we're having," he said meekly and then looked toward the sky. For an early morning, the sky was violently dark. There were so many dense clouds swirling over their heads, and it looked like it was just about to pour.

Corleen abruptly turned and went back to her corner.

Bernard couldn't see her eyes, but he could feel their heat. Her eyes were hidden under a wide-brimmed straw hat. What he did see was the hard jutting frown over her chin, which mocked the red bow at her neck.

Corleen had seen plenty of Margies before. Heifers like her gave blacks a bad name. Just because she was on the lighter end of the spectrum didn't mean this devil woman couldn't speak to her properly. Margie was nothing but one of those blacks who hated their own kind, a modern-day version of *Imitation of Life*. She was as harsh and as waxy as a bouquet of fake flowers. And just because you couldn't see all her thorns didn't mean they weren't there. Corleen had noticed a few things since she arrived. Like how tired Mr. Fowler looked and how slowly he pulled his chair and how his coloring looked a bit off. You wouldn't notice unless you were the kind of person who looked for things like these. But things dramatically changed when Margie showed up. Mr. Wade said a lot of bad things were happening to the plants. He said all the eucalyptus trees became diseased and were beginning to lean on one side, and though the oranges were more colorful than ever before, they were rotten and dark brown inside. Yesterday, he'd raked up a baby raccoon. It was stuck in the thin slender forks of his rake. He hadn't seen a bad sign like that one in ages.

Corleen threw Margie a disapproving glare.

"You don't scare me," Corleen muttered, rubbing the cross at her neck. Just touching Jesus' feet made her break into a smile. "I don't care how much voodoo queen blood's in your veins. You don't scare me at all."

Margie found a nail file in her purse and began sawing the stub on her thumb. "Folks need to mind their own business," she said.

They drove the rest of the way in complete silence. No one else said a word. The radio was the only noise in the car.

Bernard gripped the wheel, bit his own lip, and finally breathed deep when the school was in sight.

When they got to the school the girl leaped from the car, but then she walked with her head hung so low to the ground that she looked like a ninety-year-old man.

"Stand straight!" Margie yelled. "Take pride in yourself." She looked at the sea of unruly-looking children.

"How can I be proud of this?" Paula asked, whirling around holding out the pleats of her dress.

Paula was beginning to test Margie lately. It was little things at first. She was very concerned about the girl.

"Let's go," Margie told Bernard.

Bernard almost waved, but Paula didn't turn around. Before she got to the school's door another kid tripped her, and she slid across the cement on her stomach.

There were peals of laughter from the other kids outside. A big girl laughed the loudest, covering her cavity-filled mouth.

Paula got up, eyed the big girl once, walked into the hall, and never looked back.

Bernard felt genuinely sorry for the girl. Kids were still as mean as they were when he was growing up. He recalled his own glum days at school and how he used to beg his father to not make him go.

Bernard was about to put the car in reverse and pull from the curb, when he noticed the girl's lunch box left on the backseat.

"She left her lunch," Bernard said to Margie.

"Oh well," Margie said, watching the children enter the building. The last thing she wanted was to go inside a school's doors. School was where the whole ugly thing happened.

Bernard grabbed Paula's lunch and opened the car door. He stared at the sea of children trampling the school lawn and bit his fingernail to the quick. Bernard hated kids. Kids made him sick.

Kids littered his lawn with their Sprite cans and chips. They trampled his hibiscus and Egyptian mint plants. They ruined his grass with their skateboards or bikes. To him kids were foul, rotten, gangs of ripped T-shirts, with horrible caked-up noses and murderous screams, legs gashed from cuts or ruined with scabs and as lawless and vile as a mob. They teased him. They mimicked the way that he walked. They laughed at his bald head and called him four-eyes or fag. They snickered or yelled in his face. Bernard hid in the scrubs if a bunch of kids came by. If he couldn't hide he'd stand as still as a plant, gripping his hose like a weapon. If he were lucky enough to stumble on one kid alone, he'd sop up their shoes with his hose. But it gave him the creeps if too many were together. If there were more than three or four huddling out near the curb, he hid in his bushes or behind the walnut tree of his neighbor or he raced to his house in the quick smacking gait of someone who's been hated for decades.

Some kids covered their mouths and laughed as Bernard crossed the grass. He was a suspicious-looking man with a rapid-fire gait who was biting his thumb as he walked. An art teacher stared at him through the slits of her blinds, wondering who the strange bald man was.

Bernard came inside the office. A thin woman was on the phone. Her cat glasses were perched on her long beaklike nose, and a gold Jesus bled on the cross at her throat.

"Yes?" she asked. "Can I help you with something?"

"The girl, I mean, Paula forgot her lunch," Bernard stuttered. An alabaster Virgin Mary smiled at him with open palms. He wished he was back in the car.

"Paula, who?" the woman barked, raising her brows at Bernard. She stared at the bald man like a suspect. Strolling to the tall wooden counter, she leaned on her elbows, and her eyeglasses slid down her nose.

Bernard stuttered. He didn't know the girl's last name.

The woman could smell Bernard's husky, robust cologne and noticed his immaculate hands. Though his nails were perfectly clipped, there were scabs around each bed, and one of his thumbs was oozing with blood. The woman looked toward the security guard in the hall.

"Let's see," she said, examining the lunch box. She opened the lid and saw the name P. Green, written on a marker inside. "Paula Green. Ah, yes. We all know Miss Green." The woman said it like she knew more than she'd like to admit. "The principal adores her. He thinks she's the epitome of perfect."

She said it like the principal was the only one who did. In fact, odd things had been happening since Paula Green got there. Things went missing, like the heads of three Virgin Marys. And half an encyclopedia set was now gone. Lots of items were stolen or singed, and there had been several crucifixes found in the trash.

"I'm Miss Taylor, the vice principal at Immaculate Heart." She stuck out her hand and shook Bernard's palm. His fingers were thick and felt like warm clay and were as smooth as a good leather purse.

"And you, sir?" she asked, still gripping his palm. "Are you Paula's father?" She looked at his tie and his buttoned down oxford. If he was, Paula obviously got her tidiness from him.

"Oh no, I'm her neighbor. I just drove her to school today."

Everybody in the office stopped working and stared. If he wasn't the girl's father, what was he doing here? Was he a pervert? Is this how they got in? The receptionist thought Bernard looked exactly like the guy from the McMartin case.

Bernard was sweating, and he began to loosen his tie. He wished Margie were in here solving this matter. "Her mother is out in the car."

"Oh? I've been trying to contact Paula's parents." The teacher walked to the window and peered through the blinds. "Paula said there was no phone, and we've sent several notes home." The teacher picked up the sandwich and found a folded piece of paper. "Here's one of our summons here."

Two days ago, the girl's mother was called to class. One of the teachers was concerned. The school nurse was consulted. There was a discussion on what might be going on at home.

In a snarling rage, Paula had sliced the crotch out of her stockings. She'd savagely attacked the center of her black opaque tights with the X-Acto knife from her art class. The diced crotch created an obscenely large hole between her legs where her skinny thighs met below the waist.

When the vice principal phoned Margie, she dismissed the ripped stockings. She told the whole school a fabulous lie. "Her grandfather just died. We had the funeral on Monday." Margie blew her nose on the phone for effect. "Paula and Grandfather were so close it was scary. I knew it would be hard on the girl, down the road."

Just then, the bell rang and a mob of kids flooded the halls. Miss Taylor pressed her lips to a short metal whistle. But before she started to blow, she stopped the security guard by the arm. "Could I speak with you a moment?" she asked.

The security guard came over to where Miss Taylor stood.

"See that man?" Miss Taylor said, pointing to Bernard. "He brought in this lunch. He claims to be a neighbor of one of our kids. I don't know. What do you think, John? Doesn't he look strange? Do you think he put something in that food, or am I just jumpy from this McMartin thing happening?"

The security guard studied Bernard in his mirrored sunglasses. He had fifty or so keys attached to his waist, and he jingled them like a bucket of nickels. He tossed his half-eaten donut in the trash and boldly walked up to Bernard.

"Sir?" the guard asked. "Can I help you with something? Do you have a pass to be on this campus?"

Bernard was very annoyed now. His wrists started to itch. He scratched them fiercely leaving long red marks on his skin. "For heavens sake, I just brought my neighbor her lunch!"

"Sir," the guard said. He was a wide muscular man. The job rarely gave him a chance to use any of his combat moves. He flexed at the thought of getting a chance.

"Her mother is sitting right outside in the car," Bernard said tartly. "Why don't you go and ask her?"

The guard and the vice principal looked through the blinds. "The gray Plymouth in front?" The guard looked at Bernard. "Yes, that's right," Bernard snapped, scratching his wrist. "There's nobody in that car, sir," the guard answered back.

Bernard peered from the window. Margie was gone. She was not on the street either or anywhere nearby. Where in God's name did she go?

Bernard angrily gritted his teeth and turned from them both. He felt like a fool. He started to dash from the office door.

"Wait a minute, sir!" the guard yelled, grabbing Bernard's arm. Forcefully shoving Bernard's face against one of the school lockers, he aggressively bent back his arm.

Bernard hollered in pain. It felt like his bone was about to pop.

Reaching in his pocket, the guard snatched Bernard's wallet. "Can I see some I.D.?" the guard asked.

Bernard's face was sweating, and he flushed with hot rage. His arm ached, but the guard pinned him, so he couldn't move. A small band of teachers filed inside the room, and they stared at Bernard with inquisitive or hard faces, wondering what crime he had done.

The security guard told the vice principal to copy Bernard's license. He wished Bernard would make a move or try to break free so he could tackle him down to the floor or shoot him in the leg with his gun.

But Bernard was passive; his whole body went limp, like he was willing to be taken to jail.

Once the copy had been made, the guard dropped Bernard's arm.

"I'm sorry, but you understand, sir. The school is on lockdown. No one gets in or out of this campus without clearance." He handed Bernard back his license.

Bernard straightened his jacket and adjusted his tie.

The vice principal put the summons in his hand. "Will you see to it that Mrs. Green gets this note from us, please? We need to see her right away."

Bernard avoided their eyes. Lots of people surrounded him and stared. He'd never been so embarrassed in his life, and his entire face turned as pink as a crab as he hurried back to his car.

The security guard didn't have a reason to keep Bernard there. But he watched him closely. There was something odd about the man. He watched Bernard hop through the Plymouth's wide door.

Bernard roared his car away from the curb. He hated these people. He hated their insinuations and questions. He hated their all-knowing looks and long, sideways glances. He couldn't wait to get back to his mortuary job where the dead people peacefully left him alone.

He found Margie walking down the street, almost three blocks away. He slowed the car down near her legs.

"Why did you leave?" Bernard was bitterly upset. It was her fault he had to endure that humiliating scene. He hated Margie on sight. "They want to speak to you in there," Bernard waved the note from the car window.

Margie read the note, crumbled it up and tossed it down to the curb.

"You going back home? I could use a lift back." Margie already had her hand on the handle of the door. She got in and plopped hard on the seat.

Bernard ground his teeth, glaring back at the school. "I don't ever want to set foot in that forsaken place again."

Though she didn't say a word, Margie shared the same sentiment. Her mind flashed to the last time she was summoned to school. Like it was yesterday, she remembered exactly what she wore. A cream chiffon suit, real pearls around her throat, and bone-colored, leather sling-back pumps. She was a teacher herself then, in a posh Catholic school. She remembered the stunned faces of her colleagues when they cuffed her and dragged her out. She remembered the child screaming and being taken away by force and the awful things they did to escape. Things so dreadful and obscene, that when it was all said and done, her pearls were gone, one heel had snapped off, and her chiffon dress was covered in blood.

6

Val

Bernard yanked on his coat and walked down to the corner. Whenever he was furious at his father, he went to the neighborhood bar. But tonight, after the events at the school, he was angrier than ever before. He wasn't even afraid of getting caught anymore. He used to sneak there to get a beer once his father fell asleep. It was a dimly-lit shack filled with day laborers and rummies. He'd been coming to the ancient bar for years.

On his way, something caught the corner of his eye. The girl was outside, though it was quite late; there she was shaking something that looked like ashes in the trash.

"Hello," he said.

The girl actually seemed startled. She snatched her hand behind her back, and whatever was in it rattled like a drawer full of forks.

"What are you doing out here in the dark?" Bernard asked. "Won't your mother be worried?"

"She's at a meeting," Paula said, twirling a curl in her hand.

Bernard stared at the child. She had round dimpled cheeks. She chewed the end of a Popsicle stick in her mouth. Watching her tiny tongue swirl across the thin suntan stick turned Bernard's cheeks a hot skillet red. He saw the lady across the street sweeping off her porch and became immediately self-conscious about talking to the child alone.

"Well, it's dangerous," Bernard said, abruptly turning around. "Haven't you been watching the news?"

The girl didn't say anything, but she kept following his steps.

"Girl's shouldn't be out here at night," Bernard snapped.

"You're out," Paula said smartly. "Why aren't you afraid?"

"I'm a man!" Bernard said. "For men it's a lot different."

The girl stopped and considered this comment and then continued to follow him a few paces behind. He could hear the mild tapping sound that came from her shoes.

Bernard stopped. He turned around and stooped to her face. "You better go home. It's not safe for young girls. It's already very dark outside!"

The girl smiled and started to skip back toward the house. But suddenly, the skipping sound stopped. Bernard looked back again, but the small girl was nowhere in sight. After this, he had the unsettling feeling of being followed. He kept jerking his head back, but there was never anyone there.

When he got to the bar, he jerked around once more, but the street was as calm as a morgue.

Removing his coat, Bernard took a handkerchief from his pocket and wiped the bar stool before sitting down.

A heavyset man sat in the corner drinking whiskey. He studied the contents of his glass. Mr. Wade was in there, too. He sat drinking alone, examining the lines in his hands.

Bernard folded the hankie and rubbed it across the bar, then put it back in his pocket before lowering himself down on the seat. Running his hands over his newly shaved scalp, he ordered an icy cold beer.

Bernard smiled while slowly sipping the gold fluid. His cold face felt good inside the warm bar. He looked over at Mr. Wade and lifted his glass. Mr. Wade nodded his head and fingered his drink in his palm like he was trying to figure out how much the glass weighed.

"Why do you come here, son?" the heavyset man grunted. He coughed loud against his arm and wiped his mouth with a gnarled wrist.

Bernard didn't bother answering the man. He took a huge swig and licked the froth from his lips. The best thing about being at this small corner bar was people drank quietly and left you alone.

Bernard touched the moist cup of his second wet draft. He didn't come there to chat.

"Hell, if I were a spry fella like yerself, I'd be in Mirabell's off Third."

Mr. Wade shot the man a cold violent look.

Bernard ignored the beafy man, but suddenly the man reached and grabbed Bernard's shirt. His hairy fist clutched at his chest.

Angrily, he glowered into Bernard's startled face. "Mirabell's got girls you ain't seen in this world." The man's bushy eyebrows rose toward the ceiling and then fell, like two kittens being dropped in a well.

Bernard snatched his shirt away and glared at the man hard. "Do you mind?" Bernard said, straightening his tie. He could smell the gin coming out of each of the man's overripe pores.

The man let go but leaned way back in his chair. "What's wrong with you? Why do you waste your time here? They have beauties!" the man screamed. "Young bodacious bodies!" The man licked his top upper lip.

"Why don't you leave the boy alone," Mr. Wade told the old man.

"Shut up!" the man said. "I ain't talking to you! And it's not like you haven't been in there before!"

Mr. Wade leaped from his seat. He was about to say something, but he changed his mind. He'd been working all day with this cracker up the street. When he finished the job, he only got half of what was promised. He would much rather enjoy his whiskey in peace than fight with somebody else.

Bernard was tired of the old man grabbing him, "Well, why aren't you there instead of here pestering me?" But as soon as he asked, Bernard already knew. The man was ninety-nine miles of miserable road. His eyes were all bloodshot, and one of them floated to one side and had such a thick milky film on the top, he was sure he couldn't use it to see. His skin was blotchy and looked jaundiced. He had a nose so big and red, he looked like he'd been in a fight.

"Go to Mirabell's," the man said. "You won't regret it." The man hobbled from the stool and gathered his jacket. Cold air filled the bar when he shuffled out the door.

"Don't listen to him," Mr. Wade said. "Mirabell's is nothing but trouble. You'd best leave that fool place alone."

When Bernard went home that night he didn't go inside. Instead, he sat in the garage in his car. The car was twenty years old, but everything on it looked new. Only the passenger seat where his large father sat was sunken and torn on one side. Except for that, everything was shiny and clean. The vinyl seats were smooth and nicely polished. Bernard used Armor All on the car every week. He liked keeping his things looking nice. He liked rubbing things down. He liked tinkering around with his hands. He was a creature of habit and followed the same dull routine. He read the *L.A. Times* every day, bought a coffee at Winchell's, ate microwave dinners or chicken pot pies and, except for the few times he snuck out of the house for a beer, he was always in bed with the ten o'clock news.

But the man's haunting words filled Bernard with wonder. He felt defiant and angry after the event at the school, and a new rebelliousness seared through his veins. So he turned on his car and drifted out of his driveway. He turned on Vine and passed Hollywood and took it all the way down to Third and spotted a tiny pink neon sign burning a mark on the curb. There was no one outside. No sign of a club at all. In fact, if he hadn't noticed the small neon blinking above the club's door he would have never had known anything was there.

He parked and entered Mirabell's slim doors. The club was so dark and smoky, he had to stand still for a while, waiting for his eyes to adjust to the haze.

Slowly things began to emerge from the fog. He saw two women laughing, wearing shimmering fabric. Their faces were velvet. They were gorgeously dressed. They smiled at Bernard, but he quickly looked down, casting his shy eyes to the cool marble floor. Another woman smiled, and so did her well-groomed companion. Bernard didn't smile. He kept his eyes low. He moved to a seat in a dark vacant corner and slowly looked around the room. Everyone looked regal. Their clothes sparkled and looked expensive. Wineglasses and champagne flutes sat in front of their necks and brilliant jewels covered their fingers and wrists. Soft laughter filled the room, but it was subdued and controlled, like the banter in a nice hotel lobby.

A blonde sat alone. Her face slowly emerged from a dense cloud. She was extremely petite and wore a tight sequined sheath with the back cut out to the waist. The woman was a beauty with an ice-cream cone swirl of hair, circling her skull like a halo. Her backless dress clung to her curves, and Bernard's eyes followed the bones along her spine. She was radiant. Her lips were a fireplace orange. Her eyes were golf course green. Her skin was so clear and flawless that she looked like a porcelain doll smoking a thin cigarette. She was so perfectly done up, she looked like she came from filming a movie. Women like this only existed on screen or in slick magazines. He'd never seen anyone look this good up close.

Bernard's head swiveled around the room; she must be waiting for someone. No one this fine would be sitting alone. The bar had two small red vinyl booths, a few tables in the rear, and an enormously large purple couch. And even though they were miles from the beach, the bar was inlaid with mother of pearl shells.

"Please," the woman said, removing her purse from the chair. "You can sit down by me." The purse was a tiny gold-beaded bag. The light danced on its delicate handles.

Without turning her head, Val gave Bernard a once-over glance. In one look, she had taken him in head to toe. It told her everything she wanted to know. She saw his cashmere coat and his pink diamond tie pin and the tassels on his brown Ferragamos.

What she didn't know was that these were Mr. Reynolds' old clothes. Mr. Reynolds gave him lots of his discarded sweaters and shoes.

Bernard carefully sat down. He didn't even wipe the seat. His eyes were locked on her face.

"I'm Val," the girl said, extending her hand. She already knew who Bernard was. She'd seen him at the funeral last week. She'd been following him for days figuring out how to rope him and decided to pay the dirty old man at the bar twenty five dollars to send Bernard here.

Her palm, soft as a marshmallow, felt like silk in his hand, and Bernard squeezed it without wanting to let go.

"Bernard," he said quickly, dropping her palm. He was so nervous that both his hands started to itch, and he scratched his wrist feverishly until both of them were raw. He wished he'd brought his lotion to kill the burn. Not knowing what to say and not knowing where to rest his eyes, he kept them latched to the television set, sneaking glances now and then, whenever it seemed she wasn't looking. He stared at her boldly while she watched the TV over the bar.

A group of young children flashed across the small set. The newsman spoke solemnly from the screen.

"The McMartin daycare has been permanently shut down. Forty-eight more counts of lewd conduct have been added to the case against Peggy Buckey and her son."

"I heard her son molested half a dozen kids at that school," the bartender said. "Both of them are bound to get cooked."

Bernard looked at the accused son who stared from the TV. He was prematurely bald and wore a tense, angry frown. He'd already been locked in jail without bail for months with no end of the trial in sight.

Val flung one hand at the screen. "I bet those dumb kids made all that stuff up."

Bernard glanced at Val and then smiled to himself.

She glared at the set, "All those silly brats are lying." Crossing her slim legs, she hoisted her round, narrow hips, trying to get a better grip on the stool.

Bernard was entranced. Val possessed such intoxicating venom.

"Don't you like children?" he asked.

Val glared at her drink, stirring the liquid with her straw. "I hate them," she matter-of-factly told Bernard.

Val was not lying exactly. Part of this statement was fact. Though she acted like she didn't like kids, it was only a front. She wanted them. In fact, she wanted some bad. What she hated was that she couldn't have them.

Suddenly, Val gave him a million-dollar grin. "You're adorable," she said, pinching his cheeks.

Just then, another woman came and sat at the bar. She wore a beautiful velvet dress and giant diamond studs. She smiled eagerly at Bernard, giving Val a conciliatory nod. She ordered a Slow Gin Fizz and brought the fluid to her lips, raising her glass toward Bernard.

"I think those kids are telling the truth," the other woman said. She leaned her body a little closer to Bernard. He could feel the warmth of her skin. "Nobody protects kids, they're easily abused. I hope the McMartin School is permanently closed!"

The bartender came over and wiped down the bar. "Look at the mother. And come on, there's something up with that son. Those mama's boy types always turn out weird." He rubbed the bar until the Plexiglas was so see-through and slick that it shined like a clear chandelier.

"Oh, please! This is a just a modern witch hunt, honey. They murdered hordes of innocent people in Salem because folks were convinced they were evil," Val said. "This is the same crap happening again."

"I don't know," the other woman next to Bernard shook her head. "There's something unnatural about a grown man living alone with his mother. Look how close he stands next to her chair."

The bartender nodded his head in agreement. "I bet the sick fuckers did it."

"Oh, come on! It's a grudge case. The kid's mother's a kook. I heard the mother made this whole story up just because her son couldn't get in their posh little school." Val had been following the story in all of the tabloids. "McMartin was the best school in Manhattan Beach. The waiting list was over two years' long."

They all looked up at the TV again. Mrs. Buckey's faded hair was pulled up in a bun. She was heavyset, eighty and wheelchair-bound. Her face was a veil of contempt.

"I think the old lady was in on it, too." The burgundy woman kept her eyes on the set. "I bet she molested them while her crazy son held those kids down. People underestimate old people. They think wrinkles, a floral dress, and bad bluish perm means miraculously these people care. But there is no age limit on violence. I remember this little old biddy at our church. She gathered up the offerings and put them right in her purse. When the preacher caught her, the shriveled up bitch threw a fit. She grabbed one of those heavy candelabras and bashed the minister to death on the altar. I tell you it took months to get his blood out of the marble." The woman opened her gold lighter and lit her cigarette tip. A smoldering trail of vapor escaped her lips.

"Let's go," Val said, gently taking Bernard's hand. "I hate breathing other people's smoke." She threw a quick look at the woman at the bar and led Bernard to a booth in the back.

Val ordered two martinis. She scooted close to his knees.

She smelled like a garden in May.

Bernard inhaled her fresh, fragrant skin.

"See this scar," Val said, showing a small mark on her wrist. "I fell on a kid's skate on my back steps. I swear, one bad kid can ruin a good pair of nylons." Val shot one of her curvaceous legs out.

Bernard stared at Val's calf. He gulped his martini.

"I shared a room with my sister. We used to have big fun. But when my sister popped her cherry and spit out that runt, I had to get the heck out of Dallas."

Val lied through her teeth. Lying was a necessity in her life. Lies sprang from her mouth without one blink or stutter. In fact, lies were the first thing to roll from her tongue. She lied to everyone she knew for as long as she lived. She'd rewritten her life story so many times that the truth was a murky chunk of distorted facts floating around her brain like a long night of too many shots.

Val wasn't from Dallas. She was from a trailer park in Phoenix. She used the fake Southern accent after seeing a Johnny Cash movie. She thought the girl playing his wife sounded cute. She couldn't say who she really was. They would have moved their chairs away. She couldn't tell them why she really left town either. How she didn't move at all but was thrown to the street. Cursed out and tossed like a bone to a dog. How she wept, begged her father to please let her stay. How her mother never once looked her way. She was fifteen, and that was the last time she saw them. Although she tried to bury her past, some things were clear. Yes, some things remained as crystal as a new piece of glass. She remembered the pool and her newly shaved legs. All the glossy slick makeup she bought at the drugstore and the turquoise bathing suit she wore. But that's where this crystal clear memory stopped. She didn't like to think about the rest.

Bernard fingered the stem of his martini glass. He let his knee graze the wonderful meat of her thigh. She was childlike and small. He loved the colorful way Val talked. There was something almost country. A hint of a sweet Georgia twang. Her hands were expressive and waved around as she spoke. He could not take his eyes off her generous lips, especially the bottom one, which was more swollen than the top and looked like she'd been stung by a bee. Bernard didn't reveal anything about himself. He was afraid he might slip. Trip himself up. Bernard's secrets stayed locked in his ice bucket skull.

"Look at those vultures," Val shook her head in disgust. "I bet those damn attorneys invented this whole scam, and those kids sucked it all up like Kool-Aid."

Bernard nodded. He knew how the kids acted around his building. Rough kids on skateboards making all kinds of noise, screaming or cursing at the top of their lungs, leaving their trash at his doors. Bernard shut his windows when children played on his street. He wished he could pluck them off like the bad fruit he found on his trees.

Bernard leaned over and ordered them both a third round.

"So what do you do, honey?" Val mildly asked Bernard.

Bernard was proud of his funeral job. He'd taken mortuary classes at night. In no time, he became a master in his trade and received a glossy certificate in the mail. He was now a legitimate member of the Restorative Society. Each body was a gift. He felt like a magician. Each body under his scalpel was a fine work of art, and his job, which he took very seriously, was to create the illusion of peace. And even though it was fiction for those last moments in the coffin, even though they closed the door on his work, locking it forever, burying it in dirt or burning it in retorts, Bernard made sure that death had never looked better. He made sure each body looked eternal and peacefully asleep, dreaming in everlasting glory.

Bernard twirled his glass in his hand. He took a big chance. He decided to tell Val the truth.

"I'm in the restorative arts," Bernard told her calmly.

"Oh, you paint! Or do you work in ceramics?"

"Actually, no," Bernard said, playing with the diamond of his tie pin. He was beginning to dread having to spell out what he did, but emboldened by the liquor, he decided to just be frank. "I dress and make up bodies for funerals."

"Well, I'll be damned." Val said, clinking his glass. "We practically have the exact same profession."

Bernard raised his brows and clinked her glass back.

"I put makeup on the old stiffs at Macy's," Val said.

"I'll drink to that!" Bernard said. He waved over the bartender and ordered champagne and the fifty-dollar caviar plate.

Bernard couldn't believe she didn't care about his job.

"Do you live around here?"

"Not far," Bernard said, smiling.

Bernard didn't want to tell her he lived with his father. "I live in a house off Hollywood way past Franklin. I used to have a nice quiet yard until the lady and her daughter came." Bernard sipped the clear liquid over his teeth. "I wish I could get them to leave."

"Shoot, I bet I could get those ponies out of the gate." Val chuckled to herself and sipped more of her drink. "Get 'em where they never want to live there again!"

Bernard looked at Val. Her eyes sparkled with fun. He couldn't stop looking at her tiny pink tongue. She was so little. So feminine and petite. She looked like a girl wearing her mother's silky gown, like a small and gorgeously dressed up doll. She had class. Her nails were long and painted bright red with diamonds drilled into the pinkies.

But suddenly, Bernard's mind began to simmer in doubt. He leaned farther away from Val. Why would this woman want him? He was worthless and bald. He lived at home with his father. He glanced at the tiny blonde woman again. He peeked at her breasts in that glittering halter. They shook ever so slightly when she talked. She must be waiting for someone. He butted in on something. Bernard panicked. His eyes scanned the dark smoky bar. The strong urge to get up and leave had his heart banging in his chest, and he violently started to wheeze. He reached in his pocket and grabbed his inhaler. Pressing the button until a cool blast filled his lungs, he bit a hangnail from his finger, downed the rest of his drink, and finally began breathing easy.

"On the pipe, huh?" Val said, sucking her straw.

Bernard nodded and said, "Asthma."

"My daddy carried around one of them breathing jobs, too. The heaving sounds he made seemed like they could wake up the dead. We lost the house when the downstairs blew up. Mama warned the poor man over and over again. She said, don't leave your Primatene Mist on the stove, but my father was a stubborn, hardheaded man. He did whatever the hell he wanted. You couldn't tell him squat. But he cried like a baby when the entire house burned down and Mom went up in those flames."

Val smiled to Bernard. There was never any fire. And her mother was still very much alive, waitressing somewhere near

Flagstaff. Her dad didn't have asthma, and there was definitely no downstairs. They lived in a horrible mobile home where one side was caved in from that time her dad crashed in the house with his truck.

Val turned and faced Bernard, cupping his chin in her soft hands. "You feeling all right, precious?"

Her piercing green eyes seemed to tear through his clothes.

"I'm all right, my mother just died." Bernard's mother had been the buffer between his harsh and demanding father and him. She was the jewel, the one sun in his drab quiet life. "She taught me all about gardening and read me stories at night. There was always a spark in her eyes. She was as beautiful and clear as the crystal vases she collected, and she polished them with care, arranging them just so, until their dazzling rainbow streams danced across their springtime rooms. She never seemed bothered by my father's rough manner. His mean words were absorbed in the rich soil or her soul. They never seemed to touch her at all."

Val loved hearing Bernard talk so sweetly about his mother. She leaned in close to his arms.

"I loved helping her in the kitchen or planting flowers with her in the yard. But suddenly, life changed during last year's rainy winter. My mother's hand began cupping her mouth every so often. She developed this dry cough. It got louder each month and rasped sometimes deep into the night. I used to listen to it all day and then late in the night, and sometimes it sounded so horrible and wouldn't let up that I had to hold both hands over my ears just to sleep.

"I knew it was bad when she stayed in the house the whole summer. And in fall, she checked into Cedars, barely clinging to life, like a plant you'd forgotten to water. My father never considered that Mom might go first. That thought never crossed his mind. He hated sickness or ailments of any kind. 'Heal up,' he would yell if any of us were sick. 'Bear it! Will yourself well,' he would say. He was perfectly fit and never visited a doctor. 'I'm not stepping foot in that godawful place. The hospital is the last stop between hell and the tomb. Hospitals are where all the sick people go.' He didn't want to breathe in any sick people's fumes. He thought the hospital was the last post between your soul and the hearse."

Val was dying for a cigarette. She watched the woman tip her ash in a tray.

"But my father did come when they wheeled in my mother. He came two or three times a day and sometimes he'd get in that tiny metal cot and sleep with my small mother wrapped in his arms.

"He clipped flowers from their garden and lined vases around her room. He dug up the yard himself and planted petunias and roses and roped bougainvillea over the porch. 'Alice,' he would say, while stroking her thin cheek, 'the tulips are all in full bloom.' "

"Oh, no," Val said, genuinely saddened by this story.

"But Mom's lids only fluttered and never opened to full moons. And the weaker she got, the sweeter he was in the end. But it was only for her. I think he wished it was me laying in that hospital bed instead."

Val rubbed the muscles along Bernard's back and breathed in the smoke from the bar.

"When the doctor told my father the lung cancer was full blown, my father blew a gasket. He yelled in the doctor's face. He smashed a fist against the hospital wall. He didn't like that young doctor. He hated every single person in the hospital. They were always coming in the room, asking him questions. He especially didn't like how they treated my mom. They'd wake her as soon as she'd finally gone to sleep. They'd stab her with needles that made her arm swell up. They made her nauseous with pills and then shoved food in her face, force-feeding her with spoons and then eventually an I.V. or making her stand up to be weighed. All of it looked like torture. It killed him to sit there and watch. There were endless stabbings and punctures. They constantly pumped her with blood. And though he'd befriend each room-mate, each roommate would always leave. They'd get wheeled down for surgery and never come back or the zigzagging com-puter screens would turn into still lines causing a siren to beep throughout the hall. Dad hated it. He hated the whole scene. He hated watching all those bodies getting weaker and small. All the kids who refused to kiss the cheeks of their lifeless fathers or the husbands who called their wives, saying they were coming to visit today and then not show up once again.

"He hated this one nurse with a skull-splitting passion. She was rough and repeatedly stabbed my mom's arm, trying to locate another good vein.

"'Get out!' he screamed, when my mother winced in pain. 'What kind of beast are you? Can't you see she's hurt! Help,' he screamed loud. 'I want another nurse in here! This bitch is a sadistic Nazi!' He tried to slug the nurse in the jaw, but she ducked and he socked the wall with such force that it cracked like a San Fernando quake.

"The doctor strolled in slowly. He looked at my father. 'I'm sorry, sir. There's nothing more we can do. The cancer has spread to both lungs.'"

"'You're wrong!' my dad screamed in the young doctor's face. 'Alice never smoked a day in her life. You better run some more tests or get your medical book, sonny! There's no way my sweet Alice has cancer!' In an angry fit, my dad lit his cigarette right there, pulling in a lung full of dense Pall Mall smoke in his chest and blowing it toward the young doctor's face.

"'It was the secondhand smoke that did it. Your smoking killed her, sir. Now put that thing out before I have you hauled out?" The doctor said this quickly and left. He'd already taken note of the dent in the wall.

"The cigarette dropped from my father's open jaw."

Val smashed her own cigarette out in the ashtray.

"My father was stunned. The cigarette smoldered on the floor. I watched the pain of realization roll all through his body. The next thing I knew we were picking out coffins." Bernard's eyes became misty. He bit his bottom lip so he wouldn't cry.

Val let her lips graze across his. "Let's go," she said, still holding his face. "I think you could use some fresh air."

She rose, and Bernard draped her black cloak over her shoulders. He guided her thin arm out the door toward his Plymouth. As he left, the other woman winked at him and smiled. Bernard kept his nervous eyes toward the floor.

Val lowered herself to the seat holding both ankles tight and carefully swung her feet in the car.

"Wow there, cowboy. Who's been riding sidesaddle? Some big corn-fed gal wearing a size fifty dress?" The passenger seat was split wide, revealing the stuffing inside, like a body prepped for open heart surgery.

Bernard looked at the deep indentation in the seat. No one had ever ridden in his car but his father. He hated anything marring perfection.

"I'm going to have it fixed." Bernard said. He said it like he was talking about more than the passenger chair.

"Well, do it soon, honey," Val added, laughing. "I don't want to snag my new panties." Her laughter wasn't cruel. Her twinkling eyes sparkled. She looked like someone who was glad to be alive.

7

Paula

Paula ran to the girl's bathroom right after lunch.

She pulled out her matches and struck a flame inside her hand and was just about to drop the hot stick in the trash when another kid came out of the stall.

"What are you doing?" the girl asked.

"None of your business," Paula snapped.

"Why do you have a lit match in your hand?"

Paula blew the match out and walked out the bathroom door. "What match?" she said as she left.

Paula hated her life. Everything was fake and contrived. But she was stuck in this prison, this game of charades, and there was no easy chance of escape. When she was away from her mother, at least she could breathe. A hot, new Paula was blooming inside. This Paula was strong. She burned things a lot. There was something dangerous and romantic about watching a flame. She liked how it moved, like a woman doing a dance, rhythmically shifting her hips. She liked how it leapt in unpredictable patterns. It was insatiably greedy, eating everything in its path. Devouring large objects whole. She loved burning her dolls' feet or packs of playing cards or prescriptions her mother got from the doctor. She burned money and big stacks of old magazines or library books she stole from the school. Once she tried to burn a complete encyclopedia set. She was on a mission and dropped one book a day in the trash, lighting a match behind the school's gym. But one of those nosy kids saw her and told the school's coach so she had to stop burning at "F."

Most of the time, she burned things in a pie pan in her room. She took lipstick from her mother's purse, heated the color in the tube until it gushed like a river of blood. But her all-time favorite thing to burn was the parts off her dolls. She would get a Bic lighter and torch her dolls' toes until they'd melt just like butter on a stove. It drove her mother crazy, but she didn't care. Her mother gave her this life. This was all her fault. Burning relieved the horror of what she had to endure. She'd amputate by flame, her dolls' arms, legs or breasts, until she got tired of looking at their dismembered frames and bury what was left in the yard.

She went to school each day skipping or twirling her skirt, but inside she blazed like a cast-iron stove.

At three o'clock, the school bell screamed through the hall. A tight pack of ten-year-olds marched across the yard. Their backpacks were hitched to their spines. Their cruelty showed in the pitch and fall of their butts, which loomed as large as the Hollywood sign.

A big girl stepped fast. She was leading the bunch. Her narrow eyes shifted toward Paula's thin legs.

"There she is right there," the big girl announced proudly, pointing her dirty finger and rapidly popping her gum. "Let's see where this weirdo kid lives."

They followed Paula all the way up to her house. The house had a giant lemon tree in front. It was brimming with ripe yellow fruit. They'd seen the man who lived in the olive mansion before. He was always alone, pruning and trimming his plants or taking his wheelchair-bound father to the store.

"Isn't that the Howard Hughes mansion? God, does it suck!"

"Mom said," the big girl triumphantly told them, "that Howard Hughes would have gagged knowing a black woman lives there now!"

"There's a black woman living there?" another girl asked, surprised. "I haven't seen any black people hanging around Hollywood Hills."

"Dad told me he saw the black lady in the post office the other day. She was holding a little white girl's hand."

The big girl yanked a lemon and scoffed at her friend. "She's not white," the girl sneered, relishing in keeping them informed. "She's passing, pretending to be white. But Mom said she's as black as the tar in the street."

"Come on! Are you crazy! I've seen that girl! She has blue eyes and her skin is whiter than mine. There's no way a kid that white is black!"

"You wouldn't know unless someone told you. Look close at her hair," the big girl said. "That ought to tell you something right there."

They all stared at Paula's long wavy locks.

Paula shot them a look and went inside the house.

One of the girls stayed quiet. She hoped none of them looked her way. Her own hair was wavier than Paula's.

"But she's so damn light! I can't believe she's black."

"Oh, she's black. Mom said it. It's inside her blood, which is as dark as the La Brea Tar Pits on Wilshire." The big girl kicked a rock to the gravelly asphalt. It crumbled against the light curb.

Suddenly, they all heard the sound of a screen door slam. The big girl's eyes turned toward the mansion again. Paula came down the steps and sat on the porch. Her freshly combed hair was sliced straight down the front. Yellow bows held a bouquet of curls. She wore a red cowboy hat with a snap button shirt and a short gingham skirt that hugged her thin thighs. Her white leather boots were polished to a shine and were fastened with silver fake spurs.

"Oh, my God! Where does she get these weird clothes?"

"I know! They look like my grandmother's stuff."

"She's in my math class. I saw her today."

"She's so white! I can't believe she's black."

The other girls stared hard at the girl across the street.

"Come on," the big one said. "Let's have some fun."

They followed her jumbo body to the mansion and stopped. Though the big girl walked over the lawn to the porch, the others kept their heels just short of the grass.

"Who does your hair?" the big girl asked, smiling.

Paula sat still. A book rested in her lap. She glanced at the girl but she never said a word. She was licking what was left of a Fifty-fifty bar. Her dress rode up on her white thighs.

"Cat got your tongue?" the big girl grinned, leaning closer. A nasty smile slid across her giant smug face. "Hey, nigger girl! What? You forgot how to talk?"

"She looks like that Brady Bunch kid, huh?" The other girls broke out in peals of laughter. The pitch could set car alarms off.

Paula sat quietly. She kept eating her ice cream. When she got to the stick, she licked the thing raw and put the clean stick in her pocket. She tugged her jean skirt farther down on her legs, which were covered in reddish brown hair.

"Hey, monkey girl! Hey, skunk knees, I'm talking to you." The big girl jabbed two fingers against Paula's shoulder. "Tell your mother to get you a razor."

The big girl laughed so loud the rottweiler next door growled. He angrily leaped against the thin, chain-linked fence, snarling toward the tight group of kids.

Now that her ice cream was finished, the small girl stood up. Although she was a whole head shorter than the much bigger girl, she stood on one step, facing the girl full-on. She stared the big girl down with her cool ice cube eyes that looked as cruel and as cold as a morgue.

"Monkey girl is mad!" the big girl chanted to the others.

The other girls chuckled but never crept on the lawn.

The big girl laughed so hard she bent right in half. Her blonde hair waved against the pavement. "I swear, you're as hairy as a squirrel," the big girl said.

Paula stood firm. She was like a tight steel pipe. Her blue eyes turned to lava, her hands balled into fists, and her neck seemed to grow a whole inch. She was now leaning into the bigger girl's jaw.

"What did you say?" Paula rasped.

The big girl laughed, but it was clear she was startled. She hadn't expected to be challenged. Flipping her hair toward her friends she managed a gloriously large, fake smile.

"I said you belong in a zoo, you white-looking chimp." The big girl placed her hands on her hips.

Paula leaned closer. Her nostrils were flared. Her small nose almost touched the bigger girl's chin, and she could smell the swamp growing in the large girl's armpits.

The big girl felt Paula's breath and gingerly took a step back. There was something she saw in the smaller girl's eyes. The girl was totally fearless, relentless in her passion. Like those crazies you see up on Sunset and Vine, banging on car windows for cash.

"What did you say?" Paula asked. She didn't say it loud; it was more like a growl, like the way someone talks to a dog that's been bad.

"What I said is, you need to be playing at Grauman's Chinese Theatre because you look like a hideous freak show!" The big girl glanced toward her friends; she wanted their help, but her ego made her too afraid to ask. She smiled but felt cornered. Not wanting to appear weak, she took a step away, yelling so her friends could all hear, "forget this dumb bitch," she yelled. The big girl abruptly turned, whipping her long hair along her back. "Why waste my time with some Hollywood Hills skank."

But suddenly Paula pounced, grabbing the big girl's hair, wrapping the length in her fist.

"Let go!" the large girl moaned. She struggled wildly against Paula's frame. But for a small girl, Paula had an amazingly strong grip. And she wouldn't let go no matter how hard the big girl struggled. In fact, the more the big girl turned, the tighter Paula's clutch, like her hair was caught in a door.

"Take it back," Paula demanded again. Her lips pulled away from her tiny spiked teeth, which protruded from her face like a shepherd.

The other girls ran away to the safety across the street.

The abandoned girl dissolved into a wet, frightened panic. She struggled wildly, pushing and twisting to break free. Her cheeks were flushed. Her forehead was sweaty. Her limp hair was stuck to her back.

Paula was so close she could smell the big girl's body. A hot flush shot through her pulsating veins. She clung to the sweater with all of her might as a smile inched across her taut face.

The big girl was trapped. Her face was flushed in terror.

"Stop!" the big girl screamed. "I'm telling my mom!" She watched the small girl's tongue race along her sharp teeth, like any second, she would bite a big chunk from her face. The big girl dissolved into such pitiful sobs that even her friends across the street watched in disbelief.

Paula's nails clawed the fabric. She tightened her clutch. A thrilling adrenaline soared through her veins as she yanked the white sweater like a vice.

"Please . . ." the big girl begged. She started to weep. Her nose filled with snot, and her eyes burned with tears. She continued to struggle but with less and less effort. Her face was a blizzard of fear.

Paula glared into the big girl's face. Her breathing was even. Her ice pick eyes never blinked. The tight smile never shifted from her lips. "Take it back," she demanded, in a matter-of-fact tone.

The big girl twisted, contorting her body again and then realizing it was hopeless and there was no way to escape, she went limp and said, "Okay! Okay, I'm sorry! I take back everything I said. Just please let go of my arm!" the girl wept.

But Paula was having too much fun to let go of it now. She enjoyed the big girl's agony. She felt powerful and strong. It felt good to feel her arm muscles bulge and to see all the strength in her hands. She laughed as the big girl pleaded and begged to be set free. She could feel the big girl's chest rise and drop with each breath. Paula inched closer. Hot air leaked from her lips. Releasing her palm from the white sweater's pulled-out sleeve, she let her tiny spiderlike fingers drift across the big girl's chest and felt the fear in her rubber tip nipples.

The big girl screamed. She started to fight back hard. She elbowed Paula's stomach. Twisting and moving her body, she bit Paula's arm. But when she tried to kick her shin, Paula shifted away, and the girl lost her footing and fell. There was an ugly snapping sound, like a branch breaking from a tree or an empty peanut shell being crushed by a shoe.

A blood-curdling scream erupted from the girl's lungs. When she fell, the whole sweater pulled off from both arms. Feeling the sweater slack off, the big girl escaped and raced to the safety across the street. Her left arm swung funny from her body.

"I'm telling!" the big girl yelled, walking quickly away. "I'm telling my mother, you freak!"

Go ahead and tell, Paula said to herself, snatching a leaf from a tree.

The girls marched down the street in a tightly woven pack. The big girl threw a final bruised look over her shoulder before turning the curve of the block.

Paula never flinched once. Even with her skin scratched and bitten and lots of purple marks on her arm, she was the epitome of calm. This was the first time she'd ever stood her ground. Blowing a giant pink bubble and letting the gum pop across her nose, she tossed the piece of gum on the lawn. When the last shoe rounded the corner, Paula's smile fell off. She caught a glimpse of herself in the front picture window. Seeing that image of herself in the crystal clear pane created a boiling rage inside her veins. Remorseful, she left the front porch and walked to the backyard, dragging the sweater behind her.

8

Bernard

Bernard saw the girl by the fig tree in back. He hadn't seen her rip the sweater off the other girl's back. He didn't hear the screams or see her pull the girl's hair or leave and go pick up a spade. He didn't see her dig a small, bowl-sized hole in the yard, or yank each silver button off first, bury the sweater fast, and pack the dirt firm with her hands. All Bernard saw was the girl's filthy palms and her rinsing them off with the hose. He watched her walk toward the front and peek over the fence. She ripped a sharp leaf from one of the trees and tore the leaf into small bits. And then looking over her shoulder once, to see if anyone was watching, she walked back to the hole and dug some of the dirt up. She took a small pair of scissors from her denim skirt pocket. Slicing an inch off of each curl on both sides, she buried her hair with the sweater.

Though Bernard hated when Margie was around, Paula was another story. She invaded his space though he rarely saw her at all. It was almost like they played this cat and mouse game, and her presence was hauntingly there. Like her schoolbooks left randomly under some shrubs or her lunch bag being invaded by black rows of ants or a branch broken off one of his trees.

The girl had a unique voice. Like she was straining to make a deep voice stay high. It dove low and then got so sugary in pitch, she sounded like a scout trying to sell you her last box of cookies.

She threw fits. And would often dig holes in his dirt. He heard the crashing of dirt rocks being thrown against the garage, or her long and agonizing sobs, gurgling from inside the scrubs.

Though she was hired to read for his father, she hadn't come down and done it once. In fact, Margie rarely let the girl come to their place at all.

"Oh, she's reading," Margie would say. Or, "she's taking a bath." But mostly she lied, saying Paula had gone to sleep.

But they could hear the girl up there. They heard her sharp tapping feet. And there were funny smells, too, like the burning of rubber, which kept floating underneath their door.

Bernard tried to tell his father. But his father acted unconcerned. He assumed Bernard was jealous. He knew his son wanted their apartment. He'd say anything to get them to leave.

But miraculously, when Bernard went out today, Paula was on the back stairs, reading all alone on the last bottom slat. Bernard stared at her. He examined her clothes. Her fingers looked pretty, with nails clipped close and scrubbed so perfectly clean, they looked like a pink princess rose.

"Hello," Bernard said, passing the girl on the steps. He tried to make his tight voice not sound so nervous. He was curious but kept his eyes low and watched her socks. He took quick staccato breaths, and his throat felt bone dry. He walked all the way down the ramp and toward the garage. It irked him that she didn't acknowledge him at all and never took her eyes from her textbook.

She held the pages so close to her miniature face that it looked like the book touched her nose.

"Maybe your mother should invest in some glasses," he joked. He said the remark sharply, thinking she'd speak to him then. But she didn't. She kept her face pushed into the spine. And then suddenly she sat back and snapped the book shut, shooting him a sharp vicious glare. There was so much gasoline in those bluish green eyes that he raced inside the garage door and locked it.

Once inside, Bernard blotted his face with a cloth. Taking deep, measured breaths, he began to feel calm. He cleaned off his frames and put the cloth in his pocket. He unlocked the door, swung the other side open, and quickly walked to his car.

Shoving his safety belt in the slot, he backed the car out slowly, using only his rear mirror to guide him. He refused to be bothered by some snot-nosed kid. There was a eulogy at six. He had a body to dress. He had to get back to the mortuary by four.

Bernard pulled up to Rosedale at 3:45. He parked in the front of South Catalina, the location of old Chapel of the Pines.

Bernard smiled at his boss and continued down the hall. He entered an antiseptic room filled with clear bottles, drawers with tools, and six-foot-long metal trays for the bodies. He opened a drawer and pulled out a large pair of pliers and a very sharp, jagged tooth saw. A decrepit chalk-faced lady lay on one of the trays. Bernard quietly began to work on her lips.

While Bernard worked, Reynolds grinned and leaned over his shoulder. "The man out in the lobby's having a hell of a time. Poor fellow. He's too old to ever consider burning his wife. He'd rather drain all his savings getting her inside the earth than ever consider cremation.

Bernard used a small pipe to hold open the woman's jaw.

"In Sweden, those guys are trying all kinds of new things."

"Like what?" Bernard asked. He loved hearing these stories.

Bernard's boss came close. He leaned in his face. "They're boiling them," Reynolds said, widening his eyes.

Bernard listened intently while using the knife. He sliced open her black dress with ease.

"Them Swedes are cooking their bodies in lye. I'm not lying! I tell you it's the honest to God truth! No dust, no bones, and no godawful smell!"

Reynolds looked at the three dead bodies and smiled. "Business is good. I can't complain. We always have a nice fresh supply." Reynolds walked out of the room to console the family outside, leaving Bernard alone to work on the bodies.

There was a fifty-year-old man with a cloth over his head who died from his own gun. The older woman in the sliced dress wore a white slip underneath. She belonged to the family outside. She was a chubby little thing with tight, unlined skin, and her black dress and white slip made her look like a penguin, casually laying on its side. Though dead, she wore the slightest hint of a smile. That smile made Bernard feel peculiar inside. He didn't want the old lady to see what he was going to do next. He came over and closed both of the old woman's lids by sticking two pins along the rim of her lashes.

Bernard was the one who smiled this time. The third body belonged to a young Mexican woman. Bernard was there when Tommy, the grave digger, wheeled her in. Tommy pulled the white mortuary van to the service doors in the back and strapped her black body bag to the gurney. She'd just been released from the L.A. County Morgue after having died the previous morning.

Bernard rolled the bag toward the neck-high refrigerators in the corner. They had to wait twenty-four hours before cremating the remains. And it was a good thing they waited. The groom's family called in. They wanted a burial as a way of paying their respects.

When Bernard zipped open the bag, he saw a smashed to bits beauty. She leaped from the 10 freeway, right where it met the 405 when her fiancé called off the wedding. She was in the coroner's office a few days, to make sure there was no foul play. And now, the would-be-bride, lay naked on the gurney. Bernard smiled at the mangled girl's face.

Quickly looking toward the door once, Bernard squirted massage cream inside his palms and rubbed his warm fingers across the dead woman's shoulders and breasts.

Bernard liked this cream. It was emollient and rich. Many funeral directors exhibited a skin condition on their hands. It was a nasty rash doctor's called "embalmer's eczema," which caused itchy bumps over their hands and wrists and came from too much formaldehyde on their skin. Some embalmers noticed a slight enlargement in their chest from all the estrogen in the massage creams they used on a corpse.

Turning her on her side, Bernard rubbed her stomach and her behind while humming "Here Comes the Bride." His mouth hovered over her lips. She was only nineteen and had survived the vicious jump but had been mowed over by a car before they could get to her body. The left lane of the 405 was sopping in blood. But you'd never know it now by looking at the girl's face. She was perfectly intact and with the burgundy embalming fluid in her veins, she had regained the rich, healthy glow to her skin. She was lying on her side like she was watching TV. Bernard lifted her limp body, pulling one leg over his shoulder. He put her panties on, he leaned her over and hooked her bra and then zipped an elaborate wedding dress over her frame.

Quickly, he glanced at the doorway again. Instead of putting her on a clean gurney and rolling her to the viewing room with her casket, Bernard heaved her body over his shoulder and carried her himself. He smiled, imagining he was carrying his bride over the threshold. He could feel the refrigerator-cool lumps of her breasts against his back. This was the closest he ever came to beautiful women like these. Taking one last deep breath of her clean, just washed hair, he stuffed her inside of a satin, embroidered casket.

Bernard slipped a big diamond ring on the young woman's hand. He stroked the woman's hair, letting it slide across his thumb. Her hair was as soft as a fat newborn's thigh. With her hair across his face, breathing the sweet fragrance in, he never felt more alive in his life.

Suddenly, the doorknob turned. Bernard dropped the woman's skull.

"How's the Valdez girl coming? You finished with her yet?" Reynolds came over to the casket and examined the woman's head. "I'll say one thing. It's a good thing a semi didn't come mow her down, or we wouldn't have nothing to put in the box."

Reynolds rubbed the girl's cheek. "Pity the wedding didn't

happen. But financially, it turned out okay for her ol' man. Her father didn't have to pay one cent for the wedding, and the groom's family sprung for her funeral."

Bernard followed his boss back to the prep room again. They stood next to a man's head. It was covered in a towel.

Though a gunshot wound had exploded half the man's skull, Bernard had rebuilt his scalp with waxes and glue, and the man looked almost brand-new.

"Oh, this is nice!" Reynolds said, lifting the towel. "You do fine work, son. His wife will be happy to see him again. It's too bad she has to do the viewing from inside her cell."

The man was an epileptic who fell down a flight of stairs. The wife came home one night and caught him in bed with the night nurse.

"Your sex drive and anger are sister emotions. You can kill someone as easily as love 'em to death. One minute she's cooking his favorite, liver and onions, and the next thing you know, she's blasting the side of his head." Reynolds laughed like a maniac, slapping his flopping hands against his legs. Cheerful tears rolled out of his eyes.

Bernard smiled at his boss. It was easy to please Reynolds. He was the opposite of his cantankerous father.

"I fixed him this morning." Bernard proudly said. Then walked over to the penguin woman and lifted her up off the gurney and easily removed her sliced-open dress.

"Too bad about this one." Reynolds peered at the dead woman's face. "Her husband came over on a bus, just sold the family car. Killed his whole savings. Used three credit cards, too. They gave me everything they could scrape. You should have seen 'em, son. Dumping coffee cans right on my desk. I actually felt bad, and you know that's not me." Reynolds chuckled while cutting off the dead woman's slip.

When people begged for discounts, Reynolds showed them the pine boxes.

"Wood was good enough for my granddaddy," Reynolds would

say with a wink. "There's no shame in being cheap. The dead can't see you now. I'm sure you got a thousand and one more important things to buy. No use wasting your cash on your poor mother's casket."

That was usually enough to make them revisit their wallets. Most folks went into grave debt, laying their loved ones out proper. The grief was colossal. It brought unrelenting pain. People were so shaken, they couldn't see straight or think. Their sorrow compelled them to compensate somehow. Buying an expensive casket was an immediate fix. Extravagance was believed to bring relief. The more money they spent, the better they thought they would feel. And for a moment, they did feel something, though it was hard to pinpoint what. But the moment was short-lived, especially when the funeral bill was due, which almost killed some people right then and there.

"Nice," Reynolds said, rubbing one of his luxury coffins. "You have excellent taste. I'm sure Laura will love it." Mr. Reynolds talked like the person was buying a new car. "She'll look good sporting this baby to heaven."

Reynolds' advantage was the mighty toll death took on folks. He was in the business of performing community events. Funerals were communal. It was your final farewell show. Hordes of people came from all walks of life. They weren't invited. No invitations were sent. People just showed up in droves. Even in grief, the vanity of the bereaved was colossal. And with the community watching, which was usually all your family and friends, no one wanted to be thought of as cheap. This was Reynolds' sword. He carefully diced his words. He knew where to stick in the knife.

"Your boss will be coming, right, so will your wife's mother." He held the stiff shoulder of the dead woman's widower husband. "You want them to know you cared enough to do it right."

And how could people not pick expensive gilded caskets? These events were entrenched. Everyone expected a standard. They expected flowers and limos and pallbearers wearing white gloves, clutching brilliantly polished brass coffins. They expected a service with singers, an interment with chairs and plenty of liquor and food at the repast.

"Gone are the days of doing everything at home. Folks used to die in bed and planned the wake in their own parlor. Then they'd bury them out back, under a tree in the yard or in a nice patch of grass on a hill." Reynolds shoved Bernard's shoulder and laughed to himself. "But if folks still did that, they wouldn't need us, right?

"Today folks die in hospitals or nursing homes snap them up. Sometimes the police call us to come down. But most folks croak right in their own home. And everybody needs someone to get the remains. No one wants to handle the body."

And Reynolds wasn't above helping the process along. He made special trips to churches. He frequented nursing homes around town. He'd schmooze with the bishops and make donations in his name. He made sure his card was in all the Rolodexes of every hospital in town and inside the coroner's office. He'd even peek in the hospital rooms just to see who was still breathing. He liked living close to his profit.

Reynolds even got money from digging people back up. People needed autopsies or DNA from hair. Sometimes families wanted to get their hands on old jewelry. People wanted to move loved ones closer to the rest of their family and dug their graves up and put them on trains.

Reynolds had Tommy, the grave digger, shovel them in or back up. While digging, Tommy made videotapes of himself opening up the graves. This was to ensure nothing was ever removed or taken from those coffins. But Mr. Reynolds was always there when Tommy lifted the lid, and he was the one who decided when to turn the videotape on.

Reynolds reached for one of the tools laid out on the table. He took a large set of pliers and rammed it across the roof of her mouth, yanking out her back teeth so her mouth would close neatly, Reynolds quickly sewed the woman's mouth tightly shut and massaged her cold face with cream.

"I showed 'em lots of stuff those poor folks coulda got cheaper, but that man's mind was set. Told me he didn't want to see nothing but the cream of the crop. Said his wife deserved only the pick of the litter, and he shelled out the extra fee for a Saturday funeral, too. But I watched his daughter. She didn't do nothing but weep and moan. Now I see crying in this place, all the time, right? But this was different. This crying clawed my bones and the soft tender spot in my chest. I tell you it was a terrible thing to have to endure. I ended up selling him one of my Cadillac caskets. Cost him twenty-four grand when it was all said and done, and to tell you the truth, I would have given it to 'em, just to get his poor daughter out of my room."

Reynolds pulled a pipe and tin of tobacco from his pocket. He stuffed the brown earthy slivers inside the pipe bowl and struck a match, holding the flame in the air.

"I found out later the ol' man ran over his wife."

The penguin woman was now completely out of her clothes. She was hooked to the embalming machine. "He got pissed at his wife and sped from the driveway." Reynolds blew out the match when the flame reached his fingers, and the pipe bowl burned like a furnace. "The daughter screamed bloody murder, but he thought she was fussing at him too, so he kept his foot smashed on the gas." Reynolds sucked his pipe hard and blew the smoke out the window. "Poor woman never had a chance."

Reynolds pulled a clean blue dress over the woman's head. He funneled the elegant dress over her rigormortis body. And since the dress didn't fit right, he reached inside a drawer and used a nail gun to attach the dress to her skin.

"Folks'll spend a gang of money to lay their relatives out proper. But guilt . . ." Reynolds' lips smiled around his black pipe. "Guilt will get 'em to lay out every red cent they have and go into ten years of hard debt just to finance the rest." Reynolds winked at Bernard and bit the tip of his pipe. "Guilt is the profit in the funeral business."

Reynolds pulled the embalming hose and sewed the woman up quickly. Bernard liked to watch Reynolds work. He wasn't hurried or untidy. His movements were careful yet firm.

Reynolds scratched his head. He looked very concerned. "You see that family out there?" Reynolds tilted his head to the side. A black family was crying together on a bench.

"Those are real nice folks, real decent," he said. Reynolds said it like he was surprised and still trying to convince himself. "You know we used to not bury black and white side by side. In fact, Rosedale was the first cemetery to integrate in L.A. Caught holy hell for it. Lots of whites like to have died. And we had to dig deeper holes to drop those black bodies in if a white soul rested nearby."

Reynolds cracked up, laughing like the joke was on them. "To appease some, Rosedale started burning those bodies." Reynolds looked at the domelike structure of Chapel of the Pines. Built in 1903, it was the oldest crematorium in town.

"I tell you, Bernard, things sure have changed. We used to bury our treasure and burn all our trash. Now with landfills and crematories, we bury our trash and burn our bodies." Reynolds saw a woman crying near the crematory's doors. "Some people have a time getting used to that.

"L.A.'s earliest cemetery isn't there anymore. They called it 'cemetery on the hill' or 'Los Angeles City Cemetery' and it was built due east of downtown. In fact, it's right where L.A. Unified is sitting right now. I think that's why the schools are having such a ghoulish time now. They're running their business right on top of all those petrified graves."

"They built the school board on a gravesite?" Bernard asked his boss.

"That's right, but they moved all those old bodies first. But you better believe lots of arms and legs are still there. Rosedale got some of them. Evergreen got a few more. Go to the east side of our fence, you'll see these tiny ancient markers, some of them are so old they've busted and fallen down. Some have names, but lots of them just have numbers, those are all City's disinterred graves. Shoot, eighty bodies were discovered downtown the other day. You didn't see it in the paper? It was all over the news. They were excavating for a high school and stumbled upon a site. They found coffin handles and lids with the word 'Mother' etched in. They found metal combs and nails, a bracelet or two or some buttons, and lots of bone fragments and wood. One of them lucked up on a well-preserved corpse, sitting inside a red velvet casket." Reynolds laughed so loud it sounded like he might croak. "Remains that old are usually just discolored soil, which is all that is left after a hundred years in the ground."

Reynolds shook his head and studied his feet. "I don't like disinterment. Too much paperwork involved. It's more than just digging the casket back up. The funeral game has become a bloody, cutthroat business. The big boys are snapping all the mom and pops up. Oh, they look the same and they keep up the old family names, but corporations are running the bone business now.

"Did you see that man I was talking to in the hall? I had to talk to that man 'til I got blue in the face. He said he heard things. Things that weren't right." Reynolds crossed the room and looked down a dead woman's throat. "He's rattling my chain, trying to get me spooked, talking mess just to get me to sell."

"What about that guy in the paper today?" Bernard asked.

"Them damn crazy parlors give us good ones bad names! Take that Lake Ellsinore man. He started mutilating his clients. Instead of burning them in retorts, he sold them for parts. That man made money from toenail to beak, sold from both ends, so to speak. He sold the organs, arteries, and veins and then started harvesting bone. Those dental surgeons are paying top dollar for this stuff! Look at all them implants we got going on now. They're selling cadaver all over town. Plenty of folks are walking around with dead folks drilled in their mouths. Plastic surgeons are turning into body snatchers, too. They want muscle, fat, or skin for all their reconstructions. They put together a face from a girl wrecked in her car, and all the parts came from a corpse. Even big schools like UCLA made the news for buying dead bones under the table.

"I'm telling you, Bernard, you picked the right business. Dealing in death has really shot wide open." Reynolds' left arm flew out from his body. "Some say it's up in the billions."

His boss's eyes twinkled while talking about this subject. Especially when he mentioned the Lake Ellsinore man. The fact was, his boss admired the guy. He wished he had thought of it first.

"Man had a steady flow of medical school money. He'd hand 'em a body, and they gave him straight cash. No questions asked. Research, they call it. Research my ass! Some of those bodies never even made it to class. You saw it! I know you saw it, Bernard! Story was all over the paper. Got the FDA champing at the bit about the mess. A slew of folks came down with hepatitis from a diseased corpse. The FDA put the nails in that coffin but quick. We have to fill out a bunch of forms now to make sure we don't pass HIV."

Bernard knew that funeral homes were notorious for selling parts, especially the many parts of women. Women were usually more fleshy and had less damaged tissue. People wanted their teeth and their breasts and their egg-bearing wombs, but Reynolds didn't get involved in any of that, especially now, with the police hunting through parlors. No, Reynolds sold the easiest thing he could, and it didn't break any laws he knew of. He sold the newly shaved scalps of dead women's hair. Reynolds would ask the bereaved family to fill out a form. "It's for cancer patients," he told them. "It helps them make wigs." But Reynolds never sold one strand to any cancer patient. Each month, a well-dressed man would come to the parlor. Smoking a big fat cigar, he gave Reynolds straight cash, and Reynolds handed him a bag so large the man struggled to get it in his car. It was bulging with dead people's hair. The man came monthly, like clockwork, and only at night. Their routine looked like the drug deals you see on Sunset and Vine.

Reynolds loved his job. His father had done it before him, and his granddad had started the business. "We've been peddling death more than eighty-four years. You can't say I don't know this trade. Eternity's my middle name!" Mr. Reynolds stopped talking and watched Bernard use the saw. His whole hand almost fit in the dead woman's open jaw.

"How's your father been holding up?" Reynolds peered at the woman's tonsils. "I hear he's got that woman and girl living in his house?" He smacked Bernard's shoulder and laughed real hard. "Tell the old man Reynolds said hello, hear? Don't forget, son. I hope to be seeing him real soon."

9

Bernard and Val

"She's an incorrigible little brat!" Bernard neatly folded his napkin. "Goodness knows, I could have fallen down and died."

Val finished her burger and all of her fries and then reached over and stabbed her fork in the sausage on his plate.

"I could have wrung her thin neck, she scared me so bad. Had the nerve to do a cartwheel and laugh."

"She's heartless. I've seen plenty of rugrats like her." Val knew firsthand how cruel kids could be. "They tease you, they lie, and they'll rob your ass blind. They're all just a waste of small shoes."

Bernard gnawed the callused skin surrounding his pinkie. Anger turned his white cheeks a bloody persimmon red.

"My father loves the girl and her fat floozy mother. I can't believe he rented the apartment to them. And now he's hired the fool girl to come over to read him the paper. I can't turn without the blasted little girl being around!" Bernard banged his fist against the restaurant table. A few curious patrons looked their way.

"I bet there's a way to get back at them both," Val waved for the waiter and ordered pie à la mode and another cup of piping hot coffee.

The waiter lingered a while, trying to catch Val's eye. Bernard shot him a look, and the waiter hastily walked away.

"Listen, don't sweat it. I had a kid sister, once. She was a royal pain, but I fixed her wagon but good. I can help you with this kid if you want."

Bernard admired Val. Her appetite was vast. She didn't pick at her food like his father did, moving it around with his fork and finally just laying the fork down. It was always too greasy, too salty, too tough. He spat, or chewed too loud, or choked on his meat and gagged it back out on his plate. Eating with him was a lesson in disgust. Bernard usually ate alone in his room.

Val relished these free meals and liked eating them slow. All she had at home was one lonely peanut butter jar and a stale loaf of saggy wheat bread.

Bernard gazed at Val. She was as small as a child. He reached over and gently began fingering her hair. He had never been so forward with a woman before. He was sorry he wasted his precious time with Val talking about some dumb girl.

"I bet your mother was a looker," Bernard said, smoothing her tresses.

Val smiled and gently slid her hair from his hand.

"My father's from Panama. My mother was Swedish. I got his olive skin and her platinum hair," Val lied.

Val grinned to herself when she added that part. Her mom was a coal mining, midwestern brunette who married a redneck from Texas.

"My mother was a sweetheart, but my dad was a psycho. Things infuriated him at the drop of a hat." Val placed a large forkful of pie in her mouth. "I remember the first day I ever shaved my legs."

Bernard glanced at her thin calves. She was as tiny as a ten-year-old kid. He licked the top of his lips.

"Oh my God, did my dad go berserk." Val swallowed some pie whole and dug in for more. "It took my five uncles to hold the man down."

Val winked at Bernard. It was nice being with him. He was easygoing and sweet, the exact opposite of her father. He didn't swear or wear his maleness on his sleeve. His soft-mannered ways were a comfort.

"My father was a prude. He resented my body. When I hit

adolescence, my dad hit the roof. He couldn't understand how my body had changed. He was Latin. *El Hefe!* The boss of the land. Me and my sisters had to do everything he said."

Bernard tried to go for her long hair again, but Val gently moved his hand away.

"But one time he caught me. I was wearing my cousin's bathing suit. It was so cute and tight and cut real high on the thigh and way too small, but so what, right? It was white and covered with bright flaming cherries. I fell in love with it the moment I saw it."

Bernard pictured her wearing the bathing suit in his mind. A soft pull ached underneath his buckle.

"I found some patent leather red pumps and these tiny cherry earrings. I swear I felt just like a goddess!"

Val fanned her big blonde hair out of her eyes.

Bernard watched her ribbon mouth move as she talked.

"I'd strip and put the cherry bathing suit on and parade it around whenever I was at home alone. But my uncles, who were fixing the driveway outside, peeked in the window and caught me."

Val's eyes carried the slimmest hint of tears as she stared out the huge restaurant window.

"All my uncles, they screamed. They dragged me outside the house laughing. I remember being so proud. I did this little sexy dance. Man, oh man, did they love that show! They were laughing and gulping a bunch of Coronas. One of my uncles picked me up and put me on the diving board outside. Man, I strutted down that thing like it was a runway."

Bernard gazed at Val, picturing that moment in his mind. He could see the tiny bikini and her firm ample breasts as her ass fought the tight elastic fabric. He wished he were there. He wished he was one of her uncles. He wanted to be watching her while drinking cold beer, biting his sharp teeth in a lime.

"'*Que bonita!*' they exclaimed, 'munyeka, munyeka!' They reached for my feet slamming their hands against their jeans, yelling that I looked like a doll. I felt great way up there and stretched my arms to the sky," Val stopped for a moment before going on.

"But, honey, oh my God! You could have killed me right then when my dad came out to the yard."

Val let her fork slip. She stared at her coffee. Her gay mood drastically changed.

"My uncles tried to stop him but my dad wrenched himself free. He grabbed me. He dragged me down by the hair and dunked me facedown in the pool."

She paused, sipped her coffee, lifting it carefully to her lips. "He held my head down in the sour pool water. I remember seeing leaves and small bugs swirling around. I swear, I thought I would drown."

Val lifted her hair, revealing a thin pale scar. "When they finally pulled him off, I got up and ran but slid on the brand-new cement."

Bernard stared at her face and creamy smooth skin. "You're so beautiful," he said and was about to touch her skin, but the waiter came by filling her cup with more coffee.

"I bet lots of men want you," Bernard took her hand.

Val smiled at him coyly, "Now you're starting to sound like Roy."

Bernard recoiled for a moment. Self-doubt forced his lids down. He pulled his arm away from her luxurious shoulders and rested his hand back in his lap. Who was Roy? A boyfriend? Bernard bit into his lip. A woman like this was obviously taken.

What a damn fool you are, he scolded himself. *What on earth would a woman like Val want with you?* Rapidly, Bernard began scratching his hands.

"He's my beautician." Val told him. "Roy does my hair. I wouldn't let anyone else touch it."

Val noticed the muscles tighten in Bernard's face. "You look like somebody just stole your favorite toy. Relax, sugar. I'm not his type." She wiped off her mouth and folded her napkin in her lap. "Roy's only interested in boys."

Val put on her lipstick and snapped shut her purse. "Well, I better get going. I have an appointment at three."

"Well wait a minute, I'll drop you!" Bernard blurted out.

"Are you sure it's no trouble?"

"Of course not!" Bernard grabbed the check and peered in his wallet.

The wallet gaped opened like a wide leather mouth. The inside was stuffed full of bills.

Real slick, so as no one could see, Val looked in the mirror and fluffed up her hair, but her razor eyes cut to Bernard's open wallet, and she sized up the amount in her mind.

The waiter, who patiently stood over their chairs, smiled at Bernard and grinned at the cash. He wanted to shift his eyes to Val's velvety cleavage, but he didn't, so that Bernard would leave a large tip.

"Honey?" Val said hesitantly, when they got in the car. "Do you think you can loan me a couple of bucks?"

"How much do you need?" Bernard wanted to help.

"Whatever you can spare. I'll let you decide." She tried not to watch Bernard's hands.

Last night, Reynolds paid him straight cash. He paid Bernard under the table a lot.

"No use letting Uncle Sam get all of your green," Reynolds said. "Only green I like is lining my pocket or surrounding my cemetery plots."

Lots a people paid for their funerals in cash. Old money. Money kept for decades in jars. Money hidden in mattresses or in coffee cans in attics. Silver dollars or rarely seen two-dollar bills or old wrinkled hundreds with small faces.

Reynolds shoved a handful of bills in Bernard's palm. "Don't tell anybody about the man I meet Mondays late at night. I got enough problems hovering at my door now, then having to worry about the law coming, too. You just keep doing your job, and if anyone asks you a question, tell them that you don't know squat."

"So tell me, honey, what's going on at your job?" Val inquired. Val was intrigued with Bernard's funeral job.

"I'm working on a set of twin Korean girls and their father," Bernard said. "Their bodies were so torched I had to use PVC pipe for bone and use a knife through their lids to open their melted eyes."

The twin girls had been murdered, burned alive by their father. The father had been gambling each day and was buried in debt. He couldn't bear to tell his wife their lifestyle was a sham. The Hummer. Their lavish vacations. Their kids' private school education. Rather than let anyone see what a failure he was, the Korean man drove downtown and parked their van in an alley and doused both his daughters with a can of kerosene and then threw the match in the car. When the paramedics arrived, both girls were dead. They were so badly burned; only their small heads remained, and they had to pry their skeletal bodies from each seat. But the sad part was they were able to rescue the father. He was sick from smoke inhalation and his lungs had collapsed, but he would definitely survive.

"The whole Korean community showed up in droves," Bernard said. "Those Koreans put all of their money together. One by one, they came in and dumped cash on Reynolds' desk and told him to spare no expense.

"But at the wake, the day before the funeral started, a relative came in and blew the Korean father's brains out right there. Now we're doing a triple burial service."

Val barely blinked, listening to Bernard's tale. She almost forgot about the cash.

Not wanting to appear cheap and wanting desperately to impress his date, Bernard decided to give her half of what he had.

"Oh, baby, this is great! My God, you're a saint." She kissed him but turned her head when he tried to kiss her lips, and she felt his tongue roll along the length of her jaw.

"Listen," she said, placing his palm in her hand. "If you want, I can have a small chat with that girl. Sometimes these things need finesse."

"Really?" Bernard beamed. "You wouldn't mind doing that?"

"She's a child! I'm sure we can talk girl to girl. She's at the age where she doesn't want to listen to authority anymore. She's probably a terror at school, and I bet her mother is hopeless. I'll talk to her like a big sister."

Bernard gathered some of her hair in his hands and breathed in the lavender fragrance. "I could do this all day," he said lovingly.

He watched her get out and race across the street. Bernard could still smell her scent in his car.

Bernard waited for Val to go in the shop. He saw a middle-aged man wearing a giant hoop earring and a Hawaiian shirt over loose jeans. A young man with a buzz cut rose up from the chair, and Roy slid his arms around the younger man's waist and gave him a very deep squeeze. Bernard cornered the street heading back toward Franklin. He didn't worry about Roy anymore.

As soon as Val walked into Roy's shop, she immediately felt alive. Roy loved Halloween. It was his favorite time of year. And even though Halloween was ten nights away, his shop was done up to the nines. There were skeleton lights and red spiders on cobwebs and a witch screaming out from a large smoky cauldron.

"Oh, Roy! You outdid yourself, man!"

"Hey, doll," Roy said, plugging in a hot pot of wax.

"Lord, child, what have you done with the stuff?"

Val had the top part of her hair smoothed down. Her appearance was flawless, but when she took her hair down, inside was a tangled up vine.

"He's a hair man. I can't keep his hands out."

"What else does Bernard like?" Roy knowingly teased.

Roy painted a strip of wax over her lip. He covered the hot wax with a thin piece of gauze. Patting it down gently while smoothing it out, Roy violently ripped the gauze off.

"Aaawoo!" Val said. Her mouth stung with pain. Waxing was something she'd never get used to.

"It hurts so good, huh? Remember, no pain, no gain. Ain't a chick catching shit with a mustache."

"I don't have a mustache, Roy! Just fine little blond hairs."

Roy laid another piece of candy on his tongue and then snatched the gauze fast from her face. Attached to the gauze were little blond hairs with dark, rounded roots wedged in wax.

"You don't have one now," Roy stirred the melted wax in the jar. "But you would if you didn't come to me."

Val frowned at Roy who grinned in return.

"You're lucky you're not hairy. Some of my girls have a time. I did this freak yesterday. Took me over an hour. Her stuff was so thick; it was a damn redwood forest with roots that could reach Tijuana. I said honey, next time you come; bring a chainsaw. You know that heifer had the nerve to be sensitive, too! I had to hold her head down with my elbow."

"You've been doing mine so long, it barely grows anymore."

"And if you come in more often, you wouldn't have anything at all!" Roy was always after Val to come in more often.

"So how's the sugar daddy, hon? He paying your rent yet?"

Val smiled and stuck both her leopard pumps out. Her shoes looked like two pointy knives.

"I bet you got him eating out of your fine silky hand." Roy poured more paraffin wax in the warmer. He stuck both of Val's hands in the warm golden liquid. "I bet that ol' fool's buying you candy and flowers."

Val looked at her hands and smiled at Roy. "Nothing wrong with getting some chocolate now and then. Besides, Bernard's sweet. He's not like the others. And who the hell are you to talk about old?"

"Yeah, but I don't look it." Roy posed for the mirror.

"Bernard's a civilian. He doesn't know a thing about this life. And I'm glad because I'm sick of dealing with druggies and kooks."

"Well, at least you admit it," Roy sprayed a can over her head. "My ears are still burning from the last story you told. Mercy, you sure pick some winners!"

"It's easy to please Bernard. He's starved for attention. He's been cooped up for years tending to his invalid father."

"A daddy's boy! Oh Lord. I bet his father's a piece of work."

"I haven't met his father. He doesn't talk about him much.

The only problem he has is this kid in his building. She's giving Bernard's soul the blues. I told him I'd come by and help straighten the kid out."

Roy examined her weave and sucked on his tongue. "Listen, Florence Nightingale. Please read my lips. Don't get involved with no kid."

"I'm not getting *involved*! I'm just talking to her, that's all. She's just a ten-year-old brat who's completely unleashed. I'm just going to jerk on her chain. Come on! It's my job to know women. I know how they think, and I've studied all their ways. I can wrap that dumb kid around my pinkie in one blink."

"Oh please. Didn't you see *The Bad Seed*? Don't be so cocky. You don't know this young chick. A kid bashed Johnny's head in broad daylight, okay! The kid ran up on Johnny swinging a Louisville Slugger. Poor Johnny doesn't know his own name anymore."

Val looked down at the hair on the floor.

Roy lifted up a big chunk of matted blonde hair at her nape; some of the tracks were starting to come loose. "I can color it today, but don't wait too long. You don't want this to all fall out in your lap."

"I can't right now." Val told him, looking away. She could barely afford to pay for what she was having done now. "Just hit my roots and style it as usual."

"You're the boss," Roy said, frowning at her head. "Oh my God! I almost forgot. I have something to show you. The UPS guy just brought it today." Roy ran to the back of his shop and unlocked a small closet.

"You should have seen that guy's legs. I could have died right then and there. What I would have done for a quick little ride in the back of his little brown truck."

"Dang, Roy!" Val laughed. "When do you ever stop?"

"The day they come down and drag a white sheet across my face.

"Girlfriend, look at this. I'll try to save some but I can't promise. Feel it, you're gonna die when you touch it." Roy came back holding a clear plastic bag. The inside was brimming with hair.

Val placed her small hand inside the Ziploc slot and felt the soft delicate locks. "Wow, that feels great. Where do you get it?"

Roy never let on where he got his stock. He had an excellent source. He received a shipment each month. He had to wash it good. Sometimes there was an odor. But the hair was the best-looking stuff on the market. And it wasn't like the bullshit he bought once from China that smelled like a forty-year-old dog. This was real. This was perfect. This was quality stuff. Today he got lucky and got the hair of a child. He could tell because the consistency was unmarked and pure. This hair had never been treated, never been blow-dried or dyed. It was one hundred percent virgin. It had never been touched. You weave hair like that in, and no one questions it, ever. This was one hundred percent human and totally blond. You couldn't get hair like this unless you killed a Scandinavian yourself.

Roy didn't ask the guy where he got it. But he had a hunch. He saw a small article once about a funeral home in Missouri. The undertaker sold everything, bones, veins, and skin, nothing went into the trash. If the victim was young and the family wanted cremation, the undertaker craved the body like a Thanksgiving turkey, placing various parts in large plastic bags. He had plenty of takers. There were all sorts of buyers. But until recently, no one ever considered the hair. But weaving human hair was now a multimillion dollar business. And if you were lucky enough to get your hands on some young natural strands, a beautician could easily make a killing.

Roy received bags of hair on a regular basis. Radiant reds or luscious chestnut browns. Hair so rich and dark and completely jet-black it looked like the slick back of a seal.

But blonde hair, by far, was the ultimate seller. In L.A., there was never enough of the color. Everyone went light. People were sick over the shade. Gold, platinum, and champagne were requisite colors. He had to backorder the stuff because it was in such demand. Blondes were as common as cuff links on a tux. It used to be something you only saw in Newport Beach where whole seas of blondes covered the beach. But the blonde hair migration was all over this city. Everyone from black girls sporting platinum dreads and twists or Latinas pouring peroxide all over their heads, even Asian chicks bleached the molasses from their tips.

If he wasn't weaving it in, he was dying it like crazy. Extensions, the once secret hair of the rich were now worn by anyone who had four hundred dollars. And if you wanted to go cheap and had sixty-eight bucks, you could bobby pin a nice big clump in the back.

But Roy ran a very upscale shop. Only beauties that paid dearly could step foot in his door. None of his clients knew his cemetery source, and Roy never asked questions. It was morbid, but damn, the hair was so fine! There was no way he'd pass on a deal like this. He washed it with the best shampoo he could buy and conditioned it with Sebastian, the Two Plus One line, and mixed in his own homemade concoction of olive oil and lime. Hanging the hair over a rope, he'd let it naturally dry and if you looked inside Roy's shop, real late at night, you'd see a string of faceless women strapped to the line, no bodies no heads, just hair on a strap, like a long string of freshly scalped Pilgrims. Roy brushed each one thoroughly and stored them in clear plastic bags with holes punched on each side so they could easily breathe.

There was only one time that he almost quit buying.

While brushing he heard something drop down and fall. He looked but couldn't see a thing on the floor at first. But while walking barefoot something caught under his sole. When he turned his foot over there was a giant ragged tooth, wedged between two of his toes.

Roy shuddered just thinking about finding it now. He tilted his head up to the television set, which blasted the news through the room.

"Hey, Roy," Val asked. "Have you been keeping up with this case lately?"

The television was on. It was the McMartin trial again. The woman who made the first accusation had been hauled off for psychological problems.

"Now see, I bet she made this whole story up."

"This is exactly why I don't want you to mess with that kid." Roy sucked his tongue and turned from the set.

The screen flashed, showing a group of children pointing to some dirt on the ground, then it switched to the courtroom again. The camera zoomed in on an old wheelchair-bound woman. The woman looked drab. She looked beat down and shot, like she'd been chased ten long blocks by a wild pack of dogs and resigned herself to just being caught. Her mouth, a single line, was drawn as tight as her bun. Her face was like the sky before a storm.

Roy was trying to comb through Val's tangled hair. He sucked hard on his tongue again and sighed. "What a mess," he exclaimed while tugging the comb.

"I know!" Val agreed. She thought he was talking about the TV, not her hair. "They're such vile beasts!" she scowled at the set. "I bet every one of those nasty kids are lying."

"Sure they're lying! That's what kids do. Lie and tear nice shit up."

Roy scowled, remembering a woman who came in yesterday. "This lady brought this maniac kid to my shop. I tell you, that kid pulled open every got damn drawer. When I grabbed the kid's arm, the woman swore at me and screamed, 'let go of my son, or I'll call the police!'

"It's a witch hunt, out there, honey. And most of these trifling kids know it. I wouldn't fool with that girl if I was you."

Roy finished Val's hair and spun her around.

"And listen," Roy said, smiling at Val in the mirror. "Don't wait so long between visits, and tell him don't touch it so much."

"All right, I'll come back sooner. I swear. And don't worry, Bernard hasn't touched nothing yet," Val smiled, batting her heavily made-up eyes. "I've got his hands well trained already."

"Has he seen it?" Roy naughtily asked.

"Of course not! Not everyone works fast like you."

Roy had so many one-night stands, Val could barely keep track, and some were done right in this chair.

Roy sucked his tongue but kept his mouth quiet. He didn't like this Bernard. He sounded so weird. "Just remember, if the man's got Howard Hughes' blood, your old fool may turn out to be a nut job."

"He's not old! He's just quiet with old-fashioned ways. That's why I like him. He's nothing like my other dates, who trash me like napkins after having their steak."

"All I'm saying is don't wait to say who you are. Nobody wants steak if they've ordered fish."

Roy circled Val, and his red Hawaiian shirt grazed her face. A bloody scene flashed across the television set. Roy reached over and turned up the sound. There was a string of brutal murders that were all still unsolved. The last victim, a Nevada man, survived three days before he died. He said the murderer was a woman, medium build and height and she had a small kid in her car.

"So where does Dracula live? Have you been to his house?"

"I've only seen it once, but I haven't been inside. It's a duplex off Franklin west of Vermont. It's one of those old Colonial places with wooden overhangs and columns, green with burgundy trim."

"Sounds divine," Roy said, rolling his eyes. "Now, if it was mine, I would gut the place floor to ceiling. Have you seen what the boys have done in West Hollywood, honey? We've shaken the place up top to bottom. Even the boulevard has a beautiful center divide. It looks better than Beverly Hills."

Val looked at Roy for a moment in the mirror. "You wanna go over and sneak a peek now?"

"Peek at what?" Roy shot back slyly. "You know I've been wanting to take a peek for months."

"His house, Roy! Come on. Zip up your pants. You have the filthiest mind in town. I'm serious. Do you wanna see his house or not?"

"You mean a drive-by? My God! I haven't done one in ages.

I'll put on my Halloween outfit right now!" Roy pulled off his earrings and wiped the color from his lips. Once he was in that hard hat and jeans and those big workman's boots, you'd never know he was the biggest queen in town.

"Oh, but wait. What if he's home? What about the father? The last thing I want is some run-in with a crotchety old man. Why do you think I left home?"

"They're gone. He had to take his father to the doctor. He said they were going to dinner right after that, so they won't be back until way after dark." Val put on her eyeliner and dabbed some rouge on her cheeks and smoothed on a red tube of gloss.

"Okay, gorgeous, I'm ready. Let's go see this Neanderthal's cave."

Val and Roy drove over in Roy's convertible Beemer. Val had the radio on high and was singing along, waving her hands in the sky.

"Turn that down," Roy exclaimed, reaching for the knob. "Why tell the whole street we've arrived?"

But it was too late. Mr. Wade heard the radio and stopped watering the pansies. He saw a fantastic blonde and a construction worker by her side, driving a black expensive car. They parked and walked to Bernard's front door and stopped.

It was fall, and the sun had already dipped west, turning the sky a Halloween lime.

Roy and Val peered in the front window, but the shades were all down so they walked to the back and peered over the fence.

Mr. Wade wondered why they didn't knock on the front door, and he followed them with his eyes as they opened the back fence and went in.

Whistling, to make sure there wasn't a dog. "Trick or treat." Roy whispered before stepping into the large, well-kept, luscious yard.

"I like this!" Roy said low, gazing around. Thick trees and plants kept the property secluded. Half the yard was engulfed by a giant magnolia and exotic plants and flowers were meticulously groomed and growing in grass as green as Chinese jade.

There was a ramp for the mansion's entrance below and a steep flight of stairs led to the apartment on top, with a balcony and small wooden landing. The mansion was shabby and sunken near one of the columns and looked like an old man resting against a pole. Heavy paint glued most of the huge windows shut. An unpainted garage with gigantic padlocked doors was eaten to death by termites.

Roy and Val walked around all three sides of the house. The tree's thick branches surrounded the entire upper story. Breathing the thick aroma, Val smiled to herself. She could already see herself living in this place.

Roy looked at the mansion and sucked in his breath. "Oh my God! It's a wreck! I've already seen enough. The place looks like hell on a stick." Roy turned around to walk back toward his car. "Besides, it's not like we can get inside."

But Val noticed a small window open on the side. "Come on!" she said, "give me a boost. I just want to take a quick peek."

Roy raised his eyebrows and studied Val hard, "Are you crazy? That's breaking and entering, girl! I don't want to be in jail during Halloween, honey, no telling what kind of monsters will be there."

"Don't be scared. Come on, just lift me up."

Setting his toolbox on the ground, Roy laced his two hands and lifted Val's foot to his waist. "Girl, you're a pistol in stilettos," he said. It was thrilling to be doing something so utterly sneaky. He looked over the fence and saw a gardener filling a bag up with weeds.

Val's five-inch heels dug in his skin. She struggled with the window, but suddenly it burst wide and Val tumbled inside. The next thing he knew she was at the back door and Roy rushed in the back porch.

You could see all the way into the living room up front. The living room gleamed from Lemon Pledge sprayed over the wood, and the walls were filled up with silent film posters and an enormous collection of crystal filled the shelves. Velvet green drapes hung from metal-shaped spears and the dining room wallpaper was a warped sea of flowers and an oversized wooden set of chairs.

"Talk about a time warp. Look at this baby." Roy picked up the rotary dial phone, which snaked around the house on a thick mangled cord. "I haven't seen one of these things in years."

Val walked over to the dining room table. A heavy, hand-carved crystal vase was centered on the table, casting rainbows of light throughout the room.

Roy picked up the vase. "Man, this is heavy." He held it against his stomach. "This baby must weight sixty pounds."

Roy looked at the vase and examined the bottom. "It's a Steuben. This is the best crystal you can get. It's easily worth twenty grand."

Val took the vase from out of Roy hands and almost dropped it on the floor.

"Put that heavy thing down before you break your damn neck."

Roy looked around intently. He and Val went to the kitchen. The cupboards were dingy, and large cracks lined the ceiling. They were about to walk to the bedroom when they both heard the stairs creak. Quickly, they both walked back to the back door. Something made Roy turn his head toward the grass. A carbon smell tingled inside of his nostrils, and a tiny spark danced across the succulent lawn.

At the bottom of the steps was a tiny white hand. Roy crept farther out so he could get a better look. The hand was connected to a tiny delicate arm, which led to a neck and miniature head filled with perfectly done strawberry curls. Roy pointed to the girl and put his finger over his lips. Val came out so she could see what he saw and quietly walked down the ramp. There was a little girl standing in the middle of the stairs. Val moved over so she could see the tiny person better. She saw a yellow ruffled dress with a white apron front and low-heeled leather pumps that glowed in the almost gone sun. Her hand struck something fast and tossed it out toward the grass. A harsh carbon smell filled the air.

Carefully descending the ramp further down, Val could now

see a long box of matches. The girl fiercely struck each match, watched it blaze in her hand, and then tossed it until the flame fizzled against the lawn. It was like she was aiming for the wooden garage in the back, and some of the wooden sticks came very close.

Roy whispered, "Shit, we have to get those matches from that kid. All we need is for this stupid girl to burn the place while we're here and we get thrown in prison for arson."

"Listen. You distract her while I sneak outside."

Roy tiptoed down the ramp and hid in the jasmine and then silently stepped close to the little girl's arm.

"What do you have there, doll?" Roy asked the girl.

Whirling around, the girl gave Roy a poisonous glare, and if venom was something that showed in your face, the girl was a snake pit of rage.

Alarmed, Roy immediately took a step back.

"Who are you?" Paula asked him point blank. Placing her hand on the rail she moved two steps down and stood right in front of Roy's face. There was no sign of fear in the little girl at all.

Standing close, Roy could now see her icy blue eyes. They were eerie and as emotionless as a statue.

"What are you doing here?" the girl wanted to know.

Uncomfortable, Roy managed a thin veiled smile. "Listen, doll," he said fast, avoiding her glare. "I'm with the gas company, see." He pointed to the logo on his chest. "I'm checking the whole place for leaks." Roy descended the ramp, moving fast as he talked. The little girl followed his legs down to the yard.

When they left, Val slithered out from the door and hid behind the fig tree as Roy backed from the girl.

"Have you smelled anything funny around here lately?" Roy asked. He wrinkled his nose when he got to the ground. He avoided her gasoline eyes.

"No," the girl said flatly, wrinkling her nose too. "I don't smell anything bad except your nasty perfume."

Roy stared at the girl hard. He raised both his brows. He remembered the reason he didn't like kids. Kids were a royal pain in the ass.

"What's your name?" the girl asked, taking a step closer.

"My name's Freddy, I work for the gas company like I said."

"Then how come the front of your work shirt says Steve?"

Roy looked down and noticed the name tag and grinned. "That Steve is such a prankster. I bet he purposely took mine. Honey, that stuff happens all the time."

Roy took a tiny candy bar from his pocket. He held the small Snickers bar in the palm of his hand. "Hey, look what I found. Wanna have a bite?" Roy asked.

"My mother said never take candy from strangers."

"Mothers!" Roy said. "What the hell do they know?" He was forcing a laugh, but it came out high-pitched and nervous. Trying to stall the girl, so Val could escape, Roy rolled his eyes and put one hand on his hip, "If I listened to my mother, I'd be in therapy right now, crying on some cheap vinyl couch." He could see Val duck behind a rosebush and hide. Roy wanted to leave. Maybe this girl's mother was watching. He didn't like how the girl was gawking at him so hard and her narrow legs were blocking his path.

The girl watched with calculating coldness. She looked right inside Roy's skin, like she was tying to count his bones. She had so much raw heat behind her baby blue eyes, she looked like she could drink diesel and not miss a beat.

The girl took a match, striking the tip fast across the black strip and tossed the flame in Roy's face.

"Hey, watch it! That's dangerous," Roy didn't like being here now. "Come on stop that, you could burn the place down!"

The girl laughed at Roy's fear, flinging matches toward his shirt.

"Stop it!" Roy said. "Kids should not play with fire."

"And who the hell are you, Smokey the Bear? You can't tell me what to do." The little girl shouted this last line, tossing a lit match right near Roy's eyes. Powerless around her mother, Paula exerted herself when alone, using aggression to fuel her horrible life.

Roy was so taken aback that he grabbed the girl's arm.

"Look, why don't you give me those matches, okay?" But when Roy reached for the matchbook, the tiny girl lurched away and a piercing sound shrieked from her lungs.

"Maaaaa-mmmmeeeeeee!" she screamed. "There's a man trying to grab me!"

Roy didn't wait. He didn't want to deal with the girl's mother. Roy raced toward the gate and ran back to his car.

Val heard the door slam and hid underneath the stairs. She saw Margie come out and stand on the landing.

The girl saw Val but stayed mute, they exchanged brief knowing smiles.

"What's going on?" Margie asked. "Why are you making all that racket?"

The girl stood next to a bush and plucked one of the roses; breathing the fragrance in deep she walked halfway up the stairs and handed the flower to her mother.

The girl gave her mother the fakest grin she could make. "Here, Mommy. I picked this for you."

Margie ignored the flower and abruptly went inside. "Don't call me again unless someone's dying."

Paula waited until her mother got all the way in the house and then ran under the stairs where Val was hiding.

"Hi," Paula said. "You're that cemetery lady."

"That's right. How do you like L.A?"

Paula stared at the dirt. She wanted to burn something but didn't.

"Want to see what I made?" Paula ran to the section behind the garage. Val followed her spidery legs.

"Paula!" Margie called. "Get back in this house now!"

Paula stopped in her tracks, her light blue eyes watered. Val had never seen a child so forlorn. Sadly, and with her head hung to her chest she slowly walked back up each stair.

Val walked to the back of the garage to see what the girl wanted to show her.

Lying on the ground was a row of pants and shirts, arranged on the ground like three dying scarecrows.

"What happened? I was sitting here worried sick!" Roy gripped the steering wheel and sped down the street.

"I don't know," Roy told Val, "there's something weird about that kid."

"I'm worried about her." Val looked back at the house. "Something about her reminds me of myself."

"Read my lips, Val. That tot is a whack job! She tossed matches in my face. She was trying to burn something down. You'd be crazy to fool around with that runt running around."

"You didn't really get to see her. Her eyes melted my gut. It's like she's been buried alive."

10

Margie

Margie woke the next day, to the telephone sirening through-out the room. She sprang from the bed and answered the phone.

"Hello, there," Margie said cheerily, but her face changed to a scowl.

There was an incident at the girls school. The principal was involved. One of the other girls claimed Paula had choked her and taken her sweater. Although the incident happened a few weeks ago, the school had a heck of a time getting in touch with Margie. Her emergency card was blank, and there was no phone number. Luckily they had a copy of Bernard's driver's license on file and remembered that he lived in the same building. The school explained that the sweater was a valuable heirloom and since the value of the sweater was over five hundred dollars, if Margie didn't show up, they were going to have to call the police.

Margie dreaded having to go into a schoolhouse again. She got dressed with a horrible knot in her stomach. The last thing she wanted was to see any teachers. A teacher is what started the whole thing before.

Margie paid Mr. Wade to fix her car the night before. He fum-bled under the hood for an hour and a half and after a wrench and some pliers and a whole lot of grease he got the bashed Buick to run. Margie wanted to be ready to leave when the poison set in. She needed a vehicle to run.

Margie parked her smashed car outside in the front. Laboring, she pulled her big body from the car.

The P.E. teacher saw a light-skinned black woman slam a busted car door shut. She must be coming in to apply for the janitor's job, he thought. He tilted his head back toward his class.

When Margie got to the office she stood by the counter. People floated in and out, but nobody asked what she wanted. After a while, she decided to sit in one of the wide wooden chairs. She was not used to getting up that early in the morning. It felt so good to get off of her feet that she slowly drifted off to sleep.

Margie had no idea that her daughter was sitting in the next room and that a meeting was taking place behind its frosted glass door.

Paula sat straight in her chair. She stared at the principal and smiled. A union representative stared at Paula and he smiled, too. She twirled the curls in her hair.

The other girl's mother glared at Paula with lightning bolt eyes. Her daughter's arm was in a worn sling. She wore a dirty white cast. The cast was grossly stained at the wrist, and there was so much writing on the plaster, the cast arm looked grayish black.

The cast made the girl's arm itch, and she started to scratch it, but her mother slapped her hand to her lap.

The big girl's mother quickly turned toward the art teacher and complained. "She snatched my daughter's sweater. Tore it right off her arm!" The mother motioned with her wrist toward the old soggy plaster.

The union rep jotted something down.

The big girl wouldn't look at her mother or Paula. She looked scared. Her mother was angry. The big girl was hungry, and her stomach started to growl. She wished she were eating a cinnamon roll in the yard, not wasting her precious recess in this stuffy room.

Paula placed her daisy hem neatly at the edge of her knees. "I'm sorry," she told the girl's mother softly, "you're obviously mistaken." And turning toward the principal she gave him an angelic stare. "I'm new, sir. I just started at this school. I've never even seen her before."

The art teacher knew Paula wasn't telling the truth. She'd seen Paula shoot the big girl dirty looks in her class. And lately, the big girl began missing her sessions. She thought the big girl was scared. But the art teacher didn't want to point any fingers yet. She was waiting to see if Paula would tell on herself.

Paula crossed her slim ankles. Her white socks were spotless. Roses were sewn along the top. She stayed quiet and kept her hands folded in her lap. She watched the big girl squirm in her chair.

"You're lying!" The big girl's mother leaped from her seat. "All her friends saw you. You tore two ligaments in her arm. We ought to sue for the medical bills, too!"

"Listen," the principal quickly stood up. "I won't tolerate outbursts like that. If we could just stay on the subject at hand, I'm sure we can find a solution." The principal had already made up his mind. In fact, he'd sized up the situation on the very first glance. The big girl was dingy. Her socks had no elastic at all. Her T-shirt was wrinkled and stained on one side. She was overweight and had a bad pimply face, and her mother was a thin, useless rag. It was clear. The big girl was the obvious aggressor. Besides she was poor. The big girl went to their school on a hardship award. The principal looked at her mother again. The apple never falls far from the tree. The principal glanced at his gold watch. He had a golf game at four. He needed to wrap this thing up right here and now.

"She took it, I swear!" The big girl's mother said but sat still. "My mother knitted that sweater for me. It came all the way from Holland and had silver turtle buttons sewn in the front. You better give it back to us," she said to Paula.

"I'm sorry, miss, and I certainly mean no offense, but I wouldn't be seen in some hundred-year-old sweater. I don't wear hand-me-downs from Holland," Paula chimed. "All of my outfits are new."

The big girl's mother lunged for Paula, but her daughter caught her hand. But in lunging, the mother violently knocked a chair down. It made a loud bang as it smacked the school floor. The big girl's mother didn't like the way Paula was talking. It was high-pitched and dainty and dripping with sweet. She wanted to sock Paula's face. But something made her stop. It was the way the girl stared. She had vacant doll-like eyes that would not turn away. The big girl's mother dropped her lids and stared at her lap. She didn't like the look of this girl.

Margie woke and sat up in her seat at the crash of the chair. She wondered what all the commotion was for.

Not knowing where to place her hands, the big girl's mother stroked her daughter's palm, but she accidentally scratched her daughter's bad arm and the girl yelled for her to stop.

The mother was a dishrag woman, with no hint of a chin. She had four other uncontrollable children just like this one at home. She tried to use her hankie to dab at the scratch, but the big girl shoved her away.

Miss Taylor left to get a bandage for the girl. She saw Margie sitting alone in one of the office chairs. "May I help you?" she asked the black, tired-looking woman.

"Yeah," Margie said, not scooting up. "I'm posed to be at meetin' with my chile. You happen to know where it's at?" Like gravy, Margie smothered her words in sloppy backyard speech, keeping her college degree voice in her head.

"What's your child's name, ma'am?" Miss Taylor asked. What child could belong to this shabby black lady? There were only five other black kids at this school. Two of their parents were doctors, one was a judge, another one was a state senator's aide and the last one's dad sold real estate in Bel Air.

"I'm Paula Green's mama," Margie said proudly. She didn't

like the way this young woman stared. "Is my Paula all right, Miss Lady?"

"You're Paula Green's mother?" the vice principal said, amazed. Her eyes were the size of two giant saucers. How could this sloppy black woman belong to such an impeccable child? Besides, little Paula Green was white.

Margie fanned her face with a brochure. She looked like a Southerner sitting in church.

"Uh-huh, yes, ma'am, I am," Margie said. She was used to seeing shock lodged in white people's faces. She'd seen that look of disbelief so many times before, it wasn't even a surprise anymore. Sometimes it was slow, like a car rolling backward. But most times it hit with impact and speed, like a bus slamming into a store.

"You're her mother?" Miss Taylor said it again. It wasn't a question. It was more like she was trying to calculate something. Like a math problem she tried to get right in her head. Her mouth had fallen open so wide it looked like her lower jaw fell off the hinge.

"Yes, ma'am, I am," Margie repeated. She wished this dumb woman would close her damn mouth and quit gawking so she didn't have to see the cavities in her teeth.

"Please, come with me," Miss Taylor said, grinning. She knew the principal had already made up his mind. He loved Paula. All the male teachers did except the little young fag teaching gym class.

When Margie came in the door, she ran to Paula and hugged her tight, shoving the child's face in her breasts. "Oh, baby! You okay, how's my sugar pie, huh? You being good to all these nice folk, right?"

Paula knew her role. They'd been running this game for months. When Margie smothered her in kisses Paula hugged her waist tight. "Mommy, I'm so glad you came!"

"That's okay, sugar. Ima set this thing right." Margie wore a large muumuu drenched in vivid screaming color. A yellow scarf covered her head.

All the necks in the room jerked in Margie's direction. She

couldn't have appeared more backward and country if she was carrying a broom and wearing a white apron.

The principal could not believe his eyes. This thing couldn't be the girl's mother! This little white angel looked like his own daughter. She had the same orangey mane. Similar porcelain complexion and identical aquarium-like eyes. How in God's name could this white kid be black? He studied Margie's almond-colored face. They did have the same nose and the same kind of chin. *Well I'll be*, the principal mouthed to himself. He silently sucked his teeth. He glanced at Margie's large eyes. He'd seen that face somewhere. But he couldn't remember when or where. He scoured the depths of his brain.

Miss Taylor wore a victorious grin on her face. She knew the principal was always trying to keep the minority level down. He expelled the brown kids first, regardless of fault. He made sure his staff graded those kids extra hard. He kicked them out if they were even tardy. The vice principal was almost wiggling in her seat, she couldn't wait to see what the principal would do now.

"Mother, you remember that day," Paula continued. "I stayed at home from school. I made breakfast for you and I. We had sausage patties, milk, and French toast."

"Nobody cares what your thieving butt ate for breakfast. We're talking about my sweater, you bitch!" The big girl's mother screamed. Still frightened, the big girl studied the floor, hopeful the adults would protect her.

The principal was still shocked the girl had a black parent. Black kids made white parents feel anxious and nervous. Black kids meant rap music spilling from cars or pants dropping low just like test scores. He made the mistake once of enrolling too many one fall, and all the white parents came to his office to complain.

And even though he was leaning toward the white child now, he couldn't tolerate this kind of language in his presence.

"One more outburst like that, and I'm going to ask you to leave." He was not playing around with this sailor-talking parent.

He looked at the hands of his gold watch again. He studied Margie's face trying to think of who she was.

Margie remembered the day Paula was talking about well. Paula had come home from school and went outside to eat her ice cream. Margie had heard some yelling. But the next thing she knew the house was filled up with the wonderful aroma of maple mixed with cinnamon and hot melting butter. She always got up after Paula came home from school. She never rose before three. She woke and found Paula standing there cooking in her socks. She wondered why Paula had taken off her shoes. She never saw Paula in a state of undress. She remained tiptop until the moment she went back to bed, and even then she put on her gown, slippers, and robe. But now here she was standing and cooking in her socks. Her mother's eyes scanned the floor and then looked toward the porch. There, her shoes stood on some newspaper. They were completely covered in mud. Paula was meticulous about her clothes. She never got anything dirty, yet here were both of her shoes, covered in mud. She was thinking of this as the principal watched her. But Margie sat quietly and said nothing.

The big girl's mother tried to run her hand along her large daughter's back.

The big girl leaned away, flashing her mother a mean glare.

The big girl's mother gave the principal an apologetic nod. She didn't know whether to believe her daughter or not. All her kids had been in so much trouble before. But she knew one thing for sure, that little brat took her sweater, and she was not leaving until she got it back.

"Now listen," the big girl's mother turned to the principal again. "We're not rich, like little Missy Proper over there. We're common folks. We work hard for our things. But we don't expect our items to get stolen off our backs, especially at such a prestigious school. I think we should at least go and search this girl's locker right now. Then we'll see if this little bitch is telling the truth."

Oh shit, the big girl's mother clasped her hand over her lips. She wished she could learn not to swear!

"All right! That's enough," the principal said abruptly. He immediately stood up. He'd already heard too much. There obviously weren't any liability factors. Even if it did happen, the incident happened off the school's campus. He straightened his tie and coughed loud for effect. He was just about to bring this discussion to an end when the vice principal cut in.

"Maybe we should separate each girl," Miss Taylor said, "and let them tell us privately what happened." As the vice principal, many teachers came to her and complained first. They didn't want the principal to think they couldn't handle their classes, especially when it came time for raises. Miss Taylor was not convinced that this matter was solved. And there was the other matter of Paula being seen burning trash. Miss Taylor told the big girl and her mother to stay there and told everyone else to follow her to the art room.

They all walked inside a huge well-lit classroom. It smelled of turpentine and paint and was covered with drawings, from small works to huge five-foot posters. Lots of 3-D objects hung from the ceiling.

Miss Taylor smiled at Paula over her slender horn-rimmed specs. "Miss Davis," she said, addressing the art teacher now, "would you like to speak first?"

Like any good con artist, Margie sat back and listened. She pretended to smile with her evil mind spinning, trying to figure out a way they could win. She noticed a coffee tin of buttons sitting in the back, brimming with an assortment of color.

The art teacher looked at the floor. She avoided Paula's eyes. She was new, and this was her very first job. She didn't want any more trouble.

"Now Paula, are you sure? Could you have taken it accidentally? I remember you showing me a turtle button in class, you glued it on one of your paintings last week," the art teacher said.

"Oh really," Miss Taylor stood up now. She pushed her glasses further up her nose. "I think we should all look at Paula's painting now."

The principal was pissed off. He was done with this matter. He didn't want to go look at any dumb stupid painting. He especially didn't like the vice principal taking over either.

Miss Taylor and the art teacher shared an all-knowing nod, neither one of them wanted to let Paula off that easy. They'd finally caught this little brat red-handed.

Margie sat in a chair with Paula in her lap. Silently and ever so gently, without anyone seeing, Margie yanked off two buttons from the back of Paula's dress. Then Margie said, "Oh, honey, you're getting so heavy, sit in that chair next to me."

No one could see the back of her dress flapping open.

"Now Paula," Miss Taylor said sharply. "Where did you get these buttons for this car? She unrolled the drawing for everyone to see. It was a ghastly scene of a bluish green car and a little boy crying for help. The glued-on buttons were used as the headlights.

Margie got up to go look at the drawing herself. But before she got there she palmed Paula's buttons in the tin, secretly placing them on the top. Margie pretended to admire the drawing. "This is really nice, honey. I like how you drew the car blue."

"Mrs. Green." The art teacher said, "I don't mean to cut you off. But *we* have to get to the bottom of this matter. Paula took those turtle buttons off the girl's sweater in there!"

Margie smiled at the art teacher with honey in her eyes. "Your classroom is real pretty. You have lots of nice art, but I remember Paula making this picture, she told me she got the buttons from your coffee tin right there."

Paula looked confused. She liked her art teacher. She was not sure what Margie was trying to say.

Margie looked at the art teacher with crystal clear eyes. Her face was angelic. She had a white chocolate smile. She looked as sweet as a box of See's Candy.

Margie whispered loud so everyone could hear. "Is this the teacher you were telling me about, honey?"

Paula nodded her head yes, but she didn't like agreeing with Margie.

"See these buttons?" Margie showed the tin to Miss Taylor. Then she turned to the art teacher and raised her eyebrows in concern. "Paula said you collects these, they come off the kids' clothing," Margie chose each word carefully and made sure they sank in. Margie had driven fifteen hundred miles to leave misery behind. Her blood pressure shot through the roof, just climbing the school's stairs. A Catholic school was where the first murder occurred. She was not getting caught. She didn't care who got eliminated first. But one thing was clear. It was not going to be her.

"Oh my God!" Margie looked like she'd just been shot. She gasped and held one hand over her chest. "Baby, come here, what's the matter with your dress?"

Paula's back was exposed where the back of the dress flapped opened, revealing a smooth piece of white naked skin.

"Paula told me the art teacher took her into the cloakroom, but I didn't think anything of it." Margie looked horrified. She grabbed Paula's hand. Tears welled up in her eyes.

Everyone stared at the art teacher amazed. The union representative began scribbling like mad in his pad.

The McMartin trial flashed through everyone's brain. Who was this new teacher? Did she hurt any of their kids? Was that horrible thing happening right here in their school, underneath all of their noses?

The principal was stunned. Miss Taylor gasped and looked shocked.

The principal gave the art teacher a condemning stare. He was not about to let Immaculate Heart go down in flames. He had to protect the school. That he knew for sure, he had to snuff this wild flame out before anyone got hurt. If this got out, their school could shut down completely when parents started pulling kids out.

The art teacher couldn't believe what was happening in front of her eyes. She looked inside the tin and saw Paula's missing button. It was a red fabric button with a crystal rhinestone center, the same kind that was missing from her dress.

"I'm sure there must be an explanation." The vice principal said. She stood up and looked at the room full of paintings. "There must be over a hundred buttons in here, glued to every one of these drawings."

Margie gasped and bit the inside of her wrist.

The principal put the art teacher on academic leave right away.

That night, someone phoned to say the art teacher had been fired. They found a stack of nude paintings on the art teacher's desk. Lots of kids began to collaborate Paula's story. Even though the event was a flat out, boldfaced lie, the other kids ate it up and ran with the story, adding new twists and turns to the events. This was the juiciest piece of news their dull school ever had. One boy went so far as to say he had sex with the art teacher. It was totally made up, but the boy loved attention. He was an overweight kid with a bad case of acne; this was the most attention he ever had. And even though there was no trial or any conviction and only two days had passed since Paula showed them her back, the event snowballed and was reported on several news stations, with the art teacher's picture and name. Before any police were called and while her young husband slept, the art teacher got in the tub and slashed both her wrists. Her poor husband found her in the morning, in a deep pool of red, a bloated newspaper with her picture, floating in the water.

11

Mr. Fowler

Bernard feverishly showered and shaved. He put on a suit and took a belt out of his drawer, weaving the long snakeskinned strap through his pants. It was Friday. He was meeting Val at six.

Bernard tiptoed down the hall to check on his father and poked his head into his door.

Now usually, Mr. Fowler said things like, "you're leaving me again, huh? Why don't you just take me to the living room and shoot me instead."

But Bernard's father smiled at him at the door. His usually soiled pajamas smelled like fresh bleach, and even his sheets were pressed and nicely tucked in. The wild shock of white hair that usually covered his crown was now washed, combed, and fixed in a nice tidy braid. He was a meaty, big-boned man with sandpaper hands from years doing construction and welding. Except for a bad knee, at eighty-three, he was perfectly healthy and though he was usually prison guard mean, ever since Margie came he seemed childlike and sweet.

"Hey!" he said to Bernard. "Look at my feet." His father stuck out his enormous moisturized soles. "Can you believe it? She even cleans under my toes."

His father was always showing him some new thing Margie had done. Bernard could really care less.

Though he came closer to the door, Bernard didn't go in. "I'm going to work for a few hours," he said. "I'll see you when I get back." Bernard glanced at his father's feet. He hated being around when Margie was near; he wanted to get out before she came to the door.

Usually his father said things like, "You're a waste of a son," or "You might as well pick out your own casket while you're there."

But tonight his father didn't say anything like that at all. He kept staring at his feet, smiling at each just-washed toe. "Don't hurry back," he laughed. He loved having the house alone with Margie.

This father was completely strange to Bernard. The old Mr. Fowler noticed everything Bernard did wrong. The bathwater was too cold, the sheets were too stiff, or his toast was too dry or too soft. Every day there was a constant harangue of complaints, a laundry list of errors and faults.

But now that Margie was here, his room smelled forest green. His hair was always fresh, his clothes were all ironed, and his Stacy Adams shoes were covered in polish and gleamed like a row of just waxed cars.

Margie came into the room holding a tray. In the corner was a rose from the yard. She put the tray on his father's immaculate dresser and fastened a cloth around his neck with a clothespin.

"There," Margie said. "Do you want to eat in here or outside like we did last night?"

His father smiled at Margie with real affection in his eyes. "Oh, that smells good. You made me lamb chops and greens. Girl, you sure know how to treat a man right.

"Look at this ass." Mr. Fowler smacked Margie's backside.

Margie giggled and said, "stop," but she obviously liked it.

"Your mother would never let me touch her like that." Bernard's father broke out in loud roguish laughter. "I'm finally getting my second chance at life."

Bernard propped the pillow behind his father's broad back. He wished he could smother it over Margie's face.

"I'll be back," Bernard said.

"Wait, wait! What's the rush? Why don't you sit down and eat here with us?"

Margie took off her shoes and got in his bed and placed the tray over both their knees.

"Oh, Bernard, can you rinse out your father's foot bathwater. I left the bucket next to the bed," Margie said.

Bernard looked at the scummy water next to the headboard. He thought he was going to be sick.

Bernard could work on dismembered bodies and amputee thighs. He could put teeth in smashed mouths or remove entire guts from stomachs. He could drain blood from bodies and re-attach eyes or sew on a dead baby's arm. None of this ever bothered Bernard. Dead people were serene. Dead people were easy; they were as quiet and pleasing as trees.

What he despised, what he dreaded beyond anything else in life was caring for his very alive father. It was true; his father became tender when Margie came, but the drastic change made Bernard suspicious.

He didn't like Margie, but there was nobody he could discuss his concerns with. It was just Bernard and his father. They had no close relatives or friends. Except for Reynolds and the hundred-year-old drunk at the corner bar, Bernard never talked to anyone else except for the very dead people at work.

He was always alone. He had no childhood friends. In a fit of sheer loneliness Bernard bought a blow-up doll once. With his asthma, it took a toll on him blowing her up and he had to stop twice and use his inhaler to finish. But then suddenly she was there, standing close to his face, filled with the heat of his air. He told the blow-up doll all his innermost thoughts. He brushed and played with her long, lavish locks. Sometimes, when he had the yard to himself, he'd pour himself a beer and open the suitcase up, propping her face against the case. He'd tell her the slim events of his day. She was kind, smiling at him all the time. Her mouth was permanently frozen in a round hollow "O."

But one day, when his father could still walk, he went outside the house, shuffling his legs across the grass and jiggled the handle on the old garage door.

"What's going on? Who you talking to, boy? Why the devil is this got damn door locked?" There was nowhere to hide his love, she was almost as tall as him so in a panic and without really thinking about it once, Bernard stabbed the doll, gutting her heart. The doll's body sadly danced. Her movements were maudlin. Arms swung way down, her bent frame slung in half, drained of the air that sustained her. As Bernard's father pounded, Bernard squeezed the air from the doll's body, stomping her frame on the ground. But she wouldn't deflate as fast as he wanted, so he lit a match and torched her miniature feet. He almost cried watching the colorful wad of charred plastic. She didn't burn fast, she just smoldered away slow, until nothing was left but a head full of hair.

Bernard was thinking back on this as the TV news flickered.

"Those McMartins made movies of those kids in the nude. They killed and cut up rabbits, buried them in the yard to make sure those kids didn't tell."

Mr. Fowler and Margie were obsessed with this trial. They laid in the bed each night, like two peas in a pod, eating ice cream and drooling over each gory detail. Every decapitated puppy or sliced apart mouse filled both their faces with glee.

"I bet the son did it. That mother looks too shook. I bet his dad is ashamed of his dumb slack-jawed son, you notice they never show him."

Bernard watched the television, too. He hated the McMartin case. It made Bernard fearful. He still felt the sting from where the security guard wrenched his arm. Now if he saw a kid coming, he always crossed the street or hid in the trees of his yard.

Bernard got his keys. He had to get back to work.

"Bring us a cheesecake!" his father told him.

"And a tub of vanilla ice cream," Margie threw in.

"And bring me some more water, my dadgum mouth is so dry."

Bernard went to the sink and filled a glass. His dad had been complaining about cottonmouth lately. He walked in his room and put the glass by the bed and waited.

Usually, his father reached for his wallet and cussed him while handing Bernard a few bills. But this time Margie was the one to get his dad's wallet. She opened it and handed Bernard a five and took all the rest for herself.

Margie placed a blanket more snugly around his dad's shoulders, "I have to go check on Paula. I'll be right back."

Whenever Margie slipped out of bed, his father actually looked sad. He practically held his breath until she came back.

"Bye, honey. Hurry back. I'll be waitin'."

Turning his back toward the television again, his glasses reflected a sadness that lived deep inside.

His father had changed a lot since Margie arrived. His hatchet exterior was completely chopped off. Bernard marveled at how tenderly and sweetly he treated Margie. He treated her with a kindness Bernard had never seen before, and he burned and turned beet red from embarrassment if the two were lying naked in bed. When they went to the store, Margie stayed on his father's mind. He bought things for Margie all the time. "Margie might like this," he'd say, adding it to the basket. It was like Margie was his last chance to repent for old sins.

When Margie left, Mr. Fowler swung his leg over the bed and scowled.

He hadn't always been kind while his wife was alive. Even after she planted flowers and sang in the yard and did everything she could to make his life pleasant, he still continued to treat Alice poorly. He acted like she had no worth, and sometimes he heard her weeping while scrubbing the floor or digging the hard soil he refused to turn over in her garden. He never did any of the simple things she asked. He ignored her. He barked at her when he talked. He ran through her money faster than a starving machine in Vegas, and he made her do demeaning things, too. He knew it was mean, but he hated the thought that she came from better stock. Nobody understood what he had to endure!

Being related to the Hughes family took a heavy toll on a man like him. How could he ever reach Howard Hughes' standard? The bar was forever set too high. So to drop her down a few notches and to even the score, he let his pee drip along the side of the toilet sometimes or he tracked muddy boots over the just-mopped floor. That would keep Howard Hughes' niece from getting too uppity. But treating Alice poorly was the deepest regret of his life. She was gone, and he couldn't take any of those awful things back. He couldn't make her life easy or thank her for the nice things she did. But having Margie was like digging Alice up from the grave. It was like being with her tender warm body again. It was like the cancer never happened. Like there was no sickness or death. He ignored her cremation box sitting alone in the corner. He tossed her obituary in the fire and watched the glossy sheet burn. Alice was reborn! She was here and alive, buried deep inside Margie's luscious body. He had to admit; Margie was a tad bit different. She was neat, he did give her that, but Margie was more common and had a shiftier side than his wife. But he didn't mind. He had a crafty side, too. His wife never knew that he had women on the side. How could he tell Howard Hughes' niece he was playing around? He had married a gold mine! She was bound to get something. He was hoping that when she died her inheritance would kick in, and he was bitterly upset when nothing arrived. Before she got sick, he tore up the house searching through bank slips and papers. He turned the yard into a cemetery of deep empty pits. He tore up every single plant that Alice put in, hoping his shovel would hit something firm. But all he found was the petrified skull of a dog and a broken tomahawk caked in mud.

Mr. Fowler watched the fire devour each word in the obituary. He watched the pallbearers' names singe along a fiery line and die. At least he could be his natural self with Margie. He told her about the women, and she didn't even bat an eye. For that, he was eternally happy. He could live with her in peace for the rest of his life. He showered Margie with the affection he held back from his wife and summoned all the buried love he could muster.

* * *

But things have drastically changed lately. While Margie and Mr. Fowler lay in bed, Margie turned to him and asked him a question.

"Excuse my prying, but why didn't Bernard ever get married?" Margie didn't even bother getting dressed anymore. After cleaning his room perfectly, when she first arrived, she dropped the dust mop and never picked it up again and laid around all day in her slip. And Mr. Fowler, who always demanded an immaculate house didn't even notice the thick layer of dust on his dresser where his teeth swam alone in a glass.

Mr. Fowler's hand lifted up Margie's huge breasts. He was scooping them up, one at a time, like each one was a large mound of ice cream. Without his teeth and with his white hair all over his head, his lips were attached to one of those big curvaceous mounds and he was sucking like he'd just found the fountain of youth, like an infant hungry for food.

A shiver of pure pleasure shot throughout Margie's veins. This was nothing like the St. Louis man or the Oklahoma twins. The St. Louis man ran a stationery store and had a cash register drawer filled with money, but his sweaty hands felt like an orange Brillo pad, and she didn't even feel bad when he turned black and blue after she dropped a radio in his bathtub.

The Oklahoma twins ran a dry cleaning business, and Margie really had a time getting the bank statements from one. The other became lovesick and was hell-bent on planning their wedding, when all Margie wanted was his black Coupe Deville and the strongbox he kept under the counter. When she shot the first twin dead, the other dropped to the floor, too. He fell like a stone to the bottom of a lake, and she didn't even have to use a bullet on him. Her kid saw the twin fall, but Margie rolled him under a cabinet. She took out the bullets and gave the kid the gun and said to go play in the yard.

"I've been wanting to do that from day one." Mr. Fowler raised his eyebrows and then gently closed his lids, feeling each breast like a blind man. It felt like Alice was right there in bed with him again. Mr. Fowler squinted his eyes as if trying to see a picture. A salty tear slid from his lid.

"You have a good son. I don't think Paula would stay and help me." Margie looked out the window a very long time.

Mr. Fowler hit his Pall Mall and held in the smoke. "Bernard stayed, because I made him do it. He was the only one here. My wife spoiled me rotten. Hell, I never cooked or washed clothes. I didn't even know the first thing about how to buy groceries. But all that aside, the reason why Bernard stayed so long was I just tricked him from the beginning." Mr. Fowler laughed so hard he started to wheeze.

With his wife gone, life had turned into a torturous void. Not being able to hear her voice was a knife to his gut. Anything was better than being left with his hellish thoughts of how he had caused her acute death.

Margie pulled the cigarette from his mouth and smashed the thing out in the ashtray. "Now you really need to quit doing this shit."

"What for?" He smiled big, showing a pit with no teeth. "I got no reason to be afraid. Something's bound to take me out before cancer ever will." Mr. Fowler lit another cigarette and took a deep drag.

"It was funny," he said, seeing with only lovesick eyes. "You're perfect for me. We're exactly alike. I can almost see myself in your eyes."

Margie squirmed under his girth. She didn't like this subject.

Mr. Fowler ripped the sheet back, exposing her body. "We're practically cut from the very same cloth."

But like any good con, Margie admitted nothing. She would take every lie she said to the grave. She was lying in bed in Alice's white robe. She was good. She left no stone unturned. The Shalimar perfume Alice wore was on her neck. She went to the library that first day and punched in Alice's name. She learned everything about her. Where she used to live, how she wore her hair. She even called some of her old friends and gathered stories from them and then she studied her notes all night long like a college kid before a test.

"I'm not complaining. No need to put your bra back on, honey. I know about scams. Hell, I ran a construction business. I saw lots of schemes and scams firsthand. Shoot, some of my best customers were crooks." Mr. Fowler glanced at the wheelchair in the corner. "Why do you think I'm sitting around in that old rusty chair?" Pulling her ambitious body easily on top of his lumberjack frame, Mr. Fowler smacked her ass and gave her a fat nasty grin. Then he jumped from the bed, did ten jumping jacks, and hurriedly got back in.

"I'm running an insurance scam, honey. One of my customers ripped me off. He refused to pay me after I built him a damn Taj Majal. It was an easier trick to pull off than I thought. No one ever asked questions. And in one moment it was done. I walked outside and stepped out on the tall steps we put up. I even counted how many steps there were to the ground." He sucked the smoke down, holding it in.

"I walked more than halfway down, then I really yelled loud and tumbled over the last final few steps and sued the cheap bastard right then and there."

Mr. Fowler smiled to himself. It was a simple matter of settling scores. "The man refused to pay me. I finished the damn job. If he wasn't going to open his checkbook then I forced his insurance company to do it. What the hell else did he expect?"

Margie looked at him and then pinched one of his legs.

"Ouch!" he said smiling, bringing his knee to his chest. "Don't do that, honey, it hurts."

"Well I'll be! I've even pushed you myself?" Margie couldn't believe what he was saying.

"Nobody even thought twice. They never questioned me once. They took one look at me writhing in the dirt in sheer pain and figured I fell from the top.

"It was a practical choice, of course. There was no other way. I wanted to laugh when the doctors scratched their heads, examining my X-rays. They couldn't find anything physically wrong with my legs. But I fell down whenever they asked me to stand. Next thing I knew, they ordered a wheelchair for me and helped move me downstairs. I got Wade across the street to build me a ramp and made him change a few things around so I could easily roll through each room. I even gypped that spook, too. Never gave him a dime. Even after he pushed me to the store to get cigarettes or chips and took me to look at the hot chicks on Vine."

Margie let his racist comments roll off her back. She didn't care what this silly ass white cracker thought. He'd be toast when she got good and ready.

"How can you stand being in a chair all day long?"

"It's really not too bad. It was actually relaxing. I had two bum knees already and my Achilles was shot and I had to take pills for my bad lower back."

Mr. Fowler looked out the huge window and smiled. "I kinda enjoy the smooth ride." He let the smoke swirl over his tongue and through his teeth and then he smacked Margie hard on her fat naked thigh.

"You're a cold-blooded fool!" Margie laughed at him approvingly. She downed her mint julep and refilled both their glasses from a pitcher she kept on the dresser.

"How can you even ride in that chair and keep a straight face?"

"Shoot, I'm not the first parent to manipulate their kids. My friend Fred played a similar kind of trick on his daughter. Fred pretended to have dementia. He acted like he couldn't remember his name. He acted lost and confused and stared out the window for hours until his daughter decided to move home and care for him full-time. Fred didn't want to spend any of his hard-earned on a nurse. That fool hired hookers to service him right there in bed as soon as his daughter went to work. Fred did such a crazy mind-fuck on that girl that she cried whenever she left his side."

Mr. Fowler's selfishness squashed any guilt in his heart. He didn't want to give up this comfortable new life.

"Bernard does most of the work. Keeps the yard spic and span. He doesn't mind mopping floors or changing soiled sheets."

And like his wife, Mr. Fowler could talk to Bernard any way he wanted and Bernard would never think to talk back. Who'da thought Bernard would stick around all these years.

Bernard's father laughed so hard he choked on his own smoke. Bernard was such a dumb boy. He was a pathetic excuse for a man. He didn't know the first thing about what being a real man was. He was pimply and thin with pale skin and soft hands. Just looking at him made Bernard's father grit his teeth and spit.

Serves him right, he thought, grinding his butt in an ashtray. If he had his way it would have been Bernard who got buried and not his sweet lovely wife.

Mr. Fowler smiled at Margie and grabbed her healthy body. Every time he looked at her it felt like Alice was back.

Mr. Fowler flipped Margie over using his hip bone and knee. He kissed her and tickled her down to her toes, smothering his head under the covers. "I don't care what you've done. You're a savior to me." He licked her thick calves and went up to her waist. "You're my Alice reborn," he said to each of her taut nipples and carefully placing one nipple between his gums he began to suck, "I don't care if it's right or wrong. All I know is I can breathe deep again because you took away the sharp edge of grief."

Mr. Fowler devoured her body and made love like a twenty-year-old man. He put so much hot fuel into Margie's black soul that Margie almost had second thoughts about killing this fool as her head rolled across his warm pillow.

But lately, Mr. Fowler was starting to feel hindered by this scam. The bigger his appetite became for Margie the stronger he felt as a man. Maybe she'd like to go for a stroll on the beach. Maybe she wanted to take a cruise to Mexico for the week. He couldn't do any of that stuff in a chair. He whispered this sentiment to Margie late one night, and she smiled and hugged his waist tight.

Margie didn't want Mr. Fowler walking around. The only Mr. Fowler she wanted was deep in the ground, lying inside satin, with the door nailed closed, laced in a strong metal casket.

So one day while taking one of their strolls. Margie rolled him to the corner store to get him a Coke, she slipped a sleeping pill in the can and waited for his eyelids to close. Margie pushed the wheelchair up a steep hill and let him roll until he almost hit Sunset. She watched a Greyhound bus take him under all four hind tires and drag him right into a bus bench. There was a big ugly screech and traffic was killed in four lanes and the bus driver flew through the window. But good God almighty! That crusty bastard lived! He survived the ordeal with only a few scratches. The wheelchair protected his organs and head. But one week later one of his legs began to wither and get small. It shriveled and then turned a dark grotesque black. After two weeks of his having the smelling thing in a sling the doctor had to slice it off with an electrical blade, and Mr. Fowler remained strapped to the wheelchair for good.

Margie continued to take him down to the market for his Coke. But he slumped in his chair and didn't sit haughtily anymore and one day, out of the blue, he even waved at Corleen and smiled at her as he passed.

God don't like ugly, Corleen thought looking at the man. But deep down, she felt terrible sorrow for Mr. Fowler, rolling along with one leg and a black polished shoe and a hard stump sewn inside a pants leg cropped at the thigh.

Corleen had nothing but vicious contempt for Margie.

Today, Margie was wearing Alice Fowler's two-piece tweed suit, with the yellow flowers sprinkled along the bustline. It was bunched on one side, and it fit her horribly tight, like she'd left it inside the dryer too long.

"Morning," Margie said, with springtime in her voice. She had a hat and sunglasses on so no one could see her eyes.

Mr. Wade stared, and Corleen glared at her fiercely.

"Beautiful day, isn't it?" Margie said, pushing the wheelchair along.

The sky grumbled, and a couple of drops hit the ground. The clouds looked like they were about to commit a crime.

Corleen shook her fist, but Margie didn't see. "A bad woman can take a good man down fast."

Mr. Wade shook his head like he experienced this firsthand. But suddenly Margie turned and gave him a radiant grin, and he felt lured by her smile and the curve of her rust-colored lips and the deliciously teasing weight of her bosom.

"At least he's not bitter." Mr. Wade said, tipping his hat, showing a clean rack of seldom seen teeth. He leaned slightly hoping to catch Margie's eye again. "Nothing wrong with a man wanting to die happy."

"I liked him better when he was a tough piece of jerky. If he didn't like you, at least you knew where you stood. I don't know who he is now, the old Mr. Fowler is gone." Like the sky, tears began dropping from Corleen's wet eyes. Mr. Fowler was so sweet now he was almost like a baby. But it was pitiful to see an awful change like this. "Someone should call the police."

After a dinner of fried fish and rice, Margie took out the Bible next to Mr. Fowler's bed. She read some passages to him and sang a few hymns before watching him drift off to sleep. She added some poison to his teacup every single night. Arsenic. It was colorless and tasteless and had a cumulative effect. You could add an eyedrop each day for a month and then suddenly, in midsentence, a person could drop dead from just one dab on the tongue.

Margie refused to use strychnine anymore. A San Fernando man tasted its tartness in his soup. He backhanded Margie so hard in the face; she fell against the door and chipped her back tooth. But that was okay. Some folks fought against their own funerals. Margie had all the time in the world. Besides, she was a former biology teacher with a chemistry set of concoctions bubbling throughout her brain. So the next morning, while the San Fernando man was taking a shower, she doctored up a fresh batch of vanilla arsenic coffee and when he dropped on the floor she covered him in barbecue sauce and salt and left him in the yard with his dog.

12

Bernard and Val

Reynolds stepped out of the room and asked Bernard to watch a woman drain.

"Keep an eye on this one, son. Don't fill 'er too fast or she'll bloat like a seal on the beach. I tell you, Bernard, we're either filling them with water or waiting for the bad ones to burn."

Bernard knew exactly what Reynolds was talking about. They had to wait eight arduous hours for one obese man to cremate. He'd hacked a family in Oakland and was only in the penitentiary one day, when he escaped and crashed his truck into a highway patrolman's car.

Bernard was thinking of this and not watching the pump, the next thing he knew, fluid engorged the woman's body, and she grew twice her natural size. Bernard panicked. The wake was going to start in twenty minutes. He tried to put on the woman's dress but couldn't get it over her engorged head. Even after slashing the dress and stapling it onto her back he couldn't get it to fit right around her thick waist. In a hurry, he stapled the dress to her legs and then tried to cover her fat face with a wig and used a glue gun to hold her pearls to her skin.

When the husband arrived and entered the slumber room to see his wife, he screamed and cussed Bernard out.

"Damn it," Reynolds said, rushing over to the body. He was so upset he pushed the casket out of the room by himself. He told the family he was sorry and ushered them into the waiting room himself and showed them the donuts and coffee.

"Don't worry. We'll get Laura fixed up right." Reynolds sat down and drained the body himself. He stripped the woman of her dress and sparkling white undergarments. He hung the dress and slip over a hanger so they wouldn't have to iron them again. He took off the woman's glasses and ripped the pearls off her neck. He flexed both her arms and rolled up his own sleeves and then tied a rubber smock over his clothes. He massaged the woman head to toe with a lotion, pulling her muscles and massaging her arms and her legs, bending them both at the knee.

"Mr. Reynolds?" Bernard said. He was dying to ask him about Val. Bernard didn't know the first thing about women, but Reynolds had a whole slew of them all across town, waiting for him at their doors like empty coffins.

"Death is funny," Reynolds told him once. "People's reactions run the gamut. Some people are remorseful and others feel a need," Reynolds winked at Bernard slyly, "I kinda like the last response. I'm not adverse to offering a private service for them, too."

Once Bernard had walked in the room and found a woman in a state of undress. She was pressing her lips over Reynolds' shriveled mouth as her dead husband slept in a casket down the hall.

"Mr. Reynolds," Bernard repeated again.

"Uh-huh," Reynolds said. He sat on his one shaky hand and pulled his chair right between the draining woman's legs.

"How do you know when you've met the right one?"

Mr. Reynolds rubbed the woman and bent her in half and then stretched both her knees to her chest.

"Flexibility, son. That's the key to any good woman. Make sure you get one who can bend."

Once the pump was engaged, he started the machine and fluid left her hips, legs and her arms, draining the woman to her natural slim shape. Bernard watched Mr. Reynolds skillfully handle the pump. But then suddenly he noticed a mild shake in Reynolds' hands. The pump leaped and flew around the room spraying red fluid across the walls and all over Reynolds' rubber smock.

"Damn it!" Reynolds said, yanking the cord hard. "Tommy," he screamed to the grave digger down the hall. "I need a cleanup right now!"

Bernard wanted to tell Reynolds about Val before Tommy came in. Tommy teased him and mimicked his speech.

"I met this girl," Bernard said quickly. "I was wondering where to take her."

"Glory be! Are you courting someone, son?" This statement made Reynolds actually look in Bernard's face. He turned off the loud suction pump.

Bernard was gushing to tell someone about Val. He watched the fluid leave each organ as the machine sucked her clean, deflating the woman like a leaky balloon.

"I'd take her by the water. Lots of chickies love the beach. Let her stick some of her toes in the mouth of the Pacific. That ought to put some heat in her bones."

Suturing the woman closed again, Reynolds rewashed the body. "Let her suck on some shrimp or get her a big plate of clams." Reynolds cleaned the woman's fingernails using a solvent to remove stains. And even though there was no sign of spilled fluid in the woman's hair, Reynolds washed it and scrubbed her scalp clean.

"There," he said, smiling up at Bernard. "You think you can handle 'er from here?" He smacked Bernard's back so hard that it stung. "As far as the ocean, you better bring a blanket just in case; you never know where you can roll up and get lucky."

When Reynolds walked out, Tommy the grave digger came in. "So this ol' stiff's got a girl?" Tommy grinned at Bernard showing a railroad track of jacked teeth. Tommy had mud on his boots and his fingernails were black and even though they used tractors to lift the earth from the ground, he was as dirty as a farmer in March.

Tommy looked at the dead woman and stared at Bernard. "Is this your lady friend?" he asked.

When Reynolds came back in, Tommy picked up the mop. Tommy got a bucket and started swabbing the walls.

In no time, the woman was back to her normal size, but her face remained grossly engorged.

Reynolds stopped and shook his head while staring at the woman's jaws. "Too bad about the face. The face is impossible to fix. Once it fills up with liquid you can't get 'er back. Some things just can't be repaired." Reynolds left the room again and Tommy stopped working and watched Bernard.

"I can't wait to see the kind of fool woman who'd stoop to be with you."

Bernard ignored this and kept working on the dead woman's skin.

"You and your daddy both got bad taste in dames."

"My father, what are you talking about?"

"Boy ol' boy, I tell you it really takes all kinds. That old broad he's got now is a doozie, I swear. Came in yesterday bawling. She was all dolled up, too. Made the whole place reek with her cheap-smelling perfume. She tells Reynolds, your daddy's just slipping away, that he's one heartbeat from the grave. Then she smears on more lipstick and she starts pricing the glued caskets in the back. I tell you that floozie's got a real heart of gold." Tommy laughed and mopped the blood-looking fluid from the floor.

"Margie was here? What are you talking about, Tommy?" Bernard let the woman's head drop and one earring fell off.

"Reynolds had her in his room for a good while, too. Next thing I know, she's leaving with a whole bunch of papers and gets in a fat yellow cab."

Tommy stopped mopping and dumped his bucket in the prep room sink. Dirt and bloody water pooled along the drain. Tommy grinned at Bernard. He wiped his mouth with his palm. "That's got to be some special lady."

Bernard took Val to dinner on the Pacific Coast Highway. They sat on a blanket watching lava waves float in, coating the white ashy sand with liquid black. Val let Bernard kiss her, but his mind was somewhere else. She let him play with her breasts and they rolled around in the sand, but he couldn't get what Tommy said out of his mind.

When they got back to his house, the automatic sprinklers were running full blast.

"Damn it!" Bernard said, watching the wet soak his concrete.

"Looks like some of the beach followed us here," Val joked.

The runoff had thoroughly sloshed up his driveway. Bernard smiled at Val. He didn't want to waste precious time being upset. Besides, it was Friday. His dad played bingo tonight. A man came and hauled him away in a van. He wouldn't be back home for hours.

Bernard nosed his Plymouth into his long sloppy driveway, but suddenly he stopped, jamming his foot against the brakes. A red twisted bike lay in his path.

"For God's sake!" Bernard said, slamming the car into park and getting out. Grabbing the bike by the handlebars with haste, he shoved it on his neighbor's front lawn.

A crazy, deadly scream made him stop in his tracks. There was a harsh metal crash as Bernard let the bike fall. He could hear the girl arguing with her mother.

Val opened the door and got out of the car.

"Noooooooo!" an angry voice shrieked from upstairs. "I won't wear it! I hate it! It doesn't even fit!"

"You will wear it and you better stop complaining or else!"

Bernard and Val watched their shadows in the upper front window. They looked like they were struggling with a tiny piece of fabric.

"It hurts; the straps dig in my skin!"

"You're wearing it whether you want to or not. I can see both your nipples through your clothes!" Margie said.

"So!" the girl screamed, "I don't care if they show."

"Good girls don't go around showing their wares."

"I don't care what girls do! You show yours all the time."

After that, Bernard heard a skin-searing smack and then the woeful sound of heartbreaking sobs.

"So is that the brat you have living at your place?" Val rolled her eyes. Although she said this, she actually felt bad for the child. Watching the shadows in the window brought back memories of home and Val's own painful upbringing.

They heard a door open and quietly close and then a soft tapping sound of someone rapidly coming down the stairs.

A leaf-rustling noise came from the ground. Bernard walked Val to the back and immediately smelled something bad. Like an animal died somewhere deep in one of his scrubs. Out the corner of his eye, he thought he saw something move. It darted behind the elephant leaf plant. He squinted his eyes. He walked to the backyard and stopped by the fig tree and looked at the dirt by his feet. He noticed a round section of dirt that looked like it had recently been turned. He stared at the soil for a very long time. It was a small spot not much larger than a bowl. If he had turned the soil, he would have found a child's buried sweater. But Bernard left the soil alone, deciding a dog must have dug the mound, burying a nice juicy bone. He looked toward the sky through the fig tree's warped branches. He couldn't see, but hanging down was the little girl's knee, dangling alone from a branch. But Bernard didn't bother to examine the leaves. Val was right next to him now. He was excited beyond compare. He hoped they could finish where they left off at the beach.

Val waited in the dark yard listening for sounds. She was just about to turn around and walk into his house when suddenly there was a scurrying noise near her feet. Val saw a pair of small legs hurry inside a bush.

Bernard grabbed Val's arm and walked her toward the back door. But when he reached the top of the ramp, his foot rolled across the ground. Though he tried to catch himself by clinging to the door, his hand slipped and Bernard fell, facedown on the floor.

"Bernard!" Val said, grabbing his arm and hoisting him back up.

His bald head smarted awful, and he winced from the pain. His breathing became labored, and he had to blast his lungs with his spray. Rubbing his scalp while scanning the concrete back porch, he saw some blue and green marbles rolling around, darting toward the porch's dark corners. He didn't have to wonder who put the marbles there. Bernard ripped the nail off his pinkie until it bled and woefully thought of the girl.

Bernard was nervous about bringing Val into his house, and compounded with that he had the feeling someone was watching him now. He imagined the girl hidden, watching his back as he brought Val to the threshold.

Although he'd never admit it, Bernard watched the girl, too. He was fascinated with her assorted parade of costumes, sailor dresses, and white skirts with tight ruffled shirts or cowboy boots with dark denim skirts and weeks' worth of well-polished shoes. Bernard admired those who kept themselves up. He brought a fresh bag from the cleaners at least once a week. He polished his shoes at the end of each day. He had to. It became part of his routine at the job. His shoes often got splattered with blood.

Paula crept toward the back door. She pulled back the shade. Holding her binoculars to her eyes she peered in the yard.

The small woman she met earlier was standing on Bernard's porch. Her cashmere black coat licked her delicate calves. Her tiny behind fought the coat's shimmering fabric. A circular dome of gold hair was piled high on her head, and it swirled like a giant cone of vanilla ice cream.

"Where's your father?" the woman asked before stepping inside.

"Bingo," Bernard said. "A van picks him up. He should be gone for four or five hours." Seeing the van wheel him out to the street was the highlight of Bernard's miserable week. He slid Val's hand inside his as she stepped up the ramp. Her fingernails were a glossy blood red.

Paula held the lenses firmly up to her eyes and peered down toward Bernard's door. When the couple went in, she tiptoed down the stairs. She stood underneath his window, hiding in the dense fig tree and stared right inside the back door glass.

Clutching Val's hand, Bernard guided her body toward the couch.

Paula followed along the house and went to the living room window near the front.

The woman walking with Bernard was so little, so exquisite. She looked like a seashell, thoroughly polished and small. Her high heels were sharp. The toes perfectly pointed. Their red patent leather glowed against Bernard's ugly rugs.

Paula wanted to see the small woman up close. But Bernard shut the window, snugly twisting the blinds and now the girl could only see shadows. She caught one last glimpse of the woman's ice-cream hair just before the Venetian blinds closed.

The girl loved ice cream. She saved her small coins to buy it. She especially liked the soft swirling kind from machines. Bernard had watched her sneak away from the yard. He saw her race eight and a half blocks to buy some from the gas station man down the street and walked slowly back licking a cone.

Paula circled the house again and came to the window on the other side. She hid near the trees, easing her face to the pane.

Bernard's hairy hand cupped the woman's slim shoulder. He guided her waist toward his room. The woman's red pumps sunk deep into the carpet and left tiny marks in the pile.

The girl wanted to see more. She leaned closer to the glass, pressing the binoculars up to both eyes. The yard had grown dim. The sun ducked behind the garage, turning the young egg yolk sky into a cool evening gloom. The girl's hot breath began frosting the glass.

"You-hoo!" a singsong voice called.

Oh my God, it was Paula's mother. Bernard didn't want Margie to tell his father about Val. He hurried Val out of his house and onto his porch where they could hide until Margie went back inside.

Margie was leaning against the balcony rail by her door. She had been pestering him lately. She opened her back door whenever he was outside, begging him to come in or fix something in her place, which reeked with the ripe scent of onions or fish.

Margie descended the steps slowly. Her heels slapped each slat. She didn't see Val at Bernard's door as she sashayed her hips down the stairs.

Margie was fully done up, out of her usual slippers and robe. Her skull that once bulged under a scarf full of rollers now showed off a candy tray of brown shiny curls.

"Hey, Bernard!" she called. "I got a pie on the stove." The girl's mother let her finger trace the length of her cleavage. "I was wondering if you wanted a slice?"

Bernard feverishly tried to get his key in the lock's slender mouth, but in his anxiousness he dropped the keys on the ground. He ignored her completely. He hoped she would see he was busy and leave.

But Margie came down and leaned right next to his car.

"Wow," Margie said. "That's suuuurrrre's a nice ride." She grazed her fat hand across the sparkling hood. "How do you keep it looking so good?"

Margie's own car was dead. She needed transportation. She'd found an old bankbook, while cleaning and poking around their house. But the bank's closest branch was in Manhattan Beach. Margie needed to take Bernard's car to get there.

"I've got a pie on the stove and some crab legs on boil, I'd love to have you over for supper . . ."

Margie stopped midsentence. There was a woman next to Bernard's arm.

Holding a hand to her chest, Margie said, "Oh, I didn't know you had company."

Margie looked at Val, adjusting her eyes to the dim. A hint of recognition flooded her eyes. "I know you! You were at the funeral, right?"

Val smiled and shook her head no. "I don't do funerals, ma'am. It must have been somebody else."

"It's Margie," Margie said, while forcing a smile. "Save the ma'ams for your mama back home." Margie was older and didn't like Val's condescending tone. Her formality hid a snotty conceit.

"Sorry, ma'am. This is how we talk where I'm from. We country folks can yes sir and ma'am you to death."

Margie marched up the ramp and peered right in Val's face. "I'm sorry, I don't mean to stare but I'm sure it was you. You *were* at Alice's Fowler's funeral. I saw you in the bathroom before the service started. You were in there with my daughter."

Bernard didn't remember Val being at the funeral at all. Why would she be there, she never mentioned it before? But Bernard didn't want to discuss any of this now. He wanted to get inside. He picked up his keys from the ground. He wanted to finish where he and Val left off at the beach before the bingo van brought his dad home.

"I'm sorry, ma'am," Val said. "You must have me mixed up. I don't ever go to funerals," she lied. She smiled at Margie. Her burgundy lips lifted. "You know you have really pretty teeth."

Margie mimicked Val's grin. But there were pitchforks in hers. This bitch was actually trying to pull one on her. Margie eyed her giant blonde hair, smelled her perfume, and took note of her vicious spike-heeled shoes. You didn't forget a woman like Val. Women like Val were hard to miss. She epitomized the Hollywoodness of L.A. She was perfectly done up from her coifed head to her red toes. You stared at women like her in stores, admiring their style and clothes, and when you caught your own reflection after seeing someone like her, you wondered when and where you let yourself go.

Margie was about to say something, but a scream stopped her in her tracks.

"Mommmmmeeeeee!"

It was a loud, threatening scream as if someone were being attacked and it was so savage and high-pitched it could easily break glass, if it wasn't so animalistic.

Margie's loose body became stiff. It was like rigormortis set in. A chill snaked through her veins and rose up to her brain. When the scream came again, Margie raced down Bernard's ramp. She was worried. She had left the girl in the bath. It's not like she was worried if the girl would slip down and drown. Quite the contrary. She didn't care if that happened. Margie worried the girl would revolt and completely blow their scam. She was right in the tail end of the con. She needed to finish. She was almost at the end. But the girl was becoming more vengeful after each of their quarrels. She seemed to grow bolder and more defiant each day. Margie never knew which way the cold wind would blow. She raced across the yard toward her steps.

Bernard and Val followed Margie toward the steps.

"Please!" Margie screamed, glaring at the tall row of stairs. "Don't come outside like that!"

The smile Margie wore earlier was ripped from her jaw and was replaced with an agonizing frown. Deep lines of worry were scissoring her brow, digging zigzagging crevices in her skin.

How could Bernard describe her face? A horror show flick. Her curls seemed to sizzle and stand on each end. The pancake makeup spackled in creases began to break out in sweat. Her clown-like mouth, rouged cheeks, and inky black eyes looked like a cheap grocery cake left out in the sun, that was finally starting to slide. What the makeup couldn't hide was buried underneath. Eyes that cried long before the invention of tears. Eyes that lived way too long in the deep grave of worry. They'd lost all sense of hope and were such a bubblegum pink, they looked like she was ready to cry. Though Margie struggled to grin, the smile only touched her teeth. The smile never reached the abyss of her slashed-apart heart. It was like trying to appear calm, while answering the door with a butcher knife jabbed against your spine.

"Stay right there," Margie shrieked to the child. Her face was a prison of anguish and strain. She carefully chose each word, pleading to the crack at the screen. She knew she couldn't climb the stairs before the child came out. She had to use honey and hide the hand grenade inside to make sure the child did what she said.

"I'm coming, sweetie, don't come out, it's cold. Wait, and I'll show you where I hid the ice cream."

Margie looked like she was staring right into doom. Like death's mighty claw had captured her neck. Her eyes never left the screen's widening crack as she bolted her weight up the stairs.

Bernard gazed toward the door. Why was Margie so afraid? Though he couldn't see the girl's face, he imagined what she wore; a green gingham frock with white eyelet ruffles, her curls lapping her shoulders like a long, gorgeous cape.

But no, that's not what he saw at all. He saw one of the girl's small legs, and he followed the leg to her waist and saw her thigh and her belly and the hint of a nipple and a greedy smile spilling over her cheeks. The girl was completely naked! She had no clothes on at all.

Bernard's hot face flushed. He nervously coughed. His tongue swam across his dry bottom lip.

Val looked at Bernard. What was he looking at up there? She stared at Bernard but his glazed eyes were glued. And like a magnet, her own head pulled toward the stairs, and Val immediately dropped open her jaw.

Paula opened the door wider. She stepped one foot out.

Margie was almost frantic. "Stop!" she called to the child. She began hurtling the stairs, hopping two at a time. Her burly girth was jiggling in an indecent way. Her terror-stricken face was drenched, her hair stood on end as her pounding heart leaped from her chest.

"There's a Popsicle in the freezer, behind the orange box of waffles; go ahead and get one right now."

But Paula stood still and didn't move at all. "I don't want a Popsicle," she tartly told her mother, like she was testing the very limits of what Margie could bear. Then she let the screen door open a little bit more.

"Stop!" Margie screamed, at the top of her lungs. "Don't you dare come out like that, or you'll live to regret it!"

When the girl widened the door an inch, Bernard saw her grin. The grin was the only thing that the little girl wore, but the door covered the spot where his eyes drifted next and though he strained he couldn't see anything more than the door handle covering the blur between the little girl's legs.

A hungry adrenaline sloshed through his skin. He couldn't take his eyes off her half-naked body and that satisfied smirk on her lips.

Finally, Margie reached the landing, by jumping the last top steps. Thoroughly out of breath she glared in the girl's eyes. She didn't have to be kind anymore. She snatched the door handle and knocked the girl inside, slamming the screen door behind them.

After a scuffle and another nerve racking yell, Margie stuck her head out of the windowsill upstairs.

"See you at dinner tomorrow, Bernard, and bring your lady friend with you. The more, the merrier," Margie said. She was forcing a smile and was visibly upset. Her curls were messed up and her makeup had run. Margie eyed Val once more before closing her shade. She'd have to speed up her plans with Bernard's lady friend around. This diva was here for something. It couldn't possibly be Bernard. She could sniff the competition a million miles away. Maybe Bernard told Val about the safety deposit box. If Bernard and Val came to dinner, she could push them up against the ropes. Margie knew what to do to get Bernard to talk, and then she'd find out which bank the safety box was in.

Margie smiled and fingered the key in her hand. She licked her orange lips and felt a warm glow over her body. She could almost feel the Howard Hughes money in her hand.

Margie stared at the child's closed door. She could hear Paula sobbing. Shoot, if worse came to worse, the child could do the dirty work for her. They could run the exact same con as before. No one suspects a kid, especially little girls. Margie popped her gum with machine gun finesse. She went in the kitchen and yanked a roast from the freezer. Holding the brick chunk of meat in her hands like a ball, Margie slammed the frozen roast in the sink. She went to her room and took out a black little bottle. A skull and bones smiled from the front. Dinner might be fun. She'd even send a plate to Mr. Fowler. Obviously Bernard was sneaking around with this tramp. Margie let the hot water blast the hard frosty ball, and then left it inside the dirty sink to thaw.

Rubbing her stomach with one hand, she thought of that Howard Hughes money. She wasn't concerned with Bernard at first. He seemed stupid and weak. He was a pale-ass fool who worked in a funeral parlor and seemed as dim as a forty watt bulb. But Val was something else altogether.

Margie walked to the back window and peered out of the shade. She liked living here. Hollywood Hills was easygoing and quiet. She liked the weather in California. Her hips didn't hurt and her feet didn't swell. She could live on this hillside forever.

Margie's lids fell back down to the image downstairs. Val's blonde flowing hair almost reached her waist. This was definitely the same bitch she met in the bathroom. Val's nosy ass was throwing a wrench in her plans. She couldn't have anyone around in the middle of her con. She had to be dealt with finesse.

"Should I bring anything?" Margie heard Val ask.

Margie peeled the shade some more but didn't say a word. Yeah, she thought to herself. Bring your skinny butt up here. Margie stared at the drawer where she kept her knives. I got something here for your ass.

Margie picked up the phone and dialed a number. "Hello! Is Mr. Fowler still there? Could you please tell him to come home right away, there's something wrong with his son."

Margie smiled when she put the receiver back down. She went to the living room and poured herself some wine and waited for the van to bring Mr. Fowler. Bingo would have to wait tonight.

13

Bernard and Val

When they got to his house, Val lowered herself to the couch. Holding both ankles tight, she swung them across the floor. Val picked up the *L.A. Times* and saw another McMartin story. One of the kids admitted being coached into telling a lie. But Val didn't want to talk about McMartin tonight and instead read about the new observatory on Vermont.

"Have you been to the observatory?" Val asked Bernard. "Looks like they've remodeled the old thing."

"Yes," Bernard said, holding a glass of champagne. He was beaming. No woman had ever been inside his house. "I haven't been up there in ages."

The moon beat against his white knuckled fists. Bernard tried to breathe easy as his heart whipped against his chest.

Only last month he felt old, like the sweet life had passed him. But now here he was with a beautiful woman inside his home. And not any woman either. This was a slick magazine beauty. She was a head to toe stunner with radiant skin and straight teeth that were real because when she laughed big he checked.

Bernard circled his arm around the crystal lamp and clicked, turning their bodies into black silhouettes. Bernard started breathing deep, filling his lungs up with air. He could smell Val's perfume, a soft rose mixed with something reminding him of spice. It enticed the cool dewy air.

Bernard had never been alone with a grown woman in his life. His lungs almost burst through his overstarched oxford. The excitement was so intense that it tittered near full-blown panic. To be safe, he took a hit from his Primatene Mist, letting the medicine roll into his lungs. The inhaler worked fast, but so had the champagne, and his breathing slowed into a euphoric staccato.

"You must be feeling good. You've been smiling all night. What the hell are you thinking?"

"I was thinking, the last time I was at the observatory. It was the summer I turned twelve. My mother took me to the observatory for my birthday. She surprised me by letting me wander through the whole museum alone. Being left was a fluke, nothing my mother planned on letting me do, but after parking and walking up a steep hill, Mom was panting so hard she put both hands on her knees and told me she had to go back to the car to lay down."

"She was probably getting weak by then, huh?" Val said.

"If she was, she never let on and kept a stiff upper lip." Bernard remembered how they parked near the white mausoleum-like dome, which looked like a machine gun gutting out from a tank.

"That was the first time I'd ever been out of my parents' sight." Bernard sipped his champagne and grinned.

He remembered pressing his right eye against the cold metal shaft and tightly squeezing shut his left. Closing his eyes now, Bernard could see it all in his mind—there was a galaxy of stars that littered the black velvet calm, like a large Easter egg dunked in a multitude of grays.

Though he was tapped, Bernard didn't want to give up his turn. The man behind him tapped his shoulder twice, but Bernard was way too excited to leave. Reluctantly, he climbed back down the ladderlike stairs, hanging his chin to his chest.

When Bernard got to the floor he enviously looked back. The man behind him was lifting this little girl up. She couldn't have been older than five. The man pressed the little girl's face to the lens. Bernard glanced around the observatory again and saw another little boy looking under the girl's dress. He stood staring. He stayed for as long as the girl took her turn.

The older boy was a whole lot bigger than Bernard and had the pimply, mustached face of a teen. The boy began to follow the girl around the museum, and Bernard followed the little boy, too. When the little girl went through the marbled bathroom arch, the boy waited outside the door.

The girl's father was reading a paper outside and waved the small girl away like a fly.

Bernard watched them play freeze tag and hide and go seek, while the girl's father sat on a park bench and smoked. Ducking inside some jasmine, the older boy scrambled next to some thorny roses. He started whistling low, so the young girl would find him, and she smiled as she scrambled in, too. Quietly, Bernard crawled on his hands and his knees creeping closer so he could see. When a large twig scratched the entire length of his arm, he didn't even cry when it bled.

The older boy was panting. His face was flushed with excitement. He loved the warmth of her tiny round mouth over his and the girl smiled back with big walnut eyes. Then his hands moved under her white eyelet dress. The little girl grinned. She liked this new game. She giggled, but the boy whispered for her to be quiet. He told her the silent one wins. The obedient girl clamped her pink lips. She let the boy do whatever he wanted. His hands ran all over her miniature body, exploring and kneading her flesh.

But suddenly a scream speared inside Bernard's ears. A high pitch yell that drowned out all other sound. Bernard panicked. His whole face was broken in sweat. He quietly peeked further into the deep bush again. He saw the older boy holding one hand snug over her jaw. But the girl was squirming and fighting him hard. Then the boy covered her, letting his grown body smother hers, to keep her from making a sound. When the girl heaved beneath him, he forced himself down harder and stopped her from moving around.

A twig snapped, and the boy turned and looked right at Bernard. Bernard couldn't see the small girl's body anymore. The boy grabbed some dirt and tossed it in Bernard's eyes and the boy scrambled from the bush on the other side.

Bernard saw the small girl's body. Her dress was pulled over her waist, her still eyes never blinked once. She looked just like those oversized dolls you see in stores. Bernard pulled down her dress. He tried to shake the girl awake, but the frozen girl's frame remained limp. Bernard crawled from the bush, too. He saw the older boy running. He got into a large yellow bus.

Bernard ran to the car. He told his mother he felt sick. He leaped in the back and laid low in the seat as his mother tooled the car down the slim narrow hill. The last thing he saw was the little girl's father. He frantically raced around, shouting the girl's name over and over; chunks of his hair fell into his agonized face. Some kids pointed toward the parking lot, right at Bernard's car. Bernard slid farther down in the Plymouth's vinyl seat. The next thing he knew, his mother was back on Vermont. That was the last time he'd ever been up there.

Bernard snuck a look at Val while biting the nail from his pinkie. She reached for his hand and placed it down in her lap. At forty-eight, he was twenty-three years older than Val. She was a small luscious beauty with succulent lips and skin that felt smoother than glass.

Val wrapped her arms around Bernard's clammy neck.

Bernard was too excited to speak. He was holding his breath. He wanted to tear off her clothes and grab her long hair. He wanted to pull back the length of her neck and suck the soft meat along her throat. But instead, Bernard held the arm of the couch, as his heart banged against his tight shirt.

Val rubbed his back, and Bernard inhaled her scent. His brain almost exploded in his head. This was so different from his plastic blow-up doll in the yard. Val was real. Val winked at him and talked. She was vivacious and warm with thick gorgeous hair and when she let her hair fall over his face and his shoulder, it smelled like lavender and vanilla and was as soft as a silk scarf.

Around her thin waist lay a silvery chain. A heart charm dangled inside the cavernous hole of her navel.

Bernard fingered the chain. He let the inside of his thumb touch it. Without thinking, he let his other hand fall from the couch and his hand rounded her slim, dainty waist. But when his wrist reached the lace of her thin undergarments, that's when she finally stopped him.

"I'm so sorry," Bernard exclaimed. His chin sank to his chest. He could feel the red heat slide over his skin. He felt like he stood near the incinerator door with all of the burners on high.

"That's okay, honey. Man, oh man, do you have strong arms. You're like my little retarded brother, Al." Val unscrewed her lipstick. A glimmering crimson hue emerged. She circled her mouth with the color.

"You have a brother?" Bernard was happy to change the subject. He'd talk about anything but the awkward moment that just passed.

"Oh I wish you could meet him! Al is such a sweetie, really. At five-two, he could snap you in half with one arm. He was in good shape like you."

Bernard watched Val smear the color across her lip. Bernard wasn't large like his father. He told people he was 5' 9", but that was pushing it an inch. But he prided himself on how he cared for his body. He was compact and firm and did push-ups each day and ran in the morning if the weather was right or rode his stationary bike if it rained.

"Al was a wrestler. Used to pin me down in our yard. Poor Al. He's sitting in a prison cell now." Val added more black eyeliner to her lids. "I told that cheerleader to stop playing with Al. Retarded men are stronger than hell!"

Val smiled at Bernard. She didn't have any brother. Where these crazy tales come from she didn't have a clue. Val smiled at herself while looking in the mirror. Juicy lies were such fun to tell.

Val grabbed Bernard's fingers. "You have such strong hands."

She kissed each finger on Bernard's trembling hand and Bernard wanted to scratch them madly but didn't.

"There's no need to hurry, sugar, I'm not going to melt." Val kissed his cheek and the side of his neck. He was adorable, even with his breathing problems and morbid job. She liked him. She wanted to smother his face with her lips.

Bernard was numb from embarrassment. He kept his head down. He was more excited than he'd ever been before and burned like raw beef on a skewer.

"Bernard?"

"Yes, doll?"

"I have something to tell you." Val had been holding these words in since the first day they met.

"I want to be totally honest. I don't want to hold anything back."

Suddenly, the living room flooded with light.

Bernard yanked his head up and looked all around.

He heard the van's sliding door open. He heard the wheelchair come down. He heard the squeak as the tires worked their way up the ramp.

His father was home! What was he doing back so early? Bernard searched around the room but there was nowhere to hide. He couldn't leave because the van was blocking his car.

Bernard looked at Val and panicked. He had to hide her somewhere. Bernard bit his nails and shifted his lids around the room.

"What's wrong with you? You look like you've seen a ghost. I know it's Halloween, but damn, man, what is it?" Val had no idea what was wrong.

"Quick!" Bernard whispered. "Hide in my room!"

"Hide? Are you serious? Why do we need to hide? Are you afraid of that crazy lady upstairs?"

Bernard was spiraling down quickly. He was struggling to breathe.

"No! It's my father!" Bernard sputtered and choked. His head spun when he heard the lock turn on the back door. "He can't find you in here. He'll kill me, I swear!"

"What for? We haven't done anything wrong." Val watched the petrified look on Bernard's face. She tried to rub his palm to calm Bernard down, but Bernard snatched his hand away fast.

"You don't understand. I can't have women here. He's going to be terribly upset." Bernard bit his nail until blood rose from the bed.

"You're the one upset."

Bernard was shaking in fear.

"Get a hold of yourself, man. You're acting five years old! You're grown. He can't order you around anymore." Val wondered why Bernard was so afraid of his father.

Bernard heard the door open and listened to the wheelchair roll inside. He was so panicky he couldn't breathe at all. His inhaler was in his pocket, but he left his jacket in the car. The other one was inside his room, and there was one in the bathroom cabinet, but the bathroom was near the back door.

Doubled over in fear and having convulsions from no air, Bernard rolled from the couch to the floor.

"Oh my God, Bernard! Where the hell is your spray?"

"Get my inhaler! It's inside my room!"

"Which room?" Val said. It was a huge and intricate house.

Just then the telephone began sirening throughout the walls.

Val ignored the phone and ran to Bernard's room. She ran to a cabinet and started opening drawers.

"My nightstand . . . way . . . back . . ." he strained.

Val was inside Bernard's bedroom, looking around, just as Mr. Fowler wheeled himself over the threshold.

He rolled to the living room and found his son on the floor.

"Son? Are you alright?" Mr. Fowler raced along the floor toward Bernard. He grabbed a water bottle from his wheelchair pouch and spilled it over Bernard's lips. "Breathe, fool," he ordered his son.

Mr. Fowler was actually worried. When he got the call he was annoyed at first, but then Margie said something was wrong with his son. She said he fell down and was wiggling on the floor. On the way home he was filled with an overwhelming dread. Was Bernard dead? Was his only son gone, too?

Bernard sputtered from the water but managed to get some air. The phone was still ringing, but Bernard squeezed both his eyes. He waited to see what his father would say after seeing Val. He figured it was best to keep his eyes shut.

Much later, gingerly, Bernard opened one eye. Val wasn't there. His father wasn't either. He looked in the kitchen, but Val wasn't inside. He peeked in the bathroom and kept walking down the hall. When he got to his room, the wind blew the shade in his face. His bedroom window was left open wide.

14

Bernard, Margie, Val, and Paula

The next evening, Bernard left his house and picked up Val and brought her back. She had wrapped a Boy Scout survival guide in the comic section of the paper as something to give the young child. As they approached the door, they both heard a rumbling inside the apartment. It sounded like people pushing furniture around. What on earth could those two be doing, he wondered, pushing his thumb on the buzzer. He heard Margie's cheap shoes beat the wood in the hall.

"I'm a comin'!" Margie called through the door.

Bernard heard the short sliding scratch of the latch and the dry awful hiss of cheap fabric.

Her perfume hit him first. It was a heavy magnolia mixed with the harsh scent of lemon. The aroma ate the uncooked skin in his nostrils.

Gripping the inhaler inside his pocket, Bernard held it tight, keeping it locked inside the oven of his fist.

Margie grabbed the wrapped present, holding it up against her chest. "Oh, thank you." she said, beginning to undo the twine. "How very kind of you, Bernard."

"Actually, Val brought the gift for the child," he said.

Val smiled at Margie.

Margie smiled back at Val. "Well of course you did, sweetheart, how thoughtful and nice." Then she dropped the gift quickly as if it was diseased, and it bounced on the pillows of the couch as Margie walked out of the room.

Bernard was embarrassed about the gift. He wished they had brought something better. A survival book! Didn't Val know this was a girl? She'll probably look at the book and laugh or toss it in the trash where it belonged. He wished they'd gotten her a locket or a charm or even some flowers. Anything was better than some used Boy Scout manual, but he could never tell Val how he felt. Val was radiant. She was wearing a red dress and a speckled cheetah coat. She looked fierce, and he was happy to have a woman like her on his arm. She didn't seem afraid of Margie at all.

Suddenly, Margie burst from the kitchen again.

Bernard immediately pulled from Val. He didn't want Margie to spill all the beans to his father. But Margie looked at him knowingly, and Bernard tried to avoid her eyes and placed his on the blinking TV set instead.

The McMartin case was closing in on the son. It looked like Roy Buckey did it and was about to do some serious time.

Margie came over and clicked the TV off. "I'm tired of hearing about all that mess," she said.

"Is Paula here?" Val asked.

Margie whipped around and stared. "That's strange. I don't remember telling you my daughter's name."

"Oh," Val said, realizing her mistake. "Bernard told me her name in the car."

"Where is she?" Bernard asked, while looking around.

They both noticed the eagerness in his eyes.

"She's in her room," Margie said tersely, "She's plotting to do you in," she teased. She stared at Bernard with a twinkle in her eyes. "What, are you part of the McMartin clan, too? Do you want to peek at her bloomers?"

Bernard was insulted by this remark. "I don't even like kids," he snapped.

But as soon as he said it, he knew it wasn't quite true.

"Please," Margie said sweetly, edging Bernard toward the couch. "Why don't you two sit down?"

Bernard and Val took side-by-side seats on the orange couch.

But Margie wedged her large hips in between both their thighs. She opened a bottle of wine and sat out three glasses. "There," she said, sitting back. "Isn't this nice?"

Bernard sat at the couch's edge. The wooly cushion itched his arm, but he was absorbed with the show happening under the girl's door. As the light seeped from underneath the jamb, he could see the girl's feet, and he followed their faint blur in the dim.

Margie placed a glass in Bernard's hand, but when she poured Val her wine, the liquid sloshed on Val's arm. "Excuse me, I don't know why I'm so clumsy." She placed a plate of crackers and cheese near their legs.

Val looked at her face. Did Margie do that on purpose? Bernard told her Margie just showed up out of the blue and now was living in his house. Why was she at Alice Fowler's funeral that day? She didn't believe Margie was a relative or friend.

"So do you have any family pictures?" Val asked, looking around. She wanted to know if any photos proved Margie's relationship to Alice.

Margie started wiggling on the couch like a puppy, "Oh, Howard Hughes, now there was a real man for you."

Val leaned up to listen.

"Alice and I go way back, honey. You were still pooping your diapers when we met."

Val smiled at Margie and bit a tiny piece of a cracker, letting the crumbs drop down on her floor. Margie's comment was insulting, but Val gave her a stockbroker grin. The kind you got when they told you about your losses.

"Well," Val said, adding her own dig. "In a few short years you'll be wearing them again yourself!" Val broke her cracker and put half in her mouth and smiled triumphantly at Bernard.

"Did you ever meet him?" Bernard asked. Howard was an elusive family figure. He'd never seen him once. There wasn't even a picture of him in the house.

Margie handed Val her drink and smiled at her coolly "Meet him?" Margie lied. "Why the man practically lived at our house!" She scooted the cheese platter closer to herself and Bernard and shoved endless pieces of greasy cheese in her mouth. "Howard was a different bird, but he was practically my uncle." Talking while mushy cheese gushed over her teeth, "he had a thing for biscuits and cranberry jam. He used to come by for fresh bread and coffee."

"You ate jam with Howard Hughes?" Val acted like she was about to pee right there. She scanned Margie's chubby feet and her monstrously thick calves. It looked like Margie hadn't missed one hot roll since then, either.

Margie hurriedly got up and went back to the kitchen, and Val chuckled underneath her cupped hand.

"She's a trip! I think she's an out-and-out liar. I got a high radar for imposters."

Game recognizes game, Val thought to herself. She had no idea Margie was in a whole other league.

Bernard was studying the light under the little girl's door. He was bored with any story about Howard Hughes. Howard never gave a dime, and this ramshackle mansion was proof. Bernard turned his head toward the little girl's door and watched the slot on the floor. The shadowy feet were now right near the threshold.

Margie poured more wine in their glasses. "Alice Hughes was such a dear. She loved my sweet Paula." Margie pulled a small photo from her wallet.

"This is the only picture I have left. The others were lost in a fire." Margie held a small picture of a tiny cute baby. The child was sitting in the lap of an elegantly dressed man, but the man's head and legs were abruptly burned off so you couldn't tell who he was. A blue ruffled bib was tied to the baby's fat chin.

Margie looked at the picture lovingly, holding it away so they both could see.

"This picture was taken in Howard Hughes' limo in Texas.

See the pearl inlaid steering wheel and the carved minibar and the silk drapes over the side windows. Those drapes were specially made and flown in from Spain, Every stitch was sewn in by hand." Margie was flat out lying but never fluttered a lash. This was the campaign manager's car. He let her take this last picture and then he mocked her and refused to admit Paula was his and rudely tossed her out to the curb. After her husband's accidental death, he was her first brutal killing. That's why Margie burned off his face and his legs. The picture showed him screaming, a bandanna in his teeth and his feet tied while burning completely alive in the backseat of his luxurious car. Meeting him was the worst mistake of her life. Her husband would be alive if it wasn't for him. She planned to burn the campaign manager and the child together, but Margie snatched the child out of his lap before the gasoline flames got too high. Margie assumed this was why the child was fascinated with fire. The child was almost consumed too, baked away with its father, but in the last second Margie reached in and changed her mind, carrying the baby away on her hip.

"Wow, I can't really see the car, but look at her, Bernard. She's such a cute baby," Val grinned at the picture. "You're so lucky to have a cute girl," she told Margie.

Bernard glanced at the picture. He didn't care what she looked like as a baby. He sat back and stared at the narrow slot at the girl's door.

Margie smiled, bringing the picture up close to her face. She looked at Bernard and put her arm across his shoulders.

"Your mother never had one herself, but Alice was partial to girls." Margie studied the photo, like she was trying to remember something else.

And then all at once, like something was grabbing her throat, a horrible recognition began souring her mouth, wrinkling her brow in a mixture of sorrow and pain, making her face bloodless and as pale as a corpse left in a lake.

"I had the child late," Margie started rubbing her belly. Her chubby legs barely scraped the wood floor.

Bernard stared at his drink. He didn't know what to say. He was studying all the greasy fingerprints on his glass.

"The doctor said at forty-six I was pushing the limits of safety," Margie threw her head back and gave a really good laugh. "Oh God, that doctor couldn't even look in my face!" Margie laughed but that moment created a tragedy of her life. Even the doctor had sucked in his breath and avoided Margie's eyes. Though Margie had run off with the campaign manager, she eventually came back. The campaign manager didn't want Margie at all. She was a plaything, a challenge, something to do when he was bored. The campaign manager liked women like Margie. They were such easy prey. He had a dozen or so of them all over the state. Sad lonely housewives, starved for attention, the kind that watched *Days of Our Lives* every single morning and would melt on the floor like ice if you ever looked their way. She was beautiful and smart but the last one to know it. She was fun for a minute, like getting a new record to play. But he didn't love her. She was colored! He wouldn't dare cross that line. He was a white man in the deep South, with a powerful job in Memphis. He'd never admit a colored kid was his. Ashamed and dejected, Margie attempted to go back home. She wasn't showing yet and used to rub her stomach with grease and then she laid her big belly out in the sun hoping the child would come out with some color. Her husband was so happy. He wanted to have a baby. He began cooking her meals and telling her to sit down and giving her ginger ale to sip on the couch. But then that orangey hair seeped from the lip of her crotch and that white-looking child crowned and was placed on her chest, creating a soggy pale glob on her skin. All the blue-eyed evidence was there, staring at everyone in the room, transforming Margie's quiet life, into a sinkhole of misery and doom.

Margie's eyes began brimming and filling with tears, but the pain became rage and she rushed into the kitchen. She pulled the roast out of the oven and picked up the poison bottle and shook some out and hurriedly made all their plates.

Bernard didn't know where to look and decided to scan the contents of the apartment. There was a discolored credenza with end tables to match and golden thread damask chairs. A grandfather clock sat upright against the wall and the dining room table, the queen of the room, rose up from the floor like an intricately carved tomb. But these items were ruined by the woman's bad taste. Fake violets slept in orange plastic vases. Hideous floral prints were scattered without heed or care. Moth-eaten doilies covered every wood surface, making the room look like an old spider's web.

"Your father's been such a dear. We had no furnishings of our own." Margie carefully laid paper towels down as place mats.

Staring, Bernard began to recognize these items. The slow shock that set in made his rusty skin itch. The carved chairs, the angel torch lamps, the grandfather clock in the corner. All of these things were his mother's! They all came out of the garage. Even the slim vinyl ottoman with the side part ripped out from the short time that she had a cat.

"Your father let us take whatever we wanted. He didn't like having any reminders of her." Margie used the knife skillfully and sliced through the meat.

"I got lucky," Margie said to Val, "Bernard's father's such a good man. I hope he lives to be a hundred years old."

Bernard couldn't believe it! His father let them take his mother's things! He looked at Margie sharply. She was wearing his mother's necklace and dress. She had on the peach and brown tea length dress his mother wore to his mortuary class graduation and her sapphire choker and ring. He could feel the taut skin on his face going flush. His breath turned into a vicious staccato.

"You're . . . wearing?" Bernard stammered, too angry for words.

"Oh, you noticed!" Margie twirled around for Bernard. "Good glory, your mother and I are exactly the same size! I didn't have to stitch in one inch. I told your father, I said, 'Edward, you're the epitome of a generous Christian.' The Lord says to share and share alike. It's not God-like to horde things that others can use. That's not being a giver. We all need to offer our souls to the Lord. It's right on page ninety-two in the Bible." Margie grabbed a Bible from out of the window. She was using it to hold a window open, and when she took the book, the window fell like a guillotine.

Margie ignored Bernard's rage. She was content with examining herself in the mirror. After drawing on her lipstick in a perfect orange heart, she opened her purse and counted the money inside. Now that she had a steady supply of cash, fresh from Bernard's father's wallet, she had a standing appointment at Lucy's on Vine. She kept a picture of Alice Fowler inside her purse to make sure the hairdresser did it right. It was so easy, she thought, running these funeral scams. She was constantly amazed at folks opening up their homes just because someone claimed to be kin. Margie smiled at herself and added more rouge. She blew herself a kiss and then snapped her purse shut and went back into the kitchen. "I'll be back in a jiffy," she told Bernard, strolling through the kitchen's swinging door.

Bernard was steaming! He wanted to confront his father. Giving them the apartment was bad enough, but this was too much. This woman was wearing his dead mother's things! She hadn't been in the ground a month! He was about to say a cruel thing but stopped.

"Where's Dad?" Bernard asked Margie through the door.

Margie ignored him and kept tossing a salad.

"Where's my father? He wasn't in his room when I left. I thought you said you were going to send a plate down for him?"

Margie turned around and gave Bernard a genuine smile. If she was alone with him, she would have sliced his neck with one of her knives.

"Bingo. He's on a winning streak. Your father is the luckiest man I know."

Suddenly, a high-pitched, controlled voiced filled the room.

"Mommy?" the small voice called from the door.

Margie's smile turned into a stiffening gaze. "Just a minute," she said, rushing her big frame down the hall, hurrying into the girl's room and closing the door. Before the door shut, Bernard caught a glimpse of the child. She was wearing a knee-length robe made of powder blue velour; the belt was dangling down between her legs.

"You certainly can not. I don't care if you're hot. You have to wear pajamas underneath!" Margie said.

There was a short argument, and suddenly the girl emerged from her room and walked the short distance to the bathroom across the hall. Bernard could feel his heart jump inside his rib cage.

Margie opened the bathroom door, and he heard Paula scream.

"Get out of here!" she said meanly. "Can't you see I'm not dressed?"

The girl's voice sounded funny. It kept modulating in tone.

"Well, hurry up. We have guests," Margie said.

The girl went back to her bedroom, and Bernard glanced down the hall. "Is she out?" he asked. He wanted to use the bathroom now.

Margie peeked down the hall. Paula was back in her room. "All clear!" Margie said.

Bernard crept down the hall toward the small bathroom door. But instead of the bathroom he stopped at Paula's door instead. He could hear music playing inside.

Ever so carefully, Bernard began turning the door's knob. Slowly, he began to see Paula's slender frame, growing along the door's crack. She was standing in front of the mirror with the towel around her waist. She was swaying to the music, using the doll's legs as a mike and mouthing each line to the song. Her flat nipples were dark with no hint of growth yet. But there was a lot of long hair under her arms.

Suddenly, the floor creaked, and Paula whirled herself around. Bernard snatched the door closed before she could see. Paula raced to the lock and looked in the keyhole and saw Bernard going into the bathroom across the hall. After a moment, Bernard went to the living room again.

It was agonizing, waiting for the girl to come out. Bernard was trapped on the couch between Margie and Val who were talking about all the movie stars they'd seen.

And then, silently, and in socks, he heard her feet in the hall. She was now wearing a nightgown underneath the velour robe, and the robe was tightly knotted at the waist.

She scooted her young body right next to Val, which made Margie madder than hell. She had planned to keep the girl locked in her room the whole time, but now here she was on the couch.

"Hi," Val said, looking directly in Paula's face.

Paula remembered Val. She was the nice woman from the bathroom! She gave her candy and a sweater when she was freezing in the car.

Val tipped over her glass, and the burgundy liquid spilled over the table.

When Margie rushed to the kitchen, Val winked at the child and held her finger over her lips.

The girl smiled at Val. She liked playing secret games.

Bernard was so busy looking at the outline of her feet that he didn't even notice this exchange.

Almost immediately, Margie was back with a rag. It was a small, balled up pair of little boy's briefs. Rapidly, she started rubbing the table with them in her hand. "Recognize this lady?" Margie asked Paula.

"No," Paula lied, shaking her head back and forth. She stared at Val harder as if she were a puzzle she couldn't figure out.

"Who is she?" Paula asked. "Is she a teacher from my school?"

Margie was very upset that Paula didn't remember Val. But she hid it just like she hid the poison bottle in the kitchen, "Excuse me," she said to Val. "Could you help me a minute?" Margie held the kitchen door ajar.

"Sure," Val told her. She didn't mind lending a hand. She uncrossed her legs and rose slowly from the couch as her silk dress clung to her curves.

Next to Margie she looked like a model from *Vogue*. Even Margie took note of how stunning Val was. Gritting her back teeth, Margie gave Val a marmalade smile. She was thinking of how quick poison gets in your veins and how good Val would look in a coffin.

When Margie and Val went into the kitchen, Bernard peeked at the child. She immediately distracted his burgeoning rage. He was charmed by her presence. But much too timid to look at her full on, "How are you," he said, slightly turning his head. His arm felt the nap of her robe.

"My mom says you work on dead people. What do you do to them?" Paula asked. She stared at him so hard with those clear aqua eyes that Bernard yanked his eyes toward the rug.

"Now, Paula, honey," Margie, said from the kitchen, "you don't ask people that. What folks do to make a living is their private affair." Margie continued sharpening a knife while smiling at Val. She could see her red dress in the blade.

"It's okay," Bernard said quickly. He didn't mind talking about his job. It was the one subject he felt comfortable with.

"I make dead people look at peace. Like they're taking a nap." He wanted to touch her pigtail and run his fingers along the ridges and play with the blue satin bow tied at the tip.

"Why do dead people have to look good? They're just going inside dirt. Isn't your job just a big waste of time?"

"Paula, be nice!" Margie called from the door.

"What?" Paula said, flashing an annoyed look toward the kitchen. "He preserves people just like pickles in a jar. Like those stuffed elks we saw nailed up in that restaurant in Memphis." Paula grinned extra wide while looking at Val.

"You're right, honey," Val said, laughing with Paula. "Why waste all that good makeup on something you burn. That's like filling a car with gas that you're just going to sell."

Margie quickly came in the room and tightened Paula's belt. She shot Paula a look that could ignite a Riverside fire. The child knew better than to discuss where they were from. "Look," Margie told her. "It's time for you to go to bed."

But the child ignored her mother and scooted closer to Val. "What do you do first? Do you cut open their skulls? Do ya slice apart their skin and fill it with stuffing?"

"Actually, that's taxidermy, a re-creation of the body, using only the dead creature's skin. The first thing we do, is make sure we have the right body."

"Really," Paula said. Her blue eyes got big. She and Val shared an all-knowing smile. "Have you ever been wrong? Have you buried the wrong person? I saw this show once, where a doctor made a mistake and amputated the wrong leg on this man."

Bernard shifted in his seat. He didn't like this part of his job. Reynolds made him swear to never admit any of their faults. But there were plenty of mistakes in the funeral business all the time. Awful mistakes that would shut them down for sure if any of them ever oozed out. Like the time the compression machine broke and all the bodies in the cooler soured and ended up smelling like a tank of bad meat. They had to embalm them in Pine Sol then soak them in soapy cologne. Once they accidentally sawed off a little boy's foot. Reynolds turned away once to talk on the phone and the sawing knife slipped from his hand. He had to go out and buy the boy a pair of boots so the parents didn't discover the truth. Sometimes someone from the L.A. coroner's office came in to take pictures. They were always looking for criminals or for people who went missing. They came in all the time looking for identifying marks or tattoos. They gutted bodies and brought them back in on gurneys with their organs in sloshy black trash bags. Some of those bags opened, got mixed up, or leaked. Dark liquid would spill all over the mortuary floor, and Bernard's rubber apron would get splattered with gunk and many of those organs went back inside the wrong bodies. But the worst mistake of all was when they buried the wrong body. They accidentally got two similar names screwed up. Mr. Reynolds was cremating the wrong one when he realized his mistake. Hurriedly, he cut the machine and pulled the smoldering man out. The flame burned half his body but hadn't eaten the face yet. Reynolds sawed the man's head off and attached it to a body they were cremating that night. Luckily for them the two men had similar builds. Reynolds ran home and yanked one of his own turtlenecks from his drawer to cover the man's sawed off head.

"Has someone ever woken up?" The girl opened her eyes wide. "I saw this movie once, and this dead woman woke up and screamed." The little girl's eyes danced with glee.

"Oh no! That only happens on TV. I've never seen anyone wake from death's heavy nod. It's a quiet job really. There's plenty of people to see, but nobody ever talks back."

"What do you do next?" the girl wanted to know. Her robe opened, and he could see her lace gown and the white milky skin of her calves.

Margie came in and filled Val's wineglass to the brim. Then she yanked Paula's gown down and tightened the knot of her robe. While she was tying it, the girl gave Margie a smirk, and then she stuck out her tongue when Margie went back in the kitchen. Val pinched Paula's pink leg and laughed.

Bernard was so close he could smell the sweet soap on the girl's body. She smelled just like Johnson's Baby Shampoo, the same soap he used on the babies at work.

Bernard leaned a bit closer to her legs.

"Well, let's see, first we strip them, remove all their clothing, inventory any jewelry, and thoroughly wash the body, head to toe, with a specially made germicide soap. We moisturize the face and use baby powder over the skin to give a more pleasing fragrance. We put caps under the lids to keep the eye nice and round, and we use insertion trays for the ones without teeth so there aren't any sunken-in mouths. For babies who have died prematurely, we embalm their bodies, filling them until they're water balloon plump, adding lipstick and blush for a robust appearance. We cap the eyes and stuff the mouth with cotton, keeping the lips parted slightly to create the illusion of sleep."

"How do you make them look so peaceful? They don't die looking like that. I saw a man die, and he had a savage and insane look on his face. How do you make that wild nasty face go away?" The girl made a gory face and started choking her own neck and then fell to the couch like she was dead.

Suddenly, a burning smell floated into the room. They could hear a window open and an oven door bang. "My apple pie!"

Margie screamed. She bought the pie and was heating it up to make it seem homemade, but she was so worried about Paula, and what she might do or say, she'd forgotten about the pie in the oven.

"Val," Margie yelled. "Can you help me a second?" Margie wanted to get Val alone.

The girl scooted over to Bernard as soon as Val left. Her bird-like face was so close to his, she was like a blind person reading his lips. "What do you do to smooth the face to make them seem happy?"

"First we glue down the eyes and suture the mouth shut with a needle and thread, or sometimes we just use adhesive. Super-glue works best. Ever get any on your skin? I have a heck of a time getting that stuff off."

"I got some right here once." The girl licked her thumb. "I had to gnaw on it forever to get it to go away." The girl bit the juicy white meat of her palm.

It made him nervous to see the girl's tiny pink tongue. He thought of Val and felt funny thinking of the girl in that way. He could feel a hot ripening between his thighs and clamped his knees, hoping the feeling would go away.

Bernard coughed in his napkin and looked down at his hands. "We put a stain in the solution, just like the stain in wood. It makes the skin peachy and plump to the touch, just exactly like blood. After we get the faces to look right, we use rose and orange-colored lights to make the dead bodies appear lively."

Margie studied Val's face. Val wore lots of foundation. And almost all of her features were carefully drawn in.

"You must be stealing Bernard's cadaver makeup. Your skin is too flawless and smooth." Margie smiled at the burned crust and kept talking.

"When my Aunt Mildred died she looked better than me. We found her in the basement being nibbled away by strays. Half her face was gone and what was left was a sight, but the morticians worked magic on Aunt Mildred's skin." Margie stared at Val's heavily made up face. "I guess lathering it on thick is the trick."

Val smiled at Margie, taking the insult in stride. "I like to moisturize," she said, fluffing her hair and pursing her lips. "I keep mine nice and subtle." Val said it like she was talking about way more than skin. She rolled her eyes over the burned pie. "I would hate to look baked, like a plate of dried food, left out in the hot burning sun."

Margie eyed Val hard. She walked up to her face. "Listen, honey, just tell me something, huh?" Margie let her eyes roll from Val's feet to her hair. "Does Bernard know, because I peeped your hole from day one? So don't come in here trying to play Miss Prissy with me." Margie tapped her own breasts and slapped her fat behind. "See this? This is real shit, honey." Margie's smile was so wide she showed all her back teeth. "Now, I may be old, with one foot near the grave, and my ass may be big and as wide as Alaska." Margie's face turned as cold as a grave digger's shovel. "But no fake bitch like you will ever get to this realness. For as long as you live," Margie glanced at her watch like it wouldn't be long, "you'll always be a cheap imitation of life. A want-to-be version of a real woman like me."

Val clapped her hands, mocking applause. "Wow, what a trip. I should really be taking notes. I mean, when do I ever get to meet a genuine woman in the flesh. I should have known from your dyed black hair or your body in Bernard's mother's clothes," Val picked up a Marie Calendar pie box in the trash, "or the apple pies you're pretending to bake." Val's voice dropped a whole seven octaves. "So what if you know." She crossed her arms across her rib cage, "I'm not hiding shit, from nobody, okay! But I know someone who is. I wonder if Mr. Fowler knows your real name? Bernard told me some things, and I've been doing some checking. I bet you never even knew Alice Fowler."

"What are you saying? I've known Alice for decades!"

"I saw you make a beeline to Mr. Fowler from the back of the parlor."

"Alice is my friend. I was paying my respect."

"Cut the crap, honey. I had you checked out. You never lived in Texas, and you never knew Alice Hughes." Val grinned like she knew where Margie really was from "You're one bad bitch," she added, "I will give you that. Don't worry, I won't tell Mr. Fowler. No need to get your reinforced panties in a bunch."

"Well of all the nerve. I mean, my word, what exactly are you implying?"

Margie wanted to grab the butcher knife and slice out Val's lung. Instead, she reached for a dish towel and sobbed into the fabric, yelping like a puppy with a paw stuck inside a door.

Val was just bluffing. She didn't know a thing about Margie. If she knew she was dealing with a cold-blooded serial killer, she never would have opened her mouth. But she didn't. All she knew was she made Margie cry.

Val was actually touched. Margie heaved and cried deeply. Val was bluffing about what she knew; hoping Margie would take the bait and tell on herself.

"Please," Margie said, wiping her eyes with the towel. Half of her makeup was rubbed off on one side. She looked much older than she was.

"Alice Fowler helped raise me! She was the only relative I've ever known." Margie choked, trying to stifle her cries. "I'm just a plain ol' single mother from the old dirty South. But you wouldn't know about that. You just want to come in here and judge. Mr. Fowler treats me sweet. He treats me and Paula real nice." Margie covered both cheeks with her trembling palms and wept.

"I'm sorry," Val said. She patted Margie's back. Margie reminded her of her sweet aunt in Phoenix.

Margie was so upset that when she reached for the stack of dinner plates they shook violently in her hands.

"Could you carry these for me, please?" Despair poured out of each word.

"Of course," Val said, taking the plates from her hands.

Margie smiled as soon as Val walked out the door. The ball was already in motion. She wouldn't have to worry about Val much longer. But there was a brief moment in the kitchen when Margie almost dropped her glass. It was when Val lifted the pie box out of the trash. If Val had looked closer in the trash can, she would have noticed a black bottle with a skull and bones symbol for poison.

When Val and Margie returned to the living room, Bernard was describing how fast bodies burn.

"Why do some bodies take so long to burn?" the girl asked.

"Well, large people burn slower because of all the fat in their bodies. We had a man once who took a solid nine hours. You have to burn big people slowly or they could explode or start a grease fire from all the fat stored in their skin."

"What about bad people? Do they take longer to burn, too?" The girl stared at the cross on their living room wall. At her Catholic school, her teachers had been whispering about her lately. She heard words like "damnation" and "glorification" and talk of the indwelling of Satan inside flesh and innocent bodies turning into vessels of sin.

Her math teacher stopped her at lunch and made her utter these words.

"Wretched man that I am! Who will deliver me from the body of this death?"

After rubbing ashes on her forehead, he gave her a cross to take home and told the girl to keep praying for her soul.

With rampant sex scandals all over the news, religious schools took this scourge particularly hard. When small fires started at Paula's school, some thought this was a sign. Many teachers felt uncomfortable or nervous around the kids, and the kids began exerting their power. Faculty and even parents began to feel a haunting and impending doom. And when the art teacher took her life under atrocious accusations, even though the old teachers didn't like her, they began to sympathize with her plight. Some even went so far as to put lilies on her grave hoping the scandal, like a horrible and out of control fire, would not blow any flames their way. And none of them knew what to think of Paula Green. Was she the image of Jesus or some possessed anti-Christ? People were scared of her. They crossed the hall when she passed. The sweater incident spread like wildfire across campus. The story got larger each time it was told, and some said they saw Paula gobble the big girl whole and then spit her out on the lawn. She was pint-sized but walked like a hard metal pipe and was so white she could pass as a saint or a ghost but no one could ever decide on which. One kid claimed, he saw the word "*hell*" spelled in a vein along her calf, but nobody dared to get close enough to check.

Val delicately placed each plate on the table. But when she got to Paula, Val dropped her plate on the ground and it cracked right in half like two blue perfect moons.

"Oh, I'm so sorry. It just slipped right out of my hand." Val looked at her fingers, which were trembling a little. She sat down and placed both hands under her thighs.

"Are you all right?" Bernard looked at Val's face. She looked like she was tying to focus.

"I'm fine, just clumsy today." Val gave everyone a tired sheepish smile, but when she looked at their faces, all of them looked blurry and it felt like she couldn't get her face muscles to work.

"I don't like hearing about cremation. That goes against God. How can people just burn their loved ones in ovens?" Margie shook her head in disgust.

Placing a large juicy roast in the middle of the table, Margie heavily sat down, and the hickory smoke smell filled the room.

"I want a big funeral. Bury me in a pretty cemetery where I can see. I want everything peaceful and green. All of my kin were put down in the sweet ground of Memphis. That's where I was born and raised, and that's where I plan to die." Margie looked at Bernard quickly, hoping he didn't catch this infraction. She'd told him she was from Texas when they arrived. She kept talking fast hoping to hide this mistake. "Cremation is for the poor who can't afford to buy land or for fools who don't have sense to lay their folks out proper."

"Not anymore. Cremation is on the rise. Half the people who die are cremated now. It doesn't have the same stigma it once did."

Margie scowled in her drink. "I don't like burning bodies, and I discussed this with your father and he's not keen on it either. He wants a big service with lots of gladiolas."

Val could hear but couldn't get her thick tongue to work. Why would Margie be discussing Mr. Fowler's demise? She looked at Bernard, but he didn't catch the remark. He was too busy listening to Paula.

"What's the big deal?" Paula asked. "Who cares if you're burned?" Paula liked fire. She wasn't afraid of it at all.

"It's wrong. Cremation is a abomination. Ask your father, Bernard. He agrees with me on this. No good Catholic would ever consider flames."

Bernard looked at Margie. He missed what she said. He was watching the way the curls danced over Paula's shoulders.

"I saw this TV show once where these tribe people built piles. They laid the dead person on all these tall wooden slats and then torched it while everybody stood there and cheered." Paula looked gleeful. Her brilliant eyes sparkled.

"That's a suttee," Bernard said. "It's an old Hindu custom."

Margie belched in her hand. She hated this discussion. "I saw that show. The whole thing made me sick. Especially the women! My God, were they dumb! I couldn't believe what this fool woman did! She ran up and jumped right in the mouth of the flames, just to show her devotion to her husband."

Val raised her glass and clinked it with Margie. "No woman I know would ever do a stupid thing like that!" Val felt woozy but was glad her thick tongue still worked. She was too tired to fight Margie and happy to have reached some kind of truce.

"What about babies?" Paula asked. "Have you ever embalmed them?"

"Paula!" Margie said, cupping her mouth with her hand.

"I've handled four-month-old infants and one-hundred-year-old men and everything else in between. I've done parrots and dogs and thick, giant pigs. There's a pet cemetery running along the rim of the premises. Everything you can name is buried in there."

"How do you do dead babies?" The girl asked again, daring her mother to speak.

"Same as if they were living," Bernard said, matter-of-factly. "We wash them in Johnson & Johnson, using a soft brush for their hair. We massage the body with an emollient, and moisturizing cream, and we sprinkle them with baby powder and deodorizers for fragrance. For babies who've died prematurely, we over-embalm their bodies, plumping them up with lots of pink, orangey fluid to make their coloring more robust and alive. We apply a cosmetic cream to smooth their skin and cover any blemishes. We use lipstick and blush for a healthy appearance and then stuff their mouths with cotton, leaving their lips slightly ajar, to keep a sweet peaceful expression of sleep on their face."

Paula had seen a dead baby once. Margie poisoned a Detroit man by tampering with his milk. But the man had given the milk to his infant son, too, and Paula watched the baby turn blue. Margie bought a baby casket fitted with glass, with a window for the little baby to be viewed. The baby's dull skin wasn't blue anymore and was back to his original peaches and cream.

"The face is the focal point in a viewing. The mouth and its expression are very important. It determines the way we relate to casketed bodies. All human remains, that are going to be viewed, are sewn shut or glued and then thoroughly waxed.

"Is that when you put the Superglue on?"

"Actually, some embalmers swear by that substance. But I'm a bit old-fashioned. I like needle and thread. Catgut's the best. It holds skin nice and taut, and wax prevents cracking or flakes.

"Okay, that's enough." Margie was done with this subject. "Let's eat before dinner gets cold."

Margie placed sliced pieces of roast on each plate. The undercooked meat bled and swam in a small lake of red.

Bernard looked at the meat, bringing his napkin to his nose.

He hadn't been able to eat red meat since he started working for Reynolds. Just looking at this flesh turned his stomach.

"I'm sorry," Bernard blurted. "I don't eat meat anymore"

Margie eyed him suspiciously, but took the slab off his plate. "My daddy said a man who don't eat meat or taste whiskey, is not any kind of man at all."

Val's appetite was vast, but she barely touched anything tonight. All she did was swallow her burgundy wine and slink way back in her chair.

"What do you do if a dead person is so beaten or messed up, you can't even tell who they are?" The little girl was sitting so close to Bernard, she was almost inside his lap.

"Well, there's dental records, and sometimes we get DNA scans. Once we figured out who a dead woman was by her breast implant serial numbers."

Margie looked down, admiring her own chest. "Well, they wouldn't find any serial numbers on these." Margie elbowed Val's perfectly, sculpted pair. "Ah, to be young. Do yours have serial numbers, too?"

Val coughed. She was struggling to focus on Margie's face.

Bernard missed the dig and kept talking to the child. "DNA tells you everything. Whether you're a woman or man. Your race and your age, everything is stored in your cells," Bernard said.

"Look, I think we heard all we need on this subject." Margie sliced more meat on her plate.

Val was sizzling. She started fanning herself. "It's sweltering! Doesn't anyone else feel hot?" Val got up and stood by the window.

Margie smiled at Val while munching her salad. She thought of the empty poison bottle asleep in the trash.

Bernard mildly smiled back.

"Do you study history?" Bernard asked the girl.

"Of course," Paula said proudly. "Come on," the girl begged. "Ask me anything you want to know."

"Who was the eleventh president?"

"Abraham Lincoln," the girl shot back.

"Did you know Lincoln's embalming was the reason we have the kind of funerals today. People used to die at home in their beds and got laid out in plots in the back of their house. But after Lincoln's death, an embalmer preserved him so well that when they exhumed his body about twenty years later, Lincoln still was perfectly intact. Except for one thing." Bernard bit the salad off his fork.

"What?" the girl asked, her blue eyes searching his.

"Lincoln's skin turned a tar black."

The girl and her mother both exchanged looks.

"Paula," Margie said. "It's time for you to go to bed."

"I don't want to go to bed." the girl pouted. "I want to stay up."

"Remember, you're punished." Margie reminded her sharply. "Have some ice cream but take it to your room on a tray." Margie sloshed more fluid inside of Val's glass, as Paula glumly walked back to her room.

After a few minutes, Margie went inside Paula's room. Her bed was filled with old junk. An empty pillowcase lay by her toes.

"What is all this stuff? Where did you get it?"

Annoyed, Paula refused to look at her mother. She tried to cover the contents on the bed with her body. "It's nothing. Just some little things I found."

Margie came over to examine the bed's contents herself. Sticking out from under the child were lots of old-fashioned toys. There were silver metal planes, tins full of old games, a silver cap gun and a real sheriff's badge. Mr. Fowler had given her these things out of Bernard's room.

But sparkling alone across the bedspread was a pair of diamond men's cuff links. The diamonds had small emerald stones circling around. They looked like they cost fifteen grand. "Who gave that to you? Those look expensive."

Paula's eyes rolled to the loaded cap gun.

Margie snatched the gold cuff links and turned toward the door.

"Stop!" The child screamed, pointing the cap gun at Margie's chest.

Margie knocked the gun across the room to the floor. She pushed past the child, heaving her husky body through the door. She hated to confront the child. She was getting harder to control. But the last thing she wanted was trouble at her door now. She couldn't give Bernard's father a reason to put them out. Not now, not before she finished this con. There was no place to go. There was nothing left except the ocean, and neither of them knew how to swim.

"Not for no got damn cuff links," she mumbled to herself. She held the cuff links so tight in her hand that her inner palm turned into slime.

The child leaped from the bed and tried to snatch Margie's arm, but Margie was strong and wrenched her arm free.

Margie was determined. The last incident started like this. The child plucked a wallet from the Jiffy Lube man. That man chased Margie and the girl all across Nevada. Next thing Margie knew they were racing for the state line. She was not going to stand here and let it happen again.

"Nobody in their right mind gives away gold diamond cuff links. I'm sure it must be some mistake."

"Nooooo!" The girl screamed, chasing after her mother. "Give them back, I said! He did let me have them!" She tried to pry the cuff links from her mother's tightly balled hand. "Give them back! I told you they're mine!"

Margie lurched from the girl, pushing past her body, heading for the living room's arch.

Bernard and Val heard them pushing and screaming and exchanged worried glances.

The girl flew past her mother and blocked Margie's path.

"Give them back to me or I won't let you pass." Paula held both walls with her thin outstretched arms.

Margie grabbed Paula's wrist and twisted it hard until the burn made Paula's eyes tear, and she let her break through. Margie hated to hurt her child, but she had to be sure. If the girl took Mr. Fowler's things, he'd surely kick them out. The father originally hired Margie to clean their apartment. Cleaning people had to be honest. They had to be trusted. People tested you by leaving a few bills hanging out, or maybe they'd leave an expensive ring on a counter, wanting to see if you'd take it. People needed to see if you could work around nice stuff and not rob them. That's why it was important to give this right back. Bernard's father knew Margie was shady but thought she was honest with him. That's how cons worked. They dismantled their subjects. People began to feel safe, and they let their guards down. That was the best time to take them.

Margie could see hot venom spilling from the girl's eyes.

"I'll tell," the girl said.

Margie stopped in her tracks. Real fear was etched across Margie's face.

"I'll tell them everything." The girl slightly lifted the ruffle on her gown. She was speaking to her mother in a serious and much deeper tone.

Margie turned and stared into the girl's steel blue eyes. She could see she wasn't playing. This was no idle threat. The girl lifted the peach frock farther up her thin thigh.

This was too much for Margie. She rushed toward her daughter and yanked her nightgown down hard. The girl smiled and opened her tiny pink palm and Margie placed the cuff links inside.

Abruptly, the girl turned and went back into her room, slamming the door loud and tossing the cuff links on the bed.

Bernard glanced at the girl's closed door and gloomily moved his pie around with his fork.

For the moment the girl's door was open, Val had looked inside. The girl's room looked cool. There was a chair next to her bed. Val felt dizzy and was really burning up inside, she wanted to try to calm down.

"Can I read her a story?" Val stumbled to the girl's door. She was trying to stand straight, but the floor kept on moving and floated under her toes like a boat.

"Sure," Margie said, following Val. "Now make sure you stay all the way under the covers," she told Paula. Margie clicked off the overhead light and turned on a soft pink-toned lamp. "There, that's much better," she said.

Val immediately flopped in a chair by the bed. She couldn't read the type in the book, her eyes were so blurry. She tried to say something to the child, but her lips wouldn't move.

Paula was under the covers watching Val's eyes flutter in the chair.

"Thank you for the book," Paula said.

Val tried to raise her hand, but it was too heavy to lift, like rigor mortis had seized all her limbs.

"Want to know a secret?" Paula sat up and asked Val.

Val's head shifted unconsciously back and forth as Paula talked. She looked like she was having a bad dream.

The girl got out of bed and pulled out an old box of clothes. Val tried to look at the box, but she couldn't move her neck or use any of her muscles to speak. She could hear wild music coming from the next room. She tried to move her legs, but her knees wouldn't budge. The next thing she knew, the room went black.

"So," Margie said, plopping back on the couch. She threw one large arm over Bernard's hunching shoulder. "Let's talk about something a little less morbid, okay?" Margie wanted the bank account information from Bernard. She had searched the house frantically but couldn't find anything that made sense. Then one day while sprucing up Bernard's father's room, she found a sole silver key under the base of a lamp. The key had a number stamped on one side. It was the number to a safe deposit vault. Margie frantically searched the house whenever she had a chance to be inside.

They had to have a bank statement or something that told where this safe deposit vault was.

Bernard was annoyed. There was never any Howard Hughes money. And if there was, his father had probably blown it at the track, since money only served to burn a hole in his pocket. Bernard didn't like being alone in the living room with Margie. She looked like she could suck out his blood. He removed her warm arm from the back of his neck. The apartment was sweltering, especially for November. The heater must be set all the way on high. Bernard liked to keep his place at a cool fifty-nine. Anything warmer than seventy felt scalding.

And so, the rest of the evening was doomed for Bernard. He checked on Val, but she was totally knocked out cold in a chair. He tried to call her name and move her head back and forth, but she barely fluttered her lids.

"Let her sleep," Margie said, closing the door to Paula's room. "Poor thing just needs some rest."

Margie thought Paula was asleep, but she was hiding under her sheet. She was holding the survival book Val brought and studying her face for any kind of movement.

Bernard was worried about Val, but she looked so peaceful and serene that he let Margie grab his hand and lead him out from the room. He watched the glowing light creep from underneath the girl's door, and there were no more shadowy feet under the slot.

And now Val wasn't here to take the edge off the evening. And the girl went to bed so there weren't any more questions. He was alone and all he wanted to do was go home. He loathed being here with Margie! She had a mean scary laugh. She danced suggestively, and to make matters worse, she played loud music and drank, gulping straight from the bottle until the booze oozed out of her pores. Her cackling laughter made his tender ears pound. She danced wildly, shoving her breasts in his face and shaking them both with such force and such vehement need that they sloshed like big bags stuffed with warm melted cheese. Her stretched-out knit dress rose over each kneecap, and there was no hint of a girdle or slip. She danced barefoot with a dizzy and frantic abandon as her feet ate the burgundy shag. She grabbed Bernard's hand, pulling him close to her chest. Her whole fleshy frame was smashed against his. He smelled her stale perfume, and her drenched-in-sweat back. He jerked his hand away when he touched it. Bernard tried to break free, but Margie was big boned and strong.

"Come on!" she begged. "Shake a tail feather, Bernard. I know you can dance if you're anything like your father."

Bernard heard Margie and his dad dancing together all the time. They did it in his father's room with the door gaping wide. Bernard clutched his hands over both of his ears when they did, but Sam Cooke still leaked into both his palms and he heard the wheelchair roll and skid or suddenly brake. Margie would stomp her flat feet so hard the house shook like a 6.4 quake.

His father was completely changed. He'd become a lovesick buffoon. He was almost a cartoon character of his former self. As his father's affection grew, Margie matched him in size. She was as slimy as an open can of sardines. But his father didn't see this saccharine role as an act. When she bought him small things from the 99-cent store, it was as if she'd spent five thousand dollars. She got more and more dolled up for their dates, wearing things straight from Alice's closet. She kissed him right in the street, holding both his cheeks in her hands. She called him pet names like Boogaloo and Sugar Toes and Dr. Good Love, but mostly she just called him Daddy. Mr. Fowler would just glow rolling along in his chair. He thought each little name proved her undying love. He started getting into the habit of referring to Margie as Alice, and Margie never corrected him once. He began wearing his wedding band again and started sporting suit coats with fresh boutonnieres cut from the yard. And when they went down the street together, overly dressed for L.A., they looked like two aging teens going off to the prom.

Their affair became the talk of the neighborhood. Margie looked like Marilyn Monroe twenty years past her prime and left on the stove way too long. Mr. Fowler rolled along, wearing suits and dark shades, looking like an old, injured James Bond.

Mr. Wade shook his head whenever he saw them. He raked the last leaves of November inside the trash by the curb. He snapped some dead branches across one of his thighs. He thought Fowler was a fool and that anyone living could see, but old fools rarely admitted the truth. They kept standing like trees in a lumberjack-filled forest, pretending to not see the ax.

Corleen assumed Mr. Fowler was vexed. She told everyone she saw that Margie was a vintage voodoo priestess. She saw Margie holding a Barbie, pitted with marks and said they were put there by all sorts of hot stabbing pins just like those voodoo dolls she'd seen in New Orleans. She told them Margie had special powers from wearing dead people's clothes, and that she put a Love Jones on ol' Mr. Fowler's poor soul, using ointments and rosebuds she got from his yard.

All the neighbors had similar stories of their own. Everyone had an aunt or some wild crazy cousin who became lost in some woman or man's hungry eyes. None of them could see the storm waiting for them around the corner, ready to pour on their weak, lovesick minds. These stories had been around since the beginning. Since Adam and Eve. They'd sloshed around since Noah but sounded original each time. People listened because almost everyone could relate to its core where once the sick tale was about them.

But nobody had ever seen someone flip as fast as Mr. Fowler. Mr. Fowler used to wheel around with his jaw jutted out, with a scowl and never a kind word to save a soul. Now he smiled and tipped his hat whenever he passed and would often stop and buy treats from the ice-cream truck man, taking them home to that strange kid they kept locked inside.

Bernard witnessed this transformation firsthand. His father was a man who used to bitch as if it were a sport. He used to lay around unkempt and spit in a cup by his bed. But now he sat on the porch with his arm around Margie, drinking green-leafed mint juleps in the November freeze with one leg carved off at the knee. He saw them laying in bed, with Margie in her slip and his father wearing his perfectly pressed pajama bottoms with a satisfied look on his face as the television blazed in front of his glazed eyes.

Margie would smile at him too. "Good night, son," she'd say cheerily. She was wearing his mother's sky blue, see-through peignoir, and he could see all the ripples in her skin.

All of this tore through his mind as Margie gripped Bernard's shoulders and the radio gargled in static.

Bernard wanted to leave, and it was getting harder to breathe. Half his face was buried against Margie's wet cheek, and even with his back arched to keep her frame off his body, she was still close enough to make him feel nauseous.

Bernard glanced toward the couch and noticed Val's purse.

Suddenly he felt worried. Was Val really okay? He decided to go check on her himself and tell her it was time to get going. In an effort to break free, Bernard burst from her arms. But Margie grabbed him again, and he had to squirm from her wrist, kicking the radio over in his efforts.

He grabbed his jacket from the couch where it was carelessly thrown. He snatched his inhaler, spraying it deep toward his tonsils and took a blast of the air into his lungs. He felt sick. He told Margie they had to leave. It was already late. In two seconds he was holding the handle to Paula's bedroom door.

"Wait," Margie screamed. "Don't wake her up!"

But Bernard was inside the room, scrambling to find the switch and flooding the girl's room with light.

15

Bernard and Val

Later that night Bernard peeked in on his father after laying Val on the couch. His father's eyes were bloodshot. He shook like a leaf. He was laying on the floor, out of his chair. "Don't leave me. Don't leave me alone with those people." His father's enormous shoulders shuttered from the thought. He cried like he could never be consoled, like some of the people who came in to see Mr. Reynolds.

Bernard watched his old man with a pair of new eyes. Lying on the floor looking at his dad through his wheelchair spokes made his father look so vulnerable and old.

"Dad, did you fall? Are you feeling sick?" Slowly, Bernard lifted him up. Rubbing his poor father's shoulders, he tried to soothe the old man's fear.

"It's all right, son." Bernard couldn't believe his father's response. His father was shaking, and tears streamed down his face. In all his life, his father never revealed anything but pride or anger and righteous contempt.

His father still shook from tears as Bernard wheeled him to his room. Bernard put a clean change of clothes neatly across his bed and then brushed his white hair in the quiet of the mirror. Before Bernard would have hated this task, but today he did it lovingly, letting the brush run through each strand.

His father was almost asleep when he suddenly grabbed Bernard's hand.

"Son," he rasped, his age-spotted hand gripping Bernard's wrist. "I'm so glad you're here." His eyes drifted shut and then burst open wide. "There's something evil in this house, and I let it in." His hand fell to the bed, and he started to weep. Bernard watched his father's lips quivering in fear. There was nothing worse than seeing him crying like this.

"What evil, Dad? What are you talking about?"

Mr. Fowler handed Bernard a story from the *Los Angeles Times*. It had been torn from the front page last week.

"Read this," he said, handing Bernard the article. It shook in his hand like a December leaf.

It was a story about a vicious serial killer, but before Bernard could finish, Margie entered the room and plucked the story out of his hand.

"Oh my goodness, I was looking all over for that!" she said. "Your father's been so sweet clipping these articles for me." She bent down and kissed Mr. Fowler's white cheek. "Thanks, honey, I can't wait to read this juicy one. You know how I love the macabre." Margie kissed his forehead and swished her hips out of the room.

Mr. Fowler looked down. He was completely defeated. He had dry mouth and difficulty swallowing and breathing, his one eye was loose and wouldn't stop drooping, and now he had a bad bout of double vision and an acute high-pitched ringing in his ears. But he refused to admit to anyone he was sick. Sickness was a dead sign of weakness.

Mr. Fowler saw two versions of his son standing in his room and spoke to the one closest to his chair. But when he tried to talk, his dentures felt glued together.

"I did yit. Lookaaaa." He tried to make his mouth work, but he was slurring his words. He tried to lift his left hand, to show off his ring but he couldn't get his muscles to move. All he could do was flick his wrist slightly, and the ring caught the light from the soft lamp and gleamed.

"That's your wedding band, Dad. It's okay if you wear it." His father looked grief-stricken and filled with regret. "Don't beat yourself up. Mom probably thinks it's nice that you have it on again."

Bernard's father wept bitterly. His body shook from the effort. "You dooooon unnerstan. I diyit today."

"Did what? You're not making any kind of sense." Whatever it was his father had done radically changed his spirit. He looked like he'd seen Satan himself.

Then his father seized up and his sockets got big and his dentures dropped right out of his mouth. Bernard started to put him to bed, but he heard Val sighing on the couch so instead he wrapped a blanket around his dad's shoulders and gently closed the door.

"I'll be back," Bernard whispered low.

If he had looked behind the door, he would have seen Margie there. She had a cord in her hand just in case Bernard had any ideas. She took the article from her pocket and picked up Mr. Fowler's lighter and burned the newsprint in the ashtray next to his bed. She watched her face, which was buried at the end of the story, burning slow in the mouth of the flame.

She came up to Mr. Fowler's face and kissed his soft cheek. "It won't be long now, honey," she said to him and left.

If Bernard had stayed in his father's room, he wouldn't have missed his last words. They leaked from his tongue like a funeral hymn, haunting and heavy with despair. And though his other words were slurred, these three were crystal clear.

"I married Margie," he said.

Just the thought of it made him sizzle in his chair. He was burning and something was seizing his throat. He tried to kick, but his leg muscles were stiff. Only the fatty stump twitched in the chair. The poison worked its way from his toes to his scalp, and he felt like his skin blazed with fiery steam, like he was cooking from the inside out.

Drastically, the wheelchair tipped over on its side and he was trapped under the heavy metal spokes and the bed.

"Honey, I'm home," Margie whispered to Mr. Fowler. She kicked his chair and watched him writhe on the floor and then covered his mouth with both hands.

Margie closed the door and waddled down the hall. She was whistling when she saw Bernard and Val on the couch. Margie wasn't worried about either of them. Val would be dead before the sun came back out, and Bernard would be as easy to kill as a gnat on a sleeve. Margie happily went back upstairs.

16

Bernard and Paula

Val was groggy and hadn't fully woken up. Bernard kept checking her temperature and applying compresses on her face.

The girl had to climb a magnolia branch just to see all the way in his house.

She edged her slim body along the branch near Bernard's window. A row of dense ivy rimmed the trunk. Some of the ivy had crept up and the tree's leaves and scratched the girl's naked ankles.

The girl inched toward the window. Her small hands clutched the bark. She was so close to the window's glow, the light illuminated her skin. She was tilting her head up to look through the frame when Bernard burst out the back door. The girl was so shocked she let go of her hands and immediately dropped to the ground. She laid flat in the dense sea of green, waxy ivy. The dark leaves covered the girl's entire body. A beetle crawled next to her arm.

"Damn it!" Bernard said, putting something burnt on the steps. The rancid smell filled the girl's nostrils. He had not heard her fall because of the noise his screen door made when he came from the house. But Bernard's frown turned to a smile as he looked at the plants. The jasmine was blooming, the thick scent hypnotic. Bernard took a deep breath inhaling the scent. His long-sleeved dress shirt was completely unbuttoned revealing a forest of gray bushy hair.

The girl stared at his legs and his black low-cut socks. He was standing so close she could hear his deep breathing and the gravelly sound of his lungs.

Bernard stood up and turned on the hose. The girl watched him rinse the black bottom of the pot. He left the pot out on the stairs. She watched him roll the hose into a spiraling wad. He wiped his wet hands on the back of his pants before going back up the ramp.

The girl slowly rose from the foliage again. The ivy's wet leaves had splashed in her face. She lifted her dress until her white panties showed; they gleamed in the beam of the moon.

She heard Bernard's door close, so she crept up the ramp toward the rear window again when a light clicked on in the bathroom. The girl saw a shadow appear near the frame. But the bathroom light clicked off and the living room light clicked on so she inched her back along the cold stucco wall until her eyes reached the living room window. She saw the back of the woman. Her head was hunched down. Bernard was rummaging through a vast cosmetic chest. The black chest was trimmed with hard silver corners with a heavy metal handle drilled in the top. The case held the most unimaginable colors. Stunning fluorescents, multiple pastels, shimmering powders flecked with silver and gold. Bernard dabbed her face and applied some more lipstick. He powdered her shimmering nose. When Bernard called the woman's name, her thin body stayed still, like her frame had turned into stone.

"Val," Bernard called the woman again. Bernard studied the contents of her makeup case as he eyed himself in the mirror. He adjusted her hair and puckered her lips once before taking out a wand and applying more blush.

The girl watched with large eyes. Val was really something. She looked like a groomed poodle fresh from the shop and was breathing just as fast and as hard.

The girl moved her face closer to the large picture window in the front so she could see Val's face a lot better. The window was high. The girl glanced around the street. The sun was long gone and the street was pitch black. Nobody was out this late but crooks. The window was hard to see even standing on tiptoe and in boots, and her tiny legs began to grow weak. Squinting, the girl scanned the front yard. She saw an old mangled chair in a trash can across the street. She ran across just as a car sped by, and the driver had to zag and madly honked his horn. The girl waited to see if anyone came outside before bringing the chair back to the window. Placing both her feet on its seat, her heart pounded in both ears. She leaned close to the pane, taking her binoculars out and putting the twin lenses to her eyes. She could see the fireplace going, and a purse was on the floor. There was a cabinet and a chair and a large purple couch where the girl saw a dangling foot. She followed the foot all the way up to a neck and saw Val's beautiful face lying there.

Val's' face was amazing. Like an actress in a play. She was lying on the couch, perfectly straight, like a mannequin that had fallen down in a store. Her crimson mouth was such a deep bloody red it looked like juicy pomegranate seeds. Her eyelashes looked like an umbrella of black lace, hovering over a rainbow of eye-shadowed lids. She looked happy. Her dress sparkled with colorful sequins, and the flame blinked in each piece until her entire body twinkled like a Beverly Hills jewelry store.

The girl couldn't hear a thing. It was like watching an old silent movie or setting the television on mute. But then suddenly, Bernard pushed open a window on the side, and his voice boomed out to the trees.

"I hate using those horrible microwave bags. I always end up burning them."

He was unconsciously twisting and squeezing a sponge. A pool of water formed by his shoes.

Bernard smiled, revealing a row of cleanly brushed teeth. He looked guilty and wore a crooked grin on his face. He'd already kissed Val half a dozen times, and if he had any hair left on his sparkling head, it would have looked tossed and disheveled from rolling around with her on the couch.

"I shouldn't eat the stuff. Popcorn's the worst. I always get it stuck in my molars." With the burned pot of popcorn left in the yard, a new warm batch sat in his lap.

Bernard tried to put some popcorn inside Val's mouth but the lone kernel fell to the floor. There was a little moisture forming in the corner of her lips. Bernard dabbed her mouth with a hankie. He re-outlined her lips and filled in more color from the makeup case on the floor. He was so happy to be alone with Val again, and though his father was asleep in the very next room, he was so excited his heart almost burst from his chest.

The little girl stared with quiet amazement. Bernard looked so funny. His face was hypnotic. He shook Val's foot, but she never blinked. He slid his knees under his thighs and let Val's head roll in his lap. The giant cosmetic case lay at his feet.

"I like my job," Bernard said. He looked in the case again and took out a charcoal pencil and skillfully ached both her brows. "I love creating. Bringing out the best qualities in people. It's kinda like portrait painting, I guess." He bit his own lip and stroked the back of his bald head, which glowed under the dim lamp like a pumpkin.

Paula studied Bernard for a very long time. He looked sneaky, like a kid who had gotten away with something bad, like a boy getting caught playing with dolls.

He was explaining things to Val as if she were his toy.

"Bodies are ninety percent fluids, you know. If you don't embalm them soon, you'll end up with a mess. There's this funeral parlor being investigated right now. The place was tanking from bills. The owner was buried in debt, so the funeral owner decided to skimp on some of the cost. He stopped embalming and cut all refrigeration. But that's how the funeral owner got caught. People started getting sick at the services he held. One minister passed out cold on the altar. Lots of pallbearers complained, saying they heard sloshing inside the caskets as they carried them from the chapel."

Bernard poured more champagne into Val's glass. He raised her limp head and spilled some into her mouth, but the small drops slid down her chin.

The girl listened intently. Her teeth were chattering in her head. But as her morbid curiosity thrived, so did her worry. Why wasn't Val waking up? Why did she look so sick? She had a whole lot of colorful makeup on her face, but she still looked as pale as a zombie.

Bernard let his thumb roam over Val's mouth. "You're so lovely. So well put together. I admire how you keep yourself up." Bernard lifted Val up to his chest, but her body was so limp she immediately fell back down.

Bernard buried his lips inside her neck, but Val didn't respond. Her lips looked more and more moist.

Bernard unbuttoned Val's coat and folded it neatly, draping it on the back of a chair. Her torpedo breasts tugged her form-fitting dress. Turning his head over his shoulder, as if wondering if someone was watching, he touched her, rubbing his hands across her chest. He turned her around, unzipped her dress and fingered her perfectly shaped breasts.

Bernard moaned. He felt such desire in his loins. He kissed Val hungrily. She tasted like wine. Her smeared lipstick had the faint hint of dark red bing cherries. He let his mouth take each nipple and roll it around his tongue. He was about to run his hand along her perfectly bare thigh but stopped when he heard something outside.

A mosquito bit deep into one of Paula's taut calves. She lost her balance and fell flat against the glass.

Bernard leaped at the noise. He walked to the window. He leaned close to the pane and stared at the dark for a very long time. But it was so light in his house and so black outside, he couldn't see the girl lying at the ledge. Bernard turned around and went back to the couch.

"Must be one of those nasty possums. They always come out on trash day."

Val's hand slightly quivered. She tried to raise her eyes. It felt like a giant weight was holding her down and something awful was digging a hole in her gut.

"Don't worry. I've got traps all over the yard and gallons of sweet-smelling poison."

Bernard pressed his lips against the back of Val's neck. He shook her head slightly, but she didn't respond. Squeezing her back against his, he slowly raised her up.

"You're so perfect," he whispered, touching her aqua lace bra. He brought his nose to the center of her chest and ran his tongue along the length of her cleavage. He roamed along her neck until his teeth reached her ear, sucking the cubic zirconium stud in her lobe.

Bernard was astonished at how wonderfully warm her limbs felt. He was only used to the cold, dead fish, skin of a corpse. But Val was sizzling. She felt as hot as a stove, and he burned inside just being beside her.

If he'd taken her temperature, he would have seen she was sick. Her fever reached astronomical heights as the poison wreaked havoc in her body.

Paula watched wide-eyed. She pressed her face against the pane. Val didn't look right, even with all the cosmetics Bernard painted on. Her skin looked ashen, her eyes rolled inside her head, and a puddle of drool formed at the side of her mouth. Paula sucked her pink bottom lip hard. Her breath made small-fist-sized clouds on the glass. She stood rigid, balancing her tiny, dime-sized feet. Her fingers made greasy prints on the pane.

"Paula!" Margie screamed. "Come take out this trash!"

Paula left the front window and raced up the steps. She wanted to get in before Margie caught her outside. Grabbing the trash bag out of the plastic kitchen bucket, she hurried back down the steps again. But in her haste, she snagged the trash against a thorny rosebush and the bag burst over the walkway.

Paula hurriedly tried to put all the items back inside. Slimy cans of corn, bloody pieces of meat, coffee grinds, orange peels, empty liquor bottles, and a bunch of nasty, used napkins. When her hand went to pick up a moist napkin ball, a round cylinder fit in her hand. Paula unrolled the napkin and saw a black plastic bottle. A skull and bones smiled in her face. Poison! Her mother had poisoned somebody! Paula had seen Margie use this bottle before. The last time she saw a bottle like this, she saw a lady and her husband lying in bed almost green and her mother digging in their pockets for cash.

But who did her mother poison? Who recently died? An instant realization flashed across Paula's mind. Val! Her mother poisoned Val. That's why Val's face looked so gray and her eyes were half-mooned crescents.

Paula dropped the trash and snuck back up her steps. Her mother was in the kitchen drying off the dishes. Paula crept inside her room and picked up the survival book off her bed, clutching it close to her chest. Maybe the book said something about how to save Val. She snuck out of the house and ran up the ramp and gently knocked on Bernard's door.

Bernard panicked! He immediately dropped Val's skull and it bounced up and down on the couch. Bernard tiptoed to the back to see who it was. He looked out the peephole, but no one was there. Then a tiny voice said. "Help, open up now! That lady is dying in there!"

Bernard opened the door and let Paula in. The girl raced past his legs and went straight to the couch where Val was laying.

"Hey, wait a minute, what are you doing? Does your mother know you're here?"

The girl violently shook Val's shoulders, but she didn't wake up and her head rolled back over the pillow when she let go.

"Hey, wait a minute. Stop shaking her, you're going to wake her up." Bernard went over to the girl and pulled back her arm.

"She's not sleeping," Paula screamed, wrenching her arm from Bernard's and shaking Val's head again. "She's dying! She drank poison from my mother!"

"What are you saying?" Bernard looked at Val. She had a gentle smile on her face. Her lips were relaxed as if she'd peacefully fallen asleep. "Val's just tired. She's been working long hours lately. She's not dying; don't get so excited. She's probably just resting her eyes."

Just then, Val's irises disappeared inside her head. Both eyeballs turned to eggshells; they were completely white and smooth, like Val was trying to read something written deep inside her brain.

"She's been poisoned! I've seen this before. First, your eyes roll and then your mouth starts to make bubbles and then you get hot and stop breathing for good."

Paula's tiny head hovered over Val's painted lips.

"See," the girl said. Her lips almost touched Val's teeth. "She's starting to make baby bubbles already."

Bernard looked at Val's mouth. It was starting to froth.

"And look at this!" The girl said proudly, opening her hand. A Jolly Roger skull and crossbones smiled on the vial in her hand.

"Where did you get this?" Bernard snatched the bottle. He thought it was the poison bottle from his garage.

"What did you do?" Bernard towered over the child. Their shadows cast giant black pictures on the wall and made Bernard look seven feet tall.

Paula took a step back. She was right in front of the raging fire. Her spine grew immediately warm from the flame, which leaped like it wanted to taste the small ruffle on her dress.

He was about to shake the girl's shoulders but stopped. He heard his back door open and close and the sound of feet coming down the hall.

Her shadow appeared first like a gruesome enlarged rat groveling along the wall and the ceiling.

"Hello, everybody. Oh, is Val still sleep? Poor dear must be awfully exhausted," Margie smiled to the girl. "Oh, here you are, honey. Come on home now. I have some chocolate milk on the stove. I'm sure Bernard wants to be alone with Val." Margie gave Bernard an all-knowing wink.

Paula vehemently protested but Margie held her tight. "There, there, dear, no need to get so excited. I told you not to eat any of that old Halloween candy."

Bernard watched Paula leave under the firm arm of her mother.

"Call 911," Paula tried to scream. But Margie placed her hand over the girl's lips before she got the words out and dragged her polished shoes back upstairs to their apartment.

Bernard looked at Val. Maybe she really wasn't well. He opened the Boy Scout book and started reading while Val slept. He came to the part on insect wounds and snakebites and how to survive various kinds of poisons. Bernard read a list of the symptoms. Muscle spasms, lockjaw, frothing of the mouth. Bernard watched the bubbles increase between Val's painted lips. Maybe the girl was right. How could he afford to take a chance? One of the rescue suggestions was to get the person to purge. Bernard got a big wooden spoon from the kitchen. He went to the back porch and came back with an empty bucket and shoved the spoon all the way down Val's throat.

17

Val

After the poisoning incident, Val's front tooth became loose. It started with a small spot and got progressively worse. Roy made her swear never to see Bernard again. He made her promise on a Bible and a picture of the Virgin Mary to leave that whole freaky family alone.

Val wouldn't return any of Bernard's phone calls or any of his notes. He contacted her all the time to see how she was doing. Even when he wrote about the funeral of his father. Though it hurt really bad to see Bernard suffer, Val continued to ignore all his calls. The truth was Val was suffering, too. She missed Bernard and kept staring at his picture under her pillow. It was the family shot from Alice Fowler's obituary.

Val had never met someone so mild-mannered and kind. He was adorable and sweet, not to mention he had saved her life. Though when the doctors pumped her stomach, they found no traces of poison. But Roy told her some poisons were impossible to detect. Val knew something happened to her body right after being at Margie's, and she hated the fact that Margie was still on the loose. She had a funny feeling about Margie and the death of Bernard's father. She wanted to tell Bernard to have his father exhumed and test him for arsenic or strychnine.

As she became sick, Val became angry with the women who came to her job. When they held the cosmetics or opened a tube to take a whiff, Val demanded they buy the thing right then and there or snatched the tubes out of their hands. She began to get sloppy, and got mascara in their eyes. She drew huge clownlike eyebrows over their heads. She put so much powder on this one woman's nose, the woman started to choke in the chair. That's when Macy's got fed up and asked her to leave and Val rolled her makeup cart out the door.

For the three weeks, Val took painkillers and stayed high all night. Staying high blinded the sickness raging through her body. She was viciously sick and also felt doubly bad that she didn't speak up and tell Bernard the truth. If only she had stayed that night in his room instead of sneaking away out his window, hiding from his father, leaving his house like a thief. She planned to tell him that night after dinner at Margie's. She could feel him undress her and play with half her body. She tried to tell him, but her lips wouldn't move and the next thing she knew she couldn't see anymore, like a dark curtain had fallen over her eyes.

Sad and depressed, Val stopped fixing herself up and wore dark sunglasses around the house. She only showered and got ready if someone came over. But lately no one ever did.

In no time, she slid back into some very bad habits. She watched the paperboy throwing the gray wads at each porch. She caught a reflection of herself in the kitchen mirror and winced. Her blonde hair looked crooked on her head. She couldn't go out like that. Someone might see her. Her tormented face was a nightmare of caked makeup and lipstick smeared down to her chin. Val lathered her face and neck with soap, rinsed and patted it dry. She moisturized her face and applied a layer of foundation. But when she twisted her lipstick up, she threw the tube down and cried. Her hair was all snarled. She was too drained to fix it and barely had money for food. She pulled the clear bottle of Jim Beam from under the sink. She pulled down a glass and filled it halfway with juice and topped off the rest with straight whiskey. She drank two full glasses and smoked three cigarettes.

After fixing some toast, she attempted to do her face again. Val opened her large metal makeup box. She pulled out mascara, concealer, and gloss, two shades of powder, a peach-colored blush, and a good pair of long, black, false eyelashes. She got brushes and Q-tips and a small cotton cloth and an expensive, good pair of tweezers. After checking and rechecking herself in the mirror, she finally stuck one foot out the door. Leaning her head out, she checked her right and then left. She tightened her terry cloth robe around her waist and she raced the five steps it took to get the paper. Val snatched it up quickly, peering around for her neighbors. The sun exposed the black stubble on her legs. She quickly went back in the house. Val sat at the table and opened the newsprint. The front page picture showed two children playing with anatomically correct dolls. A psychologist from the McMartin hearing was making a case for sexual abuse by trying to make the kids reenact the sex crime with dolls.

Val threw the newspaper down on the floor and killed the sun coming in through the blinds. Her tongue slid back and forth in the empty hole where her front tooth used to be.

Three weeks ago, it was an insignificant dot. It was a tiny spot at first, barley visible to the eye. But each day the spot grew a little bit more and the tooth rapidly became loose. She tried bleach kits and peroxide, but none of it worked. The dentist said her calcium level had dropped down so low the whole root was bad and grossly infected, and he said the whole tooth had to go.

Val told him no. She couldn't loose her tooth now! Not the one in the front. How was she supposed to get a job? Wasn't there something else he could do?

Val begged that dentist not to pull her front tooth out "Please," Val said, "can't you cap it or something?" But the dentist explained that the infection could spread.

"If it gets to your gums and begins to abscess your roots, the other teeth could start going bad, too. I'm sorry," he said, "I'm going to have to take it."

"No!" Val screamed, turning away. But without any effort there it was in his hand. He put the dead tooth in a yellow envelope for her to take home. He showed her how implants worked, but they cost too damn much and took way too long to fix. How could she go around with a big hole in her mouth, waiting six months for the implant to heal? How could she work? How could she ever sell cosmetics? Who'd hire a girl to stand and sell makeup to women with a big hollow slot in her mouth?

Roy suggested she go to his dentist. Roy's dentist told her about a Marilyn, a tiny fake tooth that slips off and on. The tooth stood alone on a fake flesh-toned palate. The palate would fit snug in the roof of her mouth. She could have the thing done in a week and a half. Val almost felt hopeful. She almost smiled but caught herself. But when she tried to get the Marilyn, her credit card wouldn't take.

"I'm sorry," the nurse said. "Your card's been declined."

Val rummaged through her purse and pulled out a stack of shabby dollars. She handed the woman all the cash she had.

The nurse looked at the money as if it were diseased. "Honey, this is a business, not an L.A. free clinic." She leaned farther back from the counter.

"Come on!" Val pleaded. "Have a little heart," she begged.

"I'm sorry," she said smugly. "We all have to eat. Come back when you have the money."

Val closed her purse and rushed from the office. Her tongue floated into the hole below her gums.

Val knew one thing for sure, the most beautiful woman in the world could look like hell overnight if there's no front teeth in her head.

Val was desperate. She didn't know what else to do. She got acne bumps from all the stress. She took more and more pills and drank a bottle of booze and began hating the face in the mirror.

Val paced the floor like a dope fiend. She peeked through the drapes. She avoided the blinking light on the phone, knowing Bernard had left another message.

She realized the only way she could get her hands on some serious quick cash was on Santa Monica Boulevard at night. It was hard work, and she hadn't done it in years, but what else could she do?

Val hopped a bus and then walked the rest of the way down. The grocery store parking lot, near Santa Monica Blvd. and Poinsettia was a magnet for chicks exactly like her and for johns with interesting palates. Lots of girls were teetering around in high heels, sticking their necks into idling cars.

Val hadn't stood in this deadly lot in ages and fell right in a pothole as soon as she got there. She kept peeking over her shoulder. She didn't want anyone to see her face. If she worked four nights straight, she could rake in a grand. That was enough to get the dental work done.

Val stood in the cold night for more than an hour. She saw lots of other girls getting inside cars, but nobody came up to her. Suddenly a large Bentley cruised up to her knees. She couldn't see inside because the headlights were blinding. But once the driver clicked them off and rolled down the window, Val leaned in toward the red cigar blazing inside.

"Need a ride, miss?" a baritone voice asked.

Val looked at the large smiling man in the car. His shoulder blades almost took up two seats. His thick thighs were spread wide like pliers. The steering wheel dissected his knees. He sucked on the cigar real slow. He was an older white man with a humongous gut.

"Get in," the man said, opening the passenger side. Val looped around the headlights and pulled on the handle. When the door opened a light went on inside. The large man wore jeans. He had on a brilliant white Stetson. His black boots were shining, and he had a diamond on his pinkie. His shoulders were quarterback wide.

"Mm, Mm, Mm," the smiling man said, eyeing Val's breasts. His back teeth clamped deeper into the meat of the cigar.

"What are you?"

"I'm your miracle, honey," Val's heart felt like lead.

"Sugar, you've been blessed with all the parts I need. I like white and dark meat," he said. The man said it like he wasn't talking about any meat at all, and his gut jiggled over the seat. He drove silently with the scowl etched in his jaw. He tooled the large Bentley around residential streets, winding and twisting through the lanes. Val was wondering if the man was ever going to stop, when he finally pulled over at a black dead end lot.

The man took the key out slow and turned to Val's face. "So what kind of slice are you giving me tonight?" The man violently grabbed Val's body, flinging her over the backseat, circling her waist tight, until all the windows fogged. She thought these days were all over. She had abandoned this life. She no longer had to kill her soul in the back of another car. But here she was trapped in this dungeon again. Ready to mold herself around some complete total stranger. Giving her essence, letting him devour her like a steak, letting him take what he wanted and spit out the rest, like a kid tasting something and deciding it was nasty. Val hated this moment the second before it happened. The not wanting but knowing there was no way to stop. Knowing she'd decided as soon as she'd locked her front door. Decided while she was applying her liquid concealer. Decided as soon as she got up that morning, but hoping down deep she'd be able to change her mind. And now here she was in the prison of his car. The exact same spot she'd been in three years ago, smiling while steeling herself like a pole.

The man was forceful and strong and so large that she had to gnaw on the seat belt to stop the urgent pain. Val couldn't see a thing. All the windows were steamed. The only thing alive in that cold, darkened car was the heartless cigar in the ashtray.

Val stayed with the man for three and a half days. When she got home, she was horribly banged up and bruised. She soaked in the bath for hours, soaping herself up and crying, slamming her fist against the glass shower door.

Finally, she got out and tied on a robe. She lit candles in every room of her house and made a fresh glass of tea. She lined up the hundreds right there on the couch. After seeing him three times, she had the money she needed for her teeth. She could get her job back at Macy's and maybe return Bernard's calls.

Val tried hard to smile. She missed Bernard badly. But the hurt in her bones kept on weeping inside, long after the salty tears dried.

But now it was over. She endured it, and it was done. She got her tooth fixed and started smiling again. But her smile was not quite as wide as before. There were lots of girls like her, shattered by life, wearing their burgundy hearts right on their little satin sleeves, hearts that were so pounded and carved they felt hollow inside, like a Halloween pumpkin left out for months wilting on the hard porch of doom.

Even though Val never went to the parking lot, she kept seeing that Bentley. It followed her in her mind. Its headlights burned a hole right between her thighs and crept along the length of her spine.

18

Bernard

Bernard was dying to see Val. It had been over a month since he last saw her. The Halloween decorations were replaced with Christmas stuff now. He tried to find her, but she no longer worked at that store. He'd been walking around with a diamond ring in his pocket, waiting for Val to allow him to take her out. He'd slipped the ring off the dead bride they just buried. He knew it was wrong, and he'd never done anything like that before. But Bernard didn't make the kind of money to get the ring Val deserved. So after Tommy, the grave digger, washed the hearses one night. After he planted three bodies and put the tractor away. After he trimmed the weeds by each crypt and folded the plot survey map up, Bernard snuck over to the chapel and asked Tommy a favor. He paid him nine hundred to dig the 6 x 6 plot. When he dug up the bride's grave and opened the casket, Tommy snagged her ring, shutting the torso lid back and handed the band to Bernard.

"Pleasure doing business," Tommy said, wiping the dirt on the back of his pants.

Bernard was horrified seeing the bride's face. It was grossly decomposed and all his fine makeup work had caked in her hair. He practically raced to his car.

Bernard was thrilled to finally see Val again. She'd been putting him off for five weeks. He planned to ask for her hand at Mirabell's, the place where they met. He'd been pacing his floor, fingering the ring in his pocket, wondering if she'd say yes. And then one day out of the clear blue, she called to say hi. When Bernard heard her voice, his tender heart soared. He been dying to see her, to touch her again, to feel her softness against his.

He shaved and got ready, putting his best black suit on, splashing his neck with expensive shaving lotion and adding a gardenia from his yard to his lapel. He put the ring in a pale blue Tiffany's box and placed it inside his coat pocket.

Margie wasn't there. She had gone out that night. Since his dad died, she'd been seeing the Chinese man down the block who recently lost his spouse in a freak accident in the tub. Margie had been going over there bringing him barbequed duck and beer. She made Paula sit in the Chinese man's living room alone while Margie told sexy stories and jokes while massaging the bones over his ears.

As they drove to Mirabell's, Val stayed unusually quiet. But Bernard didn't mind. He was out with his girl. He didn't notice the huge circles under Val's eyes. He spent so much time happily chattering himself, he didn't notice that she rarely responded. Besides, she clutched him so tightly when they got out of the car; everything was beginning to feel like Christmas.

Bernard drove through the streets merrily enjoying the holiday lights, which burned red, yellow, and green little holes in the lawn.

He was saddened by the death of his father, but it had a liberating effect, too. He'd never enjoyed so much freedom in his life. He dressed better, hummed a few tunes around the house, and watched porn right in the front room.

When they entered the bar, the people stared at Bernard. The glamorous-looking men wondered. The coifed women gawked. Why did Bernard have this awful-looking thing on his arm? He was so put together. So pressed and well groomed. He obviously had money. It was clear he had class. Why did he have this sad sack attached to him like that? Why didn't he leave her outside in the street where she belonged? But Bernard couldn't see anything wrong with Val. He knew she'd been sick. She looked vaguely pale. But he was so happy, so hell-bent on completing his mission. So thrilled she'd finally agreed to come out at all, he couldn't tell that she was scared and depressed. But the other women recognized that pain in her eyes. They didn't want her sitting nearby and turned away from her face, hoping her desperation didn't rub off on them.

Bernard gently placed her coat around the back of her chair. He ordered champagne. He ordered two crème brulées. He smiled as the waiter filled their flutes up. He leaned across the table. He put Val's palm in his hand. He was just about to say how beautiful she was. He was just about to tell her how tormented he'd been since she wouldn't see him. He put one hand in his pocket, fingering the Tiffany box while the other hand gently stroked Val's hair. He was ready. The moment was now. He scooted his chair and leaned close to her face.

Val leaned up, too. She had something to say first.

"Val, baby!" A deep voice shot through the bar. "Girl, where the hell have you been?"

Val looked up, panicked. As soon as she saw the large Stetson, she buried her head in Bernard's jacket.

"Aw, come on, girl! Don't play me, okay? Everybody remembers Big Eddie!" The man did a quick dance step, twirling around and smiling at everyone at the bar. His pants were so tight, they bulged obscenely at the seam, and the fabric near the zipper was worn.

Bernard could see Val's annoyance and immediately took charge. He didn't want anything to spoil his special evening.

"Excuse me, sir. The lady prefers to be left alone, please." Then he got close and whispered inside Eddie's ear. "It's kind of a special evening for me, buddy."

"Oh, you don't have to tell me. Every evening with her is special." Big Eddie let his knee rub across Val's thigh. He smiled when she flashed him a glare.

Bernard tried to ignore him, but he stood over them now.

Eddie could care less about the scrawny dude Val was with. He acted as if Bernard wasn't there. "I've been looking for you, girl. Where have you been hiding" He let his hand rub the length of her spine.

Val freaked. She bolted up from her chair. She grabbed Big Eddie's wrist and snatched him to a corner, whispering all fast in his ear. Big Eddie stroked Val's face. He kept trying to kiss her mouth and it wasn't until Val opened her purse and put some cash in his hand that he finally went to the bar and gave her some peace. But he kept turning back. He even sent them some drinks.

"He's my coworker," Val lied. "Can't hold his liquor. He's a stupid damn fool when he's drunk."

Bernard patted her shoulder as Val sat back down.

But Eddie kept coming over and leaning against Val's chair.

Bernard had no choice but to confront the large man again.

"Look, can we please be civilized here? This evening is special for my girl and me. I'd appreciate it if you left us alone!"

Big Eddie stood up, too. "Your girl!" Eddie scoffed. "Boy, you don't know what you're talking about. Val ain't nobody's girl!"

"Leave us alone!" Bernard banged his fist on the bar and knocked over somebody's drink. He was shocked at his own anger and didn't know what to do next, but Eddie settled that for him when he leaped from his chair and coldcocked Bernard in the jaw.

Val screamed. She ran and picked Bernard up from the floor.

"Come on, Val!" Eddie grinned. "You don't need this chump! Look at him. He looks like he lives with his mama."

Val helped Bernard put his jacket over his shoulder.

"Hey, baby," Eddie said. "Come give Daddy a taste. I know you miss all this good gravy."

Eddie began vulgarly grinding his waist.

The bartender threatened to call the police if Eddie did not sit down or leave.

Val cupped Bernard's head. There was blood on his collar. She tried to dab his face with a napkin.

"Let me go!" Bernard steamed. He marched back to his car.

His jaw ached. He'd never been hit in the face before. He didn't hold Val's door for her either. He just got in and slammed his own door.

"Bernard, pleaseeeeee." Val cried as Bernard started the car. "I swear I don't know him. He's an asshole, that's all. Just a stupid ass drunk. The kind who gets in your face and talks shit." Val's worried face was swimming in fear. Her makeup floated on top and turned blotchy. She looked up toward the dark swirling, manic sky, which was howling with fat pregnant clouds. One splashy drop landed on her toes, and Val lifted her purse up to cover her head.

"He seemed to know you pretty well," Bernard snapped. He refused to be an old cuckolded fool, like his father. There was definitely something between Val and that man. And besides, Val hadn't let him get close to her yet. Since they met, she kept him panting, hanging on a cliff, holding back his hands or his hot anxious wrists and then disappearing just before he got close.

But he couldn't bear to leave her out there in the cold. Besides, she was getting wet in the rain, so Bernard reached over and pulled the latch.

Val slinked into the seat and sat in dead silence. She dabbed her face in the front rearview mirror, hoping to catch Bernard's eye.

When they got to his house, Bernard slammed the car door.

"What are you saving it for?" Bernard screamed, twirling Val's shoulder. "Obviously not for me. Eddie's already had a taste, hasn't he?"

Bernard raced like a maniac back to his house.

Val jerked her arm away, but she didn't leave. She saw the light on in the window of the upstairs apartment and stopped.

"Wait a minute, Bernard. Is Margie still here, even after your dad died?"

"Yes, and so what? Don't try to change the subject." He took out his key and opened the door. He was so angry, he started to shake.

The house was completely dark. Val followed behind Bernard's legs. She didn't like that Margie was still living in his house. And after everything that happened the last time she was here, she felt weird being back in this mansion again.

"Bernard, listen." Val whispered. "You have to get Margie out! She poisoned me, and your dad mysteriously died the next day! Doesn't that make you suspicious?"

Bernard hadn't turned a light on, and they crept along the floor, tripping on the wood and over the Oriental rug like two thieves casing a house.

"You weren't poisoned. Paula made that stuff up. Margie said the girl has a wicked imagination. All you had was a bout of the flu."

Bernard snatched her hand and led Val to the couch.

But Val snatched her hand back and faced Bernard full-on.

"I didn't have the flu! Margie poisoned me, Bernard. I was terribly sick, and I even lost a tooth." Val pulled the Marilyn out of her mouth. A solitary tooth sat on a pink gummy half moon. "Your teeth don't just fall out of your head from the flu. She poisoned me, and I bet she poisoned your poor father, too."

"Sit down," he said tersely, almost pushing her down. "Dad died of a diabetic coma. He slipped into it in his sleep."

"Come on, are you sure? Did you do an autopsy?"

"No!" Bernard stared with unblinking eyes. "We don't do autopsies on eighty-three-year-old men." He ignored what Val said. All he could think about was Eddie. Eddie's knowing smile, Eddie's white Stetson hat, the worn fabric over his zipper. He could still see Eddie vividly inside his head. Bernard's dad's death was the last thing on his mind.

Val sat down, but suddenly bolted up from her seat. "How can you take Margie's word? You should have him exhumed."

"I can't!" Bernard screamed, pushing Val back down.

"Why not?" Val yelled back. "At least you'll find out the truth."

Bernard could see his fingernails from the moon streaming in. The nail beds were bloody and dried up with scabs. "I can't. We cremated him last month."

"Cremated! You told me he never wanted that. You said he and your mother had side by side graves."

"Dad wanted it, okay! Margie said those were his wishes." Bernard frowned like a kid who'd gotten all the answers wrong on his test. He was surprised he'd never thought of this twice. He was so involved in making sure his father had an elaborate funeral that he hadn't had a chance to think of anything else. Margie and Reynolds had lots of secret little meetings. They didn't want to trouble Bernard. He was bereaved. He was too upset. And that's how Margie found out where the hidden bankbook was and the old chest coins he found in the yard. Bernard needed it all to pay for the funeral.

"Bernard, he was *your* father! That's not for her to say." Val felt nothing but sorrow for her friend. Bernard was so easily duped. He was almost childlike to her now. But she knew it was dangerous to be in this house. There was a vicious aggressor living right over her head.

Bernard began to feel a hot flush in his skin. He was furious. This is not what he wanted to talk about at all. He glanced out the window. The sky was pitch black, except for a heavy full moon that reminded him of Eddie's Stetson hat.

The truth was, Margie had already been poisoning him, too. For the past three weeks, she'd given him four drops of pure arsenic. One more dose, and she would be dragging him out by the feet.

The poison began boring a hole in his gut. Bernard thought it was gas or severe indigestion. He sucked Tums and drank Maalox, but it would not go away. Now it was a boiling heat surrounding his heart, and it agitated Bernard to no end.

"Bernard, we have to get out of this house!"

Bernard looked angry and confused. His brows started to set. He reached for Val's knee and held the bone down.

"Wait a minute, Bernard. I want to say something first."

"I've heard enough!" Bernard lost all control. The poison was boring a hole in his skull. He flung Val across the couch like an old sack of clothes and viciously yanked up her dress.

"Always saving it. Always putting me off!" He pushed her pink half slip down to the ground. Her round, smooth, tight ass laughed at the moon, and Bernard started slapping it hard.

It was late in December, but the heater was on. Even though the house was toasty and warm, Val's trembling skin was covered in goose bumps.

"No! Honey, wait. No! Not like this!" Val frantically twisted underneath Bernard's girth. She was small, and he was someone who worked out each day.

Bernard wouldn't wait. He was completely deranged. His dad's death hadn't hit Bernard until then. All the emotion from finding his father pinned down behind the bed, his stump caught beneath the wheel and the pure horror on his dad's face, was too much for Bernard to bear. All his anger at Margie flooded his body with rage. He hated her. His hatred was deep and complete. That morning she announced she was selling the house. She found a cute little three bedroom right on the beach and said that Bernard would love the fresh air. Bernard wanted to break something, snap something in half, and Val was the only one there.

Her squirming flesh only excited him more. He'd longed for her ever since the first day they met. She was the same size as the child-women he stared at behind scrubs. He wasn't going to wait one more day. His fist grabbed her neck. His knee held her down. Val's dress was hiked up over her waist. The thong panties carved her in half.

Bernard unzipped his pants. He was going to teach Val something.

She screamed, but he didn't care anymore. He was tired of her games and her sidestepping lies. All that was over. He was getting his now. He held her neck and Val's locks shook to and fro like a doll dangling down from a rope. Bernard tried to reach her soft inner flesh. He didn't smother her face with kisses like he'd dreamed. He didn't hand her the diamond ring in his pocket. No. Instead he held one hand over her lips and tried to burrow himself in her skin. He felt like he was taking back something that was his. Like he was branding her. Pounding her into submission so she'd never think of any other man. He licked her neck and face with his tongue. He pushed up against her, thrusting himself harder and harder. Her makeup was smeared. Her eyes were shut tight. Her face was a knotted expression of pain. Bernard melted when he saw tears streaming out of Val's eyes. He didn't want to hurt Val. Val was his friend. But his body was already full throttle now. He couldn't slow down. He was well past his peak. He tried reaching between her legs, but Val shifted away. He sucked on her lobes and told her he was sorry. Couldn't she see what he felt for her inside? But Val kept twisting and screaming under his hand and this only angered him more. Why was she complaining? He wasn't that rough. He loved her. Why did she keep whimpering like this? Her sadness only made Bernard mad. He jerked at Val's clothing, and her whimpering stopped. So that's what she wanted. She wanted him to get rough. Bernard snatched at her clothes until they all fell away. Her breasts were so perfect. Her nipples so erect. Bernard was a bonfire of strength. Never in his life had he wanted something so much. He tore inside Val's body. He scrambled between her thighs. Bernard was panting and thrusting, but something was wrong. He looked at Val, but she had both hands over her face.

Suddenly the living room burst into light when Bernard clicked on the lamp.

The horror he saw was almost too much to describe. Val wore a thin G-string under her thong. It tied down a small erupting lump. Bernard fell back on the couch. He held his hand over his mouth. He couldn't believe it. How could he have missed this? How could he have been so completely wrong? He let this thing kiss him and lick the hairs on his neck.

Bernard placed his fists around Val's slender throat.

"Bernard . . ." Val choked. "Please, Bernard, don't." Her makeup smeared over the white damask pillows. A rainbow of color slid across the ivory seat. She was biting the pillow. Her teeth gnawed a small hole. Bernard flipped her and started choking her from behind. His body was still hot. Val could feel his skin. But the shock of not breathing was weakening her heart.

He wanted to kill her. Put a knife in her body.

"Noooo!" Val screamed. It was a loud awful howl. Like a dog being hit by a truck.

The little girl upstairs heard it. She grabbed her binoculars and ran downstairs. She pulled two phone books together and peeked in the living room window. She couldn't believe what she saw.

Bernard was strangling Val! Her small body shook. But Val didn't look like Val anymore. Her face was so strange. She looked less like a girl. She was somewhere between a woman and a very tiny beautiful young man. The girl smiled and held the binoculars closer to both eyes.

"You tricked me!" Bernard said. The veins popped from his head.

Val's narrow hips rose as she arched her slim back. Her body contorted as her lungs strained for air, but Bernard's fingers tore into her neck.

Suddenly, Bernard stopped. He heard the low rumbling sound of the old Buick. He heard the rickety door slowly creak open. Margie was back home again!

Val screamed when she heard the car, but Bernard held his palms over her mouth. Val tried to mouth some words, but nothing came out. Val's brain was hazy. She couldn't think straight. She saw the swing in her yard and a pool filled with water and the length of a diving board from her town's local pool. She was fading. Everything turned a dull oozy gray, there was nothing left but the faintest of sound.

The door slammed, and Margie's stilettos came down the long driveway and her key fumbled in the lock inside the back door. The girl climbed around the house and came up the ramp and crept in behind Margie, hiding in the bathroom down the hall.

Bernard's thick hands let go of Val's mouth and throat.

"Hello, Bernard, I'm home. I got you some ice cream," Margie hurried in the door with shopping bags full of stuff.

Val heard the sound of crinkling plastic bags.

"Just leave it! I'm busy," Bernard blared toward the kitchen.

Bernard let go of Val's neck but still held Val's mouth as he looked toward the archway, holding his breath, waiting to see if Margie would come through the door.

Val wasn't struggling beneath Bernard's body anymore.

"I got butterscotch. I know that's what you like."

When Bernard didn't answer, Margie came into the room.

She was totally shocked to see Val under Bernard's chest; she could barely hold back her glee and her scorn. She thought he was done with this slutty little bitch. Trannies like her needed to be on the street where they belonged. She was planning on killing Bernard violently tonight, and Val had spoiled her plans. But Margie was an expert at masking her feelings. She'd just kill two birds with one stone, she thought. One shopping bag was brimming with yards of rope and a hatchet. The other bag had a gigantic jug of sweet-smelling weed killer she bought from the hardware store man. The last bag held a gallon of butterscotch ice cream and a CD of vintage Sinatra. Margie was singing "Nice and Easy" when she entered the room.

"Why, Val," Margie said. "What a pleasant surprise." Margie dropped the bags and came over to the couch and sat near Val's head. "You look so flushed, doll. Are you feeling okay?" She put her hand across Val's sweaty forehead. "My goodness, you're hot," Margie said, faking concern and giving Bernard a sweet Kool-Aid grin.

"I've got your ice cream. Butterscotch like you said. I can fix you both a bowl right now. Margie rushed inside the kitchen and closed the swing door.

Val was shocked! Margie didn't even say anything about Bernard gripping her mouth. Roy was right. All these people were crazy! All she wanted to do was get out alive!

When Bernard followed Margie into the kitchen, Val secretly gathered her purse and slipped on her shoes.

"Wait!" Bernard said, before going into the door. He ran back and held Val's thin arm.

"It's all right." Val tried to humor him now. She began stroking his hand and smiling in his face, anything to distract him and keep at ease until she could slip out the door.

"Bernard, you feel hot. I think you need to get some air." Slowly she tried to coax him to the door.

But Bernard grabbed Val's wrist hard and made her sit down.

"Well, look at that!" Val said, pointing at the large Steuben vase. She secretly slithered her coat on both arms. "I can see a dozen rainbows in there." For the first time in her life she was really afraid. She was trying to appear calm as Margie sang in the kitchen and Bernard firmly held her hair. She tried to appear detached while taking little panting breaths to stop her legs from trembling in fear.

"There you go, my dears," Margie came out with a tray. She put the tray down at the coffee table near their knees. There were two blue twin bowls and two silver spoons. She was wearing Alice's pink apron with the pale ivory trim, and it lapped the fat meat on her thighs.

Bernard looked at Margie with hot venom in his eyes.

Val saw that same look only moments before.

Val wasn't going to eat one damn thing from this woman! She had to get out! She had to leave right away. All she wanted was to go home, put this ugly nightmare behind and snap her locks and yank down her shades.

Bernard kicked the tray and it skidded across the floor.

Margie gave Bernard a sinister smile. "Oh, no, you had an accident, honey. I'll go get you a rag." Margie wanted to go to the kitchen to pick up the hatchet.

Bernard chased Margie and grabbed one of her pink apron strings. Margie screamed and kept running, trying to get to the kitchen door.

Val used this opportunity to leap from the couch. Like a wild woman, Val was able to tear down the hall. As Bernard tried to grab Margie, Val moved leopard quick and escaped into the bathroom and locked the door fast.

To her shock, the little girl was inside. Val begged Paula with her eyes and pressed her pointer to her lips, compelling the girl to be quiet.

Margie swore at Bernard and tore the apron off to get away. She circled the table, knocking a porcelain vase down. She picked up a piece of crystal and pitched it toward Bernard's head, but she missed and it crashed on the wall. Bernard caught her and slammed her head against the china cabinet doors. With pure violence in his veins he choked her thick neck. But Margie was able to snatch a bowl from the shelf and smash it over his head. She screamed again, this time so loud and so long, one of his neighbors turned on their lights. She was able to break his clutch and dashed toward the kitchen door, but one of her heels got caught in the rug. With one shoe firmly lodged in the pile of the shag, Margie's body flew forward and slammed against the table's corner, and she tumbled and dropped to the floor.

The force rocked the huge Steuben urn back and forth. It rolled across the dining room table like a crystal bowling ball and smashed on top of Margie's skull.

Bernard grabbed her neck and squeezed his thumbs on her windpipe.

"I'm yo—ur mo—ther!" Margie choked. But her prone obese body lunged one final time and then a thick trail of dark blood trickled out from her nose. Her limp body moved once and then didn't move again. No air passed from her lips.

Bernard was still squeezing Margie's neck with all of his might. But when he let go and saw Margie's clothes, all he thought of was his mother. Margie was wearing an outfit of his mother's that he loved. It was the fuchsia and yellow suit with the extra long coat.

And for a moment, something snapped inside his warped, twisted mind. In Bernard's head, this was his mother, Alice, laying here. Rocking her tight and biting a clump of her hair, he held her head close to his chest like a doll, swaying her skull to and fro. He didn't let go until he heard the creak of a door. Instantly, he remembered Val and the girl, and he dropped Margie's head until it thudded against the wood. He saw the thick phone cord leading into the bathroom.

"Val," he said low, trying to tiptoe to the bathroom. But suddenly he panicked. What if she was calling the police? If the police found Margie dead with red strangle marks around her neck, he'd be going to jail for sure. Bernard cut the phone cord with a steak knife. He looked around the room, studying the scene, trying to make his brain think of what he could do. There was no way the police would believe this was an accident. There was nothing else to do but try and cover it up.

Bernard gently placed Margie's head on the shag. He removed the shoe from where it had stuck in the rug. What should he do? Where could he put Margie's body? He struggled to think as he rinsed the melted ice cream and he watched the creamy lumps slide down the sink.

Bernard stepped over Margie's body, still wracking his brain. He picked up his mother's purse and both of her shoes. And after scanning the room for one lunatic moment, he slowly began rolling her up in the rug.

Bernard panicked every time he heard a car going by. Margie was big-boned and heavy and hard to pick up, but he had to get her out of the house.

But what should he do about Val? Everyone at the bar had seen him leave with her. They'd seen him angry. They heard him curse her or worse! If she told the cops that Bernard had tried to strangle her, they'd be on the lookout for him, for sure.

Bernard jiggled the lock on the small bathroom door.

"Val, honey. You can come out. You don't need to worry about her anymore." Bernard glanced at Margie's dead body and bit deep into his fist. In his sick, polluted mind, this rug contained his mother, and he winced in pain when he saw it.

"Val, really," Bernard pounded harder. He jiggled the lock. "I just need to talk to you for a minute." He was holding a poker from the fireplace in his hand. The hand was hidden behind his back.

"Val's not here." Paula said, smiling at her friend.

It was the girl! What was she doing in here?

"Where's Val?" Bernard pounded with all his might. "Open up this door, now."

"Val's gone," the girl lied, smiling excitedly now.

When did the girl come? Bernard wondered. Did she see him with Val or worse, strangling and killing her mother? And if Val had gone home and Margie was dead, was it just he and the young girl in the whole house alone? A sick smile spread across Bernard's lips.

Bernard knocked the door lightly. "Open up, honey, your mother made us all some ice cream."

The girl's eyes got big, and she almost turned the lock. But Val held back her hand and shook her head no.

Every car coming by showered the living room in light. Bernard wiped the wet that ran from his brow. It pooled at the edge of his rough, stubbled chin. Bernard went back to the dining room and squatted near Margie's body.

"Maybe she didn't see anything," he said out loud. He hurried with Margie's body, tying his belt around the rug's middle to make sure it didn't unroll. But what if the girl did see? Bernard looked at his hands. What if she saw Bernard rolling her mother in the rug and decided to go call the cops. Bernard's heart raced. He was rattled with fear. He got up and rushed to the bathroom again to see if he could see anything in the keyhole and try to coax the girl or Val out. But the bathroom door was open, and the girl and Val were gone. Bernard raced up the back stairs taking two steps at once. He couldn't chance leaving this small stone unturned. He couldn't risk either of them calling the police. The wood steps creaked violently as he dashed up the stairs, but suddenly he was there at the top of the landing. But just when he touched the knob, the girl's hand pulled the shade and he heard the cold snap of the lock.

A thunderbolt roared over his scalp, and lightning tore up the sky.

Peering inside the slim space between the shade and the frame, Bernard pressed his face against the dirt on the glass. He heard the refrigerator's cold hum, saw the floral linoleum and the paint buckets he used to clean. And just when he thought he could make out a small frame, someone clicked off the lights.

Bernard strained to see, but it was no use. All he saw was an ocean of black. Bernard thought of jimmying his way in, and then remembered his passkey. Bernard kept the spare keys inside his garage. He ran down the steps to go get it. A cat leaped from nowhere, and Bernard whirled around, and then snatched the key off of the wall.

A smile spread across Bernard's oily face when he got the keys. The kind of smile you see on gamblers in Vegas when they finally hit a big streak. In no time, Bernard was back on the girl's porch again, sliding the key into the jaws of the lock. He turned it and heard the heavy bolt click.

But then suddenly he stood straight and sucked in his breath. What was that? Straining, he heard a mild wailing noise. Was that the low moaning roar of a siren? Oh my God! They already called the police. He was too late. The police were heading this way! Bernard couldn't be caught with a dead body in his house and quickly raced back down the long wooden steps. He had to do something before the police came.

Bernard dashed into his house. He ran down the hall. Dragging Margie across the living room floor, he stopped and tightened her up like a scroll. Then he kicked open the back door.

To his horror, it was pouring rain outside. The sidewalks were slushy, the flower beds were drenched, and the ramp had turned into a water slide.

He lifted the wool rug as far as he could and laboriously dragged the tight roll down the ramp and toward his car. But wait a minute! His car wasn't there. In his haste to get Val in quickly, he'd parked his car in front, right near the mansion's front door. It was at the end of the driveway facing the street, where anyone looking could see.

The little girl watched Bernard drag the rug from her window. The rug was so heavy, it flattened the soft grass, digging a path in the freshly cut lawn. Bernard struggled mightily with the rug's heavy weight. He was gasping and wheezing, using all of his strength to lift the thing up to his car. He wanted to stop and rest, just to catch his breath, but the siren made Bernard force himself to keep going. Margie's dead weight and the dense roll of wool were more than Bernard's meager frame could take. His body was drenched. Sweat raced down his back. But he couldn't stop now. He had to keep going. The sirens howled just down the road.

Tugging the rug with all of his might, he finally got it inside his car. He pushed the rug to the backseat, folding the roll across the vinyl. But then, all of a sudden it wouldn't go in any farther. The rug was stuck. Bernard panicked. He couldn't get the thing to move. The sirens were almost at his corner now. The sound blasted inside his ears. Bernard struggled with the rug. He grabbed its thick waist. Fighting and twisting, he pushed at the roll, but the godawful thing wouldn't budge. The veins in his head bulged. They felt like they would explode. He dabbed his forehead with the sleeve of his shirt. His breath was staccato. He couldn't get any air. His tight chest struggled for a breath, but nothing came down his throat. He was having an attack. He patted his pants pocket for his medicine and realized it was in his coat pocket inside the house.

The sirens roared. They were on his street now. Every single house turned an ambulance red. Bernard ripped the tie from his wet neck. He couldn't breathe but he couldn't get caught either. He wanted to roll Margie's rug body down to the ground, but it was too late to do anything now.

The sirens had come. The sirens were here. Their blinking red lights flooded his driveway and porch. His face turned into a fun house of fear. The car door was still open with the rug hanging out. He could see the black curls from Margie's dead head. Bernard closed his eyes and waited for the police to cuff his wrists or bark for him to raise his hands and step from the car. Holding his breath, Bernard laid there, refusing to breathe. The blinking lights turned him into a horror show flick. The sirens soared loud. They slowed to a stop. Bernard dropped down and rolled completely underneath his car. Slowly, Bernard pried open his eyes. What he saw was not a cop car at all. The red lights belonged to an ambulance. It pulled right in front of his driveway and was parked at the curb. Three men dressed in navy burst from its doors. One carried a large valise in his fist. The other two yanked a gurney from the back of the truck. They came to his neighbor's door and knocked. The door flung open wide. The navy blue men went in, leaving his neighbor's door ajar. In seconds, they were wheeling his neighbor back out. Bernard saw her feet sticking out of the thin sheet. Her pale face was woven and drawn. Her ivory robe dragged across the asphalt. A pitiful knee poked out of the sheet. They wheeled her inside the van, and one of the men jumped in beside her. The other two got back into the front and slammed their doors. Red and yellow lights twirled like a carnival ride and the siren raged wildly once more.

Only when the van left and the street was completely black again, did Bernard began breathing once more. Lying on the ground was relaxing, but he hurriedly got up, working faster than he had before. He couldn't take any more chances. He had to get going and fiercely pulled the rug up over his legs.

Bernard yanked the rug roughly, pulling it frantically inside his car, moving its thickness by sheer grit alone.

He went to the other side of the car and snatched the door open. He got all the way in, pulling the rolled body inside until it lay straight across the backseat like a fat wooly scroll. Bernard slammed both back doors and got in the front seat, but he didn't start his car right away. He didn't want any one to hear him leaving this late. A few porch lights were still on. He couldn't chance being seen. So he put the car in neutral and opened his door. He pulled the car down the driveway like it was a scooter, dragging his shoe across the concrete until the heavy car rolled. When he got out of the driveway, he turned the wheel a hard left and rolled the car all the way down the street. It wasn't until his car was at the end of the block that Bernard finally switched the ignition on. With the engine on, Bernard let the old Plymouth roar. He tore down the lane like he was in a street race, ignoring all of the stop signs and lights.

Bernard drove aimlessly for a while, considering where he could go. He decided to take the body to the ocean. He took Sunset all the way to the Pacific Coast Highway. Gladstone's was there, but it was dark and closed. The restaurant was his mother's favorite place for dinner, but it had moved farther down from its original spot after the whole thing burned down from a fire. Bernard remembered that night. It was a very strange evening, seeing the building engulfed in a hurricane of flames, burning while completely surrounded by water that had no power to snuff the flame out.

Bernard pulled into the lot. There weren't any cars. All he saw was an endless sea of black rolling waves. He watched them foaming in and out. But every wave that went out came sliding back in faster, dropping shells and seaweed farther up the sand. He couldn't chance leaving Margie out here. She'd probably wash ashore before morning. And besides, the long stretch of sand was expansive. He'd easily be seen dragging the rug to the shore.

So instead, he decided to try for the mountains, aiming his car toward the luscious Angeles National Forest, but after driving twenty minutes he could see the translucent moon jeering. It wouldn't be long before the eager sun saw him. He turned his car away from the forest terrain and headed for the easier more obtainable slope of Griffith Park. He began winding his way around the dense foliage. He parked up near the top, around the side of the mountain. He opened the backseat and started to pull Margie out. But suddenly a pair of lights flashed up against his car. Bernard ducked next to the car, panting like a chased dog. He waited for the large lights to fade. He was about to pull Margie out again when another pair of lights hit him. He was standing there frozen with both hands on the rug. He couldn't see who it was. The blaring lights were blinding. All he heard was a radio blasting loud music. They dropped two cans of Pepsi and skidded away into the night. Bernard didn't like this. There were too many distractions. Too many cars coming meant he could get caught. He shoved the thick wool rug all the way back in, and aimed the Plymouth toward the city.

Where could he go? How should he hide it? He wracked his brain, gripping the steering wheel tight. His whole back was sticky with sweat. His hot breath fought hard to get out of his lungs. He had to do something fast. He looked over the dash at the dark fading sky. The flimsy moon mocked him. A sprinkling of stars winked their eyes. The sky was no longer pitch black anymore. In a few hours, it would be morning.

Bernard fought the urge to look in the backseat. It was pouring outside, and he forced his eyes on the wipers, watching their aggressive slushy dance over his dashboard. But his eyes won the fight, and he took one quick glance. Margie's hair was sticking out of one end, and when he caught one of Margie's eyes in the glass, Bernard almost veered off the road.

Bernard pounded the wheel. He had to get a grip. He couldn't lose it now, or he was going to jail. But it was hard to believe that he murdered someone and she was here in the back of his car! He flipped the rearview mirror all the way up so he wouldn't risk seeing Margie's face again.

A semi pulled up to him at the next light. The tall cab could easily see inside Bernard's car. Bernard quickly looked up, but he couldn't see the driver. He sat in a smoke-filled cab of pitch black and the rainwater created a screen over his window. All he saw was the squat glow of a cigarette butt, jabbed between two gritty fingers. The burnt fumes seeped inside Bernard's open window, and he watched the fingertips drum against the cab's metal door. Bernard was quivering in fear. The truck towered over his car. Could the man see the body? Could he see Margie's hair, waving from the rugs rolled up neck? The hand waved at Bernard, but Bernard kept his face straight. He watched the cigarette hand from his peripheral vision, fearing the man might say something to make Bernard speak. After an eternity, the light finally turned lime, and Bernard firmly pressed on the gas.

Don't make waves, he thought. *Don't do anything to get noticed*. He drove, keeping his frame as firm as a stone. He was delirious with worry. Each breath was a struggle. Where in God's name could he go!

And then suddenly he spotted a large lit up window. Caskets were lined up, shining like clean brand-new cars. They sat silently; their torso doors open wide, like they were patiently waiting for bodies.

This was perfect! Why hadn't he thought of going there before? The thought caked like the crusty red blood on his hands. Bernard turned his car around and took Norton straight down. Rosedale. Rosedale was perfect! He aimed his car toward his mortuary job. In a moment, he was at Rosedale's door. He turned off the headlights and sat in the dark, drumming his thumbs on the dash.

Sometimes a body would show up at night. Some folks didn't like people knowing someone died, and so they cremated or buried their bodies at dark. He had to be sure no one was working inside and studied the building for any signs of life.

Bernard looked around and then quickly got out. But as soon as he stepped down, his foot fell in a puddle and his shoe and sock filled with slush. He sloppily walked to the large golden doors. He found the new key on his chain and slid it into the hole. He didn't know why he snuck out and had the key made. Maybe it was because Reynolds wouldn't let him have one when he asked. He only wanted something to add to his ring besides a car key and the solitary key to his house. Bernard wanted a ring that was jingly and substantial. Something that sang like a metal toolbox in his pants. Something to make him feel more like a man.

So one day during work while he was arranging flowers on this casket, he noticed a dented locksmith truck parked out along the curb. Bernard secretly took the mortuary key off the hook and snuck out the back, ducking his head in the locksmith's van. He came face-to-face with a weathered Chinese woman. Her hands looked like meat from a grinder. Bernard was surprised. He'd never seen a woman with this job. He asked her if she would cut him a copy of Reynolds' key. The locksmith angrily snatched the key from Bernard's hand. She examined it with her stubby binocular glasses, holding it under the lamp, rubbing it across smudged, greasy fingers. She flipped the key over and over with her thumb, studying each hill and valley, each jagged tooth and then did the same thing to Bernard's anxious face. "Can't copy," the Chinese woman told him point blank, dropping the key back in his palm. There was a tense moment when Bernard and the woman locked eyes. Bernard understood what that clenched moment meant. When he opened his stiff, engraved, cowboy wallet and pushed a crisp fifty inside of her palm, the gruff locksmith smiled and finally released his eyes and grabbed the key back from Bernard's sweaty hand. "I do, for you," she said, revealing twin silver choppers. She clamped the key into the heavy machine's vice, and the van shook with the rough sound of drilling.

Bernard pushed the key inside the slim narrow lock. He'd never used the newly-made key before. It was ragged and sharp and not a good fit and nothing like the other two keys on his ring which were smooth and as clean as a bone.

He twisted the key back and forth. But the bolt wouldn't turn. Madly wiggling it around in the unrelenting hole, he thought of the locksmith and her neat silver teeth. She'd obviously taken Bernard for a ride. She's probably poring scotch in her rotten mouth now, laughing it up with some skeletal friends. Bernard bore into the lock. The key reddened his fingers. But the key didn't work no matter which way he turned. It was a worthless piece of carved detailed metal, as useless as a slug when only a real quarter would do. He was about to pitch the key across the harsh gravel lot when he heard the soft click and release of the lock. My God! The key worked! He could hardly believe it. He sighed deeply, taking a strong cleansing breath. A smile loosened the taut muscles that yanked his clenched jaw. Bernard was just twisting the handle to open the door when two headlights torched his whole frame.

Bernard froze. A police car rolled up to Rosedale's gates. Bernard was paralyzed. He quietly sucked in his chest. He flattened his thick frame against the mortuary's brick wall sliding all the way down to a squat. Crawling behind the thin branches of the dead-looking ficus, Bernard found that the tree barely offered any protection at all and the light still ate his quivering frame. He was a flashlight show of shadow and black. Ghoulish black fragments exploded across his skin. There was no place to go. He held the air in his lungs. His knees ached. His legs were beginning to burn. He couldn't see a thing except the blurred headlight's eyes, ripping a blunt steamy stream through the black. Maybe they were running a make on his plates. Maybe they could see the lone key in the door. Bernard bit the globe of his fist like an orange and feverishly scratched his wrists. If they got out and came over to look in his car, he'd get the gas chamber for sure. The sweat made a halo of light on his head. One leg began to go. It wouldn't stop shaking. He dug his teeth deeper into the flesh of his hand to stop the scream from working its way up his throat. And just when he thought he would explode from the terror. As hysteria seized the slim shell that held in his brain. While the cold wet leaked out of each follicle or pore, he suddenly became drenched in the dark calm again. The browbeating headlights moved on. Bernard collapsed and let out a long haggard gasp. He sat behind the massive planter, wiping the sweat from his eyes before racing back up to the door.

Bernard opened the mortuary door, leaving it slightly ajar. He ran back and unrolled Margie from the wool. Lifting her large lifeless body was more than a chore. She was big-boned and thick, and death added its own ounces making her a hundred times heavier than she really was. Wet salt popped out all over his whole body as he grunted and carried her up the vast steps. He flung the mortuary door open with one leg. He swung Margie across his shoulder and back and quickly locked the large heavy gates.

Bernard didn't turn on a light. He cowered in the dark. Margie's body was wrapped across his neck like a scarf. Using the small pinhead flashlight he kept in his car, he looked around and found a metal empty gurney and laid Margie flat on its bed.

Bernard sighed. Finally, this part was easy. He could roll Margie down to the crematorium with ease now that she rested on the gurney.

Fingering his hand across the wall, he found the red incinerator switch and the knob for the large ceiling fans.

The retort ovens were just like the ones used in Germany only smaller. He put Margie on the long receiving pan. He rolled the pan to the deck and closed the huge door. Flipping the giant red switch he heard the billowing sound of flames. Giant flames that came from the top and sides immediately seizing Margie's body.

The oven heated the room, filling the walls up with steam. Bernard wished Margie were small. Then she'd burn quickly. She was the typical "stinker," and he'd have to endure the heat and the long hours she'd take burning slow. If he did her too fast, and her grease heated too quickly there was a possible chance of explosion. Working fast, he didn't bother removing Margie's jewelry. It was cheap costume stuff that would melt away in minutes. The burning smell usually didn't bother Bernard. He could go day after day and never think of the odor. But this time it hurt. The sugary smell scorched his nose. It turned his pink lungs into a fiery hell. He could hardly believe this was happening to him. He committed murder and was burning the person at work. He played with the engagement ring in his pocket. A chance of life with Val was permanently over. A lone tear rolled down his blazing hot face.

Bernard walked over to the prep room where the other dead bodies lay. This was the room where he worked. Defeated, he never minded being around dead people before, but this time the bodies seemed to mock him or sneer. He couldn't bear looking inside their stony cold faces. So he rolled a gurney out to the hall, sweating profusely and nibbling what was left of his nails, he laid on the gurney waiting for Margie to cook. It was agony to wait. He tossed and turned on the metal bed. After an hour, Bernard couldn't wait anymore. He had to look and see. Quickly he rose and stood on pins and needles feet, which had fallen asleep in his shoes. He got up and checked the clock. Sixty-eight minutes. Bernard drank some water, splashed some more in his face and sank down on a gurney again.

After a horrible ninety-six minutes, he had to go check. He could see the dial register which read 1,875 degrees. Bernard stopped the machine and put the gauntlet mitts on. Fighting the nausea that lived at the back of his throat, he struggled against the urge to be sick.

The leather gauntlet gloves covered his forearms. Bernard slowly raised the crematory door. He had to crack it slow or else the explosive heat would escape and torch the skin straight off his face.

Though cracked, the heat steamed his skin like a sauna. His face turned a deep lobster red. Saline streamed from his armpits and sloshed down to his legs, turning him into a wet rag of sweat. Bernard could see the cremation in progress. All of Margie's flesh was gone; he could see her skeletal torso. Her skeleton was so much smaller than her larger flesh suggested, but she still hadn't turned into decalcified bone so he slammed the doors shut and gave it thirty more minutes. In thirty minutes, the oven automatically turned off. Bernard opened the door again, but raised them too high and began gagging inside one of his gloves. He was engulfed in a large smoky cloud. The roaring crematory fans filled the room up with sound. Bernard was coughing so much that tears streamed from his lids.

Margie was no longer a skeleton anymore. The only thing left of Margie was a stack of bone fragments. They were smoldering in a pan of hot grease, littering the thin pan and stretched to the back like a large scattered batch of burnt cookies.

Bernard held his breath, scraping her remains into a pan. With the bristled, long-handled brush, he wiped the pan clean into the chute at the front of the unit. He carried the pan over to the "processing station" where a large oval grinder pulverizes bone into powder, the grainylike substance called ash. The processor, with its twelve rotating balls, began pulverizing all Margie's bones. No one gets ash. Ash was a misnomer. The only thing people bring home, packed in urns or square boxes, were bone chips that look as fine as the sand on the beach.

Bernard held his hands over his ears. A horrible, rumbling, scraping sound ate his eardrums and brain. A sound so intense it devoured his clothes and grated against his taut skin. It sunk in and dug into the quick of his nails. It climbed each twitching disc of his hunched-over spine, vibrating the freshly mopped floor. Everything in the room shook with a harsh violent force. The light fixtures swung. Gurneys rolled back and forth. The ointment bottles clanked like a draw full of tools, laughing in Bernard's anguished face. Bernard wiped his bald head with a towel. He cupped both his ears with the palms of his hands, but the nagging tumbling clamor forged its way through his fingers, forcing his brain cells to listen to the fierce grinding blades.

And then a singular thought made the agony stop. It soared across his head like a searchlight in his mind. It brought a chilling gruesome smile to Bernard's wet sweaty face. The girl. The girl was alone in his house! Margie wasn't there to block his hot hunting eyes. Val was gone, and his father's ashes were asleep in their grave. Nobody was home but Paula, in her pink little frock waiting for him like a plump juicy steak. Bernard put on his coat and grabbed his three keys. He placed Margie's ashes inside a square box and edged his way back up to Hollywood Hills.

But before he got home, he stopped at a small pocket park. The park was buried in a residential area near Franklin. The park had a swing set, a teeter totter, and one short metal slide. He'd been coming to that same park for decades. He'd park across the street, pretending to read the *L.A. Times* while watching sweet pubescents play in the sand. He got out of the car and walked across the wet grass. He stopped at the curb that contained a round sandbox and he sprinkled Margie's ashes inside, tossing the ash box in the trash. Before he got to his car, he rubbed his hand along the slide. He smiled and jingled the chain of the swing. There was only one thing on his maniac mind. The girl. The girl was home by herself. Bernard twisted the key and smashed his foot on the gas. He couldn't wait to get back to his house.

19

Paula

It was five in the morning. Paula couldn't sleep. She watched the moon creep from her Windex clean glass as the orange smoke rose through the trees. She sat with her head cocked out toward the street. An arm from a pickup tossed newspapers on lawns. The arm was strong and completely covered in fur. The newsprint turned the fingers to coal. A dog sniffed and peed his way up the walk. His rib cage poked out from a ruined coat of hair.

It was Thursday. The street was littered with black plastic cans. Trash stuck out from the top and the sides, and some of it fell in the road. The dog edged his way, nosing for bones and old dinners. He'd lick and then rip the tied trash bags in half, chomping and swallowing food whole. Coming the opposite way was a slow moving possum. It did its waddling dance against the bashed in gray curb. The dog was busy tearing up a big plastic bag. He lucked out and found a lone meaty T-bone, deliciously covered in flesh. The dog trotted down the street with the bone between its teeth and plopped on the soft lawn to gnaw. The dog's tail rose and wagged and fell over the curb, touching the slow walking possum. The possum stood still. It didn't budge one inch. It was as calm and as still as a tombstone. But the startled dog went crazy. It immediately felt threatened. He started barking and snarling, showing yellow fanged teeth, daring the possum to leap.

The dog kept circling, surrounding the small furry runt, trapping him against the stone curb. The possum stayed glued. Still as a brick. Though its black and white fur was standing on end, only its wide, blazing eyes moved around.

The girl stuck her head all the way out of the ledge. A smile drew across her small slender face. She had just clipped one of her braids all the way off and was holding the dead rope of hair in her hand.

The frightened dog barked mightily. A house light came on. But the tiny possum stood firm and held its ground.

When the dog got too close, the possum reared up. It stood on the claws of its mini hind feet. Its bared mouth was gleaming with razor sharp fangs, and it hissed just like it was a snake. The dog barked but backed up. He eyed the small possum's size, reared up and ready to fight. But the dog made a mistake and came way too close and the possum clipped the dog over his long nose, leaving deep bloody grooves across his snout. The dog roared, dropping the red meaty bone. It growled and barked loud but wouldn't come closer, and eventually the dog trotted to easier trash across the street.

The little girl pulled the shade and got back in her bed. She was tired from all the excitement last night. She could hear the soft rumbling of Val's heavy snores and felt safer because she was there. Both of them had just recently gotten into bed. The girl couldn't sleep, and Val kept reading her stories until the moon was a translucent ghost in the sky and the sun was trying to sneak over the trees.

The girl couldn't really sleep. She felt worried being there. She pulled a pillow over her one-pigtailed head. When she heard a door shut, she got out of bed and glanced across the street. The gardener across the street was watering the lawn. The lawn didn't look like it needed any water, since yesterday it rained really hard. But the gardener stood under her window holding the hose. He looked up toward the small girl and waved. He was hoping he'd see Margie, like he usually did every morning, putting her bra on or shimmying into a slip or zipping up an ultra-tight dress.

The old lady across the street was standing out there, too. The old lady rarely stepped out of her house, but she thought she heard screams coming from Bernard's place and thought she'd peek out and see. She held a hose even though she had a complete sprinkler system. But watering gave her an excuse to see what was happening on her block.

Last night, the girl had taken a medical book from Bernard's shelf. While Val slept, the girl scanned the book's contents. She looked at people whose limbs were covered in rashes. Or people who had white sores that bore into their fat tongues. There was a section on first aid, mouth-to-mouth resuscitation and infectious diseases of children. The girl looked in the back. She found the word she wanted. Asthma. The girl flipped the worn page. She read that pungent and irritating odors, such as turpentine and smoke or even gasoline, can have a terrible effect on asthmatic lungs. Sometimes feeling a hint of bitterness, or failure in one's life, can precipitate horrendous attacks.

Paula read while dragging her finger over the words. She read about chloride, and how dust mites led to horrible inflammations and remembered the bleach kept underneath the sink.

So that night, she took a batch of it and searched for the vacuum cleaner bag and emptied the dust in a white plastic sack.

Paula snapped the book shut. She watched Val's eyes flutter and went to her mother's bedroom.

She approached her mother's room with a steady, adventurous eye. As soon as she came home from school, she would rush inside the dark room of her mother's and rifle through all of her drawers. Under the soft undergarment fabric, were lots of letters and cards. She pulled envelopes out and read the letters inside. Most of them were condolences for people who had died or sympathy cards that sometimes contained money. There were lots and lots of pictures of men with pleasant-looking faces or nice-looking suits. But there was one particular box Paula loved best. It was the cardboard box her mother kept on the shelf in her closet. She'd been searching the closet for weeks before she found it again. The box was carefully hidden inside a larger older box. The girl lifted the top off, placing it on the bed. The girl carefully began examining its contents. She knew every single item inside. Each piece was a small detail of life. The box was all that she had of her former self in Memphis and the person she was before. Before she closed the deep box, she let her fingers run across the assortment of fabrics and freshly cleaned neatly stacked clothes. And even thought most of this stuff didn't fit anymore, she carried it to her room like a treasure chest of gold.

Bernard rolled the rain-filled Plymouth quietly up his drive-way. It had stopped pouring by now, but the sidewalk was soaking. Bernard was wearing yesterday's soiled and stained clothes, and his pants were missing their belt. He hoped nobody would see him pull in.

"Hey, Mr. Wade." Bernard was startled to see his gardener. He was never happier to be home in his life. "Nice weather, we're having," Bernard said, watching his house and briskly walking up to his door.

Mr. Wade gazed up at the bullet-holed sky. He watched his disheveled neighbor get out of his car and practically race to his door.

"Morning, Bernard," Mr. Wade said, and adding in a low voice that was more for himself. "You up at the crack of dawn for a Thursday."

Most Thursdays, Bernard went to work late. For some reason death slowed down toward the end of the week and gave the grave diggers a rest.

Bernard hadn't heard his gardener. He was focused on his doorknob. He kept his head down until he touched the knob. But suddenly he felt something at his back.

Bernard turned around sharply. There was an old lady at his door. He had the key inside the lock when the lady grabbed his arm, and he almost jumped in the rosebush. Bernard hadn't even heard the lady come up. She was the last neighbor on the street from his parents' generation, and she was as old as she was skinny and mean. She'd never spoken to Bernard once in these forty-seven years, except to call him a heathen when he was just six and his ball went up on her lawn.

"I heard some terrible screaming last night," the old lady said, holding Bernard's elbow and not letting go.

Bernard faced her ancient face and told a bald-faced lie. "I'm sorry I disturbed you," he said. "I was watching an Alfred Hitchcock movie. I must have had the volume turned up too high."

"Too high. It sounded like someone was dying in there, boy!" The skinny woman was looking at the back of his collar, which was filthy and grimy from sweat and old skin. His pants were wet, one leg was torn on one side, and his whole face was covered in a light dusty ash.

But Bernard was too impatient to chat. He went in and locked the door. He couldn't believe he was finally here! The girl was alone. The girl was waiting here in his house! That's all he kept saying on the torturous drive home. Dodging police and trying not to race any lights. The girl was alone. The girl was alone. The girl was inside. Waiting for him like dessert on a tray.

Paula heard Bernard and looked over at Val. She wanted to protect Val and didn't want Bernard to know she was here, so the girl pulled the cover up and around Val's slim shoulders and over her face like a corpse.

Paula got out of her bed, slid into her slippers, and gathered her robe around her waist. She dressed and combed her curls fiercely, clipping the final braid off and arranging her hair in a soft curly halo around her head. She viciously brushed her teeth, scrubbing her tiny face raw, carefully placing the cloth on the rack. She put the teakettle on and walked down the back steps. The girl stood on the last step and held in her breath. When she finally breathed deep, the cold air stung her lungs. A white cloud drifted off from her lips. Climbing the tall stairs to her apartment again, she peeled the shade back slightly and stared out the front window, holding her small body against the wall so she wouldn't be seen. Bernard was there. She heard him come home. He must have parked in the garage.

The little girl glanced at the clock. It was ten minutes to six.

She cracked the back door, sneaked down the steps, ran up his ramp, and peeked in. Bernard looked crazy. He tore off his shirt. He was singing to himself wearing only his undershirt and pants. The undershirt was stuck to his skin. His face was covered in ashes. His blazing eyes looked mad, like he wanted something bad and couldn't find it. When he looked toward the back door the girl quickly ducked down and hid under the window's short screen.

But it was too late. He saw her. His angry face turned to joy as he chased her up the steps to her apartment.

Bernard tapped on the door lightly. The glass window mildly quaked.

"Paula!" Bernard said. "Your mother called me, she's sick. She asked me to take you to school."

Paula didn't know what to do. She didn't want him to come in and find Val, so she quietly got dressed, choosing an outfit for her crime and faced Bernard on the porch.

When Bernard saw her, he immediately started licking his chops. Her curls were shorter and probably wrapped in a bun, but her angelic face was still beautifully there. She wore a red cowboy hat and a blue denim shirt, and though it was cold, she had on a billowing pink skirt that rose high up on her legs.

She walked a few paces behind Bernard in her white patent leather shoes, and gingerly got in his car. She refused to get in the passenger seat next to him and sat in the back like a queen.

Bernard drove to the school and stopped at the yield sign. But instead of slowing down and parking his car against the curb, he kept his heavy foot down on the gas.

The guard looked out the window just as Paula Green passed. He saw them come to the school and slow down but not stop. He could see the small girl look toward the school and panic and saw Bernard keep driving the car faster.

The guard picked up the phone and dialed the police. He was glad he had copied Bernard's license.

"Hey," Paula asked, "why aren't we stopping?"

"Oh," Bernard smiled. "I know you like ice cream. I thought we could go and get some at the pier. The have the best ice cream in L.A."

Paula loved ice cream, but she became really concerned when the school faded from her rear window.

Bernard was determined. He didn't know what the girl saw. He could have one chance of fun, one luscious filthy moment and then he'd get rid of her body. But maybe he could keep her, like the doll in his garage. Bernard stuck one hand in the well of his pocket. His fingers touched the vial he took from his job. A teaspoon of that would certainly do the trick; it could knock the small girl out for hours.

Bernard glanced at the girl in his rearview mirror. He drove to the 10 and took it all the way until he saw water and the beautiful long sandy shore.

When he got to the coastline and was about to pull over and park, a motorcycle cop pulled alongside his car. He smiled at Bernard and looked at the girl in the backseat.

"Good day for the beach!" The cop told Bernard.

Bernard gripped the wheel. His face erupted in sweat. He wiped his face and his neck with a handkerchief from his pocket and was just about to pull from the light when the cop put on his lights for him to pull over.

"Yes," Bernard said. "It's a beautiful morning." The clouds looked like a typhoon was turning the sky.

"Sir, it's Thursday? Shouldn't your daughter be in school?"

"I'm not his daughter," Paula told the cop.

"What school do you go to, honey?"

"Immaculate Heart."

"Why aren't you there?"

"He's taking me to get ice cream," Paula said.

"Who is he?" the cop studied Bernard's stubbled face and the scratches around his hands and arms. He was filthy. There was a spot of blood on his shirt. He wasn't even wearing a belt on his pants, and he looked liked he hadn't slept in weeks.

"Will you step out of the car, sir?" the cop asked Bernard.

Bernard didn't step out, instead he took off, wheeling the old Plymouth, making a treacherous U-turn and speeding recklessly down the Pacific Coast Highway.

He cut across the road and drove the wrong way, causing on-coming cars to blow their horns or swerve and forcing a few off the road. The motorcycle cop stopped to call his car in before hopping back up on his Harley.

Going through alleys and side streets and parking inside an abandoned car wash off the road, Bernard saw the motorcycle cop dramatically whiz by.

The child looked happy. Like the whole experience was fun. But actually she was glad to get back to her plan when Bernard drove back to his house and pulled into the garage.

Bernard went into the house and put on a clean shirt. He walked to the refrigerator and took out the butterscotch ice cream and set two bowls and two silver spoons on the table. He secretly poured in the vial from his pocket and mixed it up with the ice cream. Putting the sedative batch inside a large plastic bag, he shoved it back in the freezer. After the police incident, he knew he couldn't keep the girl long. He would have her one time, one time alone, and then he'd sprinkle her away like her mother.

"I've got some homemade ice-cream, would you like some?" he asked.

Paula followed Bernard to the kitchen and stood by a chair.

"Your cowboy outfit's cute." His eyes scanned her hairy legs and decided not to say anything about them.

"Come on," Bernard said. "Have a seat." Bernard had two servings ready, a spoon rested next to each bowl.

The girl watched Bernard take the ice cream from the bag.

"Why is the ice cream in there? Why do you have it in a bag? Shouldn't it be in a container from the store?"

Bernard remembered why he hated kids over ten. They acted too grown up and smart.

"Well I like to mix it in the bowl, and then I put it in here. That's the way homemade is done."

The girl seemed convinced and sat down at the table. "I don't have a napkin," she told him.

Bernard slapped a pile of napkins in front of her bowl. He hoped she didn't notice his severe irritation. He started scratching his hands.

The girl watched Bernard put a nice scoop of ice cream in her bowl. She licked her small lips leaving her hands in her lap. But she didn't touch a thing. She didn't even lift a spoon. Bernard stared at the girl. He tried real hard to smile.

Just eat the damn ice cream, he said to himself. *Why are you just looking at it, go ahead and have some now!*

"Where's yours?" the girl asked. She was permanently polite. "Aren't you having any?" she wanted to know.

"Oh, I had mine right before you came in," Bernard grinned.

"Well, it's rude to just sit and eat in front of someone else. I'll just take it home if you don't mind."

"No," Bernard said quickly. "I'll eat some, too." Reaching back inside the freezer he pulled out the bag. But just after putting the ice cram in his bowl, he stood up and went to the freezer again. He turned his back to the girl and placed his bowl in the freezer and replaced it with another bowl he had waiting in there instead.

The girl patiently waited for Bernard. Her hands stayed in her lap. She was busy eyeing everything inside that room. It was very neat. Very clean. Nothing out of place, but she did notice the old rug was gone.

"What happened to the rug?" The girl asked.

"I got allergic to it," Bernard said fast. "Hurry up or it's going to melt."

She stopped and looked at Bernard's bowl again.

"That's funny," she said.

"What's funny?" he asked.

"Well your bowl's all cloudy, like it's been in the cold, and mine is warm like it was just washed in hot water."

"Oh, I keep a fresh bowl in the freezer for me. I like my ice cream in a cold bowl," he said.

"So do I," the girl said. "I want mine cold, too!"

Bernard was really getting impatient with this inquisitive child. If she didn't look so tender and good, he would have stood up and taken her right there. But his mood was too good to be spoiled by this. He had the girl. There was no one here but her and him. He couldn't help but smile to himself.

Bernard smiled at her broadly. He tried to touch her hair, but Paula jerked her head from his hand.

"Then let's switch," Paula said, without blinking a lash.

She stared at him with giant saucers for eyes. They revealed nothing but a curious nature.

Bernard was angry. He couldn't switch bowls now! It was too late! The girl's bowl was glistening with poison.

Bernard's overworked brain struggled to think. He had to come up with something to throw Paula off. His hand fingered the Primatene Mist in his pocket; suddenly a thought jumped in his head. "I have to take mine cold because it helps with my asthma. The cold from the bowl keeps my sinuses clear." Bernard pulled the red inhaler from out of his pocket. "If I don't eat it cold enough, I could have an attack." Bernard was beginning to feel that familiar tightness in his chest. The kitchen suddenly felt close and hot. It was harder to breathe. It felt like the girl sucked all the air from the room. He could smell her. Smell the rich nauseous soap on her neck. He was beginning to get sick to his stomach. He didn't know Paula had poured pure bleach on the floor, and the fumes were working in his lungs.

Bernard stood up and struggled with the side kitchen window. He violently tried to pry it up with both of his hands. It was jammed. The stiff air was beginning to feel agonizingly thin. His chest heaved up and down with each breath. But the window was old. The ropes were broken on both sides. The paint on the frame had been laid on too thick, and it fastened the frame shut like cement.

Bernard struggled with it madly. His bald head perspired. Finally with one hard jerk, the window flew open wide, and Bernard hung his head out of the sill and breathed deeply. He hadn't had a good breath since yesterday morning. Bernard stayed like that for a couple of minutes. He looked around to find something to hold the old window up and saw a Bible on one of the chairs.

"Hand me that book!" Bernard snapped at the child.

"That's the Bible!" Paula said concerned.

Bernard grabbed the Bible himself, shoving it inside the warped sill.

The girl watched Bernard's back. She looked at his inhaler on the table. She slid her fingers around the smooth metal tube. It was a bright metallic red, a bit larger than a tube of lipstick. It was still warm from being next to Bernard's skin. The girl picked it up, rolling the tube in her hand. But as soon as she did, Bernard saw her do it and came over and snatched the tube back. He held the inhaler way down in his mouth and sprayed a long dose down his throat. He took three deep breaths, then put it back inside his pocket. The girl studied this routine with amazement. The slight hint of a smile slid across her thin lips and then she looked down at Bernard's ice cream again. The cool frosty layer was starting to drip.

"Make mine cold," the girl said, staring back at him boldly. "I want mine to be chilled just like yours."

The large rain-filled clouds outside turned grotesque and dark. It was early in the day, but it could have been midnight as dark as the sky had turned. Bernard was just about to get up and flick the kitchen light on. But he thought better of it. No, this was much better. This was actually cozy. He sat down in his chair; no one would see them in here.

The little girl stared at him intensely. She never flinched once. Bernard smiled. After the inhaler blast, he felt more relaxed. This was fun. He could do whatever he wanted. They were alone, and no one was ever coming back. He liked sitting here, in the dimness of his kitchen without interruptions of any kind, including light. He'd never seen her this close. He'd never been able to stare at her this long. She was an absolute beauty even with chopped hair. Her curls framed her face like the robe of the Virgin Mary. Her cheeks were fresh and scrubbed. Her neck so clean it sparkled. Her skin looked as smooth as fresh polished marble.

She scowled, glancing down at her ice cream again.

"Make mine cold, now," the girl coolly demanded. She moved her bowl until it was right next to his. Her delicate fingers touched Bernard's hand.

Bernard didn't know what to say. Anger flared under his skin. He'd never been in the company of such an impertinent child. He hated her smugness and knocked her hat to the floor. But he immediately felt sorry and tried to put the hat back, but the girl left the hat on a chair. But there was another part of him that could not be ignored, and it banged at him like a rent-seeking landlord. He was excited beyond reason. The flush tore through his skin. He wanted to smother her miniature mouth under his. He bit his own lip imagining the taste of her tart flesh. He did his best to hide these thoughts within the scorched contents of his skin.

The girl gave him a vague yet acknowledging smile. She understood what he wanted. She'd seen that look many times before. It was on the faces of her mother's friends. Or bus drivers or Scout leaders. It was on some of her teachers who sat too close to her in class. Even the principal at Immaculate Heart tried to hug her one time, smashing his body over hers against the cold metal lockers when they were alone in the hall.

Bernard couldn't stop staring at her crystal blue eyes. *Snap out of it, Bernard,* he thought to himself. He had to stay focused. He couldn't be distracted by her nature. He had a nasty job to do, but he was going to have fun first. A fun he felt he deserved. But his nerves were on end, and his underarms were soaked. His hands began to itch until he scratched them. She was so deliciously wicked. Incredibly horrid. He'd love to taste the rich hatred that flowed throughout her limbs. She was a puzzle. A riddle he could not understand. Just swallow the damn ice cream, he said to himself. He knew she wanted it. She'd already tasted it with her tongue. Hell, she'd be knocked out in less than ten minutes. He would embalm her and be able to play with her for life. It was almost too glorious to fathom. But what if he tasted her while she was still warm? Just a nibble before he put her to sleep. Bernard's eyes traced the curve of her white peachy cheek. What if he took a small piece before freezing her completely, while the little thing could still see? It would be quick. She would be cold in six minutes. He could have a wild episode, and no one would ever know. At that thought, Bernard almost lost it right there. His bones began smoldering again.

"Why are you staring at me like that?"

"I wasn't aware that I was staring,"

Bernard quickly looked down. He fiddled his thumbs. His eyes only rose as high as his inhaler on the table. It lay near the edge of his napkin.

"Why are you looking at me so funny?" the girl knowingly asked. She dipped her finger in the ice cream and licked the tip with her tongue. Her wet tongue darted in and out of her mouth like a lighter. Bernard's own body burned with desire. He still simmered from his unfinished business with Val. Something inside needed feeding. He imediately felt starved. Letting one hand gently drop, he massaged the knot between his pants. Yes, that was it. His body responded to his own touch. This was what he wanted, and he wanted it bad, even if he had to steal it like he'd done before. His eyes rose and stared at the young girl again. She sat there looking just like a sweet slice of cake. He smiled at her again, but the girl only scowled. He had to work to hold his throbbing self down.

"See that look," she said. "You're doing it now."

"Am I doing something?" Bernard asked the girl calmly. He tried to make his face look as blank as a chalkboard, without any lines, words or marks. He tried to make his voice even. Though it quivered and shook. But he couldn't help but smile when he glanced in his lap. He couldn't ignore that for long.

"You're weird," the girl said. Her voice sounding triumphant. Like she had finally figured him out.

Bernard should have felt badly. She was only a child. But she was at the age where girls were aware of their power. She had a wonderfully, sweet, intense face. And staring at her, seeing those swimming pool eyes, made his guts feel like a volcano. He was too excited to speak. He felt a deep pent-up need. He'd never known his body to shiver with such desire. It was agony to try to look calm.

He laughed, but the laughter came out like a grunt. His hand was extended under the table. If he could just get his forefinger under her dress, if he could do it now while her tiny tongue licked the bowl, he knew he would go straight to heaven.

Paula became impatient. She didn't want to sit and wait. She wanted what he had promised when she entered the apartment. She wanted ice cream. She wanted her bowl nice and cold.

"Come on! Where's my bowl?" she demanded.

But her anger only ignited Bernard's burgeoning lust. He was so hot, he was practically exploding right there. He wanted her. He wanted to grab her hair and part her pale legs with his knee. All of this was swirling around in his head as he tried to look Sunday morning calm. He despised her for making him sit here this long. He hated her hands and the quaint doll-like way that she sat. He hated the white napkin lying perched in her lap. Balling one hand in a fist, it was all he could do not to bust the smug look off her face.

"See!" she said exasperated. "You're doing it again."

Bernard stopped looking long enough to rip a cuticle with his teeth. He used everything inside to relax the knot between his thighs. He saw himself in the kitchen mirror and eased the grooves in his brow. He smiled, trying to look as nonchalant as possible as his skull smoldered inside.

"You're strange," the girl said, flipping her curls.

Bernard wanted to reach up and catch a curl in his hand and clench it tight in his fist. But instead, he dabbed the sweat around his moistening brow, wadding the napkin into a small ball.

Something happened when he saw her hand fly behind her pink neck. He couldn't hold himself back. He was boiling now. He stood up to grab the girl, but she immediately stood, too. She dragged her chair to the freezer and opened the door. She climbed on the chair as her dress lapped each calf, and she went to go get the ice cream herself.

"Here, let me help." Bernard said, coming behind her. He stood near her body as she yanked the cold door. Freezing air flew into Bernard's blazing face. He breathed deep and smiled widely inside. She was close enough to touch. He could hold her and not let go. "Don't fall," he said, putting a hand around her waist.

The girl whirled around and faced him. A knowing smirk was on her mouth. "What is it, Bernard?" the girl craftily asked, using his first name as if she'd said it all of her life.

Bernard was so stunned he looked down on the floor.

"What? You can't talk, cat got your tongue." the girl smiled and slowly got down off the chair. She was completely unafraid, and it had taken him by surprise.

Bernard babbled. "Why of course, you can have a chilled bowl, too." Bernard began folding and unfolding the green kitchen towel. He hated sounding dumbfounded. The girl smiled, narrowing her eyes. She lifted her dress up a few inches from her knees.

"Say pretty please," she cooed. "You have to be nice." It's so rude to take things without asking."

Bernard's eyes scanned the dim room. He saw the glasses and plates; he couldn't bring himself to look at her thighs. The girl lifted her dress further showing the beginnings of a pink slip. Bernard couldn't take it. He lunged for the girl. The chair fell and the girl wound up on the floor. Bernard was on top of her, but she managed to slip away. She was laughing loud and kept on saying his name.

"Oh, Bernard, where are you. Come find me," she said. The girl had gone in his room and hid under his bed.

He looked into the bathroom, inside the linen closet's doors. Where was she? Where in the hell did she go? He heard some laughter and saw the girl on the back porch looking in. She stuck her small tongue out at his face. He got to the door, but she hopped up the steps fast, taking two and three at a time. He chased her up the stairs, straining to breathe until he had to stop midstep to catch a good decent breath. She stopped, too, and laughed. She came a few steps down.

"Bernard," she said, whirling her skirt over his head.

Bernard choked and stared. The need to live killed his lust. He reached in his pocket to get his inhaler. But his inhaler wasn't there. Then he remembered. He took it out of his pocket and left the red tube on the table. Bernard raced back downstairs but was now breathing really hard. He had to stop twice to catch his breath, dragging himself slowly over each step.

The girl laughed wildly. Her shrill voice, hacksawed his skull. He pulled himself along the railing. He had to get to the inhaler. His chest heaved uncontrollably. His ribs went up and down like a pump. He ripped at his collar. Three buttons flew off. He couldn't breathe at all. He could feel a weakness run through his arms and around his knees. He dropped to the floor, catching himself with one hand before falling backward down the long stairs. The girl was right there. She had a smirk on her face. She put her ear right next to his wide open mouth like she was watching a large slimy fish on a boat that had just been pulled from the water.

Bernard rolled around the girl, rotating his useless body. His shirt had come up from his pants, but after resting a minute he managed to get to his knees and crawl toward his back door. He swam up the ramp and fell across the back porch, forcing himself to take mini breaths instead, he rested next to a bucket and mop. Yanking the mop handle, he managed to pull his frame around the door. But the door violently swung back, pinching his fingers in the crack, Bernard screamed sucking his thumb and his knuckles. He swore to himself, cursing crudely under his breath.

"That bitch!" Bernard said. "That little fucking cunt!" Bernard grunted, swinging his exhausted frame. He was running out of strength. His lungs told him there was no time.

He wanted to scream, but when he tried nothing came out. He

had to get to the kitchen. His inhaler was there. Pulling himself more, he forced his arms and legs, elbowing and kneeing himself along the floor, using the mop like a paddle. He could see the kitchen door. Only a few feet to go. Bernard's chest felt deflated. He was fading inside. The events of last night had left him helplessly weak and the bleach fumes were eating his tongue. He stopped two more times strangling some air through his lungs. It killed him to breathe. Razor blades ate his chest. He was totally drenched, and his whole body ached. He didn't think he was going to make it.

But then, finally he was there. He was looking under the table-top. The underside of the table was unpolished but clean. Tongue and groove slats of wood wove an efficiently neat pattern. He reached his hand up and fumbled around trying to feel for it first, but his hand only felt a cold bowl. He used all the strength he had to lift himself further up. He pulled the mop and flung his gut over a chair. He lifted his head until his eyes cleared the flat top. But immediately he knew it was over. The inhaler was gone. Bernard willed his weak body to strain and rise higher. But it was clear that the inhaler was no longer there. Bernard began to sob. Where in God's name was it? He leaned down trying to see if it had fallen to the floor. Maybe it fell and rolled to a corner. But no, the inhaler was gone. Bernard racked his brain trying to think.

Suddenly two little white shoes appeared under the table. Bernard followed the shoes to two twin spindly calves where dense hair wove its way up to her thighs. Her legs were right next to his face. He followed them to a pink skirt that screamed its color to his empty lungs.

"Are you looking for this?" the little girl teased. She smiled looking down at Bernard's ruined face. Very slowly, she put one hand on her hip and equally as slow, pulled the inhaler from her small, embroidered pocket.

Bernard felt like someone held a blowtorch to his skin. He burned with such ferocious and uncontrollable rage. He was determined. The will to live made him feel like a savage. He grabbed one of her legs. He could feel the hair under his hand. She wiggled, but the girl could not get away. He had her. He tightened his grip around her ankle. A cruel smile wedged on his face. He could feel the thin bone under his fingers and thumb. The girl struggled fiercely, but Bernard wouldn't let go. He wanted to bring her face next to his on the floor, and he started to pull her frame down. But the little girl was fierce and struggled magnificently against his hand. His palm was getting sweaty, and he almost lost his grip so he dug his ripped fingernails into her skin. The girl screamed, but Bernard really had her this time. Nothing could stop him. He'd never let go. Even if the building became completely engulfed in flames, he wouldn't let go of her skin. He couldn't breathe, but this time he had the girl good. He tightened his grip. He brought his other hand down and around one hand and began trapping her next to his body. But the girl continued to struggle and kicked his face hard. The pain made him set her hand free. As Bernard tried to tighten his grip on her leg again, the girl kicked him fiercely, knocking him right in the nose. Shockwaves filled his brain with excruciating pain. The impact of her shoe against the tip of his nostrils made Bernard release and open his hand.

As soon as she was free, she scrambled away. But Bernard knew that she didn't leave.

Bernard kept wheezing, trying desperately to catch his breath. All his insides felt empty like the wind had been knocked from his lungs. His pale skin was turning a dull grayish hue as the little oxygen he had left, left his brain. There was something he could do, but he had to act fast. His body began to shake in minor convulsions. Swinging himself past the table, Bernard pivoted his whole frame until he was now facing the long wooden hallway. The hall to his bedroom looked incredibly far. It was like trying to swim to Catalina from Santa Monica's pier. How in the world could he ever make it? Dragging himself, he became driven by pure need and hate and a burning hot animalistic, criminal lust that could have turned Charles Manson to stone.

There was another inhaler on the nightstand next to his bed. He dragged himself, panting and sweating along the floor. His eyes closed and rolled back inside of his head. But he kept moving his legs. He kept swinging his arms and hoped he wouldn't black out before hitting the door.

Suddenly the girl was there. She was holding something behind her back. She brought the thing forward, but Bernard couldn't tell what it was. He only realized after it was too late.

Shaking the big bag of dust in Bernard's doomed-looking face the girl emptied a vacuum cleaner bag right inside Bernard's face.

Bernard's whole body went into revolting convulsions. He turned green. A yellow slime seeped from his tongue. This was the end, Bernard thought, he'd never take another breath. He sputtered and choked on the dust bag.

He heard the girl laugh and run out of the room.

But Bernard remained determined. He had to go on. He was going to get that inhaler if it was the last thing he did. He willed his limp body to move.

Finally, he felt the rough carpet rub against his cheek. Though his mouth felt like a bag of dried leaves, he smiled at the ceiling, wiping the sweat from his eyes. This was his room. That was the shag underneath his skin. There was the choo choo wallpaper. He almost laughed at the sweet tender glory of it all. He never felt more relieved. He could almost feel himself breathing again. He looked out of the window and saw the fig tree. Everything was going to be all right. The sky looked like the sun was about to peek out. It was going to be okay. He was going to live. But when he looked up the girl was inside the room, too. She started laughing so hard it seemed like she was crying. She held his second blue inhaler tightly in her fist.

"Looking for this?" She began prancing around the room.

Bernard grimaced. It took all his effort to speak. "Plea—" Bernard said, willing his vocal cords to work. His voice wheezed. His whole body heaved from the effort. A cold sweat pooled around the base of his spine. He couldn't catch much air at all anymore. Every vein strained. His corpuscles stretched.

The girl walked up and stared upside down at Bernard. "I know what you did." The girl told him slowly. "I saw you," she said. "I saw the whole thing." Bernard ignored the girl. He rolled his body away. He remembered a semi-empty inhaler inside the small drawer. He struggled to his knees and flopped his arm on the bed, willing himself up to get it.

The girl was standing so close; that when he flung his arm wildly, he smacked her thigh with such force she fell down and she could feel Bernard's hairs graze the meat of her leg.

Feeling skin, Bernard grabbed, squeezing her thigh like a snake. With all the strength he had left in his body, Bernard brought the girl down on her back to the bed. The thought of capturing her brought a new strength to his body. He covered her thin frame with his.

Bernard exhaled in her face deeply, and the girl squirmed under his girth. The covers were ruined as she thrashed, and she turned but there was no way she could escape. She screamed with all of the power in her lungs, but Bernard smothered her lips with his palm.

With his free hand, he moved it up next to the dresser. With some effort he reached up to the drawer. He was fueled by the cool flowing from the girl's nostrils. Almost half-dead, he never felt more alive. The girl. The girl was right under his waist, her soft lips felt like butter in his hand.

Bernard's fingers hunted for the drawer handle, and suddenly he felt the calm metal. With one steady jerk he yanked the drawer to the floor. A *Playboy* magazine fell out and some Vicks menthol rub, a fake mustache, assorted pairs of glasses with no prescriptions in the frames. And then tied together bound by a fat rubber band was an assortment of Polaroids of girls. A girl in the park. A girl on the swing. Two girls going down a stubby short slide, and a girl digging a hole in the sand. Bernard wiped the pictures aside and grabbed the inhaler. He popped up the lid with his thumb. Holding the blue tube right next to his dry tongue, Bernard was about to spray the mist inside his mouth. He'd prayed for this day. He wanted the girl bad. Had lusted after her since the first day she came. He wanted to profess this secret desire, but he didn't want to waste any energy using words.

He pushed his finger on top of the spray. He couldn't wait for the life force to enter his lungs. He could almost taste the sweet mist at the back of his throat, could almost feel the surge coming back in his brain and like the nectar of his roses rising up from his yard was the wonderful scent of the girl. All this and more passed through his head. All those thoughts occurred in less than a second because in the next instant Val stood over his face. She smiled at Bernard and snatched the inhaler away.

Bernard screamed, but no sound came out, only this long, vulgar, puppy dog wheeze. He collapsed on the bed and slid down to the floor, facedown. Only a small amount of air inched from his strained passages. He didn't gasp anymore. The whole world became silent. It felt like he was falling down a long soundless hole. His red eyes stopped blinking. Though his face twitched against the shag, he never spoke again. His arms and legs went limp. He curved into a tiny fetal ball. One hand was clinging to his neck. The last thing he saw was the fringe on her sock and the pure polished white of her shoe. And in his mind, once his eyes closed, he imagined seeing the soft curve of her lovely face, the slender contour of her beautiful chin and the whisper pink of her mouth. Bernard sucked his lips hard as if imagining the taste and never opened his eyes again.

"Paula?" Val called.

"Paula, are you all right?" Val pulled the girl from the weight of Bernard's dead body.

Paula got up and smoothed down her dress.

"Come on!" Val said, yanking the girl by the wrist. "Help me get him back into bed. Taking his head and his arms she instructed the girl to take his feet and together they turned Bernard straight in the bed and covered him with the sheet, laying it up to his neck, until he looked just like he was sleeping.

Val took the inhaler and put it in Bernard's hand. Though he couldn't hold it, she forced his fingers around the tube, so that if he let go it would roll on the right place on the floor.

"Come on!" Val said. "Get your stuff now; we're leaving."

Paula pulled a large trunk from under her bed. It was filled to the brim with old coins and solid gold jewelry.

"Where did you get this? This stuff is worth a fortune! Val grabbed a pair of emerald gold cuff links. Another pair was twinkling with diamonds.

"This was Howard Hughes' old stuff. Where did you find it?"

"I saw Bernard hide it in the garage," Paula said.

Val scooped up a handful of gold coins in her palm. She'd never seen so much money and fine jewels. But in the distance she could also hear the faint hiss of sirens. She closed the box hurriedly and pushed it by the door. "Come on, we have to get out now!"

Val was snatching down the girl's dresses and ripping the hangers from the neck, stacking them quickly on the girl's bed.

Paula knocked the stacked dresses to the floor. She went to her closet and opened a box and took out an old stack of clothes. There was a stack of boy's pants and some freshly starched oxfords and lots of old ties and belts.

Val stared at the clothing. She didn't understand. She looked for answers in Paula's tortured eyes.

"My mother made me do it. She didn't want to get caught. The police were hunting for a woman and her son so she made me dress up as a girl."

There was a moment of confusion, wracking Val's brain.

Paula's eyes blazed and flashed around the room like a torch. "None of this is me. All of it is fake!"

Paula took off the dress and removed the pink ruffled slip. She climbed in the pants and buttoned up the white shirt.

"My name is Paul." His voice dropped a few octaves. And then gazing at the stack of frilly dresses on the bed, "I never want to be Paula again." He didn't cry, but his eyes turned a deep red and his bottom lip started to quake.

Val stood with her mouth gaped. "Oh my God!" she screamed. "You even fooled me, and I'm an identity queen!" Giving the child a naughty smile, she lifted her weave and said, "My real name's Valdez, but don't ever call me that in public."

Val smiled and gave Paul a wink.

"I still can't believe it! I'm totally shocked. But hell, we live in Hollywood. Everybody's in drag."

Val picked up Paul's dresses and tossed them all in the trash.

She gathered the jewelry and coins in a sheet. "You got to walk to the beat of your own drum, honey. And mine's going to always play cha cha," Val did a little spin and wove her hand through Paul's arm.

"Let's go spend some of Mr. Hughes' money on Melrose."

Paul scanned the room one last time before he left. A lone matchbook sat on the stand by his bed. The word "Mirabell's" was etched in gold on the flap. Paul jammed the matchbook in his pants.